20篇：英美现当代散文

（修订版）

Twenty Pieces: Modern and Contemporary English Essays

(Revised)

陆谷孙　丁　骏　朱绩崧　张　楠 ◎ 选编

Selected and Annotated by
Lu Gusun, Ding Jun, Zhu Jisong, Zhang Nan

復旦大學出版社

图书在版编目(CIP)数据

20篇英美现当代散文:英文/陆谷孙等选编. —修订本. —上海:复旦大学出版社,2021.5
ISBN 978-7-309-15540-2

Ⅰ.①2… Ⅱ.①陆… Ⅲ.①英语-语言读物 ②散文集-英国-现代 ③散文集-美国-现代
Ⅳ.①H319.4:Ⅰ

中国版本图书馆CIP数据核字(2021)第088413号

20篇:英美现当代散文(修订版)
陆谷孙 丁 骏 朱绩崧 张 楠/选编
责任编辑/谢露茜

复旦大学出版社有限公司出版发行
上海市国权路579号 邮编:200433
网址:fupnet@fudanpress.com http://www.fudanpress.com
门市零售:86-21-65102580 团体订购:86-21-65104505
出版部电话:86-21-65642845
上海四维数字图文有限公司

开本787×960 1/16 印张17.75 字数309千
2021年5月第2版第1次印刷

ISBN 978-7-309-15540-2/H·3060
定价:39.00元

Foreword

by Zhu Jisong

This anthology is based on the textbook and notes of Professor Lu Gusun's "Contemporary British and American Essays: Selected Readings for Seniors Majoring in English," a canonical Fudan University undergraduate course that he took over from his poet-advisor, Professor Y. M. Hsü (1906-86), and has been teaching for more than twenty years. I took the course eight years ago, got four credits, and then audited it twice, as I felt sure that revisits would enhance my understanding of the literary texts and, speaking broadly, of human life, past and present, as is reflected in them. Even today, a faculty member myself, I will occasionally sit in his classroom as a "back-bencher," a native returned from the Wasteland of pomo-babble to the Wonderland of sense and sensibility. That he sometimes cracks the same joke for the same topic adds to my secret amusement.

Meanwhile, this peppy polymath, now an early septuagenarian, manages to perform a textual aggiornamento of the reading list for the course on a semestral basis, missing neither Noam Chomsky's peacenik interpretation of the September 11 terrorist attacks nor Barack Obama's post-racial Philadelphia speech, "A More Perfect Union," the prelude to the first non-white presidency of the United States. In his own words, Professor Lu finds "a new tide to swim with," as he wants himself and his students to boot to "stay afloat." Yet it is no accident, I am afraid, that his two decades' worth of striking arms in a troubled sea of worldwide words charts a mapping, though not intended to encompass the marine multitudinousness, of the latest century-long rising and receding of a genre that Montaigne named, in his serene *château* life, *Essai*. In this sense, the present volume, an annotated anthology, eloquently bespeaks Professor Lu's art and craft of pedagogy and scholarship.

Etymologically, *anthology*, a word of Greek origin, is the gathering of flowers. Of flowers, we expect petals, styles, stigmas, and, above all, fragrance. What do we want, then, from an anthology, one of essays in our case, apart from selection, random or with sagacious system, of personal, peculiar writings by divers authors, to the pleasant scent of which the anthologist is allured?

Present-day China, a nation firmly in the grip of English fever, has witnessed a boom of anthologies of English essays. Most of them, however, prove to be loose motleys that, despite their claims about preserving the essence of Englishness, fail to show any insight into the heart and mind of the English-speaking peoples. To me, a non-native speaker of the tongue, such anthologies are but "an vnweeded Garden/That growes to Seed" (*Hamlet* I, ii) in which even an otherwise red, red rose will wither, owing to lack of cultivation and watering by the hand of the gardener. What's wrong? Bacon, Johnson, Lamb, Hazlitt, Thackeray, and Thoreau—aren't their names a warranty of intense delight? Most obviously, the problem lies with the anthologist, who used to be looked upon, to quote the formidable C. S. Chien, as "one who makes the good things in literature accessible to many and thus spreads aesthetic joy in the widest commonality." Indeed, it must not be forgotten that an essay, argues Christopher Morley, is more a mood than a form, a mood in which someone feels impelled to share, in an artfully natural fashion, something touching her- or himself to the quick in real life and that traditionally, it has been the role of the anthologist, as if an avatar of the essayist, to transport readers into the mood. Since in this Age of Information, the Internet has theoretically brought about, once and for all, the universal accessibility to and commonality of literary gems, the anthologist, with her or his communicational burden thus removed, is supposed to concentrate on infecting readers with "aesthetic joy," or in Virginia Woolf's introspective description, on shutting them in, not out of, the curtain of esoteric ecstasy that a genuine masterpiece draws around. This shutting-in, this infection, is the atman of any essay anthology worth its salt.

Whereas some anthology-smiths may be living a life of sedentary ease and doing brisk scissors-and-paste work on their laptop, Professor Lu, with the assistance of his disciples, Ms. Ding Jun, Miss Zhang Nan, and, last and least, Yours Humbly, has taken strenuous, sometimes hair-splitting, pains to teach the pieces first and then anthologize them, endeavoring to convey to the Chinese who love English for English's own sake the sweet, soul-stirring smell of the "flowers" that he has handpicked for them. By doing so, he is actually doing literary criticism in the Bloomish sense, which is primarily appreciation and fuses analysis and evaluation (Bloom viii).

Most of the twenty essays included here, half of British authorship and half American, were written in the previous century and are of the "familiar" type.* It needs to be further pointed out that although the anthologist famously believes in elitism, some lesser authors, such as James Herriot, Gilbert Norwood, and David Owen, have also found their way into this book, attesting to a soft spot for the plebeian and practical. Ten are provided with annotations of philological, historical, or philosophical nature that, in the electronic proofs for me, fill the margin to the full and often spill out of the page frame, so that readers are well (not over, hopefully) equipped for embarking on a learned odyssey with Professor Lu as their Mentor. To the other ten is left far more space for a hunt for opulent breath to be undertaken largely by readers themselves.

Lo and behold, here come the essays!

"Are they unusual?"
"Do they set you thinking?"
"Do they make you recall things you have seen or read?"
"Do they urge you to find more in your surroundings, and read more, and try to express yourself more clearly and more interestingly?"

John M. Avent raises these questions in the introduction to his *Book of Modern Essays* (xiii). When you find yourself pondering them as you turn over the pages that follow, you will agree with me, I bet, that this tiny anthology—a word of caution—is aromatically contagious.

August, 2011

* For a definition of "familiar essay," see Chevalier 578-81.

References

Avent, John M. Introd. *The Book of Modern Essays.* Ed. Avent. 1924. Whitefish, MT: Kessinger, 2005. Print.

Bloom, Harold. Preface. *Essayists and Prophets.* By Bloom. Philadelphia: Chelsea, 2005. Print.

Chevalier, Tracy, ed. *Encyclopedia of the Essay.* London: Dearborn, 1997. Print.

Chien, C. S. Foreword. *Selected Modern English Essays for College Students.* Ed. Y. M. Hsü, D. Z. Zia, and T. W. Chou. 1947. Shanghai: Fudan UP, 2007. Print.

Morley, Christopher. Preface. *Modern Essays.* Ed. Morley. New York: Harcourt, 1921. Bartleby.com: *Great Books Online.* Bartleby.com, 2000. Web. 6 Mar. 2010.

CONTENTS

Intensive Reading

Extensive Reading

Intensive Reading

Too Many Books[1]

by Gilbert Norwood

When Julius Caesar[2] allowed the Library of Alexandria[3] to burn, excellent people[4] no doubt exclaimed: "Lo,[5] another cord added to the scourge of war!"[6] Certainly countless students since the Revival of Learning[7] have looked upon that conflagration as one of the world's disasters. It was no such thing,[8] but a vast benefit. And one of the worst modern afflictions is the printing-press;[9] for its diabolical power of multiplication has enabled

---

[1] *Too Many Books*: The most striking feature of this essay is its tinge of British humor, a poker-faced joke told in mock seriousness. Bear this in mind while reading the essay.

[2] *Julius Caesar*: (100-44 BC) Roman general and statesman, he established the First Triumvirate of Rome with Pompey and Crassus. After a civil war with Pompey, which ended in Pompey's defeat at Pharsalus (48 BC), Caesar became dictator of the Roman Republic.

[3] *the Library of Alexandria*: Once the largest of its kind in the world, it is usually assumed to have been established at the beginning of the 3rd century BC during the reign of Ptolemy II of Egypt. The library is estimated to have contained at its peak 400,000 to 700,000 parchment scrolls. Its destruction has remained a mystery, but one of the most popular beliefs is that when Julius Caesar torched the Egyptian fleet of Cleopatra's brother and rival monarch, the great library of Alexandria was incinerated with about 40,000 volumes burned, and many grammarians, librarians, and scholars killed.

[4] *excellent people*: Mark the ironic tone as if the author were talking on behalf of literary snobs.

[5] *Lo*: archaic and poetic form for "look," often used in "lo and behold"

[6] *another cord...of war*: another evil committed by war; *cord* and *scourge* forming a sustained metaphor

[7] *the Revival of Learning*: the Renaissance

[8] *It was no such thing*: an emphatic denial

[9] *one of...the printing-press*: echoing Benjamin Disraeli (1804-81), the British prime minister who said "Books are fatal: they are the curse of the human race. Nine-tenths of existing books are nonsense, and the clever books are the refutation of that nonsense." Also, he remarked that "[t]he greatest misfortune that ever befell man was the invention of printing."

literature to laugh at sudden mischance[10] and deliberate enmity.[11] We are oppressed, choked, buried[12] by books.

 The beginning of the essay gives readers a foretaste of the author's mock seriousness, the tone that is to pervade the entire writing and characterizes British humor as well. On the surface, Norwood stresses in a matter-of-fact way the negative effects of the invention of the printing-press, making the destruction of the Library of Alexandria appear as a blessing in disguise. However, readers will come to find the irony in the author's claims. Bear in mind that the author's proposal is not to be taken at face value.

Let not the last sentence[13] mislead. I do not mean that we, or some few of us, are asphyxiated[14] by barren learning;[15] that is another story. Nor am I adding yet another voice to the chorus which reviles bad literature—the ceaseless nagging at Miss Ethel M. Dell.[16] I have read none of her books; and in any case that, too, is another story. No; I mean good literature—the books (to take contemporary instances) of Mr. Arnold Bennett[17] and Pierre Loti,[18] of Schnitzler[19] and Mr. Max

[10] *sudden mischance*: primarily such natural disasters as floods and fires

[11] *deliberate enmity*: like banning and burning on purpose. Books need not fear either natural disasters or organized banning and burning thanks to the reproducing power of printing.

[12] *oppressed, choked, buried*: the three consecutive verbs growing in intensity

[13] *last sentence*: the last sentence of the previous paragraph

[14] *asphyxiated*: a formal word meaning choked or suffocated

[15] *barren learning*: unproductive, useless learning

[16] *Ethel M. Dell*: (1881-1939) British woman writer of popular romance novels; her works are severely criticized by some for their sentimentality and lack of intellectual depth.

[17] *Arnold Bennett*: (1867-1931) British novelist, dramatist, and critic; his most renowned works include *Anna of the Five Towns* (1902), *The Old Wives' Tale* (1908), and the *Clayhanger* series (1910-18), most of which depict life of the lower middle classes.

[18] *Pierre Loti*: (1850-1923) French novelist; his voyages as a naval officer provided the exotic settings for works such as *Pêcheur d'Islande* (1886) and *Matelot* (1893).

[19] *Schnitzler*: Arthur (1862-1931), Austrian dramatist, novelist, short story writer, and critic, known for his psychological dramas such as *Anatol* (1893) and *La Ronde* (1897) and sometimes erotic novels

Beerbohm,[20] and countless others ancient and modern, European, American, Asiatic, and Polynesian (an epoch-making novel from Otaheite is much overdue).[21] And when I say "good," I mean "good." I have no intention of imitating those critics whose method of creating a *frisson*[22] is to select the most distinguished author or artist and then, not call him bad, but imply that he is already recognized as bad by some unnamed and therefore awe-inspiring coterie.[23] They do not write: "Mr. Hardy[24] is a bungler," but: "Unless Mr. Jugg[25] takes more pains, his work will soon be indistinguishable from Mr. Hardy's."

The author emphasizes that his focal point is commonly accepted good literature. A list of four writers led off by Mr. Arnold Bennett represents it.

It was a famous, almost a proverbial, remark that Sappho's[26] poems were "few, but roses."[27] What should we say if we found roses on every table, rose-trees along the streets, if our tramcars and lamp-posts were festooned with roses, if roses littered every staircase and dropped from the

---

[20] *Max Beerbohm*: (1872-1956) British essayist, caricaturist, and critic, whose major works include *Caricatures of Twenty-Five Gentlemen* (1896) and the novel *Zuleika Dobson* (1911) criticizing Oxford academics

[21] *an epoch-making...much overdue*: Otaheite is an old name for Tahiti, an island in the central South Pacific, one of the Society Islands in French Polynesia. The whole sentence is a bitter satire suggesting the abuse of such critical clichés as "an epoch-making novel." The author means to say that critics have looked for such a novel in the deserted island of Otaheite for too many years but, to their disappointment, in vain.

[22] *frisson*: [French] a shiver or thrill

[23] *coterie*: a small and often exclusive elitist circle

[24] *Hardy*: apparently Thomas Hardy

[25] *Mr. Jugg*: a randomly chosen name, anybody who aspires to a writing career

[26] *Sappho*: (early 7th cent. BC) Greek lyric woman poet who lived on Lesbos; called by Plato the Tenth Muse, she had a large following of women.

[27] *few, but roses*: a remark by Meleager of Gadara, the compiler of an ancient anthology entitled *Garland*

folds of every newspaper? In a week we should be organizing a "campaign"[28] against them as if they were rats or house-flies. So with books. Week in, week out, a roaring torrent of novels, essays, plays, poems, books of travel, devotion,[29] and philosophy, flows through the land—all good, all "provocative of thought" or else "in the best tradition of British humour;" that is the mischief[30] of it. And they are so huge. Look at *The Forsyte Saga*,[31] confessedly in itself a small library of fiction; consider *The Golden Bough*,[32] how it grows.[33] One is tempted to revolt and pretend in self-defense that these works are clever, facile, and bad. But they are not; far from it. The flood leaves you no breath.[34]

 The author points out the predicament confronting modern readers, that is, their helplessness in face of a surfeit of multitudinous and voluminous good books. One needs only to browse a nearby bookstore to realize the truth of it.

What is to be done? Various remedies are in vogue, none efficacious, indeed—that is my point—all deleterious. There is nothing for it but burning nine-tenths of the stuff.[35] For consider these remedies.

---

[28] *campaign*: a sanitary campaign

[29] *devotion*: religious sermons or prayers. John Donne, author of the famous "For Whom the Bell Tolls," is especially noted for this genre of writing.

[30] *mischief*: harm, disaster

[31] *The Forsyte Saga*: a voluminous trilogy written by John Galsworthy (1867-1933). A *saga* means a collection of fiction or an odyssey.

[32] *The Golden Bough*: Sir James George Frazer (1854-1941) composed it. He collected a host of materials from Polynesian and other tribes. The entire work contains 12 volumes, recording superstitious rituals performed by various primitive peoples in order to conjure up the blessing by God. It is a comparative study of superstitions.

[33] *grows*: The verb is ingeniously selected to collocate with the *bough*, a large tree branch, to form a sustained metaphor.

[34] *The flood...no breath*: This brings back the feeling of asphyxiation in the previous text.

[35] *burning nine-tenths of the stuff*: Mentioned for the first time is the author's proposal, which is extremist, unrealistic, specious and, above all, made in a jesting spirit.

 Pay attention to the author's manner of argument in the following text. He pretends in real earnest in an effort to convince readers of the validity of his proposal of burning the majority of books by refuting available remedies first and then supplying solutions to supposed technical difficulties, putting it in effect in a logical and systematic way. In the process is revealed the quintessence of his humor: his mock seriousness and deadpanning.

 Following is an account of four categories of readers that the author classifies: (1) the non-reader, (2) the selective reader, (3) the literary snob, and (4) the cream reader. Try to sum up their respective characteristics.

First, of course, comes the man who simply gives up, who says: "I haven't the time," and goes under.[36] Virtue, they say, is its own reward.[37] Not for him. He tries to pass it off blusteringly[38] but he is ashamed of himself till death.

Second is the man who, swindler though he be, yet merits applause as paying back the "everyone" journalist[39] in his own base coin.[40] He defines in his mind the little patch of literature that he can read, then condemns all the rest on general grounds evolving a formula which shall be vaguely tenable and shall vaguely absolve him. An eager youth asks: "Pray, Sir, what is your opinion of Mrs. Virginia Woolf?"[41] He replies: "No opinion of mine, my dear Guildenstern,[42]

---

36 *goes under*: disappears from view as a ship being submerged

37 *Virtue, they...own reward*: an English proverb meaning being virtuous is a reward in itself

38 *pass it off blusteringly*: dismiss the issue of reading in aggressive terms decisively

39 *"everyone" journalist*: those who publish their articles regularly in newspapers and say that everyone must read them

40 *base coin*: "To pay somebody back in his own coin" is an idiom meaning to retaliate somebody by similar means. The word *base* is added to denote the inferior quality of the metal.

41 *Virginia Woolf*: (1882-1941) English woman novelist and essayist; for more details, see *The Death of a Moth* in the present anthology.

42 *Guildenstern*: This may be an allusion to the gullible character in *Hamlet* by Shakespeare. Guildenstern and Rosencrantz were Hamlet's friends at the University of Wittenburg, who were sent by Claudius to spy on Hamlet but were consequently trapped by Hamlet.

would be of much use to you, as regards Mrs. Woolf. I fear I am an old fogey. These modern people seem to me to have lost their way. Fielding[43] and Jane Austen[44] are good enough for me." Guildenstern retires, suitably abashed,[45] and vaguely classing Mrs. Woolf with Mrs. Bertram Atkey,[46] Alice Meynell[47] with Ella Wheeler Wilcox.[48]

The second type of readers single out a certain patch of literature that every literate person is supposed to read. Then they justify their neglect of other books on the pretext of personal taste by extolling this limited amount of must-reads. In fact, it is a cunning way to conceal their ignorance.

The third man gallantly faces the insoluble problem by following the fashion.[49] Setting his jaw,[50] he specialises in the moderns of whom one reads

---

[43] *Fielding*: Henry (1707-54), one of the earliest British novelists; his works include *Joseph Andrews* (1742) and *Tom Jones* (1749).

[44] *Jane Austen*: (1775-1817) British female writer, well-known for her penetrating observation of middle-class manners and morality and for her irony, wit, and meticulous style; her novels include *Pride and Prejudice* (1813), *Sense and Sensibility* (1811), and *Emma* (1815).

[45] *suitably abashed*: The eager youth was embarrassed because he was led to believe that his taste was not classical enough.

[46] *Bertram Atkey*: (1880-1952) a minor woman writer of crime novels in the early 20th century, a contemporary of Virginia Woolf's. The sentence means that Guildenstern receives the false impression that Virginia Woolf was no different from a cheaper writer from the way she was mentioned by the "old fogey."

[47] *Alice Meynell*: (1847-1922) English woman poet and essayist, quite influential for a while not only for her literary achievements praised by, say, John Ruskin but also for her involvement in major socio-political issues of her time. Obviously, she is not to be mentioned in the same breath with Ella Wheeler Wilcox.

[48] *Ella Wheeler Wilcox*: (1850-1919) American woman poet who is commonly regarded as second-rate. *Times Literary Supplement (TLS)* once remarked that "she was the most popular poet of either sex and of any age, read by thousands, who, however, never opened Shakespeare."

[49] *following the fashion*: swimming with the tide, being with-it, jumping on the bandwagon

[50] *Setting his jaw*: a gesture of painful determination; biting the bullets

most in the *Times Literary Supplement*. Feverishly he cons[51] the work of all authors enshrined[52] in that austere mausoleum;[53] feverishly, because he may at any moment be caught napping by some more alert practitioner.[54] This third section forms the bulk of the educated class. Members are everywhere and spoil everything. Literature has two great uses: The fundamental use is that it creates and satisfies a keener taste for life;[55] the superficial use is that it provides a precious social amenity.[56] Our third man not only knows nothing of the first; he ruins the second.[57] Decent people[58] converse about books with a view to finding common ground and exchanging delight (deep or frivolous) thereon. But the Third Man is mostly anti-social.[59] He selects some voluminous[60] author and catechises[61] his victim till he has found a

---

[51] *cons*: a colloquial word meaning commits to memory

[52] *enshrined*: a verb that accords well with the following metaphoric *mausoleum*

[53] *austere mausoleum*: a sarcastic metaphor for *Times Literary Supplement (TLS)*; a little unfair in the editors' opinion

[54] *practitioner*: practitioner of such a conning art. The snobs are trying to remember as much as possible from *TLS* so that they can talk about it to show themselves off on social occasions. If you know about some authors and books that others do not know, then you triumph over them.

[55] *The fundamental...for life*: The author is being serious and means what he says.

[56] *social amenity*: The author is more or less jesting in assigning the second superficial use of literature to enliven social events when people have books to talk about.

[57] *Our third...the second*: He ruins it because he is always trying to rake in as much as possible that is not known to others. For example, he may pose a lot of strange questions to others so as to make them feel embarrassed not being able to answer them. The third type of readers read books not to acquire a keener sense of life. Nor do they contribute to discussion of books at social functions.

[58] *Decent people*: in contrast to showy, morbid, or abnormal people like the snobs; decent in the sense that they wish to exchange real pleasures they derive from their reading experiences

[59] *anti-social*: in the sense that they tend to ruin social amenity

[60] *voluminous*: A voluminous author is key to the third reader's finesse because only from such a writer can he find topics for discussion that most others are not well read up in.

[61] *catechises*: a religious word meaning "poses questions" as by a pastor in a kind of liturgy or religious sermon wherein the congregation are supposed to answer

work which the victim has not read. With a hoot of joyous disgust[62] he leaps upon the confession and extols the unread book as the finest of the list. Such a man will always be found smacking his lips in public over Stevenson's[63] "Wrong Box" to Lewis Carroll's[64] "Sylvie and Bruno." Chief of this tribe, apparently, was no less a person than Coleridge, of whom Hazlitt reports: "He did not speak of his (Butler's)[65] 'Analogy,' but of his 'Sermons at the Rolls Chapel,'[66] of which I had never heard. Coleridge somehow always contrived to prefer the unknown to the known."[67] Exactly; for the great aims of such people are (1) to avoid being scored off; (2) to score off others.[68] It is this ignoble competition which has ruined taste, for to carry it on we must needs[69] follow the crowd. It would never do to enter a room full of persons discussing Masefield[70] or Walter de la Mare[71] and explain wistfully: "I've been reading Whittier[72] all day." Masefield and de la Mare are good—

---

62 *a hoot of joyous disgust*: a very vivid description of the snob. *Hoot* is an onomatopoeic word showing contempt and disgust mixed with joy of triumph.

63 *Stevenson*: Robert Louis (1850-94), Scottish novelist, poet, and travel notes writer, whose most representative works include *Treasure Island* (1883), *The Strange Case of Dr Jekyll and Mr Hyde* (1886), and *Kidnapped* (1886)

64 *Lewis Carroll*: (1832-98) English writer of children's classics, the most famous of which include *Alice in Wonderland* (1865) and *Through the Looking Glass* (1871)

65 *Butler*: Samuel (1612-80), English poet remembered primarily for his three-part satirical poem *Hudibras* (1663-78), not to be confused with his 19th-century namesake who wrote *Erewhon* (1872)

66 *the Rolls Chapel*: an archive in London, first constructed by Henry Ⅲ

67 *to prefer...the known*: a bad habit of snobbery typical of the third type of readers

68 *to avoid...off others*: These two sentences boil down to one idea: to get the upper hand. By splitting one idea into two sentences, the author achieves the desired effect of satirical emphasis.

69 *needs*: an adverb meaning ever

70 *Masefield*: John (1878-1967), British writer most notable for his poetry, including the colloquial *Everlasting Mercy* (1911) and *Reynard the Fox* (1919). He became Poet Laureate in 1930.

71 *Walter de la Mare*: (1873-1956) English poet remembered for his verse for children

72 *Whittier*: John Greenleaf (1807-92), American poet and staunch abolitionist. He is best known for his poems on rural themes, especially "Snow-Bound" (1866).

yes, maybe;[73] but we keep up with them not for that reason, but because they are the gods of the literary weeklies.[74] Our notion that commerce is the first of human activities has ruined the noble art of reading; for though competition is the life of trade it is the death of social intercourse and of social arts. The greatest things in life flourish by being shared, not by being monopolized.

 Mark the underlined sentence above. The author's criticism of the snobbish reader reflects his attitude toward arts and social communication. Also, reading is a highly personal affair, and there is no point competing with each other over who has read what.

Our Fourth Class is by far the most respectable.[75] It advocates what may be termed the Cream Theory. "Since we cannot read all the good books, let us attempt to know the best that has been written in all times and places."[76] So after a solid[77] banquet of English, they move off to Dante[78] (a great man for this class, and read by scarcely anyone else),[79] Goethe, Tolstoy, Racine, Ibsen, Cervantes, Virgil, Homer.[80] A respectable kind of person, we said; but not necessarily sagacious. In fact, they are utterly, almost horribly, mistaken.

For it is an error to suppose that because an author has by the world in general been placed upon a pinnacle, every reader can derive much good

---

[73] *yes, maybe*: Second thoughts make the statement tentative.

[74] *literary weeklies*: such as *TLS*

[75] *Our Fourth...most respectable*: ironic

[76] *to know...and places*: Traditionalists like Harold Bloom, a Yale University professor of literature, may be counted as a modern exponent of the Cream Theory. He compiles *The Western Canon* (1994) and likes to draw up booklists for students. Similarly, the "Great Books of the Western World", 443 in number by 74 authors, espoused by Robert Maynard Hutchins and Mortimer J. Adler of the University of Chicago in the 1950s embody such a theory.

[77] *solid*: very filling, substantial

[78] *Dante*: Dante Alighieri (1265–1321), Italian poet, author of *The Divine Comedy* (c1308-20)

[79] *read by scarcely anyone else*: What an anticlimax!

[80] *Goethe, Tolstoy...Virgil, Homer*: respectively German, Russian, French, Norwegian, Spanish, ancient Roman, and ancient Greek masters of some great books, all well-known enough to deserve an individual note

from him. Do we not see[81] that a bright boy of twelve finds nothing particular in Milton or Thackeray? (Someone objects: "Oh, but he does!"[82] One in million,[83] my friend; anything beyond that is propagandist falsehood.)[84] Why? Because he is not yet ready for them. They are magnificent, but they wrote for adults—as, unfortunately, most authors have written. Let him[85] gain by experience the needful equipment, and he will appreciate them well enough. And the analogous proposition is true of the Cream Theory. Take a person who has completed the first stage, namely a reading of English, and place him suddenly before those foreign Great Ones. They will bore him to tears. Any dramatic canons drawn exclusively from Shakespeare prove that Racine is a simpleton;[86] any poetical canons, that Virgil is affected, Homer childish, and Dante no poet at all; any psychological canons, that Ibsen is "a dirty old blackguard" (a quotation, this, from a man deeply read in English). Yes, they are bored to tears; but since our national temperament understands not aesthetic right, only moral right, they feel that they must be wicked if they are bored by great authors.[87] The familiar result follows. Thousands of otherwise[88] honest folk sit flogging themselves[89] through *Andromaque*[90] or *Don Quixote* with a dazed sense that they are making the

---

[81] *Do we not see*: Note the rhetorical *not* in the question, the expected answer to which is "Yes."

[82] *Oh, but he does*: Oh, he does derive much good from reading Milton or Thackeray.

[83] *One in million*: This is my answer.

[84] *propagandist falsehood*: a downright lie with a view to brainwashing

[85] *him*: the said boy of twelve

[86] *Any dramatic...a simpleton*: In the author's eyes, Shakespeare eclipses the well-known French dramatist in terms of diversity, poetic beauty, in-depth psychological probing, and so forth. In a word, Shakespeare's works are nonpareil, especially to the native English. And comparing across the boundaries of national cultural backgrounds is beside the point.

[87] *they feel...great authors*: The readers feel ashamed that they must have been morally deficient in failing to appreciate those great foreign writers.

[88] *otherwise*: except in matters concerning literary appreciation

[89] *flogging themselves*: expressing what a tough time they had reading the following works

[90] *Andromaque*: a tragedy by Racine

Almighty somehow their debtor.[91] Works like these depend for their true effect upon a whole literary tradition, a whole national culture, unrevealed to the worshipper. Every writer needs a considerable equipment[92] in his reader, and it is precisely the greatest writers ("simple" though they are called by the critics) who demand most. They sum up gigantic experiences of the race in politics, religion, philosophy, literature.

Nevertheless our friend[93] plods on, head bowed and muscles tense. The Cream Theory, even for its most genuine and respectable adherents,[94] is a delusion.[95] That is not the way in which literature "works," or life. As well[96] saw off[97] the topmost six feet of the Jungfrau,[98] set the mass up in your back-garden,[99] and take your guests out to admire the terrific grandeur of the scenery.

The Cream Theory finds its best expression in those dreadful lists of the World's Best Books. Everyone who has glanced through those catalogues knows how repellent they are; but does he realise why? It is because they are inhuman.[100] The list is nobody's list, though it contains something which would be in everybody's list.[101]

---

[91] *making the...their debtor*: They feel as if they were fulfilling a moral obligation, thus discharging a debt to the Almighty God.

[92] *equipment*: not only reading skills but also intellectual preparedness or the capability to appreciate the unique beauty and profundities of these Great Books

[93] *our friend*: the fourth reader who subscribes to the Cream Theory

[94] *genuine and respectable adherents*: honest members of the type. The adjective *respectable* is no longer ironic here.

[95] *delusion*: an imaginary thing

[96] *As well*: to put the theory into practice, one may as well

[97] *saw off*: cut off with a saw

[98] *Jungfrau*: literally "young lady," the name of a mountain summit in the Bernese Alps of south-central Switzerland

[99] *set the...your back-garden*: like a massive "rockery" in a Chinese garden. What grotesque imagination with which to reify the Cream Theory!

[100] *It is...are inhuman*: The booklists are awe-inspiring, distancing, off-putting—anything but human. At the sight of the books, you are afraid that you will not finish reading so many books within such a short lifetime unless you are superhuman.

[101] *The list...everybody's list*: There cannot be a one-size-for-all booklist considering the different predilections and tastes of each and every reader.

Now prepare yourself for the absurdly interesting proposal of first blacklisting the books to be burned and then of systematically submitting them to "wholesale destruction." Read the following with an open mind, though, so that you know how true humor tells itself apart from cheap jocosity.

So much for the various types of reader. None of them solves the difficulty. What, then, is to be done? It is no answer to say: "Read what you can, and leave the rest," because the size[102] of the unread mass has positive and evil effects. In the honest it causes worry, a sense of waste;[103] in the dishonest it causes snobbery and the desire to outshine.[104] There is but one remedy: a wholesale destruction.[105] Quite[106] nine-tenths of the good books should be burnt; of the bad we need say, here as elsewhere, nothing—they are drawn towards the pulping-machine by a force persistent as gravitation.[107] "But," say some, quoting perchance[108] their own reviews, "your suggestion raises more difficulties than it solves." Scarcely; but I see two problems, which are by no means so hard to solve as might appear: What are we to destroy? How are we to destroy it?

Let me answer the second question first. When a book is condemned, all public libraries burn their copies with whatever rites[109] may seem fitting

---

[102] *size*: great size

[103] *In the...of waste*: in the honest reader, like in the case of the non-reader

[104] *in the...to outshine*: an echo of "to avoid being scored off and score off others" in the previous text (Cf. Page 10, Note 68)

[105] *a wholesale destruction*: a book holocaust, so to speak

[106] *Quite*: no less or fewer than

[107] *they are...as gravitation*: Bad books are automatically reduced to pulp, automatically as in a free fall.

[108] *perchance*: by chance, perhaps

[109] *rites*: extremely funny to think of burning books in public with elaborate rituals such as playing of dirge music with someone making a mourning address. Some say the statement is an unfortunate prophecy of the Crystal Night (Nov. 9-10, 1938) in Nazi Germany, when, among other things, fires were lit, and Jewish prayer books, scrolls, artwork, and philosophy texts were thrown into the flames.

to its subject-matter and the occasion. It becomes illegal to possess, buy, sell the book or to expose it for sale. All copies secretly preserved are stripped of their value by an enactment that any person quoting them, referring to them, or in any manner whatsoever seeking personal credit from them, shall be prosecuted under a Disturbance of the Realm Act.[110] A fixed sum should be paid for each copy handed over to the police;[111] that is the way, more or less, in which wolves were extirpated.[112] That great army of persons who thrive on the various forms of bibliography,[113] the booksellers, the librarians, the makers and printers of catalogues, the ghouls who (like vultures on the battle-field)[114] hover over the twopenny box[115] should be told that the state is not robbing them either of livelihood or of excitement.[116] "Of whatever thing a man is a smart guardian," says Plato, "of that he is also a smart thief."[117] Let these experts continue their function of tracking books, but for destruction, not preservation.[118] They will not care. What they love is their hard-won knowledge of the quarry,[119] its appearance, methods of concealment, and habitat; not its ultimate destiny. Does the enthusiast who

---

[110] *All copies...Realm Act*: Law is appealed to make the whole business appear all the more formal and real.

[111] *A fixed...the police*: as compensation

[112] *that is...were extirpated*: The author compares books to wolves or annoying pests such as flies and rats, which are to be eliminated, an echo of the earlier "sanitary campaign" (Cf. Page 6, Note 28).

[113] *bibliography*: the book industry

[114] *ghouls who (...the battle-field)*: blood-sucking profiteers like vultures preying on the war dead

[115] *twopenny box*: a very small, cheap booth selling magazines, newspapers, and so on

[116] *of livelihood or of excitement*: They do not have to worry about their bread and butter and can continue to enjoy the delight of hunting in a new social order of booklessness.

[117] *Of whatever...smart thief*: It means the more ingeniously you guard a thing, the smarter a thief you become of it. 钱锺书 translated this sentence into 彼欲慎卫之，彼亦巧窃之.

[118] *but for...not preservation*: Only the *why* changes, while the exciting *how* remains the same.

[119] *quarry*: a game bird or animal; the prey

follows the scent of a First Folio[120] across England and at last runs it to earth in an apple-loft,[121] sit down forthwith and read *The Merchant of Venice*? Not he. If he ever reads the play at all (which is highly doubtful) he prefers a popular edition with pink pictures[122] of the Rialto.[123] For him the chase is all. The new regime will alter his life and enjoyment surprisingly little.[124] He will give interviews with the title, "How I Stamped Out Fielding."[125] Nor is this the only way in which our newspapers will be brightened. During the first years of the new Golden Age[126] we shall read of a fanatic who, hearing a Cabinet Minister quote the words "as well almost kill a man as kill a good book,"[127] instantly shot him through the head,[128] and of detectives at peril of their lives raiding a den of Wordsworth-printers.[129]

Before we consider the second problem in its main aspect, the selection of the extant works which are to be banned, let us complete the minor

---

120 *First Folio*: the first effort ever to produce a complete Shakespeare in 1623, seven years after the playwright's death, edited by two of his theatrical friends. A *folio* is a book consisting of large sheets of paper that are folded in half to make two leaves or four pages. (Compare a quarto.) About 1,000 copies of it were printed, of which 200 or so—mostly dismembered or in bad shape —have survived to this day as very expensive collectables.

121 *apple-loft*: an attic, supposedly an unnoticeable place

122 *a popular...pink pictures*: an edition for children indicating poor taste

123 *Rialto*: an island of Venice where a market of hustle and bustle was and is situated

124 *The new...surprisingly little*: He did not care at all if the books he had dug up were to be destroyed ultimately.

125 *How I Stamped Out Fielding*: an example of the excitement of a hunter of Fielding's works with a view to annihilating them

126 *Golden Age*: an age of booklessness ironically

127 *as well...good book*: from John Milton's *Aereopagitica*: "As good almost kill a man as kill a good book: who kills a man kills a reasonable creature, God's image; but he who destroys a good book, kills reason itself, kills the image of God, as it were, in the eye."

128 *shot him through the head*: another hypothetical sensational incident, a forerunner of present-day terrorism

129 *detectives at...of Wordsworth-printers*: yet another imagined sensational incident resulting from banning Wordsworth

task of diminishing heavily the future output. I should favour the absolute prohibition of all novels for the next ten years.[130] Then, during five years[131] only those novels, hitherto held up, should be issued which both publisher and author still thought worthwhile. After that, if people persisted in writing novels, the Government might refuse permits to those treating the following topics: (a) the Great War,[132] (b) girls dressed in salad[133] and living beside lagoons,[134] (c) imaginary kingdoms with regents called Black Boris,[135] (d) any type of "lure."[136] As for indigenous works other than novels, they might be allowed freedom of publication so long as the price were[137] not less than one penny a page.[138] This would keep down the output effectually and would also give Cambridge University Press[139] an equal chance with other publishing concerns.

There remains[140] the chief and most arduous task, to decide which books already extant should perish. The work is enormous, and must be spread over many years. Ten thousand per annum[141] seems a likely figure, which

---

130 *I should...ten years*: overall moratorium: an unlikelihood everybody, the author himself included, is aware of

131 *five years*: five years out of the ten. Mathematical precision helps enhance the credibility of the incredible.

132 *the Great War*: WWI standing for the theme on violence

133 *salad*: creamy or flesh-colored material looking good enough to eat

134 *girls dressed...beside lagoons*: waterside nymphs standing for the theme on sex

135 *Black Boris*: another name for the devil; the theme on devilry

136 *any type of "lure"*: a list of all bad things that can conveniently come under this rubric like "其他" in Chinese

137 *were*: Note the subjunctive.

138 *As for...a page*: As long as the price is bargained down, the book sellers will not have much money to make. As a result, publications may increasingly phase out.

139 *Cambridge University Press*: standing for all prestigious university presses

140 *There remains*: introducing, as it were, a perfectly logical sentence that, however, expresses sheer illogicality

141 *Ten thousand per annum*: being mathematical again to reinforce the false impression of being scientific

could be rapidly increased as the public grew accustomed to the system and observed that the sky did not fall.[142] A committee of fifty (ten of whom must, and all of whom might, be women)[143] should each year promulgate its list, to appear simultaneously with the New Year Honours list.[144] The Committee should contain representatives of every class and—an unusual thing in committees—of every age.[145] First, that[146] the more nervous might be in some degree reassured, they would make a list of books which in any case should be preserved—books which almost everyone really likes and really reads. It would be a surprisingly small list,[147] but there is no danger of our losing Shakespeare, most of Dickens, the Sherlock Holmes stories. This done, they would on each New Year's Day promulgate their list of ten thousand books.

Nothing, however, is further from my intention than tyranny.[148] All I aim at is effecting what the public in its heart desires.[149] Therefore any of these ten thousand may be saved if it can be shown[150] that the public really wishes to save it. The proof must, however, be given in deeds, not words as heretofore[151] and should be conducted on the following lines. The list is promulgated on January 1st, but the destruction does not begin until August 1st.[152] During July all publishers and librarians are to make

---

142 *the sky did not fall*: a phrase corresponding to 天不会塌下来. Find other examples showing different cultures at times converge, although they basically diverge.

143 *ten of...be women*: as if he were making a serious proposal

144 *New Year Honours list*: a list of recently conferred peerage

145 *age*: age group/bracket

146 *that*: in order that

147 *small list*: This indicates that the number of the truly popular books is indeed small—a sane, truthful observation embedded amidst absurdities.

148 *Nothing, however...than tyranny*: Tyranny is by no means my intention.

149 *All I...heart desires*: I only verbalize or speak aloud what the public secretly wishes.

150 *shown*: proved

151 *heretofore*: up to that point of time

152 *The list...August 1st*: On Jan. 1 every year, a list of outlawed books is made. However, they will be left at large and given seven months as a grace period during which these books can prove their innocuity or usefulness.

a return of the number of persons who during the preceding six months have purchased or read each of the books prescribed.[153] Anyone claiming to have read a book owned by himself would be subjected to a brief oral examination.[154] The works would then be arranged in three categories.[155] Any which had been read by ten thousand people should be struck from the list and given immunity for fifteen years.[156] Those which had been read by less than ten but more than five thousand should be immune for five years. Each work which had found less than five thousand supporters should be retained for one year if any single person could be found to prove his love for it by making a sacrifice to ensure its preservation. This would form the sound test of that "revelling in" authors of which we hear so much.

 The time slot from Jan. 1 to Aug. 1 and "the three categories" are especially interesting. Consider the last category, for instance. Is 1-5,000 a viable range? The only possible conclusion from such much ado about nothing is that in the end NO book is actually burned!

Author

Gilbert Norwood (1880-1954) was born in Sheffield in northern England on Nov. 23, 1880. Early in his life, he evinced an aptitude for learning classical languages and won a classical scholarship to St. John's College, Cambridge. After winning distinctions of every kind in his undergraduate career, he held appointments at Manchester and Cardiff. He

---

[153] *During July...books prescribed*: July will be the last month of the grace period as well as a Month of Reckoning in which statistical research is to be carried out on how popular or unpopular the books in question are so that the final decision on whether to destroy them or not is eventually made.

[154] *a brief oral examination*: to check if the person's claim is true or false

[155] *The works...three categories*: a total Utopia to follow, which would sound very realistic though

[156] *Any which...fifteen years*: In that case, many of the newly published Chinese books in the mainland of China would have been compulsorily destroyed as each of them runs hardly more than a couple of thousand copies and sells fewer.

went to Toronto as Professor of Latin in 1926 and became Professor of Classics two years later, a position he held down until retirement in 1951. He died as Professor Emeritus of Classics at University College, Toronto in 1954. Norwood is best known for his work on Greek drama, publishing among others *The Riddle of the Bacchae: The Last Stage of Euripides' Religious Views* (1908), *Greek Tragedy* (1920), and *Plautus and Terence* (1932). He used to be an avid collector of books. It is very thought-provoking for a true book lover to write about burning books.

Text

Apparently revolting at an increasingly profit-conscious publishing industry and an indiscriminate reading public, he wrote this essay in 1920, which was widely read among the literati of the time. Some called it caustic; others ludicrous, but all agreed that it was "amusing" (*TLS*). For those who doubt the essay's applicability today, American woman writer and critic Evelyn C. Leeper's remark may be quoted: "If one replaces *The Forsyte Saga* with *The Wheel of Time*, and *The Golden Bough* with *Discworld*, nothing else need be done to make it as true today as then, or to note that it was as true then as today."

Further Reading

"On Destroying Books," J. C. Squire
Selected Modern English Essays, Humphrey Milford
《书太多了》，吕叔湘
"The Decline and Fall of Literature," Andrew Delbanco

The Death of the Moth

by Virginia Woolf

Moths that fly by day are not properly[1] to be called moths; they do not excite that pleasant sense of dark autumn nights and ivy-blossom which the commonest yellow-underwing[2] asleep in the shadow of the curtain never fails to rouse in us. They are hybrid creatures, neither gay[3] like butterflies nor sombre[4] like their own species. Nevertheless the present specimen, with his narrow hay-coloured wings, fringed with a tassel[5] of the same colour, seemed to be content with life.[6] It was a pleasant morning, mid-September, mild, benignant,[7] yet with a keener breath[8] than that of the summer months. The plough was already scoring[9] the field opposite the window, and where the share[10] had been, the earth was pressed flat and gleamed with moisture. Such vigour came rolling in[11] from the fields and the down[12] beyond that[13] it

---

1 *properly*: in the strict technical sense

2 *yellow-underwing*: a kind of nocturnal moths, having brightly colored hind wings visible only during flight

3 *gay*: bright in color

4 *sombre*: dark-colored, gloomy-looking

5 *tassel*: The wings end in loose threads as if for decorative purposes.

6 *content with life*: the moth's lack of movements for the moment being emphasized in sharp contrast to the vigorous scene outdoors depicted in the following

7 *benignant*: temperate, pleasant to live in

8 *keener breath*: a cooler and more crisp wind

9 *scoring*: ploughing, cutting asunder

10 *share*: ploughshare, the cutting blade

11 *rolling in*: rushing in, suggesting invasion with force and in plentiful sequence

12 *down*: low round bare hills in southern England

13 *that*: grammatically required by the beginning *such*

was difficult to keep the eyes strictly turned upon the book. The rooks[14] too were keeping one of their annual festivities;[15] soaring round the tree tops until it looked as if a vast net with thousands of black knots[16] in it had been cast up into the air; which, after a few moments sank slowly down upon the trees until every twig seemed to have a knot at the end of it.[17] Then, suddenly, the net would be thrown into the air again in a wider circle this time, with the utmost clamour and vociferation,[18] as though to be thrown into the air and settle slowly down upon the tree tops were a tremendously exciting experience.[19]

 Mark Woolf's appeal to the senses and her evocation as well as representation of vivid moth imagery from the very beginning of the essay, which, among other things, characterize the style of her *belles-lettres*. Pay attention to the qualifiers of color: *dark*, *yellow*, *hybrid*, *gay*, *sombre*, and *hay-coloured* in the description. They combine to add to the intensity of the imagery and manifest Woolf's emphasis on perception for both modern writers and readers alike.

 Pay attention to the underlined sentence. Temporal reference comes after the moth imagery with which Woolf is apparently preoccupied. The sentence itself is typical of a familiar essay style with *mid-September* occurring as an afterthought.

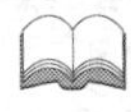 The temporal reference serves as an axle around which the focal point is shifted from the moth to the outdoor scene. This forms the basic level of the contrast in this essay, i.e., the moth/indoors vs. rooks, etc./outdoors or interiority vs. exteriority.

 The imagery of rooks rising and falling appears in many of Woolf's novels and essays, including *Mrs. Dalloway*, *The Waves*, and "On Being Ill."

---

14 *rooks*: black European crows noted for their gregarious and clamorous habits

15 *annual festivities*: festival celebrations with the word *annual* suggesting that it was the season when rooks are particularly active

16 *a vast...black knots*: a metaphor, describing a large flock of black rooks frolicking as if spreading a net

17 *a knot...of it*: a bird perching on every twig

18 *clamour and vociferation*: noise and loud din as if numerous confused voices spoke up at once. The use of the two words intensifies the vigor and vitality of the outdoor scene.

19 *a tremendously exciting experience*: as if the observer/narrator were feeling vicariously on behalf of the birds

The same energy[20] which inspired[21] the rooks, the ploughmen, the horses, and even, it seemed, the lean bare-backed downs,[22] sent the moth fluttering from side to side of his[23] square of the window-pane. One could not help watching him. One[24] was, indeed, conscious of a queer feeling of pity for him. The possibilities of pleasure seemed that morning so enormous and so various that to have only a moth's part in life, and a day moth's at that,[25] appeared a hard fate, and his zest in enjoying his meagre opportunities to the full, pathetic.[26] He flew vigorously to one corner of his compartment,[27] and, after waiting there a second, flew across to the other. What remained for him but[28] to fly to a third corner and then to a fourth?[29] That was all he could do, in spite of the size of the downs, the width of the sky, the far-off smoke of houses, and the romantic voice,[30] now and then, of a steamer out at sea. What he could do he did.[31] Watching him,[32] it seemed

---

[20] *energy*: a key word; raw force of nature or *Vitalität* in German

[21] *inspired*: stimulated, agitated

[22] *the lean bare-backed downs*: Even inanimate objects seemed to be inspired.

[23] *his*: The possessive pronoun indicates that the following was the moth's territory or kingdom, tiny as it was.

[24] *One*: Instead of "I," Woolf uses the universal pronoun, thus creating a sense of invited involvement and achieving an objectifying effect.

[25] *at that*: furthermore; used when an extra piece of information is being given

[26] *The possibilities...full, pathetic*: Mark the contrast between the "enormous" and "various" "possibilities of pleasure" on the one hand and the moth's "pathetic" "meagre opportunities" on the other.

[27] *compartment*: a separate section. The word heightens the isolation of the moth from the spacious, lively world outside.

[28] *but*: except

[29] *What remained...a fourth*: This rhetorical question strengthens the futility of the moth's strenuous efforts and his "hard fate." The four corners of the compartment suggest the limitations of a very small area to which the moth is confined.

[30] *romantic voice*: whistle (of the ship) giving rise to romantic fantasizing

[31] *That was...he did*: There was a dynamic world outside, but this tiny moth just did not belong there. The sense of helplessness is thus made all the more poignant in these lines.

[32] *Watching him*: an illogical "dangling" participle phrase when one considers the subject *it*—an objectionable practice in grammar but common usage in actual writing

as if a fibre, very thin but pure, of the enormous energy of the world had been thrust[33] into his frail and diminutive[34] body. As often as he crossed the pane,[35] I could fancy that a thread of vital light[36] became visible. He was little or nothing but life.

 "He was little or nothing but life." The sentence is forceful in that it sings loud praises of life, although forms of life, big or small, vary. To be sure, the magnitude of the energy contrasts with the frailty and evanescence of the moth's life. Nonetheless, the moth's life is equally endowed with "energy" and "vital light."

 Note how prose rhythm is achieved by juxtaposing and alternating long and short sentences. An interested reader is encouraged to measure the different lengths of the sentences in the paragraph: long ones such as the 1st and the 4th and short ones like "One could not help watching him," "What he could do he did," and "He was little or nothing but life."

Yet, because he was so small, and so simple a form of the energy that was rolling in at the open window and driving its way[37] through so many narrow and intricate corridors[38] in my own brain and in those of other human beings, there was something marvellous as well as pathetic[39] about him. It was as if someone had taken a tiny bead of pure life and decking it[40] as lightly[41] as possible with down and feathers, had set it dancing and

---

[33] *thrust*: pushed

[34] *diminutive*: tiny, smaller than small

[35] *As often...the pane*: a clause of time adverbial

[36] *a thread of vital light*: Study this phrase "thread of vital light" along with the underlined "a fibre...enormous energy" in the preceding context. Woolf demonstrates that rumination has to be based on observation. The more closely one observes, the more profound one's rumination is.

[37] *driving its way*: reminiscent of the earlier "rolling in" and a "keener breath" in the first paragraph

[38] *narrow and intricate corridors*: literally the channels of a nervous system, and metaphorically the layers of consciousness. Mark how Woolf connects the objective world with the subjective one here.

[39] *marvellous as well as pathetic*: *pathetic* taken for granted because it was already mentioned, and *marvellous* is the sentiment newly felt

[40] *it*: the first time that the moth has been referred to as *it* instead of *he* because of the comparison of it to a bead

[41] *lightly*: referring to touches of the hand or whatever other instruments

zigzagging to show us the true nature of life.[42] Thus displayed one could not get over the strangeness[43] of it. One is apt to forget all about life, seeing it humped and bossed and garnished and cumbered[44] so that it has to move with the greatest circumspection and dignity. Again, the thought of all that life might have been had he been born in any other shape[45] caused one to view his simple activities with a kind of pity.

The use of the underlined qualifier *marvellous*, along with another underlined word *dignity*, denotes the subtle change in the observer/narrator's contemplation upon the moth. Pity has persisted, on the one hand. But on top of it now is admiration for marvelousness and dignity. Consider in what way the moth is marvelous and dignified from the perspective of the narrator and how the mixed feelings are mediated by the concept of life.

Note the cluster of expressions about life: "bead of pure life," "true nature of life," "all about life," and "all that life might have been." Undoubtedly, Woolf sees life in the moth above all else, however diminutive a creature it is.

After a time, tired by his dancing apparently, he[46] settled on the window ledge in the sun, and, the queer spectacle[47] being at an end, I forgot about him.[48] Then, looking up, my eye was caught by him. He was trying to resume his dancing, but seemed either so stiff or so awkward that he

---

[42] *It was...of life*: This sentence, what with *decking*, *dancing*, and *zigzagging*, is typical of Woolf's subtle and gossamer essay style. The metaphor, like an epiphany, is sustainably descriptive in an exquisite way, scintillating with a characteristic perspicacity.

[43] *strangeness*: strange in that life can be imbued in such a diminutive creature. Also recall the "queer feeling of pity" in the previous paragraph.

[44] *humped and...and cumbered*: The breathless four past participles are highly descriptive of the moth's awkward posture and ponderous movement in its futile and pitiable struggle in anticipation of the doom.

[45] *had he...other shape*: reminiscent of the horses and rooks outside

[46] *he*: using "he" again, equating the moth with you and me

[47] *queer spectacle*: Only when the observer/narrator is feelingly attentive to detail can he/she see such a "queer spectacle."

[48] *I forgot about him*: denoting the passage of time

could only flutter to the bottom of the window-pane; and when he tried to fly across it he failed.[49] Being intent[50] on other matters I watched these futile attempts for a time without thinking, unconsciously waiting for him to resume his flight, as one waits for a machine,[51] that has stopped momentarily, to start again without considering the reason of its failure. After perhaps a seventh attempt[52] he slipped from the wooden ledge and fell, fluttering his wings, on to his back on the window sill. The helplessness of his attitude[53] roused me. It flashed upon[54] me that he was in difficulties; he could no longer raise himself; his legs struggled vainly. But, as I stretched out a pencil, meaning to help him to right himself,[55] it came over[56] me that the failure and awkwardness were the approach of death. I laid the pencil down again.[57]

While the shadow of death has been cast from the very beginning, it looms large now. From the zestful dancing creature, the moth is reduced to a moribund state. Words such as *futile*, *helplessness*, and *vainly* all emphasize the irresistible force of death. The unremitting struggle on the part of the tiny moth against a formidable fate, under these circumstances, adds to the tragic intensity produced by Woolf, who has in turn experienced pity, wonder, and now helpless remorse.

---

[49] *when he...he failed*: This failure signals the beginning of the end.

[50] *intent*: concentrated, with her mind roaming elsewhere

[51] *machine*: The comparison of the moth to an inanimate machine contrasts sharply with the creature dancing and zigzagging in the previous context. Life with its vigor drained off is nothing but mechanical.

[52] *a seventh attempt*: It reflects both the observer's absorption, even though her mind had roamed, and the moth's perseverance.

[53] *attitude*: posture

[54] *flashed upon*: suddenly occurred to

[55] *right himself*: bring himself to an upright position

[56] *came over*: dawned upon

[57] *I laid...down again*: a simple enough sentence but a gesture of giving up with helplessness in face of the overpowering death

The legs agitated themselves once more. I looked as if for the enemy[58] against which he struggled. I looked out of doors. What had happened there? Presumably it was midday,[59] and work in the fields had stopped. Stillness and quiet had replaced the previous animation. The birds had taken themselves off to feed in the brooks. The horses stood still. Yet the power[60] was there all the same,[61] massed outside indifferent, impersonal, not attending to anything in particular.[62] Somehow it was opposed to the little hay-coloured moth.[63] It was useless to do anything. One could only watch the extraordinary efforts made by those tiny legs against an oncoming doom which could, had it chosen, have submerged an entire city, not merely a city, but masses of human beings; nothing, I knew, had any chance against death.[64] Nevertheless after a pause of exhaustion the legs fluttered again. It was superb this last protest,[65] and so frantic that he succeeded at last in righting himself. One's sympathies, of course, were all on the side of life.[66]

---

[58] *as if for the enemy*: Woolf knew as well as we do that if there were an enemy, it was an enemy incarnate, a force determined to destroy the moth.

[59] *Presumably it was midday*: temporal reference again in the middle of the narration; *presumably* indicates that time elapsed unnoticed.

[60] *power*: the energy in the preceding context

[61] *Yet the...the same*: the power made all the more formidable by its invisibility and by its ominous perennial presence

[62] *indifferent, impersonal...in particular*: qualifiers all suggesting that death is the Great Leveler, unfeeling and indiscriminate

[63] *Somehow it...hay-coloured moth*: For one reason or another, death has chosen as its victim of the day the unfortunate moth.

[64] *One could...against death*: This is a very powerful sentence evoking mixed feelings of sympathy and resignation. While the strenuous efforts by the tiny creature were "extraordinary," death as a massively destructive power always laughs the last laugh.

[65] *It was...last protest*: The last-ditch struggle was like a protest. Feeble as it was, the protest on the part of the weak against the strong was superb. The tagged position of the phrase appositional to *it* renders it exceptionally prominent.

[66] *life*: even though it is fragile and easily perishable

Also, when there was nobody to care or to know,[67] this gigantic effort on the part of an insignificant little moth, against a power of such magnitude, to retain what no one else valued or desired to keep, moved one strangely.[68] Again, somehow, one saw life, a pure bead.[69] I lifted the pencil again, useless though I knew it to be. But even as I did so, the unmistakable tokens of death showed themselves. The body relaxed, and instantly grew stiff. The struggle was over. The insignificant little creature now knew[70] death.[71] As I looked at the dead moth, this minute[72] wayside[73] triumph of so great a force over so mean an antagonist filled me with wonder. Just as life had been strange a few minutes before, so death was now as strange. The moth having righted himself[74] now lay most decently and uncomplainingly composed. O yes, he seemed to say, death is stronger than I am.[75]

 Described in detail in this last paragraph is the moth's last "frantic" struggle prior to death

---

[67] *there was...to know*: Death occurs every second, minute, and hour. Sad is the fact that numerous deaths happen uncared-for and unnoticed.

[68] *moved one strangely*: One was touched to the quick in a strange way by a death without a dirge or remorse felt about it. The disproportion between the moth's size and its stamina reinforces the narrator's sentiment.

[69] *life, a pure bead*: pulsating life compared to a bead again, a bead without impurities yet easily breakable that stands no rough handling

[70] *knew*: experienced

[71] *The insignificant...knew death*: This is a projection of the observer/narrator's consciousness and feeling. Try to empathize with Woolf's attitude toward the moth, life, and death at the moment.

[72] *minute*: slight, negligible as if the moth were but an accidental victim on the wayside when the force of death sweeps past

[73] *wayside*: an ingenious usage, meaning not the main target but as a collateral damage only; it enhances the incommensurability between the moth and the force of death.

[74] *having righted himself*: Note the symbolism involved: a decent, uncomplaining, composed, dignified death.

[75] *O yes...than I am*: Mingled with a sense of submission that lingers after the death of the moth is a touch of placidity, which vastly differs from the sentiment before the sweeping force of death wreaks havoc. At this moment death almost holds a placatory charm for the observer/narrator. When reading these lines, keep in mind that Woolf was to choose to drown herself at last.

agonies. Imagine seeing the thin legs "fluttering" after "a pause of exhaustion" and the tiny body finally "relaxing" and then growing "stiff." None the less, Woolf took pains to add weight to the death of the moth by presenting it not only as inevitable from the lop-sided battle between life and death but also as a termination dignified enough rather than ugly and mean.

Author

Virginia Woolf (1882-1941) is widely regarded as one of the foremost British modernist writers of the early 20th century. She was born in London in 1882, daughter of Leslie Stephen, an eminent literary critic and the founder of the *Dictionary of National Biography*. Following the death of her father in 1904, Woolf moved with her sister Vanessa and two brothers to a house in Bloomsbury, where they formed the nucleus of what was to be known as the Bloomsbury Group. In 1905 Woolf began to write for the *Times Literary Supplement* almost until her death. In 1912 she married the political theorist and critic Leonard Woolf, and together they founded the Hogarth Press in 1917. Her first novel, *The Voyage Out*, was published in 1915. Although realistic in form, it already foreshadows the lyrical intensity of her later works. Her third novel, *Jacob's Room* (1922), blazes a new path in the art of fiction with its indirect narration and poetic impressionism. Shortly afterwards, she published one of her most famous essays, "Mr Bennett and Mrs Brown," criticizing the realism of Arnold Bennett and advocating a more fluid, internal approach to the problem of characterization and so forth. This and her subsequent major novels, *Mrs. Dalloway* (1925), *To the Lighthouse* (1927), and *The Waves* (1931) established Woolf as one of the leading writers of modernism. Her other novels include *Orlando* (1928), *The Years*

(1937), and *Between the Acts* (1941). Woolf was also a prolific essayist and literary critic, publishing around 500 essays in periodicals and collections such as *The Common Reader* (1925; 2nd series, 1932), the posthumous *The Death of the Moth* (1942), *The Captain's Death Bed* (1950), and *Granite and Rainbow* (1958).

Virginia Woolf remains a cynosure of widespread scholarly and lay interest to date. Many of her experimental techniques and narrative styles, such as the use of stream of consciousness, interior monologue, and the deliberate breakage of linear chronological sequence, have been absorbed into the mainstream of fiction. However, it is noteworthy that Woolf is likewise concerned with public affairs and human conditions at large. The upsurge of feminist criticism from the 1970s onwards succeeded in bringing more attention to Woolf's novels, sometimes to the extent of pigeonholing her as a feminist pioneer. *A Room of One's Own* (1929) has become a classic of the feminist movement. Recent Woolfian studies have become more varied, promising more subtle and comprehensive understanding of her works, aesthetics, and her contribution to literature as a unique writer.

Virginia Woolf suffered from mental disorder and ill health since she was very young. The last of her attacks of mental illness led to her drowning herself in the Ouse river, near her country house at Rodmell, Sussex in 1941.

Text

Moths are recurrent, sometimes even central, images in Virginia Woolf's works and diaries. For example, in her novel *Jacob's Room*, Woolf mentions eleven types of lepidoptera. Besides, she had originally intended to use *The Moths* to entitle her novel *The Waves*. While it may smack of overinterpretation to read the moth in this essay as anything more than "a pure bead," it is nonetheless helpful to understand the possible symbolic meanings of the moth. Sometimes it suggests the metamorphic and fleeting existence of human beings. At other times it symbolizes the fluttering of the creative mind, not only the creative or imaginative power *per se* but all the sources of the imagination, including anxiety and apprehension, emotions and sensibilities, and pains and pleasures. In general, in Woolf's writings, the moth often signifies how the mind perpetually endeavors to metamorphose from chaos to creativity. In fact, the whole process of creation (its genesis, development, and composition) corresponds to the different forms of the moths (larva, chrysalis, and moth) perfectly.

Further Reading

"Woolf Rooks, and Rural England," Ian Blyth
"Hunting the Moth: Virginia Woolf and the Creative Imagination," Harvena Richter
"Butterflies and Moths: Insects in September," Virginia Woolf
The Common Reader, Virginia Woolf
The Second Common Reader, Virginia Woolf
The Waves, Virginia Woolf

Chinese Translation

飞蛾之死

陆谷孙　译

白昼出没的飞蛾，准确地说，不叫飞蛾；它们激发不起关于沉沉秋夜和青藤小花的欣快意念，而藏在帷幕黝暗处沉睡的最普通的“翼底黄”飞蛾却总会唤醒这样的联想。“翼底黄”是杂交的产物，既不像蝴蝶一般色彩鲜艳，也不像飞蛾类那样全身灰暗。尽管如此，眼前这只蛾子，狭狭的双翼显现着枯灰色，翼梢缀有同样颜色的一圈流苏，看上去似乎活得心满意足。这是一个令人神清气爽的早晨。时届九月中旬，气温舒适宜人，而吹过来的风已比夏季凉冽。窗户对面，犁耕已经开始。铧片过处，泥土被压得平整，显得湿漉漉又乌油油。从田野以及更远处的丘陵，一股勃勃生机扑面而来，使双眼难以完全专注于书本。还有那些白嘴鸦，像是正在欢庆某一次年会，绕着树梢盘旋，远远望去仿佛有一张缀有万千黑点的大网撒开在空中。过了一会，大网慢慢降下，直到林中的每一处枝头落满黑点。随后，大网突然再次撒向天空，这一回，划出的圆弧更大，同时伴以不绝于耳的呱呱鸦噪，似乎一会儿急急腾空而去，一会儿徐徐栖落枝头，乃是极富刺激性的活动。

一种活力激励着白嘴鸦、掌犁农夫、辕马，影响所及甚至连贫瘠的秃丘也透出了生气。正是这种活力撩拨着飞蛾鼓翅，从正方形窗玻璃的一侧移动到另一侧。你无法不去注视它；你甚至对它产生了一种莫名怜悯。这天早晨，生命的乐趣表现得淋漓尽致又丰富多样，相比之下，作为一只飞蛾浮生在世，而且是只有一天生命的飞蛾，真是命运不济。虽则机遇不堪，飞蛾却仍在尽情享受，看到这种热情不禁引人唏嘘。它劲儿十足地飞到窗格的一角，在那儿停了一秒钟之后，穿越窗面飞到另一角。除了飞到第三然后又是第四角，它还能做什么呢？这就是它能做的一切，虽然户外丘陵广袤，天空无际，远处的房屋炊烟缭绕，海上的轮船不时发出引人遐思的汽笛声。飞蛾能做到的事，它都做了。注视着它的时候，我觉得在它羸弱的小身体里，仿佛塞进了一缕纤细然而洗炼的世间奇伟的活力。每当它飞越窗面，我总觉得有一丝生命之光亮起。飞蛾虽小，甚至微不足道，却也是生灵。

然而，正因为它微不足道，正因为它以简单的形式体现了从打开的窗户滚滚涌进并在我和其他人大脑错综复杂的狭缝中冲击而过的一种活力，飞蛾不但引人唏嘘，还同样令人惊叹，使人感到似乎有谁取来一颗晶莹的生命之珠，以尽可能轻盈的手法饰以茸羽之后，使其翩跹起舞，左右飞旋，从而向我们显示生命的真谛。这样展示在人们的面前，飞蛾使人无法不啧啧称奇，而在目睹飞蛾弓背凸现的模样的同时，看它妆扮着又像背负了重荷，因此动作既谨慎又滞重，人们不禁会全然忘记生命是怎么一回事。人们倒是会又一次想到，生命若以另一种不同于飞蛾的形态诞生将可能变成什么，而这种想法自会使人以某种怜悯的心情去观察飞蛾的简单动作。

过了一会，飞蛾像是飞得累了，便在阳光下的窗沿上落停。飞舞的奇观已经结束，我便把它忘了。待我抬起头来，注意力又被它吸引了去，只见它在试图再次飞起，可是因为身体已太僵直，要不就是姿态别扭，而只能扑闪着翅膀，落到窗玻璃的底部。当它挣扎着往顶部飞时，它已力不从心了。因为我正专注于其他事情，所以只是心不在焉地看着飞蛾徒劳的扑腾，同时，无意识地等着它再一次飞起，犹如等着一台暂时停转的机器重新开始而不去深究停转的原因。也许扑腾了七次，飞蛾终于从木质窗沿滑下，抖动着双翅，仰天掉在窗台上。它这种绝望无助的体位唤回了我的注意，我顿时意识到飞蛾陷入了困境，它的细腿一阵乱蹬，却全无结果，它再也无法把身体挺直。我手持一支铅笔朝它伸去，想帮它翻一个身，然而就在这时我认识到，扑腾失败和姿态别扭都是死之将至的表征。于是，我放下了铅笔。

细腿又抖动了一次。我像是为了寻找飞蛾与之搏斗的仇敌，便朝户外望去。那儿发生了什么？大概已是中午时分。田畴劳作业已停止。原先的奔忙已被静止所取代。鸟儿飞往小溪觅食；辕马立停。但是，那股力量依然聚集在那儿，一股冷漠超然、非人格化、不针对任何具体对象的力量。不知出于什么原因，与枯灰色的小飞蛾作对的，正是这股力量。试图抗拒这股力量，全然无用，我所能做的，唯有看着飞蛾软弱的细腿作出非凡的挣扎，抵拒那渐渐接近的毁灭伟力。毁灭伟力，只要它愿意，本可埋没整个一座城池；除了城池，还可夺去千万人的生命。我知道，与死神作搏斗，世间万物都无取胜的可能。虽说如此，因为筋疲力竭而小憩之后，细腿又抖动起来。这最后的抗争确属英勇超凡，而挣扎又是如此之狂暴，飞蛾竟然最终翻身成功了。当然，你定会同情求生的一方。与此同时，在无人过问也无人知晓的情况下，这微不足道的小飞蛾为了维持既无他人重视也无他人意欲保存的生命，竟对如此巨大的伟力作出这样强悍的拼搏，这更使人受到异样的感动。不知怎么的，我又一次见到了那晶莹的生命之珠。虽说意识到一切全是徒劳，我重又提起铅笔。然而正在这时，确凿无误的死亡征状出现了。蛾体先是松弛下来，旋即变得僵硬。搏斗告终。这微不足道的小生命死了。看着飞蛾的尸体，看着这股巨大的伟力把这么一个可怜巴巴的对手捎带着战胜，我心头充满了惊诧感。几分钟之前，生命曾显得那样奇谲。如今死亡也是同样的奇谲。飞蛾端正了身体，安安静静躺在那儿，端庄而毫无怨尤。哦，是的，它好像在说，死神毕竟比我强大。

译后记

某日，弗吉尼亚·沃尔夫正在窗前读书，注意力忽被一只小小的飞蛾吸引了去，目光由此扫往户外，又见到白嘴鸦、拖犁辕马和贫瘠丘陵等景物。飞蛾扑腾着，挣扎着，最后力竭而死。“物色尽而情有余”（刘勰语），女作者因小见大，由此生发有关重大的生死问题的杂感，于时写下这篇随笔。

随笔是一种突破拘牵、张弛相随、笔触细腻的文体，翻译时最大的难处莫过于捕捉作者发挥想像力的大致轨迹，变通适会，同时用心于细节，把原文的意象和旨趣尽量忠实地传达出来。

《飞蛾之死》看若思无定契，其实裁章也有顺序，即前三段以写“生”为主，后两段写“死”；写“生”为主时也发怜悯，也有唏嘘，而写到死神强大时也不忘抗争的英勇和强悍。把握住这一基调，译文方可字从句顺。例如第一段末尾描写白嘴鸦的两长句，翻译时就宜尽量拆析，并以“万千黑点”“大网撒开”“呱呱鸦噪”“急急腾空”“徐徐栖落”等词语来渲染一种热闹的动态；又如第二和第三段由“as if”引起的比喻句中多用“fibre”“thread of vital light”和“bead”等意象，译时亦宜将“生的活力”作为主要的参照框架，以使比类虽繁，不失切至。

作者在摹写飞蛾的形体和动态时文字工巧，曲写毫芥，要把细节的真实翻译出来，是件极具挑战性的工作。译者煞费苦心，自问像“翼底黄”（yellow-underwing）一类的译法在求真之余不无创意，又如将“It was as if someone had taken a tiny bead of pure life and decking it as lightly as possible with down and feathers, had set it dancing and zigzagging to show us the true nature of life. Thus displayed one could not get over the strangeness of it.”两句译成现在的模样（请参见译文），译者也是比较满意的。但是，最没有把握的译法也发生在细节的处理方面。读者如果循着上引两句接着往下读，就会碰到四个以-ed结尾的补足语：humped and bossed and garnished and cumbered，现试以“弓背凸现”“妆扮着又像背负了重荷”对应之。这样的译法是“翻译过度”（overtranslation）还是刻鹄类鹜，只有请读者诸君批评指教了。

Insouciance[1]

by D. H. Lawrence

My balcony is on the east side of the hotel, and my neighbours on the right are a Frenchman, white-haired, and his white-haired wife; my neighbours on the left are two little white-haired English ladies. And we are all mortally shy of one another.[2]

Mark the underlined word "white-haired," which is repeated three times in the same short paragraph. Apparently the color white here does not appeal to the author but looks distancing, being cold, and associated with age. Remember D. H. Lawrence is sometimes referred to as one who "never outgrows his boyhood." Also consider why one of his early novels is entitled *The White Peacock*.

When I peep out of my room in the morning and see the matronly[3] French lady in a purple silk wrapper,[4] standing like the captain on the bridge surveying the morning, I pop[5] in again before she can see me. And whenever I emerge during the day, I am aware of the two little white-haired ladies popping back like two white rabbits, so that literally I only see the whisk[6] of their skirt-hems.

---

[1] *Insouciance*: nonchalance, lack of concern; the typical attitude of "who cares" or "what the hell"

[2] *we are...one another*: we avoid one another's company by all means

[3] *matronly*: From the word *matronly* we can learn three things about the French lady: age, size, and air. Like a typical matron, she is elderly and massive, carrying herself in a dignified, off-putting manner.

[4] *wrapper*: a loose robe. The morning gown befits a person of elevated social status.

[5] *pop*: move in a jerky way, swiftly and abruptly

[6] *whisk*: a light, rapid, and brief movement. Here it implies that the writer only sees a very small section of the skirts.

 Pay attention to the underlined words "matronly," "purple," "captain," and "surveying." All of them suggest an air of dignity, importance, and authority. Naturally at the sight of the French lady with such an impressively assured presence on the balcony, the writer feels involuntarily dwarfed and becomes "shyer" if anything. Small wonder that he "pops" in almost instinctively.

 Note the repeated use of "pop." The prequel to the following balcony encounter is described as a kind of hide-and-seek, highlighting again how "mortally shy" we are of one another.

This afternoon being hot and thundery,[7] I woke up suddenly and went out on the balcony barefoot. There I sat serenely contemplating the world, and ignoring the two bundles of feet[8] of the two little ladies which protruded from their open doorways, upon the end of two *chaises longues.*[9] A hot, still afternoon! The lake shining rather glassy away below, the mountains rather sulky,[10] the greenness very green,[11] all a little silent and lurid,[12] and two mowers moving with scythes, downhill just near; *slush! slush!* sound the scythe-strokes.[13]

 Notice the shift from the present tense to the past tense and then back in this paragraph. It is most probable that the author suddenly became conscious that he was relating what had happened on one bygone afternoon. And then he shifts back to the present tense in the last sentence, the effect of which is a sense of immediacy, of things as if they were happening right under his nose.

---

7 *thundery*: a rarer word for *thunderous,* especially when one speaks of clouds threatening to thunder

8 *two bundles of feet*: two pairs of feet that are completely wrapped up, a synecdoche rhetorically. By identifying the two ladies as "two bundles of feet," the author succeeds in presenting human beings as inanimate objects.

9 *chaises longues*: /ˈʃeɪzˈlɒɡ/ [French] sun beds or sofa chairs, mostly found on the sundeck on board a ship

10 *sulky*: cheerless, morose; ill-boding to the writer's eyes

11 *the greenness very green*: When a color becomes overly colorful, luridness results.

12 *lurid*: so harshly vivid that the scene creates an unpleasant sensation

13 *slush! slush! sound the scythe-strokes*: an inverted sentence with *slush* as an onomatopoeic word

 Mark the contrast between "barefoot" and "bundles of feet." One is intimately connected to Nature, while the other to artificiality.

 In contrast to "surveying" in the second paragraph, whose object is externally directed, "contemplating" signifies a passive, thoughtful, and introspective attitude of its subject.

 Gauge your own feeling as you read this paragraph. What with the weather and the scenery, the reader is not likely to get a comfortable impression but feels a little stifled.

The two little ladies become aware of my presence. I become aware of a certain agitation[14] in the two bundles of feet wrapped in two discreet steamer rugs[15] and protruding on the end of two *chaises longues* from the pair of doorways upon balcony next me. One bundle of feet suddenly disappears; so does the other. Silence!

 Mark the contrast between brevity of the first sentence and wordiness of the second where the author takes pains to trace the bundled feet all the way to their issuance. The former is a statement of fact; the latter carries a certain amount of fiction, reinforcing an impression of inanimate objects.

 Most of the second sentence is none other than repetition of what appears in the previous paragraph. Lawrence is never tired of repetition. He uses lengthy expressions, purposely prolonging lines of words to enhance the effect of artificiality of inanimate objects as contrasted with unadorned humanity.

 Note how prose rhythm is achieved: a short sentence, a long sentence, a short sentence again, a shorter sentence, and a one-word sentence. A good writer knows how far he can freewheel and where he has to apply the brakes. If you tilt your ears to listen as a habit, you will be able to install an inner clockwork of the language that tells you where to begin and where to stop.

Then lo![16] With odd sliding suddenness a little white-haired lady in grey silk, with round blue eyes, emerges and looks straight at me,[17] and

---

[14] *agitation*: fidgeting

[15] *steamer rugs*: rugs used to keep one warm on a voyage, a cruise, etc.

[16] *lo*: see Page 3, Note 5; used to draw attention

[17] *with odd...at me*: The encounter is rendered dramatic not only by the suggestion of suddenness of the sliding motion but also by a succession of uncomfortable cold colors: white, grey, and blue.

remarks that it is pleasant[18] now. A little cooler, say I, with false amiability.[19] She quite agrees, and we speak of the men mowing:[20] how plainly one hears the long breaths of the scythes.

 Mark how painstakingly the author has prepared his readers for the transformation of a bundle of feet to a three-dimensional little lady as big as life.

 The way the author was forcibly pulled into conversation after the previous hide-and-seek is interesting: exchange of remarks about the weather with a reluctant Lawrence responding against his own free will.

By now[21] we are *tête-à-tête.*[22] We speak of cherries, strawberries, and the promise of the vine crop. This somehow leads to Italy and to *Signor*[23] Mussolini.[24] Before I know where I am, the little white-haired lady has swept me off my balcony, away from the glassy lake, the veiled mountains, the two men mowing, and the cherry trees, away into the troubled ether[25] of international politics.

 Mark how the conversation develops from the immediately empirical to the illusorily abstract. "The glassy lake, the veiled mountains, the two men mowing, and the cherry trees": they are all existentially important to the author but unperceived by the old lady.

 The time clause, "before I know where I am," accentuates the swiftness of the topic shift. It is obvious that the author's "false amiability" has persisted, and he is unaware of what is going on: he is totally absent-minded since all the topics brought up by the old lady sound irrelevant to him.

---

[18] *it is pleasant*: it is nice, weather-wise

[19] *with false amiability*: The phrase suggests the author was loath to talk but was being amiable dutifully.

[20] *mowing*: The colon serves the function of expressing "why," i.e., introducing the reason for speaking of the men mowing.

[21] *By now*: the next I find myself

[22] *tête-à-tête*: an exaggeration: a head-to-head conversation, as if we were old friends

[23] *Signor*: /ˈsiːnjɔː(r),siːˈnjɔː(r)/ the Italian equivalent of Mr.

[24] *Mussolini*: Benito (1883-1945), Italian Fascist statesman, known as Il Duce (the leader)

[25] *ether*: atmosphere

I am not allowed to sit like a dandelion on my own stem. The little lady in a breath blows me abroad.[26] And I was so pleasantly musing[27] over the two men mowing: the young one, with long legs in bright blue cotton trousers, and with bare[28] black head, swinging so lightly downhill, and the other, in black trousers, rather stout in front, and wearing a new straw hat of the boater variety,[29] coming rather stiffly after, crunching the end of his stroke with a certain violent effort.

 D. H. Lawrence believes that beauty resides in youth and vital nature, which is manifest in the contrastive description of the young mower and the old one. Note these antithetical pairs of phrases: long legs/stout in front, bright blue cotton trousers/black trousers, bare black head/wearing a new straw hat of the boater variety, lightly/stiffly, and swinging/crunching with a certain violent effort.

I was watching the curiously different motions of the two men, the young thin one in bright blue trousers, the elderly fat one in shabby black trousers that stick out in front, the different amount of effort in their mowing, the lack of grace in the elderly one, his jerky[30] advance, the unpleasant effect of the new "boater" on his head—and I tried to interest the little lady.[31]

 Apparently this paragraph is merely paraphrasing the previous one. But this repetition serves to reinforce the author's keen interest in actualities, i.e., what is around him, here and now.

---

[26] *I am...me abroad*: a sustained metaphor reiterating the fact that the little lady "has swept me off my balcony" and cut me from my root in Nature by pushing me into a world of meaningless ideology

[27] *musing*: contemplating; note the past tense, meaning before she chatted me up.

[28] *bare*: hatless

[29] *a new...boater variety*: a flat-crowned straw hat, originally worn while boating, later a kind of garden party hat; here the older mower looks ridiculous to the writer, because he wears a party hat while doing manual labor.

[30] *jerky*: unsteady, shaky as a result of uneven over-exertion

[31] *and I...little lady*: indicating that the writer had talked to the lady about the two mowers at length, making a vain effort to interest her

But it meant nothing to her. The mowers, the mountains, the cherry trees, the lake, all the things that were ACTUALLY[32] there, she didn't care about. They even seemed to scare her off the balcony.[33] But she held her ground,[34] and instead of herself being scared away, she snatched[35] me up like some ogress,[36] and swept me off into the empty desert[37] spaces of right and wrong,[38] politics, Fascism and the rest.

 Pay attention to the word *care* that is to appear repeatedly in the following context—all underlined. The difference between "insouciance" and "care" is supposedly the thematic thread running through the whole essay.

 Mark the transition from the earlier "hide-and-seek" to the fight to sweep each other off his/her feet.

 It is noteworthy that Lawrence lumps together "right and wrong," "politics," "Fascism," and later in the text "abstract liberty"—things he had never brought himself to believe in.

The worst ogress couldn't have treated me more villainously.[39] I don't care about right and wrong, politics, Fascism, abstract liberty, or anything else of the sort. I want to look at the mowers, and wonder why fatness, elderliness, and black trousers should inevitably[40] wear a new straw hat of the boater variety, move in stiff jerks, shove the end of the scythe-strokes

---

[32] *ACTUALLY*: emphasizing that these are real, perceivable things, as opposed to such abstract, intangible stuff like international politics

[33] *They even...the balcony*: My mention of what is right before our eyes almost blew the little lady off the balcony just as her talk of international politics "swept me off my balcony."

[34] *But she held her ground*: She did not back off; she did not budge an inch. In other words, she was NOT the type so easily scared off the balcony.

[35] *snatched*: suggesting unthinking haste and careless heavy-handedness

[36] *ogress*: female demon; sorceress

[37] *desert*: barren or lifeless

[38] *right and wrong*: referring to any kind of ethical judgment

[39] *The worst...more villainously*: The subjunctive throws into bold relief the fact that to the author, she is worse than the worst ogress.

[40] *inevitably*: unavoidably, as if such things naturally go together

with a certain violence, and win my hearty disapproval,[41] as contrasted with young long thinness, bright blue cotton trousers, a bare black head, and a pretty lifting movement at the end of the scythe-stroke.

Why do modern[42] people almost invariably ignore the things that are actually present to them? Why, having come out from England to find mountains, lakes, scythe-mowers and cherry trees, does the little blue-eyed lady resolutely close her blue eyes to them all, now she's got them,[43] and gaze away to *Signor* Mussolini, whom she hasn't got, and to Fascism, which is invisible[44] anyhow? Why isn't she content to be where she is? Why can't she be happy with what she's got? Why must she CARE?

 It is only natural to suppose that the little lady came all the way to France to do sightseeing, to relax herself and enjoy good weather as well as scenery. Yet she ended up not seeing or feeling anything in Nature at all, anything France had so generously to offer.

 Mark the underlined sentence, uncharacteristically long and with so much information packed in it, only to be followed by a series of queries increasingly shortened. Mark again the syntactic rhythm here: short, long, short, short, and shorter. The arrangement is almost identical to that in the fourth paragraph. The language clockwork within is heard ticking again.

 Pay attention to the sense perceptions valuated by Lawrence as opposed to abstract ideologies.

I see now why her round blue eyes are so round, so noticeably round.[45] It is because she "cares."[46] She is haunted by that mysterious bugbear[47] of "caring." For everything on earth that doesn't concern her she "cares." She

---

[41] *hearty disapproval*: a case of oxymoron, translated by 钱锺书 as 冤亲词. Other examples include "bitter sweetness," "mute eloquence," and "intimate stranger."

[42] *modern*: The word is used sarcastically in Lawrence's context, carrying, among other things, connotations of urbanized, worldly-wise, and hip. Of two possible translations: 现代的 and 摩登的, the latter is opted for.

[43] *now she's got them*: a parenthetic clause with *now* similar to "now that"

[44] *invisible*: not seeable or tangible, pointing to the illusory nature of any ideology

[45] *round*: The word is used three times in breathless succession. Study it in connection with words like *ogress* and *bugbear*. Mark how a feeling of disgust is created.

[46] *It is because she "cares"*: Her pupils are diluted by care, i.e., irrelevant worries.

[47] *bugbear*: an object of oppressive, obsessive fear; some recurrent unpleasant thought

cares terribly because far-off,[48] invisible, hypothetical[49] Italians wear black shirts,[50] but she doesn't care a rap that one elderly mower whose stroke she can hear, wears black[51] trousers instead of bright blue cotton ones. Now if she would descend from the balcony and climb the grassy slope and say to the fat mower: "*Cher monsieur, pourquoi porlez-vous les pantalons noirs?*[52] Why, oh, why do you wear black trousers?"—then I should say: What an on-the-spot little lady![53]—But since she only torments me with international politics, I can only remark: What a tiresome off-the-spot old woman![54]

They care![55] They simply are eaten up[56] with caring. They are so busy caring about Fascism or Leagues of Nations[57] or whether France[58] is right or whether Marriage[59] is threatened, that they never know where they are. They certainly never live on the spot. They inhabit abstract space, the desert void[60] of politics, principles, right and wrong, and so forth. They are doomed to be abstract. Talking to them is like trying to have a human

48 *far-off*: either an adverb or an adjective, meaning far-away

49 *hypothetical*: in that one only reads about them in, say, news stories

50 *black shirts*: Members of the Italian Fascista had a black shirt as part of their uniform.

51 *black*: same color as that of the Fascista uniform, a color incongruous with the stifling weather and the "boater," which is usually white

52 *Cher monsieur...pantalons noirs?*: The English equivalent is given immediately below.

53 *an on-the-spot little lady*: a little lady who lives the moment to the full

54 *a tiresome off-the-spot old woman*: a boring old woman who has not the faintest idea about *carpe diem*, in which Lawrence evidently believed

55 *They care!*: a forceful, vehement sentence

56 *eaten up*: consumed totally

57 *Leagues of Nations*: The League of Nations is the antecedent to today's United Nations. "Leagues of Nations" in the plural refers to organizations like the League of Nations. Meanwhile, a slighting irony is detected.

58 *France*: Anatole (1844-1924), French novelist and critic who won the Nobel Prize in literature in 1921

59 *Marriage*: the upper case M used to emphasize marriage as a social institution

60 *void*: emptiness, nothingness

relationship with the letter x in algebra.[61]

There simply is a deadly breach[62] between actual living and this abstract caring. What is actual living? It is a question mostly of direct contact. There was a direct sensuous contact[63] between me, the lake, mountains, cherry trees, mowers, and a certain invisible but noisy chaffinch[64] in a clipped lime tree. All this was cut off by the fatal shears[65] of that abstract word FASCISM, and the little old lady next door was the Atropos[66] who cut the thread of my actual life this afternoon.[67] She beheaded me, and flung my head into abstract space.[68] Then we are supposed to love our neighbours![69]

The first sentence of the paragraph puts in a nutshell the unpleasant encounter of the afternoon.

Mark the underlined word *clipped*. Depicting a lime tree with its top "clipped," the author prepares the reader for the cutting off of his own head. Or we might say that when he uses the word *clip*, the word *cut* is already surfacing in his subconscious. The cutting

---

[61] *Talking to...in algebra*: It is impossible to engage them in natural, day-to-day, human conversation.

[62] *breach*: rift, gap, chasm

[63] a direct *sensuous contact*: contact through the five senses uninterrupted or interfered with by anything abstract

[64] *chaffinch*: a kind of French sparrow

[65] *shears*: big scissors, usually used in wool-shearing

[66] *Atropos*: one of the three Goddesses of Fate in Greek Mythology, known as the Fates; Atropos is the one who cuts the thread of man's life at death. Clotho, the Spinner, spins the thread of life, while Lachesis, the Disposer of Lots, assigns each man his destiny.

[67] *the little...this afternoon*: My afternoon was utterly ruined by the little old lady.

[68] *She beheaded...abstract space*: a sustained metaphor that further illustrates my being victimized by her. It is a very graphic "cruel" sentence, showing the author's intense aversion to the kind of interest in the abstract. Lawrence believes "caring" of this kind is draining and devastating.

[69] *Then we...our neighbours!*: an ironic jab at the Biblical tenet of "loving thy neighbors;" *neighbours* here used in the literal sense of the word, considering they stay in the contiguous hotel rooms

of the thread of life and then of the head, the beheading, and then flinging the head: although metaphorical, the heinous cruelty of the process is made proportionate with the abhorrence the author feels.

When it comes to living, we live through our instincts and our intuitions. Instinct makes me run from little over-earnest ladies; instinct makes me sniff the lime blossoms and reach for the darkest[70] cheery. But it is intuition which makes me feel the uncanny glassiness of the lake this afternoon, the sulkiness of the mountains, the vividness of near[71] green in thunder-sun,[72] the young man in bright blue trousers, lightly tossing the grass from the scythe, the elderly man in a boater stiffly shoving his scythe strokes, both of them sweating in the silence of the intense light.[73]

 The term *instincts* means the innate aspect of behavior that is unconscious and unlearned, while *intuitions* means understanding or knowing in the manner of immediate experience without reasoning.

 Though Lawrence seldom makes assertive statements in this essay, the first sentence of this last paragraph is the one philosophical statement in *Insouciance*. To him, life is primarily a combination of instinctive behavior and intuitional knowledge. What follows the statement are literary images as illustrations of instincts and intuitions.

 Consider the implications of Lawrence's privileging of sense experience over cognitive knowledge and logical abstraction in the early twentieth century.

Author

David Herbert Lawrence (1885-1930), one of the most important British writers of the 20th century, was born on September 11, 1885, in a coal-mining

[70] *darkest*: ripest

[71] *near*: *almost total*

[72] *thunder-sun*: sunlight in thundery weather, often sickly or lurid

[73] *the silence...intense light*: a combination of oral and visual sensations, a rhetoric device known as synaesthesia, translated by 钱锺书 as 通感, or more commonly known as 联觉

town called Eastwood in Nottinghamshire. Little Lawrence was a victim of an unhappy marriage between an uncouth miner and a schoolteacher who spoke King's English, a rather "refined" woman compared to her husband. His first famous novel *Sons and Lovers* (1913) is based on autobiographical experiences of his early victimization. It had been preceded by two far less successful novels: *The White Peacock* (1911) and *The Trespasser* (1912). Other important works by D. H. Lawrence include *The Rainbow* (1915), *Women in Love* (1920), *Phoenix* (1920), *England, My England and Other Stories* (1922), *Birds, Beasts, and Flowers* (a collection of poems, 1923), *Reflections on the Death of a Porcupine and Other Essays* (1925), *Lady Chatterley's Lover* (1928), *The Escaped Cock* (1929, later re-published as *The Man Who Died)*, and *Last Poems* (1932).

Criticisms on D. H. Lawrence were varied even in his own time. E. M. Foster believed that "he was the greatest imaginative novelist of our generation." T. S. Eliot opined that he had "an incapacity for what we ordinarily call thinking" and went so far as to attack his "violent prejudices and passions, and lack of intellectual and social training." One thing that can be said for sure about D. H. Lawrence, however, is that like his thought, his works are complex and share one basic theme: the struggle for self-realization and self-responsibility. He sees himself as a complete rejection of modern life and of what it brings about or epitomizes, such as industrialism, nationalism, Christianity, science, and popular education. "A passionate religious man," as he called himself, D. H. Lawrence endeavors perpetually to achieve the total development of the self, of being, the unconscious and intuitive, as opposed to knowing, the conscious and intellectual. According to him, a true individual identity—a new oneness between the individual and others as well as Nature—is only approachable after our eyes are opened to our primitive selves, to our position in Nature, and our essential relation to the cosmos. Consequently, his works are all passionate and uncompromising but sometimes also violent and uneven. Nevertheless, they are equally sincere, intriguing, and never trivial. Through his works, D. H. Lawrence challenges vigorously the assumptions of Western civilization about itself, modernity, humanity, and man's future.

Text

Insouciance was written during D. H. Lawrence's sojourn in France in the mid-1920s. The one-word title describes his mood at the time: a carefree kind of attitude towards anything that is not both natural and actual. To achieve a better understanding of its theme and tone, one needs to pin down a number of contrasts artistically woven into the body of the essay. They are, namely, Youth (grace, ease) vs. Age (clumsiness, effort), the Aesthetic (the mowers, the mountains, the cherry trees...) vs. the Ethical (right and wrong, politics, Fascism...), On-the-spot (enhanced hedonism) vs. Off-the-spot (degenerate inhumanity), Actuality vs. Abstraction, Instincts and Intuitions vs. Intellect and Rationality, and on top of them all, Insouciance vs. Care.

The text is especially useful for an in-depth understanding of D. H. Lawrence's overall aversion to the artificiality of the civilized world and of his excruciating sense of alienation from it.

Further Reading

Either/Or, Søren Kierkegaard
Fantasia of the Unconscious, D. H. Lawrence
Psychoanalysis and the Unconscious, D. H. Lawrence
Sons and Lovers, D. H. Lawrence
"Why the Novel Matters," D. H. Lawrence
Against Interpretation, and Other Essays, Susan Sontag

Politics and the English Language

by George Orwell

Most people who bother with the matter[1] at all would admit that the English language is in a bad way,[2] but it is generally assumed that we cannot by conscious action do anything about it.[3] Our civilization is decadent and our language—so the argument runs—must inevitably share in the general collapse. It follows that any struggle against the abuse of language is a sentimental archaism,[4] like preferring candles to electric light or hansom cabs to aeroplanes.[5] Underneath this lies the half-conscious belief that language is a natural growth and not an instrument which we shape for our own purposes.

George Orwell is anxious to set the English language right, which seems to many people a futile effort. In their view, it is problematic to judge the performance of a language in terms of whether it is good or bad. All languages have their own rationale and follow their own laws. Language is a natural growth from a host of circumstances combined. Linguistic puritanism is quite dated, if not altogether harmful. Orwell questions this standpoint by drawing attention to how language is shaped and manipulated by its users.

---

[1] *the matter*: See the title.

[2] *way*: shape; but it must be pointed out that one does not judge whether a language is in a bad way or decadent. If and when the urge to comment is too strong, one may question or criticize the style a language is being abused in society at large. As far as language *per se* is concerned, any judgment of good or bad is dubious, if not altogether deleterious.

[3] *we cannot...about it*: However much we want to improve things, we can do nothing but let them take their normal course.

[4] *a sentimental archaism*: The struggle is mistimed, showing a tendency toward nostalgic mawkishness.

[5] *like preferring...to aeroplanes*: Maybe we can call such people modern Luddites?

Now, it is clear that the decline of a language must ultimately have political and economic causes: it is not due simply to the bad influence of this or that individual writer. But an effect can become a cause, reinforcing the original cause and producing the same effect in an intensified form, and so on indefinitely.[6] A man may take to drink because he feels himself to be a failure, and then fail all the more completely because he drinks. It is rather the same thing that is happening to the English language. It becomes ugly and inaccurate because our thoughts are foolish, but the slovenliness[7] of our language makes it easier for us to have foolish thoughts. The point is that the process is reversible.[8] Modern English, especially written English, is full of bad habits which spread by imitation[9] and which can be avoided if one is willing to take the necessary trouble. If one gets rid of these habits one can think more clearly, and to think clearly is a necessary first step towards political regeneration:[10] so that the fight against bad English is not frivolous[11] and is not the exclusive concern of professional writers.[12] I will come back to this presently, and I hope that by that time the meaning of what I have said here will have become clearer. [...]

 The underlined sentence reveals that the author still pins hopes on the English language—it is still salvageable in his point of view. Also mark the interplay between language and thought that Orwell dwells upon.

---

[6] *But an...on indefinitely*: This is like a vicious circle in which cause and effect feed on each other non-stop, and in the process things get worse all the time. The following sentence is a good illustration of this argument.

[7] *slovenliness*: untidiness, a slipshod state

[8] *the process is reversible*: The deteriorating process of the English language can be checked and shunted on the opposite course, i.e., in the direction of healing and thriving.

[9] *imitation*: blind imitation, e.g., when we parrot journalistic English unthinkingly, peace threatened is always "fragile," and drastic changes are always "a sea change."

[10] *regeneration*: rebirth, resurrection

[11] *frivolous*: not worthy of serious attention; capricious and trivial

[12] *is not...professional writers*: The fight against bad English should be a concern of every ordinary speaker of the language.

[...]

In certain kinds of writing, particularly in art criticism and literary criticism, it is normal to come across long passages which are almost completely lacking[13] in meaning. Words like *romantic*, *plastic*,[14] *values*, *human*, *dead*, *sentimental*, *natural*, *vitality*, as used in art criticism, are strictly[15] meaningless, in the sense that they not only do not point to any discoverable object,[16] but are hardly ever expected to do so by the reader. When one critic writes, "The outstanding feature of Mr. X's work is its living quality," while another writes, "The immediately striking thing about Mr. X's work is its peculiar deadness," the reader accepts this as a simple difference of opinion. If words like *black* and *white* were involved, instead of the jargon words[17] *dead* and *living*,[18] he would see at once that language was being used in an improper way. Many political words are similarly abused. The word *Fascism* has now no meaning except in so far as it signifies "something not desirable." The words *democracy*, *socialism*, *freedom*, *patriotic*, *realistic*, *justice*, have each of them several different meanings which cannot be reconciled with one another.[19] In the case of a word like *democracy*, not only is there no agreed definition, but the attempt to make one is resisted from all sides. It is almost universally felt that when we call a country democratic we are praising it: consequently the defenders of every kind of regime claim that it is a democracy, and fear

---

[13] *lacking*: *Lacking* followed by *in* is an adjective, not the continuous tense of the verb *lack* as many Chinese students are prone to mistake it for.

[14] *plastic*: as an adjective in this context, meaning artificial or pliable

[15] *strictly*: strictly speaking

[16] *any discoverable object*: anything tangible that can be pinned down precisely

[17] *the jargon words*: words peculiarly used by art and literary critics; pretentious and ambiguous words of shop talk

[18] *dead and living*: 死气沉沉 and 生机勃勃

[19] *which cannot...one another*: Around these words often one thing is professed and another practiced irreconciliably.

that they might have to stop using the word if it were tied down to any one meaning.[20] Words of this kind are often used in a consciously dishonest way. That is, the person who uses them has his own private definition, but allows his hearer to think he means something quite different. Statements like *Marshal Pétain*[21] *was a true patriot,*[22] *The Soviet Press is the freest in the world, The Catholic Church is opposed to persecution,* are almost always made with intent to deceive. Other words used in variable meanings, in most cases more or less dishonestly, are: *class, totalitarian, science, progressive, reactionary, bourgeois, equality.*

This is a typical Orwellian paragraph: excruciatingly sarcastic, full of political innuendoes (e.g., "The Soviet Press is the freest in the world") with ruthless clarity and candidness at their heart (e.g., "That is, the person who uses them has his own private definition, but allows his hearer to think he means something quite different").

Now that I have made this catalogue of swindles and perversions,[23] let me give another example of the kind of writing that they lead to. This time it must of its nature be an imaginary one.[24] I am going to translate a passage of good English into modern English of the worst sort. Here is a well-known verse from *Ecclesiastes*:[25]

---

[20] *if it...one meaning*: a very incisive remark about what Jean-Paul Sartre would later call "violence of words"; in other words, nobody would wish to define words like *democracy* in a clear-cut definitive way. Instead, deliberate befuddling is preferred.

[21] *Marshal Pétain*: (1856-1951) head of Vichy France, the government set up by the Nazi Germans during WWII

[22] *patriot*: In fact, Pétain was convicted of high treason after the war.

[23] *I have...and perversions*: I have supplied you with illustrative examples of bad English intended for deception.

[24] *This time...imaginary one*: This example has to be concocted by the author because he is talking about what the above-mentioned bad writing will most probably "lead to" and wishes to make the contrast more striking.

[25] *Ecclesiastes*: a book of the Old Testament traditionally ascribed to Solomon

I returned and saw under the sun,[26] *that the race is not to the swift,*[27] *nor the battle to the strong, neither yet bread to the wise, nor yet riches to men of understanding,*[28] *nor yet favour to men of skill;*[29] *but time and chance happeneth to them all.*[30]

Here it is in modern English:

Objective consideration of contemporary phenomena compels the conclusion that success or failure in competitive activities exhibits no tendency to be commensurate[31] *with innate capacity, but that a considerable element of the unpredictable must invariably be taken into account.*

The English of the Holy Bible is noted for its lucidity and crispness among the literati of the English-speaking world. Most of the words in the quote are of Anglo-Saxon origin, known as Old English, and the parallel sentences are very forceful. The Orwellian rewrite, however, is stilted and turgid, a jaw-breaking mouthful consisting of multisyllabic words of Latin origin and one word from Greek.

This is a parody,[32] but not a very gross[33] one. [...] It will be seen that I have not made a full translation. The beginning and ending of the sentence

---

[26] *under the sun*: a more or less archaic expression meaning in the world

[27] *the race...the swift*: The race is not necessarily won by the swift-footed person.

[28] *men of understanding*: knowledgeable men in a broad sense

[29] *favour to men of skill*: skillful persons not necessarily favored

[30] *but time...them all*: Time and chance are the factors that decide things for everyone. It indicates what Orwell subsequently describes as "the uncertainty of human fortunes."

[31] *commensurate*: compatible, consistent

[32] *parody*: A parody is a rhetoric device in which the writer writes in purposeful imitation of another person and meanwhile satirizes him or her or holds him or her to ridicule. George Orwell is known to be a great writer of parody.

[33] *gross*: grossly distorted, far-fetched or 十分离谱, meaning that the rewrite is not wide of the mark from present-day bad English

follow the original meaning fairly closely, but in the middle the concrete illustrations—race, battle, bread—dissolve into the vague phrase "success or failure in competitive activities." This had to be so, because no modern writer of the kind I am discussing—no one capable of using phrases like "objective consideration of contemporary phenomena"—would ever tabulate[34] his thoughts in that precise and detailed way. The whole tendency of modern prose is away from concreteness. Now analyze these two sentences a little more closely. The first contains forty-nine words but only sixty syllables, and all its words are those of everyday life. The second contains thirty-eight words of ninety syllables: eighteen of its words are from Latin roots, and one from Greek. The first sentence contains six vivid images, and only one phrase ("time and chance") that could be called vague. The second contains not a single fresh, arresting[35] phrase, and in spite of its ninety syllables it gives only a shortened version of the meaning contained in the first.[36] Yet without a doubt it is the second kind of sentence that is gaining ground[37] in modern English. I do not want to exaggerate. This kind of writing is not yet universal, and outcrops[38] of simplicity will occur here and there in the worst-written page. Still, if you or I were told to write a few lines on the uncertainty of human fortunes, we should probably come much nearer to my imaginary sentence than to the one from *Ecclesiastes.*

Mark the semantic contrast between the two underlined verbs *dissolve* and *tabulate*. The former calls up fluid or melting images, thus rendering the following word *vague* highly predictable. On the contrary, *tabulate* is distinctly associated with tables, clear-cut schemes or synopses, thus rendering *precise* and *detailed* predictable. George Orwell demonstrates through this pair of verbs his scrupulous choice of diction as a writer of "good, simple English."

---

34 *tabulate*: arrange and organize and then formulate; *tabulate* is a derivative of the adjective *tabular,* which is in turn derived from *table*.

35 *arresting*: catching the attention; pleasantly striking; intriguing

36 *in spite...the first*: More syllables but less meaning is the vice of such writing.

37 *gaining ground*: becoming more popular and widely accepted

38 *outcrops*: Literally *outcrop* means the part of a rock formation that appears at the surface of the ground. Here it is used metaphorically to mean at times simplicity will crop up—but only abruptly.

 The key sentence in this paragraph is "The whole tendency of modern prose is away from concreteness," which is one of the most important conclusions of this article. George Orwell deplores the fact that modern English prose writers attach undue importance to high-sounding abstractness, vagueness, or nebulosity.

As I have tried to show, modern writing at its worst does not consist in picking out words for the sake of their meaning and inventing images in order to make the meaning clearer. It consists in gumming together[39] long strips of words which have already been set in order by someone else, and making the results presentable by sheer humbug.[40] The attraction of this way of writing is that it is easy. It is easier—even quicker, once you have the habit—to say *In my opinion it is not an unjustifiable assumption that*[41] than to say *I think*. If you use ready-made phrases, you not only don't have to hunt about[42] for words; you also don't have to bother with the rhythms of your sentences, since these phrases are generally so arranged as to be more or less euphonious.[43] When you are composing in a hurry—when you are dictating to a stenographer,[44] for instance, or making a public speech—it is natural to fall into a pretentious, Latinized style.[45] Tags[46] like *a consideration which we should do well to bear in mind* or *a conclusion to which all of us would readily assent*[47] will save many a sentence from coming down with a bump.[48]

---

[39] *gumming together*: sticking together as if with gum

[40] *humbug*: nonsense, deception of a hypocritical kind

[41] *In my...assumption that*: a laboriously lengthened way to say "I think"

[42] *hunt about*: look right and left, seek high and low

[43] *euphonious*: pleasing to the ear, sweet-sounding, melodious

[44] *stenographer*: a secretary, especially one good at taking shorthand notes

[45] *Latinized style*: Writing in a "Latinized style" is to constantly employ words of Latin origins, usually long, high-sounding ones.

[46] *Tags*: a phrase, etc. added to an already complete sentence

[47] *a consideration...readily assent*: again, a typical example of laborious verbiage

[48] *will save...a bump*: By attaching these basically meaningless tags to your otherwise simple, straightforward sentences, you make them sound less direct and abrupt, thus impressing others with your tactfulness.

By using stale[49] metaphors, similes and idioms, you save much mental effort, at the cost of leaving your meaning vague, not only for your reader but for yourself. This is the significance of mixed metaphors. The sole aim of a metaphor is to call up a visual image. When these images clash—as in *The Fascist octopus has sung its swan song, the jackboot*[50] *is thrown into the melting pot*—it can be taken as certain that the writer is not seeing a mental image of the objects he is naming; in other words, he is not really thinking. [...] A scrupulous writer, in every sentence that he writes, will ask himself at least four questions, thus: What am I trying to say? What words will express it? What image or idiom will make it clearer? Is this image fresh enough to have an effect? And he will probably ask himself two more: Could I put it more shortly? Have I said anything that is avoidably ugly?[51] But you are not obliged to go to all this trouble.[52] You can shirk[53] it by simply throwing your mind open and letting the ready-made phrases come crowding in. They will construct your sentences for you—even think your thoughts for you, to a certain extent—and at need[54] they will perform the important service of partially concealing your meaning even from yourself.[55] It is at this point that the special connection between politics and the debasement of language becomes clear.

---

[49] *stale*: overused, dry, tedious, banal

[50] *jackboot*: *Jackboot* literally means a large leather boot reaching to the knee and usually serving as part of armor. Now it is frequently associated with the exercise of force or oppression, as in this quoted sentence.

[51] *avoidably ugly*: ugly, though this ugliness could have been avoided if one had tried

[52] *But you...this trouble*: What is left unsaid in this sarcastic sentence is, perhaps, "unless you are a scrupulous writer."

[53] *shirk*: evade, dodge

[54] *at need*: when you find it necessary

[55] *partially concealing...from yourself*: The author is re-stressing his point made earlier in the same paragraph: "at the cost of leaving your meaning vague, not only for your reader but for yourself."

 "The attraction of this way of writing is that it is easy"—the underlined on the previous page is a simple sentence, but it points right to the heart of the problem: mental laziness is part of human nature after all. Yet as the Austrian poet Rainer M. Rilke says in his letter to a young poet: "[T]hat something is difficult must be one more reason for us to do it." That a clear, fresh, and unpretentious writing style is difficult to achieve must be one more reason for us to learn it.

 A "mixed metaphor", the underlined compound on the previous page, is a combination of incongruous metaphoric elements, as is best illustrated in the example "*The Fascist octopus has sung its swan song*" mismating the "finned" and the "feathered."

In our time it is broadly true that political writing is bad writing. Where it is not true,[56] it will generally be found that the writer is some kind of rebel,[57] expressing his private opinions and not a "party line." Orthodoxy, of whatever colour, seems to demand a lifeless, imitative style. The political dialects to be found in pamphlets, leading articles, manifestos, White Papers[58] and the speeches of undersecretaries do, of course, vary from party to party, but they are all alike in that one almost never finds in them a fresh, vivid, home-made turn of speech.[59] When one watches some tired hack[60] on the platform mechanically repeating the familiar phrases—*bestial atrocities, iron heel,*[61] *bloodstained tyranny, free peoples of the world, stand shoulder to shoulder*—one often has a curious feeling that one is not watching a live human being but some kind of dummy:[62] a feeling

56 *Where it is not true*: where political writing is not bad writing

57 *rebel*: Compare it with the words like *dummy* and *machine* in the following context.

58 *White Papers*: a government statement giving information or proposals on a major issue, especially in the UK

59 *turn of speech*: a distinctive way of expression

60 *hack*: a writer paid to write low-quality mediocre stuff like an undersecretary mentioned in the preceding context

61 *iron heel*: Originally iron heel means an instrument of torture used to burn or crush the foot and leg. Now it has the hackneyed figurative meaning of the rule of force, the oppression of the people, etc. Jack London entitles one of his works, a dystopia, with it, which was published in 1908.

62 *dummy*: puppet

which suddenly becomes stronger at moments when the light catches the speaker's spectacles and turns them into blank discs which seem to have no eyes behind them.[63] And this is not altogether fanciful. A speaker who uses that kind of phraseology has gone some distance towards turning himself into a machine. The appropriate noises are coming out of his larynx, but his brain is not involved as it would be if he were choosing his words for himself.[64] If the speech he is making is one that he is accustomed to make over and over again, he may be almost unconscious of what he is saying, as one is when one utters the responses in church.[65] And this reduced state of consciousness,[66] if not indispensable, is at any rate[67] favorable to political conformity.

 It is interesting to note that George Orwell has a strong aversion to not only "political conformity" but all kinds of "orthodoxy," the true meaning of which, to him, is revealed in the seemingly off-hand remark "when one utters the responses in church."

In our time, political speech and writing are largely the defense of the indefensible. Things like the continuance of British rule in India, the Russian purges and deportations,[68] the dropping of the atom bombs on Japan, can indeed be defended, but only by arguments which are too brutal for most people to face, and which do not square with[69] the professed[70] aims of political parties. Thus political language has to consist largely of

---

[63] *turns them...behind them*: a very vivid image of a face with two glass discs instead of real human eyes glistening under the spotlight

[64] *The appropriate...for himself*: a speaking robot, an echo of the earlier word *dummy*

[65] *as one...in church*: apparently unthinkingly. The technical term for this kind of Q&A as a Christian rite is catechism.

[66] *this reduced state of consciousness*: implying again that man is being reduced to be sub-human

[67] *at any rate*: in any case, after all; note "in any rate" is gaining currency in present-day English.

[68] *purges and deportations*: notorious abuses of Stalinism

[69] *square with*: agree with

[70] *professed*: openly declared

euphemism, question-begging[71] and sheer cloudy vagueness. Defenseless villages are bombarded from the air, the inhabitants driven out into the countryside, the cattle machinegunned, the huts set on fire with incendiary[72] bullets: this is called *pacification.* Millions of peasants are robbed of their farms and sent trudging along the roads with no more than they can carry: this is called *transfer of population* or *rectification of frontiers.*[73] People are imprisoned for years without trial, or shot in the back of the neck or sent to die of scurvy[74] in Arctic lumber camps: this is called *elimination of unreliable elements.* Such phraseology is needed if one wants to name things without calling up mental pictures of them. Consider for instance some comfortable[75] English professor defending Russian totalitarianism. He cannot say outright, "I believe in killing off your opponents when you can get good results by doing so." Probably, therefore, he will say something like this:

> *"While freely conceding that the Soviet régime exhibits certain features which the humanitarian may be inclined to deplore,[76] we must, I think, agree that a certain curtailment[77] of the right to political opposition is an unavoidable concomitant[78] of transitional periods, and that the rigors which the Russian people have been called upon to undergo have been amply justified in the sphere of concrete achievement."*

---

[71] *question-begging*: question-inviting, especially when the question is an obvious, anticipated one

[72] *incendiary*: designed to cause fire, to ignite spontaneously on contact

[73] *transfer of...of frontiers*: The current euphemistic expression one hears is "relocation of population."

[74] *scurvy*: 坏血病

[75] *comfortable*: highly sarcastic of a transient visitor glibly speaking in defense of Stalinism as he does not have to live under it

[76] *While freely...to deplore*: a clause of concession and a very clumsy euphemism

[77] *curtailment*: cutting short, reduction, limitation, etc.

[78] *concomitant*: something that happens at the same time and of the nature of an appendage

Mark the three consecutively underlined sentences. They are examples of the language calling up vivid "mental pictures" versus the political language that is dead and intended for deception. Harold Pinter, the 2005 Nobel laureate in literature, demonstrates the legacy of George Orwell in his comment on the "humanitarian intervention" by the US army: "All that happens is that the destruction of human beings—unless they're Americans—is called collateral damage."

The inflated style[79] is itself a kind of euphemism. A mass of Latin words falls upon the facts like soft snow, blurring the outlines and covering up all the details. The great enemy of clear language is insincerity. When there is a gap between one's real and one's declared aims, one turns as it were[80] instinctively to long words and exhausted[81] idioms, like a cuttlefish squirting[82] out ink. In our age there is no such thing as "keeping out of politics." All issues are political issues, and politics itself is a mass of lies, evasions, folly, hatred, and schizophrenia.[83] When the general atmosphere is bad, language must suffer. I should expect to find—this is a guess which I have not sufficient knowledge to verify—that the German, Russian and Italian languages have all deteriorated in the last ten to fifteen years, as a result of dictatorship.

Mark the first two underlined sentences. Both are similes that create concrete images to help illustrate the author's points: insincere words hide facts as snow covers up objects; one utters ready-made phrases and sentences as a cuttlefish spits its ink. To all intents and purposes, the third underlined sentence is again one of the most important conclusions of the essay.

But if thought corrupts language, language can also corrupt thought. A

---

[79] *inflated style*: of the passage by a supposedly comfortable English professor

[80] *as it were*: a parenthesis meaning so to speak

[81] *exhausted*: used so much that they are vapid, trite, hackneyed

[82] *squirting*: ejecting liquid in a jet-like stream

[83] *schizophrenia*: originally a psychiatric term; split by extension of the meaning between what is professed and what is practiced

bad usage can spread by tradition and imitation, even among people who should and do know better. The debased language that I have been discussing is in some ways very convenient. Phrases like *a not unjustifiable assumption, leaves much to be desired, would serve no good purpose, a consideration which we should do well to bear in mind*, are a continuous temptation, a packet of aspirins always at one's elbow. Look back through this essay, and for certain you will find that I have again and again committed the very faults I am protesting against.[84] By this morning's post I have received a pamphlet dealing with conditions in Germany. The author tells me that he "felt impelled" to write it. I open it at random, and here is almost the first sentence that I see: "[The Allies] have an opportunity not only of achieving a radical transformation of Germany's social and political structure in such a way as to avoid a nationalistic reaction in Germany itself, but at the same time of laying the foundations of a cooperative and unified Europe." You see, he "feels impelled" to write—feels, presumably, that he has something new to say—and yet his words, like cavalry horses answering the bugle,[85] group themselves automatically into the familiar dreary pattern. This invasion of one's mind by ready-made phrases (*lay the foundations, achieve a radical transformation*) can only be prevented if one is constantly on guard against them, and every such phrase anaesthetises a portion of one's brain.[86]

The first underlined sentence of the above paragraph is a reiteration of the key statement of this paragraph: "The attraction of this way of writing is that it is easy." To resist the allure of "convenience," one has to be "constantly on guard against" the hackneyed phrases. In other words, be a "scrupulous writer."

Mark "a packet of aspirins always at one's elbow." Aspirins at hand are easy to reach and taken as panacea by most people, though they are never expected to solve any real health problems. That is how those ready-made phrases are: handy, convenient for employment in any given context but never used to convey any real meaning. But is George Orwell overly

---

[84] *Look back...protesting against*: See, for instance, his use of "not indispensable" in Par. 7.

[85] *bugle*: trumpet, used especially for military rallying

[86] *anaesthetises...one's brain*: partly hypnotizes one's mind; drives one to a "reduced state of consciousness"

metaphoric? Is he unconsciously affected by one of the sins he condemns?

I said earlier that the decadence of our language is probably curable. Those who deny this would argue, if they produced an argument at all,[87] that language merely reflects existing social conditions, and that we cannot influence its development by any direct tinkering[88] with words and constructions. As far as the general tone or spirit of a language goes, this may be true, but it is not true in detail. Silly words and expressions have often disappeared, not through any evolutionary process but owing to the conscious action of a minority.[89] Two recent examples were *explore every avenue* and *leave no stone unturned*, which were killed by the jeers of a few journalists. There is a long list of flyblown[90] metaphors which could similarly be got rid of if enough people would interest themselves in the job; and it should also be possible to laugh the *not un*-formation out of existence,[*] to reduce the amount of Latin and Greek in the average sentence, to drive out foreign phrases and strayed scientific words,[91] and, in general, to make pretentiousness unfashionable. But all these are minor points. The defense of the English language implies more than this, and perhaps it is best to start by saying what it does *not* imply.

In polemics a point is apt to be over-stretched. The two phrases "explore every avenue" and "leave no stone unturned," for instance, have not really phased out of the English language as Orwell wishes. The latter one, in fact, is included in almost every English dictionary as an idiom in current active use.

---

[87] *if they...at all*: Is Orwell always free from wordiness? Or is it partly a symptom of the linguistic epidemic?

[88] *tinkering*: repairing especially minor defects

[89] *owing to...a minority*: a statement somewhat running counter to an earlier one (see Page 47, Note 2)

[90] *flyblown*: literally meaning infested with the eggs or larvae of a blowfly; the word is used metaphorically here to highlight the repulsive nature of bad metaphors.

[91] *strayed scientific words*: scientific words that are inserted in the wrong place; misplaced scientific terms

* One can cure oneself of the *not un*-formation by memorising this sentence: *A not unblack dog was chasing a not unsmall rabbit across a not ungreen field.*[92]

To begin with it has nothing to do with archaism, with the salvaging of obsolete words and turns of speech, or with the setting up of a "standard English" which must never be departed from. On the contrary, it is especially concerned with the scrapping[93] of every word or idiom which has outworn[94] its usefulness. It has nothing to do with correct grammar and syntax, which are of no importance so long as one makes one's meaning clear, or with the avoidance of Americanisms, or with having what is called a "good prose style." On the other hand, it is not concerned with fake simplicity and the attempt to make written English colloquial. Nor does it even imply in every case preferring the Saxon word to the Latin one, though it does imply using the fewest and shortest words that will cover one's meaning. What is above all needed is to let the meaning choose the word, and not the other way about. In prose, the worst thing one can do with words is to surrender to them. When you think of a concrete object, you think wordlessly,[95] and then, if you want to describe the thing you have been visualizing you probably hunt about till you find the exact words that seem to fit it. When you think of something abstract you are more inclined to use words from the start, and unless you make a conscious effort to prevent it, the existing dialect[96] will come rushing in and do the job for you, at the expense of blurring or even changing your meaning. Probably it

[92] *A not...ungreen field*: George Orwell is being unfair by "pushing the envelope" in a debate. That is, exaggerating the vices of an opposite view. In fact, nobody will say or write such an imbecilic sentence, and the *not un-* kind of expression continues to be used a lot today.

[93] *scrapping*: abandoning or discarding as useless

[94] *outworn*: worn out, exhausted; note the prefix "out-" as in "outstay one's welcome."

[95] *When you...think wordlessly*: a doubtful assertion about the relationship between thoughts of "concrete" and "abstract" objects on the one hand and words on the other if one believes that thought and language take place in sync

[96] *the existing dialect*: those above-mentioned ready-made expressions

is better to put off using words as long as possible and get one's meaning[97] as clear as one can through pictures or sensations. Afterwards one can choose—not simply *accept*—the phrases that will best cover the meaning, and then switch round[98] and decide what impression one's words are likely to make on another person. This last effort of the mind cuts out all stale or mixed images, all prefabricated[99] phrases, needless repetitions, and humbug and vagueness generally. But one can often be in doubt about the effect of a word or a phase, and one needs rules that one can rely on when instinct fails. I think the following rules will cover most cases:

(i) Never use a metaphor, simile or other figure of speech which you are used to seeing in print.[100]
(ii) Never use a long word where a short one will do.
(iii) If it is possible to cut a word out, always cut it out.
(iv) Never use the passive where you can use the active.[101]
(v) Never use a foreign phrase, a scientific word or a jargon word if you can think of an everyday English equivalent.
(vi) Break any of these rules sooner than say anything outright barbarous.[102]

The six rules laid down by George Orwell are well-known as rules of the thumb throughout the English-writing circles of his time and are still upheld by pedagogues. While they may be useful for a student, we may do well in remembering in the meantime that "Never is a long word." For instance, regarding Rule (v), in an increasingly globalized world with "many Englishes" and in an age of science and technology, avoidance of loan words and shop talk

---

97 *it is...one's meaning*: as if thought and language do not happen simultaneously

98 *switch round*: turn back

99 *prefabricated*: ready-made like a prefab

100 *Never use...in print*: Do not use hackneyed metaphors or other figures of speech that have become clichés. Then how about using "to spend/kill time?" Is it not a metaphor in the first place?

101 *Never use...the active*: Compare, for instance, the wording of a public notice on a London bus: "The passengers are requested not to communicate with the driver while the vehicle is in motion" and "Don't talk with the driver when he is driving."

102 *Break any...outright barbarous*: But "rules are made to be broken." It is always better to take others' advice with a grain of salt than make them all-time musts/must-nots.

is hardly a piece of viable advice.

These rules sound elementary, and so they are, but they demand a deep change of attitude in anyone who has grown used to writing in the style now fashionable. [...]

[...] Political language—and with variations this[103] is true of all political parties, from conservatives to Anarchists—is designed to make lies sound truthful and murder respectable, and to give an appearance of solidity to pure wind.[104] One cannot change this all in a moment, but one can at least change one's own habits, and from time to time one can even, if one jeers loudly enough, send some worn-out and useless phrases—*jackboot, Achilles' heel, hotbed, melting pot, acid test,*[105] *veritable inferno*[106] or other lumps of verbal refuse[107]—into the dustbin where they belong.

Note Orwell's "black list" of overused words. True, a *jackboot* in a *melting pot* is absurd enough and an *inferno* is an inferno needing no intensifying qualifiers—fortunately either of the two is seldom, if ever, seen or heard today—but the rest on the list remain part of the common core of the English vocabulary as we learn it. Pushing the envelope or stretching a point too much can be one's Achilles' heel.

Author

George Orwell (1903-50) is the pen name of Eric Arthur Blair, one of the most widely admired English essayists of the 20th century. He was born on June 25, 1903, to British parents of a family background described by himself as "lower-upper-middle class." George Orwell is best known for his two political novels: *Animal Farm* (1945) and *1984* (1949), the former

103 *this*: cataphoric rather than anaphoric

104 *to give...pure wind*: to give false shape and substance to a thing which is by nature shapeless and without substance; one more metaphor to further illustrate the deceptive nature of political language

105 *acid test*: a crucial test; originally chemical and now a cliché

106 *veritable inferno*: real, genuine hell

107 *refuse*: rubbish, useless stuff

an allegory, and the latter a dystopian story, both being critical of totalitarianism. Other important works by George Orwell are mostly essays of journalism such as *A Hanging* (1931) and *Shooting an Elephant* (1936) and books of reportage such as *Down and Out in Paris and London* (1933), *Burmese Days* (1934), *The Road to Wigan Pier* (1937), and *Homage to Catalonia* (1938). There are three lesser novels by Orwell: *A Clergyman's Daughter* (1935), *Keep the Aspidistra Flying* (1936), and *Coming Up for Air* (1939).

To some, George Orwell is the "finest journalist of his day" (*Newsweek*), and *1984* and *Animal Farm* are selected by the *Time* magazine as one of the 100 best English-language novels from 1923 to the present. Yet there are also voices about the want of pure aesthetic considerations in his novels that are after all so overwhelmingly politically-oriented (Cf. Milan Kundera: *The Art of the Novel and Richard Rorty: Contingency, Irony, and Solidarity*).

George Orwell died in 1950. The epitaph on his tombstone was a simple line: "Here lies Eric Arthur Blair, born June 25, 1903, died January 21, 1950." No mention is made of his better known pen-name.

Text

"Politics and the English Language" was originally published in the April 1946 issue of the journal *Horizon*. Michael Sheldon, in Orwell's authorized biography, calls it "his most influential essay."

Though severely criticizing the "outworn" phrases in English, George Orwell himself is actually responsible for a number of terms that would later become overused and "ready-made" after the immense success of his novel *1984*. Here are some examples: *newspeak*, *Big Brother*, *thought police*, *doublethink*, and *cold war*. Similarly, "All animals are equal, but some animals are more equal than others," a quote from *Animal Farm*, is now a popular expression.

Further Reading

Animal Farm, George Orwell
1984, George Orwell
The Elements of Style, William Strunk, Jr. and E. B. White
Gulliver's Travels, Jonathan Swift

Thinking as a Hobby[1]

by William Golding

While I was still a boy, I came to the conclusion that there were three grades of thinking;[2] and since I was later to claim thinking as my hobby,[3] I came to an even stranger conclusion—namely, that I myself could not think at all.

This one-sentence opening paragraph sounds paradoxical: the author first claims thinking as his hobby but concludes that he could not think at all. Note the ironic tone here. The boyish "three grades of thinking" are made the pivot of the whole essay at the very beginning—a device used frequently in argumentation.

I[4] must have been an unsatisfactory child for grownups to deal with. I remember how incomprehensible they appeared to me at first, but not, of course, how I appeared to them. It was the headmaster of my grammar school who first brought the subject of thinking before me—though neither in the way, nor with the result he intended. He had some statuettes in his study. They stood on a high cupboard behind his desk. One was a lady wearing nothing but a bath towel. She seemed frozen in an eternal panic

---

1 *Thinking as a Hobby*: Pay attention to the obvious incongruity of the two concepts in the title and the irony contained therein: thinking is usually considered to be a faculty or, to some, a serious endeavor, while a hobby is something pursued in one's spare time for fun.

2 *three grades of thinking*: This is a crucial notion of the essay. The author conveys his skeptical ideas about thinking basically through the gradation.

3 *claim thinking as my hobby*: On a separate occasion, William Golding identifies his hobbies as thinking, classical Greek, sailing, and archaeology.

4 *I*: Even though it is argumentative in nature, the essay remains familiar throughout in that the author draws heavily on his personal experiences, inviting rather than demanding the reader to share in them.

lest the bath towel[5] slip[6] down any farther; and since she had no arms, she was in an unfortunate position to pull the towel up again. Next to her, crouched[7] the statuette of a leopard, ready to spring down at the top drawer of filing cabinet labeled A-Ah. My innocence interpreted this[8] as the victim's last, despairing cry. Beyond the leopard was a naked, muscular gentleman, who sat, looking down, with his chin on his fist and his elbow on his knee. He seemed utterly miserable.

 As is reflected in the paragraph, the narration is carried forward in chronological order, interspersed with episodes and anecdotes. This is arguably an effective way to make a serious topic more accessible and readable.

 Mark the humorous observations of the three statuettes, including their positions, gestures, and expressions, all from the point of view of an innocent and imaginative little boy.

 Just as beauty is in the eye of the beholder, so is misery. Take particular note of the symbolism of the statuettes, which is an essential element in the tabulation of the author's ideas.

Some time later, I learned about these statuettes. The headmaster had placed them where they would face delinquent[9] children, because they symbolized to him the whole of life. The naked lady was the Venus of Milo.[10] She was Love. She was not worried about the towel. She was just busy being beautiful.[11] The leopard was Nature, and he was being natural. The naked, muscular gentleman was not miserable. He was Rodin's Thinker, an image of pure thought. It is easy to buy small plaster models of what you

---

[5] *bath towel*: the drapery over the lower torso mistaken for a bath towel in the eyes of a child

[6] *slip*: *the subjunctive in a "lest..." clause*

[7] *crouched*: stooped or bent low as if prepared to pounce

[8] *this*: referring to A-Ah not as part of the filing catalogue but as the legible representation of a cry

[9] *delinquent*: failing in or neglectful of a duty or obligation, especially in cases of young people

[10] *Venus of Milo*: a sculptured Greek goddess discovered in the Aegean island of Milo in 1820, believed to have been created between the years 130 and 100 BC

[11] *busy being beautiful*: an interesting observation from a child's perspective as if Venus was going out of her way to catch the eye

think life is like.[12]

 Keep in mind the symbolic meanings of the three statuettes for the schoolmaster and compare how they differ from those in the view of the author as a child.

I had better explain that I was a frequent visitor to the headmaster's study, because of the latest thing I had done or left undone.[13] As we now say, I was not integrated.[14] I was, if anything, disintegrated; and I was puzzled. Grownups never made sense. Whenever I found myself in a penal position[15] before the headmaster's desk, with the statuettes glimmering whitely above him, I would sink my head, clasp my hands behind my back and writhe[16] one shoe over the other.

The headmaster would look opaquely[17] at me through flashing spectacles.

"What are we[18] going to do with you?"

Well, what *were* they going to do with me?[19] I would writhe my shoe some more and stare down at the worn[20] rug.

"Look up, boy! Can't you look up?"

---

12 *It is...is like*: Read between the lines; consider if there is anything implied in it. Does the author imply, for instance, that to the headmaster, life is as simple as purchasing the small plaster models?

13 *I had...left undone*: referring to sins of commission and omission; 动辄得咎

14 *integrated*: As a term of sociologese, it means of or pertaining to a group or society whose members interact on the basis of commonly held norms or values. The boy is in all likelihood aberrant and defiant.

15 *in a penal position*: subject to punishment

16 *writhe*: move with a twisting or turning motion; another gesture to hide guilt and embarrassment

17 *opaquely*: impenetrably, inscrutably because of his glasses

18 *we*: the royal *we*, so to speak, speaking on behalf of the powers that be

19 *Well, what...with me?*: Consider the rhetorical question, which echoes the earlier statement "Grownups never made sense."

20 *worn*: indicating many a pupil had been "called on the carpet"

Then I would look up at the cupboard,[21] where the naked lady was frozen in her panic and the muscular gentleman contemplated the hindquarters of the leopard in endless gloom. I had nothing to say to the headmaster. His spectacles caught the light so that you could see nothing human behind them.[22] There was no possibility of communication.[23]

"Don't you ever think at all?"

No, I didn't think, wasn't thinking, couldn't think—I was simply waiting in anguish for the interview to stop.

"Then you'd better learn—hadn't you?"

On one occasion the headmaster leaped to his feet, reached up and plonked[24] Rodin's masterpiece on the desk before me.

"That's what a man looks like when he's really thinking."

I surveyed the gentleman without interest or comprehension.[25]

"Go back to your class."

 The vivid blow-by-blow description of the confrontation between the headmaster and the little boy accentuates the tragic failure in human communication, which provides much food for thought.

Clearly there was something missing in me. Nature had endowed the rest of the human race with a sixth sense and left me out. This must be so, I mused, on my way back to the class, since whether I had broken a window, or failed to remember Boyle's Law,[26] or been late for school, my teachers produced me one, adult answer: "Why can't you think?"

---

21 *Then I...the cupboard*: still avoiding eye contact

22 *His spectacles...behind them*: *chilling and dehumanizing effect of the spectacles*

23 *communication*: Emphasized in the sentence is the failure of communication between children and grown-ups.

24 *plonked*: threw or placed heavily or abruptly

25 *I surveyed...or comprehension*: failure to communicate emphasized again

26 *Boyle's Law*: the principle discovered by Robert Boyle (1627-91), British physicist, that at a constant temperature the volume of a confined ideal gas varies inversely with its pressure

 Mark the author's tone of irony. Doubts about his own endowments and self-mockery are only a façade. The adult insistence on thinking as is expressed in the underlined sentence, if anything, serves to stifle a child's natural inclinations.

As I saw the case, I had broken the window because I had tried to hit Jack Arney with a cricket ball and missed him; I could not remember Boyle's Law because I had never bothered to learn it; and I was late for school because I preferred looking over the bridge into the river. In fact, I was wicked. Were my teachers, perhaps, so good that they could not understand the depths of my depravity? Were they clear, untormented people who could direct their every action by this mysterious business of thinking?[27] The whole thing was incomprehensible. In my earlier years, I found even the statuette of the Thinker confusing. I did not believe any of my teachers were naked, ever.[28] Like someone born deaf, but bitterly determined to find out about sound, I watched my teachers to find out about thought.

 The underlined phrase "mysterious business of thinking" not only attests to a child's bewilderment in the adult world but also gives an added dimension to the basic human function of thinking. Thinking happens to all of us all the time as human beings are known to be thinking animals; there is nothing mysterious about it. Only when it is interfered with by external exigencies can we say that thinking becomes anything but natural.

There was Mr. Houghton. He was always telling me to think. With a modest satisfaction,[29] he would tell me that he had thought a bit himself. Then why did he spend so much time drinking? Or was there more sense in drinking than there appeared to be? But if not, and if drinking were in

---

[27] *In fact...of thinking?*: sentences smacking of extreme irony building up and leading to the principal concern of the essay-thinking

[28] *I did...naked, ever*: Recall the schoolmaster's remark: "That's what a man looks like when he's really thinking" and enjoy the humor of this sentence. The word *ever* adds to the end weight of the sentence.

[29] *a modest satisfaction*: modest in that he admilted he had thought a bit—an understatement of satisfaction assumed

fact ruinous to health—and Mr. Houghton was ruined, there was no doubt about that—why was he always talking about the clean life and the virtues of fresh air? He would spread his arms wide with the action of a man who habitually spent his time striding along mountain ridges.

"Open air does me good, boys—I know it!"

Sometimes, exalted by his own oratory,[30] he would leap from his desk and hustle us outside into a hideous wind.

"Now, boys! Deep breaths! Feel it right down inside you—huge draughts of God's good air!"

He would stand before us, rejoicing in his perfect[31] health, an open-air man.[32] He would put his hands on his waist and take a tremendous breath. You could hear the wind, trapped in the cavern of his chest and struggling with all the unnatural impediments. His body would reel with shock and his ruined face go white at the unaccustomed visitation. He would stagger back to his desk and collapse there, useless for the rest of the morning.[33]

Mr. Houghton was given to high-minded monologues about the good life, sexless and full of duty. Yet in the middle of one of these monologues, if a girl passed the window, tapping along on her neat little feet, he would interrupt his discourse, his neck would turn of itself[34] and he would watch her out of sight. In this instance, he seemed to me ruled not by thought but by an invisible and irresistible spring in his nape.[35]

His neck was an object of great interest to me. Normally it bulged a bit over his collar. But[36] Mr. Houghton had fought in the First World

---

[30] *oratory*: high-sounding remarks made in class

[31] *perfect*: ironically used here

[32] *an open-air man*: An open-air man and a confirmed drinker at once bring forth the schizophrenia of the person.

[33] *You could...the morning*: a vivid portrayal of the teacher and of his mismatching words and deeds especially. Does such mismatching assort well with clear-headed thinking?

[34] *of itself*: as if automatically and ungoverned by thinking

[35] *an invisible...his nape*: exaggeration but very realistic childish imagination

[36] *But*: for all the tendency toward obesity as is evidenced by the excrescent fat over the collar

War alongside both Americans and French, and had come—by who knows what illogic?[37]—to a settled[38] detestation of both countries. If either country happened to be prominent in current affairs, no argument could make Mr. Houghton think well of it. He would bang the desk, his neck would bulge still further and go red. "You can say what you like," he would cry, "but I've thought about this—and I know what I think!"

Mr. Houghton thought with his neck.[39]

The anecdote is narrated in detail and with a hilarious effect. Houghton's open-air debacle, his neck turning of itself to passing high heels, and his inscrutable dislike of his former allies combine to complete the portrayal of this self-styled thinking person who thinks "with his neck" rather than with his mind, paving the way for Golding's grade-three thinking.

There was Miss Parsons. She assured us that her dearest wish was our welfare, but I knew even then, with the mysterious clairvoyance[40] of childhood, that what she wanted most was the husband she never got. There was Mr. Hands—and so on.[41]

I have dealt at length with my teachers because this was my introduction to the nature of what is commonly called thought. Through them I discovered that thought is often full of unconscious prejudice, ignorance and hypocrisy.[42] It[43] will lecture on disinterested purity while its neck is being remorselessly twisted toward a skirt. Technically, it is about as proficient

---

[37] *by who knows what illogic?*: illogicality of a self-styled thinking man

[38] *settled*: confirmed, not subject to change

[39] *Mr. Houghton...his neck*: a remark witty in an absurd way as the last say about Houghton; a reference to the neck bulging and gyrating

[40] *clairvoyance*: astute intuitive insight or perception

[41] *so on*: the whole lot of them, these deceptive adults; with Mr. Houghton portrayed in minute detail, the author becomes broad-brush with the other teachers wherein we learn a useful lesson about writing now in-depth and now with economy.

[42] *unconscious prejudice, ignorance and hypocrisy*: the author's generalization of the features of grade-three thinking

[43] *It*: thought being personified if we consider the following verbs

as most businessmen's golf, as honest as most politicians' intentions, or—to come near my own preoccupation—as coherent as most books that get written.[44] It is what I came to call grade-three thinking, though more properly, it is feeling, rather than thought.

True, often there is a kind of innocence in prejudices, but in those days I viewed grade-three thinking with an intolerant contempt and an incautious mockery. I delighted to confront a pious lady who hated the Germans with the proposition that we should love our enemies.[45] She taught me a great truth in dealing with grade-three thinkers; because of her, I no longer dismiss lightly a mental process which for nine-tenths of the population is the nearest they will ever get to thought.[46] They have immense solidarity. We[47] had better respect them, for we are outnumbered and surrounded. A crowd of grade-three thinkers, all shouting the same thing, all warming their hands at the fire of their own prejudices, will not thank you for pointing out the contradictions in their beliefs. Man is a gregarious[48] animal, and enjoys agreement as cows will graze all the same way on the side of a hill.

"Unconscious prejudice, ignorance and hypocrisy" are not thinking proper, but "feeling, rather than thought," as the author puts it. Pay attention to his incisive observation and trenchant tone. His analysis of nine-tenths of shallow people with a herding instinct is penetrating.

---

44 *Technically, it...get written*: The "as…as…" comparisons here are rhetorically called enantiosis, i.e., a figure of speech by which what is to be understood affirmatively is stated negatively. What he actually wants to say is respectively "improficiency," "dishonesty," and "incoherence."

45 *we should love our enemies*: a Christian tenet; cf. "Love your enemies, bless them that curse you, do good to them that hate you, and pray for them which despitefully use you, and persecute you" (Matthew 5:44).

46 *the nearest...to thought*: The implied meaning: if there is such a thing as a mental process at all, forming prejudices (which they call thinking) is the farthest they can go.

47 *We*: What kind of people can "we" possible be? Really and rationally thinking people without prejudices? "Grade-one" thinkers?

48 *gregarious*: social and sociable, enjoying and seeking the company of others

Grade-two thinking is the detection of contradictions. I reached grade two when I trapped the poor, pious lady. Grade-two thinkers do not stampede[49] easily, though often they fall into the other fault and lag behind.[50] Grade-two thinking is a withdrawal, with eyes and ears open.[51] It became my hobby[52] and brought satisfaction and loneliness[53] in either hand. For grade-two thinking destroys without having the power to create. It set me watching the crowds cheering His Majesty the King and asking myself what all the fuss was about, without giving me anything positive to put in the place of that heady[54] patriotism. But there were compensations. To hear people justify their habit of hunting foxes and tearing them to pieces by claiming that the foxes liked it. To hear our Prime Minister talk about the great benefit we conferred on India by jailing people like Pandit Nehru[55] and Gandhi.[56] To hear American politicians talk about peace in one sentence and refuse to join the League of Nations[57] in the next. Yes, there were moments of delight.

---

[49] *stampede*: to be part of a mob or crowd running helter-skelter

[50] *though often...lag behind*: See Note 53 below.

[51] *withdrawal, with...ears open*: an attitude of keeping away and non-involvement but with all sensibilities remaining receptively sharp enough

[52] *hobby*: The private and individualistic nature of a hobby coheres with the claimed detection of contradictions characteristic of grade-two thinking.

[53] *satisfaction and loneliness*: "众人皆醉我独醒"式的满足和孤独； Now we understand better what the author meant by saying "though often they fall into the other fault and lag behind."

[54] *heady*: dizzy, headstrong, unthinking

[55] *Nehru*: Jawaharlal (1889–1964), Hindu political leader in India: first prime minister of the Republic of India (1947–64)

[56] *Gandhi*: Mohandas Karamchand (1869-1948), also known as Mahatma Gandhi, Indian nationalist and spiritual leader who developed the practice of nonviolent or civil disobedience that forced Great Britain to grant independence to India (1947). He was assassinated by a Hindu fanatic.

[57] *the League of Nations*: an international organization founded after the end of WWI, whose primary goal was to prevent any future world war; the forerunner of the UN

 By using grade-three thinking as his point of departure, the author moves on to explicate grade-two thinking, illuminating his point by virtue of several explicitly ironic examples of showy hypocrisy. Grade-two thinking is independent and essentially critical and destructive, rewarded with a delight only the thinker is entitled to.

But I was growing toward adolescence and had to admit that Mr. Houghton was not the only one with an irresistible spring in his neck. I, too, felt the compulsive hand of nature[58] and began to find that pointing out contradiction could be costly as well as fun.[59] There was Ruth, for example, a serious and attractive girl. I was an atheist at the time. Grade-two thinking is a menace to religion and knocks down sects[60] like skittles.[61] I put myself in a position to be converted by her with an hypocrisy worthy of grade three. She was a Methodist[62]—or at least, her parents were, and Ruth had to follow suit. But, alas, instead of relying on the Holy Spirit[63] to convert me, Ruth was foolish enough to open her pretty mouth in argument. She claimed that the Bible (King James Version) was literally inspired. I countered by saying that the Catholics believed in the literal inspiration of Saint Jerome's *Vulgate*,[64] and the two books were different. Argument flagged.[65]

At last she remarked that there were an awful lot of Methodists, and they couldn't be wrong, could they—not all those millions? That was too

---

[58] *I, too...of nature*: referring to irresistible attraction by the opposite sex

[59] *costly as well as fun*: delight as reward can be expensive

[60] *sects*: religious divisions, especially small groups separated from larger, established denominations

[61] *skittles*: nine pins that a wooden ball or disk is used to knock down, probably the origin of bowling

[62] *Methodist*: a member of the largest Christian denomination that grew out of the revival of religion led by John Wesley, which stresses both personal and social morality

[63] *the Holy Spirit*: the spirit of God

[64] *Vulgate*: a Latin version of the Bible, prepared chiefly by St. Jerome at the end of the 4th century AD and used as the authorized version of the Roman Catholic Church

[65] *flagged*: fell off in vigor and intensity

easy, said I restively[66] (for the nearer you were to Ruth, the nicer she was to be near to) since there were more Roman Catholics than Methodists anyway; and they couldn't be wrong, could they—not all those hundreds of millions? An awful flicker of doubt appeared in her eyes. I slid my arm around her waist and murmured breathlessly that if we were counting heads, the Buddhists were the boys for my money.[67] But Ruth had *really* wanted to do me good, because I was so nice. She fled. The combination of my arm and those countless Buddhists was too much for her.

That night her father visited my father and left, red-cheeked and indignant. I was given the third degree[68] to find out what had happened. It was lucky we were both of us only fourteen. I lost Ruth and gained an undeserved reputation as a potential libertine.[69]

 Along with its delightful reward, grade-two thinking yields costly consequences. A verbal encounter with a girl in his adolescent years and the resultant punishment he received are indicative of how grade-two got the upper hand of grade-three but had to take the rap thereby.

So grade-two thinking could be dangerous. It was in this knowledge, at the age of fifteen, that I remember making a comment from the heights of grade two, on the limitations of grade three. One evening I found myself alone in the school hall, preparing it for a party. The door of the headmaster's study was open. I went in. The headmaster had ceased to thump Rodin's Thinker down on the desk as an example to the young. Perhaps he had not found any more candidates, but the statuettes were still there, glimmering and gathering dust on top of the cupboard. I stood on

---

66 *restively*: because he was being sexually aroused

67 *the Buddhists...my money*: meaning Buddhism boasts the most disciples; "for my money" is somewhat equal to "I bet."

68 *the third degree*: intensive interrogating or rough treatment used to obtain information or a confession

69 *libertine*: a person who is morally or sexually unrestrained, especially a dissolute man; a profligate

a chair and rearranged them. I stood Venus in her bath towel on the filing cabinet, so that now the top drawer caught its breath in a gasp of sexy excitement. "A-Ah!"[70] The portentous[71] Thinker I placed on the edge of the cupboard so that he looked down at the bath towel and waited for it to slip.

 The rearrangement of the statuettes serves as the boy's revengeful frolicking with grade-three thinking. Besides, now the Thinker is breathing down the shoulder of Venus, symbolic of a thinking boy after an unthinking girl.

Grade-two thinking, though it filled life with fun and excitement, did not make for[72] content. To find out the deficiencies of our elders bolsters[73] the young ego but does not make for personal security.[74] I found that grade two was not only the power to point out contradictions. It took the swimmer some distance from the shore and left him there, out of his depth. I decided that Pontius Pilate[75] was a typical grade-two thinker. "What is truth?" he said, a very common grade-two thought, but one that is used always as the end of an argument instead of the beginning. There is still a higher grade of thought which says, "What is truth?"[76] and sets out to find it.

 This is a transitional paragraph whereby the author moves further to explore grade-one thinking. Mark the author's detection of the limitations of grade-two thinking, which poses questions without answering them. Refresh your memory with the author's previous statement that "grade-two thinking destroys without having the power to create."

---

[70] *A-Ah!*: Cf. the interpretation of the exclamation in the second paragraph

[71] *portentous*: seemingly more serious than necessary; ominous

[72] *make for*: help to promote, contribute

[73] *bolsters*: uplifts or props up

[74] *security*: because being egomaniac results in risking oneself in many ways

[75] *Pontius Pilate*: Roman procurator of Judea in the first century AD, the final authority concerned in the condemnation and execution of Jesus Christ. Cf. John 18: 37-38.

[76] *What is truth?*: According to the Gospel of John, Jesus said to Pilate that he is a king and "came into the world [. . .] to bear witness to the truth; and all who are on the side of truth listen to my voice," to which Pilate famously replied: "What is truth?"

But these grade-one thinkers were few and far between.[77] They did not visit my grammar school in the flesh though they were there in books.[78] I aspired to them, partly because I was ambitious and partly because I now saw my hobby as an unsatisfactory thing if it went no further.[79] If you set out to climb a mountain, however high you climb, you have failed if you cannot reach the top.

I *did* meet an undeniably grade-one thinker in my first year at Oxford. I was looking over a small bridge in Magdalen Deer Park, and a tiny mustached and hatted figure came and stood by my side. He was a German who had just fled from the Nazis to Oxford as a temporary refuge. His name was Einstein.

But Professor Einstein knew no English at that time and I knew only two words of German. I beamed at him, trying wordlessly to convey by my bearing[80] all the affection and respect that the English felt for him. It is possible—and I have to make the admission—that I felt here were two grade-one thinkers standing side by side; yet I doubt if my face conveyed more than a formless[81] awe. I would have given my Greek and Latin and French and a good slice of my English for enough German to communicate. But we were divided;[82] he was as inscrutable as my headmaster. For perhaps five minutes we stood together on the bridge, undeniable grade-one thinker and breathless aspirant.[83] With true greatness, Professor Einstein realized that my contact was better than none. He pointed to a trout wavering in midstream.

He spoke: "*Fisch.*"

---

[77] *But these...far between*: Compare the proportions of the three grades of thinkers. Grade-three "thinkers" account for nine-tenths of the population according to the author.

[78] *they were there in books*: prominent great thinkers anthologized or quoted in books

[79] *no further*: than grade two

[80] *bearing*: the manner in which one carries oneself, including posture and gestures

[81] *formless*: nondescript; euphemistically for *wry*

[82] *divided*: by a communication barrier

[83] *undeniable grade-one...breathless aspirant*: he, Einstein, the former and I the latter

My brain reeled.[84] Here I was, mingling with the great, and yet helpless as the veriest[85] grade-three thinker. Desperately I sought for some sign by which I might convey that I, too, revered pure reason. I nodded vehemently. In a brilliant flash I used up half of my German vocabulary.

"*Fisch. Ja*[86] *Ja.*"

For perhaps another five minutes we stood side by side. Then Professor Einstein, his whole figure still conveying good will and amiability, drifted away out of sight.

Mark the tone of mingled fondness, aspiration and regret in the author's reminiscences about his brief encounter with Albert Einstein back in his Oxford years. To him, "pure reason" may be the hallmark of grade-one thinking. Nevertheless, in actuality, by identifying Einstein "as inscrutable as my headmaster" and by the monosyllabic exchange of "Fisch" and "Ja," he may have wanted to suggest that the much aspired-for grade one thinking does not necessarily make for human communication, realizing that artificially grading human thought, ceaseless workings of the mind as a concomitant with man, is a bit far-fetched. Note how his grade-one thinking comes to naught in the following paragraphs.

I, too, would be a grade-one thinker. I was irreverent at the best of times.[87] Political and religious systems, social customs, loyalties and traditions, they all came tumbling down like so many rotten apples off a tree. This was a fine hobby and a sensible substitute for cricket, since you could play it all the year round. I came up in the end with what must always remain the justification for grade-one thinking, its sign, seal and charter.[88] I devised a coherent system for living. It was a moral system, which was wholly logical. Of course, as I readily admitted, conversion of the world to my way of thinking might be difficult, since my system did away with a number of trifles, such as big business, centralized government, armies,

---

84 *reeled*: as a result of being overwhelmed

85 *veriest*: sheer, utmost

86 *Ja*: [German] yes, suggesting the other half of his German vocabulary is the negative *nein*

87 *at the best of times*: in the sense that society falling apart provides much food for thinking

88 *sign, seal and charter*: an idiomatic phrase meaning entirely

marriage....[89]

Recall the author's definition of grade-two thinking as lacking in creation in the previous text. Here he explains his capacity for both destruction and creation, which entitles him to the status of a grade-one thinker. However, such qualifiers as "coherent system," "moral system," and "wholly logical" indicate the idealistic nature of the pattern of life designed by the author with pure reason. Does his scenario work? Let's see.

It was Ruth all over again.[90] I had some very good friends who stood by me, and still do. But my acquaintances vanished, taking the girls with them. Young women seemed oddly contented with the world as it was.[91] They valued the meaningless ceremony with a ring. Young men, while willing to concede the chaining sordidness of marriage, were hesitant about abandoning the organizations which they hoped would give them a career. A young man on the first rung of the Royal Navy, while perfectly agreeable to doing away with big business and marriage, got as rednecked as Mr. Houghton when I proposed a world without any battleships in it.

Note how a grade-one thinker with his scenario hit a stone wall. Except a few like-minded stalwarts, men and women fled, leaving him in isolation. These men and women, perhaps accounting for the nine-tenths of the population, tend to ostracize William Golding, because they are either comfortably practical or intellectually benumbed, all incapable of the so-called grade-one thinking.

Had the game gone too far? Was it a game any longer? In those prewar days,[92] I stood to lose a great deal, for the sake of a hobby.

Now you are expecting me to describe how I saw the folly of my ways

---

[89] *a number...armies, marriage...*: Mark the deliberate incongruity between "trifles" on the one hand and on the other "big business, centralized government, armies, marriage," which are far from trivial matters by commonly accepted standards.

[90] *It was Ruth all over again*: Ruth standing for utter failure in this context

[91] *the world as it was*: the status quo

[92] *prewar days*: pre-WWII, a period of time when undiscriminating patriotism and obedience were highly touted

and came back to the warm nest,[93] where prejudices are so often called loyalties, where pointless actions are hallowed[94] into custom by repetition, where we are content to say we think when all we do is feel.

But you would be wrong. I dropped my hobby and turned professional.[95]

Mark the uncompromising quality of a real thinker, who, intolerant of "prejudice, ignorance and hypocrisy" or of "destructing without creating," would keep thinking in real earnest throughout his life. Now return to the title of the essay to see Golding's true attitude toward thinking.

If I were to go back to the headmaster's study and find the dusty statuettes still there, I would arrange them differently. I would dust Venus and put her aside, for I have come to love her and know her for the fair thing she is. But I would put the Thinker, sunk in his desperate thought, where there were shadows before him—and at his back, I would put the leopard, crouched and ready to spring.

Think of possible symbolism of the rearranged statuettes. Pay attention to the position of the Thinker sandwiched by shadows ahead—"prejudice, ignorance and hypocrisy"—and at the back by the leopard, which can be an avatar of sheer brutal force. True independent thinking is not a hobby but a serious matter involving risks. Alternatively, the shadows, the Thinker, and the leopard can represent the three grades of thinking. Feel free to come up with other possible interpretations.

Author

William Golding (1911-93) was born in Cornwall, England. He declared that he was brought up to be a scientist, but revolted; after several years'

---

93 *came back...warm nest*: sought refuge among grade-three thinkers and moved out of harm's way

94 *hallowed*: greatly respected and revered

95 *I dropped...turned professional*: "[D]ropped my hobby" and "turned professional" ought to be studied in unison. Then the meaning becomes clearer that thinking ceased to be a hobby or something to be trifled with but henceforth became my profession.

study of science at Oxford, he devoted himself to English literature. During World War II he served five years in the Royal Navy, an experience that probably helped shape his sustained interest in the theme of barbarism and evils of humanity. Following the war Golding continued to teach and to write fiction. In 1954, his first novel, *Lord of the Flies*, was published, winning widespread acclaim in England and around the world subsequently. Other major novels by Golding include *The Inheritors* (1955), *Pincher Martin* (1956), *Free Fall* (1959), *The Spire* (1964), and *Darkness Visible* (1979).

Lord of the Flies describes a group of British schoolboys marooned on a tropical island. After having organized themselves upon democratic principles, their society degenerates into primeval barbarism. The novel presents a central theme prevailing in Golding's oeuvre: the conflict between the forces of light and darkness within the human soul. Golding describes it as follows: "The theme is an attempt to trace the defects of society back to the defects of human nature. The moral is that the shape of a society must depend on the ethical nature of the individual and not on any political system however apparently logical or respectable. The whole book is symbolic in nature except the rescue in the end where adult life appears, dignified and capable, but in reality enmeshed in the same evil as the symbolic life of the children on the island. The officer, having interrupted a man-hunt, prepares to take the children off the island in a cruiser which will presently be hunting its enemy in the same implacable way."

Golding received the Nobel Prize in literature in 1983 and was knighted in 1988.

Text

Though best known for his novels , William Golding wrote a number of essays regularly—not only about topical issues but also for phenomenal themes such as Loch Ness Monster theories. "Thinking as a Hobby" is a narrative essay in which Golding perceptively defines the three grades of thinking through his own personal experiences, observations, and intellectual growth from childhood to adulthood. In a now humorous now sarcastic manner, he poignantly conveys the darkness of human nature and the loneliness and isolation confronting real thinkers. The style may seem light and familiar in general, but the theme is definitely weighty and deeply thought-provoking.

Further Reading

Lord of the Flies, William Golding
Heart of Darkness, Joseph Conrad
Representations of the Intellectual, Edward Said

A Cow That Could Never Get Up N'more

by James Herriot

I could see that Mr. Handshaw didn't believe a word I was saying. He looked down at his cow and his mouth tightened into a stubborn line.

"Broken pelvis?[1] You're trying to tell me she'll never get up n'more?[2] Why, look at her chewing her cud.[3] I'll tell you this, young man—me dad[4] would've soon got her up if he'd been alive today."

I had been a veterinary surgeon for a year now and I had learned a few things. One of them was that farmers weren't easy men to convince[5]—especially Yorkshire Dalesmen.

And that bit about his dad. Mr. Handshaw was in his fifties and I suppose there was something touching about his faith in his late father's skill and judgement. But I could have done very nicely without it.

In these paragraphs the author juxtapozes a basically illiterate farmer and an educated man, and such juxtaposition is going to persist through. The farmer's faith in his late father is in fact part of his resistance to science and of his immanent bigotry.

It had acted as an additional irritant[6] in a case in which I felt I had troubles enough. Because there are few things which get more deeply under

---

[1] *pelvis*: repeating the vet's diagnosis incredulously

[2] *never get up n'more*: "[N]ever+n'more (i.e., no more)" is a colloquial double negative.

[3] *chewing her cud*: rechewing partly digested food as of a ruminant animal

[4] *me dad*: my dad. This is the farmer's dialectal colloquialism.

[5] *I had...to convince*: Understatements of this kind abound.

[6] *irritant*: That bit about his dad irritates. Note the "-ant" suffix as in "pollutant."

a vet's skin[7] than a cow which won't get up. To the layman it may seem strange that an animal can be apparently[8] cured of its original ailment and yet be unable to rise from the floor, but it happens.[9] And it can be appreciated that a completely recumbent milk cow has no future.[10]

The case had started when my boss, Siegfried Farnon, who owned the practice in the little Dales market town of Darrowby,[11] sent me to a milk fever. This suddenly occurring calcium deficiency attacks high yielding animals just after calving and causes collapse and progressive[12] coma. When I first saw Mr. Handshaw's cow she was stretched out motionless on her side, and I had to look carefully[13] to make sure she wasn't dead.

But I got out my bottles of calcium with an airy confidence[14] because I had been lucky enough to qualify just about the time when the profession had finally got on top of this hitherto fatal condition.[15] The breakthrough had come many years earlier[16] with inflation of the udder[17] and I still carried a little blowing-up outfit around with me (the farmers used bicycle pumps),

---

[7] *get more...vet's skin*: "[G]et under somebody's skin" is an informal but descriptive way of saying "irritate somebody intensely."

[8] *apparently*: by the mere outward look of the situation; not really

[9] *it happens*: Note the terse two-worder following a relatively long sentence.

[10] *And it...no future*: And people should be able to understand that a cow lying down all the time is simply doomed.

[11] *Darrowby*: Like all person names including the author's own, place names in the story are fictitious to avoid the suspicion of advertizing.

[12] *progressive*: increasing; more and more intense

[13] *carefully*: twice

[14] *with an airy confidence*: with assumed confidence coupled with light-heartedness as if it were going to be a breeze of a job

[15] *the profession...fatal condition*: the veterinaries had finally worked out a therapy (that is the "breakthrough" in the next sentence) to deal with this disease that had been incurable up to that moment

[16] *earlier*: Compare it with *ago*.

[17] *udder*: the large milk-carrying bag-like organ with a nipple on it

but with the advent of calcium therapy one could bask in[18] a cheap[19] glory by jerking an animal back from imminent death within minutes. The skill required was minimal but it looked very very good.

By the time I had injected the two bottles—one into the vein, the other under the skin—and Mr. Handshaw had helped me roll the cow on to her chest the improvement was already obvious, she was looking about her and shaking her head as if wondering where she had been for the last few hours.[20] I felt sure that if I had had the time to hang about for a bit I could see her on her feet. But other jobs were waiting.

 With "a little blowing-up outfit" and "bicycle pumps" on the one hand and calcium injections on the other, the background is set, so to speak, for confrontation between conventional wisdom of folklore and science.

"Give me a ring if she isn't up by dinner time," I said, but it was a formality.[21] I was pretty sure I wouldn't be seeing her again.

When the farmer rang at midday to say she was still down it was just a pinprick.[22] Some cases needed an extra bottle—it would be all right. I went out and injected her again.

I wasn't really worried when I learned she hadn't got up the following day, but Mr. Handshow, hands deep in pockets, shoulders hunched as he stood over his cow, was grievously disappointed[23] at my lack of success.

"It's time t'awd[24] bitch was[25] up. She's doin' no good laid[26] there. Surely

---

[18] *bask in*: enjoy as if basking in the sunshine

[19] *cheap*: cheap in the sense of being effortless

[20] *she was...few hours*: Note the affectionately humanizing touches.

[21] *it was a formality*: I was only saying it out of professional protocol.

[22] *pinprick*: a small puncture made by a pin; it means figuratively that he did not take it seriously. Note how the frustrating situation escalated by "I did my best to be hearty" and so forth until "I felt tied up inside with sheer frustration" in the later context.

[23] *grievously disappointed*: disappointed and with grievances said aloud too

[24] *t'awd*: dialectal form for "the old"

[25] *was*: the subjunctive in an "it's (high) time that…" sentence

[26] *laid*: originally misuse for "lying" but now near-acceptable in colloquial English

there's summat[27] you can do. I poured a bottle of water into her lug this morning but even that hasn't shifted her."[28]

"You what?"

"Poured some cold water down her lug'ole.[29] Me dad used to get 'em up that way and he was a very clever man with stock[30] was me dad."[31]

"I've no doubt he was," I said primly.[32] "But I really think another injection is more likely to help her."

The farmer watched glumly[33] as I ran yet another bottle of calcium under the skin. The procedure had lost its magic for him.

As I put the apparatus away I did my best to be hearty.[34] "I shouldn't worry. A lot of them stay down for a day or two—you'll probably find her walking about in the morning."

The phone rang just before breakfast and my stomach contracted sharply[35] as I heard Mr. Handshaw's voice. It was heavy with gloom. "Well, she's no different. Lyin' there eating her 'ead off,[36] but never offers to rise. What are you going to do now?"[37]

What indeed, I thought as I drove out to the farm. The cow had been down for forty-eight hours now—I didn't like it a bit.

The farmer went into the attack immediately. "Me dad allus[38] used to

---

[27] *summat*: dialectally "something"

[28] *I poured...shifted her*: a matter-of-fact statement forming a sharp contrast to the vet's next outraged question

[29] *lug'ole*: Note the dialectal accent leaving out the /h/ sound; also, *'em* for *them.*

[30] *stock*: livestock; farm animals

[31] *was me dad*: a repetitive tag for emphasis as if the late father were "twice clever"

[32] *primly*: in a dry, formal manner

[33] *glumly*: gloomily; with brooding morose

[34] *hearty*: cheerful and looking confident

[35] *my stomach contracted sharply*: See how things escalated.

[36] *eating her 'ead off*: doing nothing but eating; the principal verb is optional such as "to laugh one's head off."

[37] *now*: The word should receive the greatest emphasis.

[38] *allus*: always, pronounced with a heavy accent

say they had a worm in the tail when they stayed down like this. He said if you cut tailend off it did the trick."[39]

My spirits sagged lower. I had had trouble with this myth before.[40] The insidious[41] thing was that the people who still practised this relic of barbarism[42] could often claim that it worked because, after the end of the tail had been chopped off, the pain of the stump touching the ground forced many a sulky[43] cow to scramble to her feet.

"There's no such thing as a worm in the tail, Mr. Handshaw," I said. "And don't you think it's a cruel business, cutting off a cow's tail? I hear the RSPCA[44] had a man in court last week over a job like that."

The farmer narrowed his eyes. Clearly he thought I was hedging,[45] "Well, if you won't do that, what the hangment[46] are you going to do? We've got to get this cow up somehow."

I took a deep breath. "Well, I'm sure she's got over the milk fever because she's eating well and looks quite happy. It must be a touch of posterior[47] paralysis that's keeping her down. There's no point in giving her any more calcium so I'm going to try this stimulant injection." I filled the syringe with a feeling of doom.[48] I hadn't a scrap of faith in the stimulant, but I just couldn't do nothing. I was scraping the barrel out[49] now.

I was turning to go when Mr. Handshaw called after me, "Hey, Mister.

---

[39] *it did the trick*: it would solve the problem

[40] *I had...myth before*: It was not the first time for me to be confronted with this folklore diagnosis.

[41] *insidious*: tricky; harmful in an imperceptible way

[42] *this relic of barbarism*: this barbarically outmoded custom

[43] *sulky*: low-spirited; morosely sluggish

[44] *RSPCA*: acronym for "Royal Society for the Prevention of Cruelty to Animals" of the UK

[45] *hedging*: dodging the real problem; avoiding committing myself; being evasive

[46] *hangment*: Farmers avoided blasphemy. So a euphemistic word was used for "hell."

[47] *posterior*: a formal word for "back" or "towards the back of the body." Its antonym is *anterior*. Note how the vet was using technical terms to keep a respectable façade vis-à-vis the farmer.

[48] *a feeling of doom*: a feeling that it wouldn't do any good; doom: sure failure

[49] *scraping the barrel out*: reaching my wit's end; resorting to the last resource at my disposal

I remember summat else me dad used to do. Shout in their lugs. He got many a cow up that way. I'm not very strong in the voice—how about you having a go?"[50]

It was a bit late to stand on my dignity.[51] I went over to the animal and seized her by the ear. Inflating my lungs to the utmost I bent down and bawled wildly into the hairy depths. The cow stopped chewing for a moment and looked at me inquiringly,[52] then her eyes drooped and she returned contentedly to her cudding.[53] "We'll give her another day," I said wearily. "And if she's still down tomorrow we'll have a go at lifting her. Could you get a few of the neighbours to give us a hand?"

Driving round my other cases that day I felt tied up inside with sheer frustration. Damn and blast the thing.[54] What the hell was keeping her down? And what else could I do? This was 1938 and my resources were limited. Thirty years later[55] there are still milk fever cows which won't get up but the vet has a much wider armoury[56] if the calcium has failed to do the job.

As I expected, the following day brought no change and as I got out of the car in Mr. Handshaw's yard I was surrounded by a group of his neighbours. They were in festive mood,[57] grinning, confident, full of helpful[58] advice as farmers always are with somebody else's animals.

---

[50] *go*: try

[51] *to stand on my dignity*: to try to preserve my dignity as a professional by refusing to do such a stupid thing upon request

[52] *inquiringly*: humanizing touches again; also note the word *contentedly* in the following line.

[53] *cudding*: chewing the food brought up into the mouth from its first stomach

[54] *Damn and blast the thing*: a very strong expletive

[55] *Thirty years later* : temporal reference to the time of writing

[56] *armoury*: a collection of available resources

[57] *in festive mood*: high-spirited, as if celebrating some festival in an otherwise uneventful village

[58] *helpful*: Note the ironical tone for such counterproductive advice and the "weird suggestions" in the next paragraph.

There was much laughter and leg-pulling[59] as we drew sacks under the cow's body and a flood of weird suggestions to which I tried to close my ears. When we all finally gave a concerted[60] heave and lifted her up, the result was predictable; she just hung there placidly with her legs dangling whilst her owner leaned against the wall watching us with deepening gloom.

After a lot of puffing[61] and grunting we lowered the inert body and everybody looked at me for the next move. I was hunting round desperately in my mind when Mr. Handshaw piped up[62] again.

"Me dad used to say a strange dog[63] would allus get a cow up."

There were murmurs of assent from the assembled farmers and immediate offers of dogs. I tried to point out that one[64] would be enough but my authority had dwindled anyway and everybody seemed anxious to demonstrate their dogs' cow-raising potential. There was a sudden excited exodus[65] and even Mr. Smedley the village shopkeeper pedalled[66] off at frantic speed for his border terrier.[67] It seemed only minutes before the byre[68] was alive with snapping, snarling curs[69] but the cow ignored them all except to wave her horns warningly at the ones which came too close.

The flash-point[70] came when Mr. Handshaw's own dog came in from the fields where he had been helping to round up the sheep. He was a skinny

---

59 *leg-pulling*: joke-making at the expenses of others

60 *concerted*: combined; performed in unison

61 *puffing*: heavy breathing

62 *piped up*: spoke up, especially in a shrill voice

63 *a strange dog*: The sight of it would hopefully give the cow a shock.

64 *one*: one dog

65 *exodus*: mass departure; a big enough word to emphasize confused stampede

66 *pedalled*: worked the pedals of a vehicle or an instrument; apparently, Mr. Smedley went off riding a bicycle.

67 *border terrier*: a kind of small hunting dog

68 *byre*: cow shed

69 *curs*: originally mongrels or inferior dogs

70 *flash-point*: Originally it means the temperature at which a volatile substance ignites. Figuratively it means the crucial moment.

hard-bitten[71] little creature with lightning reflexes and a short temper. He stalked, stiff-legged and bristling,[72] into the byre, took a single astounded look at the pack of foreigners on his territory and flew into action with silent venom.

Within seconds the finest dog fight I had ever seen was in full swing and I stood back and surveyed the scene with a feeling of being completely superfluous.[73] The yells of the farmers rose above the enraged yapping and growling.[74]

It seemed to me that all the forces of black magic had broken through and were engulfing me and that my slender resources of science had no chance of shoring up the dyke.[75] I don't know how I heard the creaking above the din—probably because I was bending low over Mr. Reynolds in an attempt to persuade him to desist from his tail rubbing. But at that moment the cow shifted her position slightly and I distinctly heard it.[76] It came from the pelvis.

It took me some time to attract attention—I think everybody had forgotten I was there[77]—but finally the dogs were separated and secured with innumerable lengths of binder twine,[78] everybody stopped shouting, Mr. Reynolds was pulled away from the tail and I had the stage.

I addressed myself to Mr. Handshaw. "Would you get me a bucket of hot water, some soap and a towel please?"[79]

---

[71] *hard-bitten*: tough; unyielding; cf. soft-spoken

[72] *bristling*: with hair standing on end as a gesture of taking on an aggressive attitude

[73] *superfluous*: out of place as an odd man out

[74] *The yells...and growling*: Apparently the farmers were more excited than the dogs.

[75] *It seemed...the dyke*: Notice the sustained metaphor.

[76] *it*: the cataphoric "creaking" sound

[77] *It took...was there*: Study the sentence along with an earlier word *superfluous*. Also note what happened next from a narratological point of view and how prose rhythm was achieved by following longer statements with shorter ones.

[78] *binder twine*: a kind of strong string used for makeshift leashes

[79] *Would you...towel please*: Note how confidence returned to the vet not only from the request but also from what he was to do methodically in the following context.

He trailed off, grumbling, as though he didn't expect much from the new gambit. My stock[80] was definitely low.

I stripped off my jacket, soaped my arms and pushed a hand into the cow's rectum[81] until I felt the hard bone of the pubis. Gripping it through the wall of the rectum I looked up at my audience. "Will two of you get hold of the hook bones and rock the cow gently from side to side."

Yes, there it was again, no mistake about it. I could both hear and feel it—a looseness, a faint creaking, almost a grating.[82]

I got up and washed my arm. "Well, I know why your cow won't get up—she has a broken pelvis. Probably did it during the first night when she was staggering about with the milk fever. I should think the nerves are damaged too. It's hopeless, I'm afraid." Even though I was dispensing bad news it was a relief to come up with something rational.

Mr. Handshaw stared at me. "Hopeless? How's that?"

"I'm sorry," I said, "but that's how it is. The only thing you can do is get her off to the butcher. She has no power in her hind legs. She'll never get up again."[83]

That was when Mr. Handshaw really blew his top[84] and started a lengthy speech. He wasn't really unpleasant or abusive but firmly pointed out my shortcomings and bemoaned again the tragic fact that his dad was not there to put everything right. The other farmers stood in a wide-eyed ring,[85] enjoying every word.

At the end of it I took myself off. There was nothing more I could do and anyway Mr. Handshaw would have to come round to my way of thinking.[86] Time would prove me right.

---

[80] *stock*: credit, reputation

[81] *rectum*: the last part of the intestine, ending at the anus

[82] *grating*: louder than creaking; a grinding or rasping noise

[83] *The only...up again*: The vet sounded as if he were being deliberately cruel than dispensing bad news. Why?

[84] *blew his top*: lost his temper; flew into a rage

[85] *stood in a wide-eyed ring*: stood in a circle, each with his eyes wide-open

[86] *would have...of thinking*: would have to change his stubbornness and accept my judgment

I thought of that cow as soon as I awoke next morning. It hadn't been a happy episode[87] but at least I did feel a certain peace in the knowledge that there were no more doubts. I knew what was wrong; I knew that there was no hope. There was nothing more to worry about.

Note the diminuendo of the account with a view to fully exploiting the following surprise factor.

I was surprised when I heard Mr. Handshaw's voice on the phone so soon. I had thought it would take him two or three days to realize he was wrong.

"Is that Mr. Herriot? Aye, well, good mornin' to you. I'm just ringing to tell you that me cow's up on her legs and doing fine."

I gripped the receiver tightly with both hands.[88]

"What? What's that you say?"

"I said me cow's up. Found her walking about byre this morning, fit as a fiddle. You'd think there'd never been owt[89] the matter with her." He paused for a few moments then spoke with grave deliberation like a disapproving school-master. "And you stood there and looked at me and said she'd never get up n'more."

"But... but..."

"Ah, you're wondering how I did it? Well, I just happened to remember another old trick of me dad's. I went round to t'butcher and got a fresh-killed sheep skin and put it on her back. Had her up in no time—you'll 'ave to come round and see her. Wonderful man was me dad."

It is interesting to note how various folk therapies have been tried: from pouring water into the lughole, the suggested cutting of the tailend, shouting to arouse the cow's attention, hoisting with a concerted effort, the sight of a strange dog, tail-rubbing, finally to a freshly killed sheep skin. Emphasized in the escalating process are the myth of omnipotent science and the eventual triumph of conventional wisdom.

---

87 *It hadn't...happy episode*: a typical British understatement

88 *I gripped...both hands*: a gesture of surprised anticipation of fresh trouble

89 *owt*: aught, meaning anything as it was pronounced with an accent

Blindly I made my way into the dining-room. I had to consult my boss about this. Siegfried's sleep had been broken by a 3 a.m. calving[90] and he looked a lot older than his thirty-odd years. He listened in silence as he finished his breakfast, then pushed away his plate and poured a last cup of coffee. "Hard luck, James. The old sheep skin eh?[91] Funny thing—you've been in the Dales over a year now and never come across that one. Suppose it must be going out of fashion a bit now but you know it has a grain of sense behind it like a lot of these old remedies. You can imagine there's a lot of heat generated under a fresh sheep skin and it acts like a great hot poultice[92] on the back—really tickles them up after a while. And if a cow is lying there out of sheer cussedness.[93] She'll often get up just to get rid of it."

"But damn it, how about the broken pelvis? I tell you it was creaking and wobbling[94] all over the place!"

"Well, James, you're not the first to have been caught that way. Sometimes the pelvic ligaments don't tighten up for a few days after calving and you get this effect."

"Oh God," I moaned, staring down at the tablecloth. "What a bloody mess I've made of the whole thing."

"Oh, you haven't really." Siegfried lit a cigarette and leaned back in his chair. "That old cow was probably toying with the idea of getting up for a walk[95] just when old Handshaw dumped the skin on her back. She could just as easily have done it after one of your injections and then you'd have got credit. Don't you remember what I told you when you first came here.

---

90 *a 3 a.m. calving*: This explains why one of the author's works is humorously entitled "Let Sleeping Vets Lie" *à la* "let sleeping dogs lies."

91 *eh*: same as "huh," meaning "you say?"

92 *poultice*: 膏药

93 *cussedness*: obstinacy especially out of bad humor

94 *wobbling*: a sound from rocking unsteadily from side to side louder than creaking

95 *toying with...a walk*: thinking of getting up for a walk as a possibility but not doing it actually yet

There's very fine dividing line between looking a real smart vet on the one hand and an immortal[96] fool on the other. This sort of thing happens to us all, so forget it, James."

But forgetting wasn't so easy. That cow became a celebrity in the district. Mr. Handshaw showed her with pride to the[97] postman, the policeman, corn merchants, lorry drivers, fertilizer salesmen, Ministry of Agriculture officials and they all told me about it frequently with pleased[98] smiles. Mr. Handshaw's speech was always the same, delivered, they said, in ringing,[99] triumphant tones:

"There's[100] the cow that Mr. Herriot said would never get up n'more."

I'm sure there was no malice behind the farmer's actions. He had put one over on[101] the young cleverpants vet and nobody could blame him for preening himself[102] a little. And in a way I did that cow a good turn:[103] I considerably extended her lifespan because Mr. Handshaw kept her long beyond her normal working period just as an exhibit. Years after she had stopped giving more than a couple of gallons of milk a day[104] she was still grazing happily in the field by the roadside.

She had one curiously upturned horn and was easy to recognize. I often pulled up my car and looked wistfully[105] over the wall at the cow that could never get up n'more.

---

96 *immortal*: utter; complete

97 *the*: the definite article used to denote the uniqueness, from which we know how small the community was

98 *pleased*: amused when they thought of what a face-losing episode it had been for the vet

99 *ringing*: resonant

100 *There*: archaic and dialectal use of *that*

101 *put one over on*: got the upper hand of

102 *preening himself*: showing himself off

103 *did that cow a good turn*: did a favor to that cow

104 *she had...a day*: The cow became low-yielding.

105 *wistfully*: in a musingly sad manner; pensively

 The concluding part is full of bitter-sweet irony at the author's own expense, which more often than not is part and parcel of British humor.

Author

James Herriot (1916-95) is the pen name of James Alfred Wight, a British veterinary surgeon and writer. Herriot started writing about his medical practice as a country veterinarian in Yorkshire when he was already in his fifties. It is for these semi-biographical stories that Herriot is best known as a writer. His writing style is noted for its simplicity, lucidness, and a strong sense of humor. Without exception, his tales radiate a genuine love of all living creatures. Two of his books, remaining on the best-selling list long in the early 1970s, have been adapted for film and television: *All Creatures Great and Small* and *All Things Bright and Beautiful*, the latter being a sequel to the former. Sociologically, the James Herriot series points, albeit indirectly, to the transition of vets' focus from draught animals to pets like cats and dogs. For all his fictionalizing touches such as using fictitious person and place names and adding dialogues, Herriot's remains excellent prose narratives that may double as examples of good essay writing.

Text

"A Cow That Could Never Get Up N'more" is an excerpt from Herriot's most famous book *All Creatures Great and Small*. It is the 32nd chapter with the title added by the current anthologizer. The book is a memoir about the author's life in the countryside of Yorkshire during the late 1930s as a young veterinarian. It covers a two-year period and stories are arranged in chronological order, from the hard beginning of the narrator's career till his success in becoming a partner of his former boss and marrying his sweetheart. The book is full of ups and downs just as life itself is. Woven into all the hardships and conflicts is the author's never-abating humor and courage. To quote Phoebe Adams, one critic of the book, *All Creatures Great and Small* continues to be one of "the funniest and most likable books around."

Further Reading

Anything by James Herriot
Silent Spring, Rachel Carson
The Unexpected Universe, Loven Eiseley

On the Morning after the Sixties[1]

by Joan Didion

I am talking here about being a child of my time. When I think about the Sixties now I think about an afternoon not of the Sixties at all, an afternoon early in my sophomore year at Berkeley,[2] a bright autumn Saturday in 1953. I was lying on a leather couch in a fraternity house (there had been a lunch for the alumni, my date[3] had gone on to the game. I do not now recall why I had stayed behind), lying there alone reading a book by Lionel Trilling[4] and listening to a middle-aged man pick out on a piano in need of tuning the

---

1 *On the Morning after the Sixties* : The title indicates the retrospective angle of this essay. The Sixties in the US is a tumultuous and dynamic period of time, which is often associated with various political, social, and cultural movements that have engendered a great many changes—notably the Free Speech Movement, the protest marches and draft-dodging to end the war in Vietnam, the growth of the counterculture, the founding of the Black Panthers and the Black Power Movement, the stirrings of women's liberation and gay liberation, and the widespread impact of the Beatles. However, throughout this essay, Didion does not dwell elaborately upon the afore-mentioned externalities in the Sixties. Instead, by focusing on her own college days in the Fifties, and accordingly, her generation's psyche and mentality, she presents in an ambivalent but emphatic manner the differences between the two peer cohorts belonging to their respective eras.

2 *Berkeley* : The University of California at Berkeley was the foremost arena for unprecedented student upheaval, protest demonstrations, and direct confrontations with the police and the powers that be. Note Didion's portrayal of a totally different Berkeley in this essay.

3 *date*: a boy or girl friend that one is going steady with

4 *Lionel Trilling*: (1905-75) American literary critic whose works include *The Liberal Imagination* (1950), *Beyond Culture* (1965), *Sincerity and Authenticity* (1972), and *Mind in the Modern World* (1972); he was one of the best-known American literary critics of his time, usually identified as a traditionalist.

melodic line to "Blue Room."[5] All that afternoon he played "Blue Room" and he never got it right. I can hear and see it still, the wrong note in "We will thrive on/Keep alive on,"[6] the sunlight falling through the big window, the man picking up his drink and beginning again and telling me, without ever saying a word,[7] something I had not known before about bad marriages and wasted time and looking backward.[8] That such an afternoon would now seem implausible in every detail—the idea of having had a "date" for a football lunch now seems to me so exotic as to be almost czarist[9]—suggests the extent to which the narrative[10] on which many of us grew up no longer applies.

 Note the three temporal references: a) 1970, i.e., the morning after the Sixties when the author wrote the essay; b) the Sixties the author was apparently called upon to comment on; and c) the Fifties the author focused upon, namely, her own college days.

 Mark what a lazy, somnolent, lethargic afternoon it was: being left behind by one's date to lie on a couch with nothing but heavy reading to amuse oneself with; a middle-aged man playing an off-key piano while drowning his bitterness and nostalgia in drink, and so forth.

 See translation as aids as appendage for the underlined sentence.

The distance we[11] have come from the world in which I went to college

---

[5] *Blue Room*: a 1926 popular song composed by Richard Rodgers with lyrics supplied by Lorenz Hart for the 1926 musical *The Girl Friend* starring Eva Puck and Sammy White. It also featured in the 1948 film *Words and Music*.

[6] *We will...alive on*: from the lyrics of the song. The wrong note at this place may arguably allude to the player's contingent skepticism about the theme of thriving.

[7] *without ever saying a word*: by means of his rendition of the tune and drinking while playing

[8] *bad marriages...looking backward*: the three things that the piano player seemed to convey, though unknown to the young author back then

[9] *czarist*: a term to suggest how outlandish and what an anachronism

[10] *narrative*: a set of ideas or beliefs such as freedom of personal choice to which Didion's generation has been conditioned. Consider all the possible interpretations of the word *narrative*.

[11] *we*: Note the change in Didion's use of personal pronouns from the first person singular to the plural. She starts to speak on behalf of her generation from now on. Consider the credibility of this *we* as a homogeneous whole.

was on my mind quite a bit during those seasons when not only Berkeley but dozens of other campuses were periodically shut down, incipient battlegrounds, their borders sealed.[12] To think of Berkeley as it was in the Fifties was not to think of barricades[13] and reconstituted classes.[14] "Reconstitution" would have sounded to us then like Newspeak,[15] and barricades are never personal.[16] We were all very personal then, sometimes relentlessly so,[17] and at that point where we either act or do not act, most of us are still. I suppose I am talking about just that: the ambiguity of belonging to a generation distrustful of political highs, the historical irrelevancy of growing up convinced that the heart of darkness lay not in some error of social organization but in man's own blood. If man was bound to err, then any social organization was bound to be in error.[18] It was a premise which still seems to me accurate[19] enough, but one which robbed us early of a certain capacity for surprise.[20]

---

[12] *not only...borders sealed*: details used to describe the Free Speech Movement at Berkeley in 1964-65; before "insipient battlegrounds," *being* is supposedly omitted.

[13] *barricades*: barriers thrown up by the students to impede the advance of the police

[14] *reconstituted classes*: basically courses with a revolutionized syllabus and with redefined teacher-student relations

[15] *Newspeak*: a term coined by George Orwell in his novel *1984*, meaning deliberately ambiguous and contradictory language used to mislead and manipulate the public

[16] *barricades are never personal*: because they have to be manned by many; but the seeming truism of this reductive conclusion is open to doubt. As material obstacles, barricades are apparently impersonal. But as a symbol of a cause or an ideal, they also denote personal commitment and determined endeavor. Didion seems to presuppose a clear-cut boundary between the personal and the public or political, which smacks of tendentious absolutism. Compare the feminist slogan "The personal is political."

[17] *sometimes relentlessly so*: unyieldingly so, suggesting that they would never exchange being personal for anything else—least of all for "political highs" in the following context

[18] *the ambiguity...in error*: descriptive of the generation of the Fifties' sense of belonging nowhere, its non-impact on history, and its deep-seated cynicism about human nature

[19] *accurate*: viable, valid

[20] *which robbed...for surprise*: which taught us a lesson when we were young that all evils were possible and probable and, therefore, unsurprising

 This paragraph sums up the message of this essay as much as Didion's own socio-political philosophy, which reveals a nihilistic belief in the meaninglessness and futility of any social agenda or movement because of the born evil of human nature. However, Didion's reasoning about the cause-and-effect relationship between man and social organization may appear flimsy and simplistic. The interplay between individuals and institutions is in fact much more complicated and dynamic than is explicated by Didion here. For example, even though "any social organization was bound to be in error," it does not necessarily follow that man should do nothing to rectify the error or try to prevent the worst error from happening.

 See translation as aids as appendage for the underlined sentence on the previous page.

At Berkeley in the Fifties no one was surprised by anything at all, a *donnée*[21] which tended to render discourse less than spirited, and debate nonexistent. The world was by definition imperfect, and so of course the university.[22] There was some talk even then about IBM cards,[23] but on balance the notion that free education for tens of thousands of people might involve automation did not seem unreasonable.[24] We took it for granted that the Board of Regents[25] would sometimes act wrongly. We simply avoided those students rumored to be FBI informers. We were the generation called

---

[21] *donnée*: [French] a set of notions, facts, or conditions that govern and shape an act or a way of life

[22] *The world...the university*: This argument echoes the "premise" in the preceding paragraph.

[23] *IBM cards*: pieces of stiff paper that contain digital information represented by the presence or absence of holes in predefined positions; in the Sixties the IBM card became a symbol of the computer, of alienation, and more generally, of anxiety about technology. It also signified the way the individual could be submerged into the mass and the resentment of individuals toward the power of large organizations. "Do not fold, spindle, or mutilate," the phrase printed on IBM cards was a cultural icon of the 1960s, which was once turned into a T-shirt slogan: "Do not fold, spindle, or mutilate, I am a human being."

[24] *not seem unreasonable*: not unreasonable because we in the Fifties maintained a balanced view that while IBM cards may have a dehumanizing effect, they contributed to open education

[25] *Board of Regents*: a committee of university officers who have general supervision over the welfare and conduct of students

"silent," but we were silent neither, as some thought, because we shared the period's official optimism[26] nor, as others thought, because we feared its official repression.[27] We were silent because the exhilaration of social action[28] seemed to many of us just one more way of escaping the personal, of masking for a while[29] that dread of the meaningless which was man's fate.

The last sentence throws into bold relief what Didion thinks of the upheaval of the Sixties — a temporary escape from the personal — and her conviction that meaninglessness is man's ultimate fate.

To have assumed that particular fate so early[30] was the peculiarity of my generation. I think now that we were the last generation[31] to identify with adults. That most of us have found adulthood just as morally ambiguous[32] as we expected it to be falls perhaps into the category of prophecies self-fulfilled: I am simply not sure. I am telling you only how it was. The mood of Berkeley in those years was one of mild but chronic depression, against which I remember certain small things[33] that seemed to me somehow explications, dazzling in their clarity, of the world I was about to enter: I remember a woman picking daffodils in the rain[34] one day when I was walking in the hills. I remember a teacher who drank too much[35] one night

---

[26] *official optimism*: a reference to post-WWII American national mood with baby-booming and so on

[27] *official repression*: a reference to, say, McCarthyism of the 1950s

[28] *the exhilaration of social action*: Compare the "political highs" in the last paragraph.

[29] *for a while*: instead of permanently

[30] *so early*: when we were in our late teens and early twenties as college students

[31] *the last generation*: No student generation after us would have assumed such a particular fate.

[32] *morally ambiguous*: Mark the slight difference between the claimed moral ambiguity and ontological meaninglessness.

[33] *small things*: Didion is noted for her obsession with details and minutiae.

[34] *a woman...the rain*: supposedly a solitary, sentimental image

[35] *who drank too much*: an echo of the middle-aged piano player in the first paragraph

and revealed his fright and bitterness. I remember my joy at discovering for the first time how language worked, at discovering, for example, that the central line of HEART OF DARKNESS was a postscript.[36] All such images were personal, and the personal was all that most of us expected to find. We would make a separate peace,[37] we would do graduate work in Middle English,[38] we would go abroad. We would make some money and live on a ranch. We would survive outside history, in a kind of *idée fixe*[39] referred to always, during the years I spent at Berkeley, as "some little town with a decent beach."[40]

 Consider if Didion's self-indulgent recollections of the small things, stressed as personal, are NOT "just one more way of escaping the personal, of masking for a while that dread of the meaningless which was man's fate."

As it worked out I did not find or even look for the little town with the decent beach. I sat in the large bare[41] apartment in which I lived my junior and senior years (I had lived awhile in a sorority, the Tri Delt[42] house, and had left it, typically, not over any issue[43] but because I, the implacable "I,"

---

36 *the central...a postscript*: supposedly the exclamation by Kurtz on the verge of his death, "The horror! the horror!" which was not revealed until the very end of the novella by the narrator Marlow, when he was asked by the fiancée what was Kurtz's last word. Read Conrad's novella.

37 *a separate peace*: It emphasizes the self-sufficiency of the personal world, no matter how tumultuous the external society might be.

38 *we would...Middle English*: something innocuous enough; so are the following choices.

39 *idée fixe*: [French] a fixed idea; an idea that dominates the mind; an obsession

40 *some little...decent beach*: a common Bay Area summer housing rental come-on phrase in the early 1950s

41 *large bare*: two adjectives accentuating a personal and solitary image; *bare* meaning unfurnished

42 *Tri Delt*: Fraternities and sororities usually choose Greek designations.

43 *issue*: major controversial matters

did not like living with sixty people[44]) and I read Albert Camus[45] and Henry James[46] and I watched a flowering plum come in and out of blossom and at night, most nights, I walked outside and looked up to where the cyclotron and bevatron[47] glowed on the dark hillside, unspeakable mysteries which engaged me, in the style of my time, only personally. Later I got out of Berkeley and went to New York and later I got out of New York and came to Los Angeles. What I have made for myself is personal, but is not exactly peace. Only one person[48] I knew at Berkeley later discovered an ideology, dealt himself into history,[49] cut himself loose from both his own dread and his own time.[50] A few of the people I knew at Berkeley killed themselves[51] not long after. Another attempted suicide in Mexico and then, in a recovery which seemed in many ways a more advanced derangement, came home

---

[44] *I, the...sixty people*: choice of being alone and personal over living in a commune-like group

[45] *Albert Camus*: (1913-60) French novelist, dramatist, journalist, and essayist celebrated for his exploration of the implications of the "absurd" nature of the human condition in his works, such as *The Outsider* (1942), *The Plague* (1947), and *The Myth of Sisyphus* (1942). Camus is often associated with the existentialist philosophy and the Theater of the Absurd. He was awarded the Nobel Prize in literature in 1957.

[46] *Henry James*: (1843-1916) American author particularly noted for his subtle representation in works like *The American* (1877) and *The Ambassadors* (1903) of his personae's inner worlds, somewhat isolated from the external disturbances, and for juxtaposing his American and British experiences

[47] *cyclotron and bevatron*: the two accelerators sitting atop the Berkeley Hill where the Lawrence Berkeley Laboratory is; while they may look like symbols of what Eisenhower would later call military-industrial complex, the "*idée fixe*" had prevented Didion from seeing them as more than a mysterious charm.

[48] *one person*: a maverick, so to speak, considering the generation doubtful of "political highs" and growing outside history

[49] *dealt himself into history*: included himself forcibly in history while "historical irrelevancy" was the staple for his age peers

[50] *cut himself...own time*: By doing so, he tried to get over his dread of meaninglessness and distinguish himself from the prevalent life-style of the Fifties.

[51] *killed themselves*: result of "dread of meaningless" and "chronic depression" perhaps

and joined the Bank of America's three-year executive training program. Most of us live less theatrically,[52] but remain the survivors of a peculiar and inward[53] time. If I could believe that going to a barricade would affect man's fate in the slightest[54] I would go to that barricade, and quite often I wish that I could, but it would be less than honest to say that I expect to happen upon[55] such a happy ending.

 The last sentence emphatically says that radicalism of the Sixties, erring on the side of being simplistic, would NOT affect man's fate. She may have added "The world is not that simple, babies. Amen!" to her essay.

Author

Joan Didion, born in 1934, is one of the most highly regarded contemporary American writers of essays and novels. Her works often explore the despair of contemporary Americans and the cultural chaos as a result of the disintegration of morality and values, using her own subjective experiences and observations as a vantage point. Didion is noted for a cool and almost brittle style that emphasizes the concrete. Her major works include the novels *Play It as It Lays* (1970), *A Book of Common*

---

[52] *theatrically*: theatrically in the sense that the said person followed a zigzag pattern career-wise with an aberrant mind

[53] *inward*: synonymous with silent and personal in the preceding context

[54] *If I...the slightest*: Mark the tone of cynical irony.

[55] *happen upon*: find by chance

Prayer (1977), *Salvador* (1983), *Democracy* (1984), and *The Last Thing He Wanted* (1996), as well as essay collections *The White Album* (1979), *After Henry* (1992), and *Political Fictions* (2001). Didion made quite a splash by the 2005 publication of *The Year of Magical Thinking*, an account of the grief-laden year that followed the death of her husband, commonly acclaimed as a new classic in mourning literature.

John Leonard, the often acerbic contemporary American critic, summarized the opinions of many others when he observed, "Nobody writes better English prose than Joan Didion."

Text

"On the Morning after the Sixties" is selected from Joan Didion's essay collection *The White Album*. Many of the essays in the collection criticize what Didion saw as the collapse of American culture in the 1960s and the shallow advocacies of members of the hippie movement. In this essay, however, Didion refrains from any direct recounting on the Sixties but dwells upon the peculiarities of her own generation's subjectivity in the 1950s instead, portraying hers as essentially personal and silent, if also solitary and inwardly restless. Her explanation for such generational characteristics reveals a strong existential conviction, although her persistent reliance on meticulous details to represent her subjects may reflect a desire to land on something solid and concrete.

Further Reading

The White Album, Joan Didion
Slouching Towards Bethlehem, Joan Didion
**Berkeley in the Sixties*, a 1990 movie directed by Mark Kitchell

Translation as Aids

1）这样一个下午，从各个角度细看，对今人来说，都是不可思议的——找个相好却是为一顿橄榄球午餐，今天看来简直是沙俄时代的域外奇谈。由此可见，我们中的许多人成长过程中依赖的叙事方式，已变得何其不适用。

2）我想我说的无非就是：我们是对政治狂热抱有疑虑的一代，内心总是模棱两可；我们从小就认定黑暗的核心不在于社会组织的某种错误，而在于人性本身，亦无所谓历史。

On Writing

by Stephen King

In the early 1980s, my wife and I went to London on a combined business/[1]pleasure trip. I fell asleep on the plane and had a dream about a popular writer (it may or may not have been me, but it sure to God[2] wasn't James Caan[3]) who fell into the clutches of a psychotic fan living on a farm somewhere out in the back of the beyond.[4] The fan was a woman isolated by her growing paranoia. She kept some livestock in the barn, including her pet pig, Misery. The pig was named after the continuing main character in the writer's best-selling bodicerippers.[5] My clearest memory of this dream upon waking was something the woman said to the writer, who had a broken leg and was being kept prisoner in the back bedroom. I wrote it on an American Airlines cocktail napkin so I wouldn't forget it, then put it in my pocket. I lost it somewhere, but can remember most of what I wrote down:

She speaks earnestly but never quite makes eye contact.[6] A big woman and solid all through; she is an absence of hiatus.[7] (Whatever *that*

---

[1] /: Note the multiplying use of the slash. Cf. s/he for "he or she."

[2] *to God*: a parenthesis for emphasis

[3] *James Caan*: (1940-) the name of the actor starring the protagonist Paul Sheldon in *Misery* (《危情十日》) adapted from Stephen King's 1987 psychological horror story

[4] *in the...the beyond*: in the backwaters, or very far away from where the action is; cf. "in the middle of nowhere."

[5] *bodicerippers*: sexually explicit, romantic stories. The story about Misery Chastain referred to here is set in Victorian England.

[6] *never quite makes eye contact*: a manifestation of some disturbing psychological problem within

[7] *absence of hiatus*: a loose phrase the author himself admits in the later parenthesis, which may suggest that when the woman talks, she does so non-stop

means; remember, I'd just woken up.) *"I wasn't trying to be funny in a mean way when I named my pig Misery, no sir. Please don't think that. No. I named her in the spirit of fan love, which is the purest love there is. You should be flattered."*

Tabby and I stayed at Brown's Hotel in London, and on our first night there I was unable to sleep. Some of it was what sounded like a trio of little-girl gymnasts[8] in the room directly above ours, some of it was undoubtedly jet lag, but a lot of it was that airline cocktail napkin. Jotted on it was the seed of what I thought could be a really excellent story, one that might turn out funny and satiric as well as scary. I thought it was just too rich not to write.

 These paragraphs show how irresistibly Stephen King was drawn to the seminal story that even made sleep impossible. It then kept germinating, fermenting, developing, and getting fleshed out so much so that it unsettled him. The lesson to be learned is that when there is such an urge to write, set pen to paper.

I got up, went downstairs, and asked the concierge[9] if there was a quiet place where I could work longhand[10] for a bit. He led me to a gorgeous desk on the second-floor stair landing. It had been Rudyard Kipling[11]'s desk, he told me with perhaps justifiable pride. I was a little intimidated by this intelligence, but the spot was quiet and the desk seemed hospitable enough; it featured about an acre of cherrywood working surface, for one thing. Stoked on cup after cup of tea (I drank it by the gallon when I wrote... unless I was drinking beer, that is), I filled sixteen pages of a steno[12]

---

8 *gymnasts*: exaggeration of the noise they made upstairs

9 *concierge*: janitor, a formal French word most frequently used in continental Europe

10 *longhand*: having words written out in full by hand as distinguished from writing in shorthand or typing; used as an adverbial here

11 *Rudyard Kipling*: (1865-1936) British writer born in India, who is most noted for his children's stories such as *The Jungle Book* (1894). He won the 1907 Nobel Prize in literature. Kipling's style is often unruly and wild.

12 *steno*: short for stenographer, i.e., secretary

notebook. I like to work longhand, actually; the only problem is that, once I get jazzed,[13] I can't keep up with the lines forming in my head and I get frazzled.[14]

When I called it quits,[15] I stopped in the lobby to thank the concierge again for letting me use Mr. Kipling's beautiful desk. "I'm so glad you enjoyed it," he replied. He was wearing a misty,[16] reminiscent[17] little smile, as if he had known the writer himself. "Kipling died there, actually. Of a stroke. While he was writing."

I went back upstairs to catch a few hours' sleep, thinking of how often we are given information we really could have done without.[18]

The working title of my story, which I thought would be a novella of about 30,000 words, was "The Annie Wilkes[19] Edition." When I sat down at Mr. Kipling's beautiful desk I had the basic situation—crippled writer, psycho fan—firmly fixed in my mind. The actual *story* did not as then exist (well, it did, but as a relic buried—except for sixteen handwritten pages, that is—in the earth), but knowing the story wasn't necessary for me to begin work. I had located the fossil; the rest, I knew, would consist of careful excavation.

 This paragraph sheds some light on the question: how does a story happen? Here Stephen King uses a metaphor. He compares a story to a fossil buried underground to be excavated, that is, to be worked on painstakingly and gingerly. It also suggests that Stephen King is the type of writer who does not believe in an overall plan beforehand when one writes,

---

13 *jazzed*: a colloquialism for excited or fascinated

14 *I can't...get frazzled*: My thoughts always race ahead of my pen. Once I start writing, thoughts keep welling up and, in my effort to catch up, I often get very tired in a short while.

15 *called it quits*: called it a day in the sense of stopping working

16 *misty*: faint, hard to describe accurately

17 *reminiscent*: reminiscent in the sense that there were giants in those days, as the proverb goes

18 *we are...done without*: referring to the totally superfluous unpleasant information that the concierge had added about Kipling writing himself to death

19 *Annie Wilkes*: the nurse's name, i.e., the woman fan

but that one writes as inspiration happens to him/her. Gradually the story will take shape. Of course, there have to be improvements and corrections, deletions and, additions afterwards.

I'd suggest that what works for me may work equally well for you. If you are enslaved[20] to (or intimidated by) the tiresome tyranny of the outline[21] and the notebook filled with "Character Notes," it may liberate you. At the very least, it will turn your mind to something more interesting than Developing the Plot.[22]

(An amusing sidelight: the century's greatest supporter of Developing the Plot may have been Edgar Wallace,[23] a bestselling potboiler novelist of the 1920s. Wallace invented—and patented—a device called the Edgar Wallace Plot Wheel. When you got stuck for the next Plot Development or needed an Amazing Turn of Events in a hurry, you simply spun the Plot Wheel and read what came up in the window: a fortuitous arrival,[24] perhaps, or Heroine declares her love. These gadgets apparently sold like hotcakes.)

 A disparaging paragraph in parentheses to laugh at writing as an artificial endeavor or a programmed game.

By the time I had finished that first Brown's Hotel session, in which

---

[20] *If you are enslaved*: if you are not my kind but believe in over-all planning beforehand

[21] *tyranny of the outline*: the overall plan or, as Virginia Woolf called it, the "dictatorship" by the plot

[22] *Developing the Plot*: a patented device as an aid to writing; see the following paragraph for a description of it. Sources say this bit of digression is "a tall tale" invented by Stephen King.

[23] *Edgar Wallace*: (1875–1932) a famous and extremely prolific British writer of crime novels, such as *The Clue of the Twisted Candle* (1916). He also wrote several plays and the scenarios for such films as *King Kong* (1933), upon which a hit remake was based in 2005, although in actuality he did not contribute much to the story.

[24] *fortuitous arrival*: such as the timely arrival of an unexpected guest or a Godsend legacy from an unknown relative so that the story can develop

Paul Sheldon[25] wakes up to find himself Annie Wilkes's prisoner, I thought I knew what was going to happen.[26] Annie would demand that Paul write[27] another novel about his plucky continuing character, Misery Chastain, one just[28] for her. After first demurring, Paul would of course agree (a psychotic nurse, I thought, could be very persuasive). Annie would tell him she intended to sacrifice her beloved pig, Misery, to this project. *Misery's Return*[29] would, she'd say, consist of but one copy: a holographic[30] manuscript bound in pigskin!

Here we'd fade out, I thought, and return to Annie's remote Colorado retreat six or eight months later for the surprise ending.

Paul is gone,[31] his sickroom turned into a shrine to Misery Chastain, but Misery the pig is still very much in evidence, grunting serenely away in her sty beside the barn. On the walls of the "Misery Room" are book covers, stills from the Misery movies, pictures of Paul Sheldon, perhaps a newspaper headline reading FAMED ROMANCE NOVELIST STILL MISSING. In the center of the room, carefully spotlighted, is a single book on a small table (a cherrywood table, of course, in honor of Mr. Kipling). It is the Annie Wilkes Edition of *Misery's Return*. The binding is beautiful, and it should be; it is the skin of Paul Sheldon. And Paul himself? His bones might be buried behind the barn, but I thought it likely that the pig would have eaten the tasty parts.

At first King had already conceived of a possible conclusion to the story. But as he wrote on, he changed his mind bit by bit as inspiration occurred. Finally, as we see from the story, after a seesaw between the two the protagonist escaped from the psychotic nurse. Here is another example of writing *impromptu* King believes in.

---

25 *Paul Sheldon*: the writer's name

26 *what was going to happen*: the rest of the story

27 *write*: the subjunctive

28 *just*: only; exclusively

29 *Misery's Return*: She had even thought of a title for the author.

30 *holographic*: written entirely in one's own hand

31 *gone*: dead if we consider the following newspaper headline

Not bad, and it would have made a pretty good story (not such a good novel, however; no one likes to root for a guy over the course of three hundred pages[32] only to discover that between chapters sixteen and seventeen the pig ate him), but that wasn't the way things eventually went.[33] Paul Sheldon turned out to be a good deal more resourceful than I initially thought, and his efforts to play Scheherazade[34] and save his life gave me a chance to say some things about the redemptive power of writing that I had long felt but never articulated. Annie also turned out to be more complex than I'd first imagined her, and she was great fun to write about—here was a woman pretty much stuck with "cockadoodie brat"[35] when it came to profanity, but who felt absolutely no qualms about chopping off her favorite writer's foot when he tried to get away from her. In the end, I felt that Annie was almost as much to be pitied as to be feared.[36] And none of the story's details and incidents proceeded from plot; they were organic, each arising naturally from the initial situation, each an uncovered part of the fossil. And I'm writing all this with a smile. As sick with drugs and alcohol as I was much of the time, I had such fun with that one.

 Revealed here is how his story took shape and evolved with twists and turns and in the process achieved a sort of autonomy of its own.

---

[32] *three hundred pages*: nothing much happens in the meanwhile; an objectionable lapse in novel writing

[33] *things eventually went*: the storyline really developed

[34] *Scheherazade*: the name of the girl who featured in *The Arabian Nights* or *The Book of One Thousand and One Nights*, who won her life by continuing to tell the Sultan suspense stories. The protagonist was playing stalling tactics in order to save his own life.

[35] *cockadoodie brat*: the endearing term that the nurse had coined for her favorite writer, meaning "You naughty or bad-mannered boy." A kind of children's language, it indicates that she was being very motherly in a sick way.

[36] *as much...be feared*: in view of her schizophrenia; *feared* taken for granted and *pitied* as a newly felt additional response

If "read a lot, write a lot" is the Great Commandment[37]—and I assure you that it is—how much writing constitutes a lot?[38] That varies, of course, from writer to writer. One of my favorite stories on the subject—probably more myth than truth[39]—concerns James Joyce. According to the story, a friend came to visit him one day and found the great man sprawled across his writing desk in a posture of utter despair.

"James, what's wrong?" the friend asked. "Is it the work?"

Joyce indicated assent without even raising his head to look at the friend. Of course it was the work; isn't it always?[40]

"How many words did you get today?" the friend pursued.

Joyce (still in despair, still sprawled facedown on his desk): "Seven."

"Seven? But James...that's *good*, at least for you."

"Yes," Joyce said, finally looking up. "I suppose it is... but I don't know what *order* they go in!"

 James Joyce represents one extremity of "how much," or rather "how little," namely, extreme literary economy, stringency, or austerity.

At the other end of the spectrum, there are writers like Anthony Trollope.[41] He wrote humongous[42] novels (*Can You Forgive Her?*[43] is a

---

37 *Commandment*: a religious term borrowed: thou-shalt-not

38 *how much...a lot?*: What is the adequate quantity of writing that passes for "much?"

39 *more myth than truth*: with the truth of the story untested; more of hearsay than a fact

40 *Of course...it always?*: It is always the work that plunged him in despair and weighed him down into this awkward position.

41 *Anthony Trollope*: (1815-82) a prolific British writer noted for his lengthy, voluminous writings. He wrote at least six novels about his hometown Barsetshire and six political novels.

42 *humongous*: huge, enormous

43 *Can You Forgive Her?*: the title of one of Trollope's novels written during 1864-65. The retitling in the following is an ironic jab.

fair enough example; for modern audiences[44] it might be retitled *Can You Possibly Finish It?*), and he pumped[45] them out with amazing regularity. His day job was as a clerk in the British Postal Department (the red public mailboxes all over Britain were Anthony Trollope's invention); he wrote for two and a half hours each morning before leaving for work. This schedule was ironclad.[46] If he was in mid-sentence[47] when the two and a half hours expired, he left that sentence unfinished until the next morning. And if he happened to finish one of his six-hundred-page heavyweights[48] with fifteen minutes of the session remaining, he wrote **The End**, set the manuscript aside, and began work on the next book.

 The other extremity is that of unrestrained literary profusion. Note the author's faint tone of disapproval about Trollope's mechanical clockwork kind of way of writing.

John Creasey,[49] a British mystery novelist, wrote five hundred (yes, you read it correctly) novels under ten different names. I've written thirty-five or so—some of Trollopian length—and am considered prolific, but I look positively blocked[50] next to Creasey. Several other contemporary novelists (they include Ruth Rendell/Barbara Vine,[51] Evan Hunter/Ed McBain,[52]

---

[44] *modern audiences*: Modern readers are notoriously faster-paced who do not have the patience to read such a tirade from A to Z.

[45] *pumped*: as if mechanically

[46] *ironclad*: not subject to change by any means

[47] *mid-sentence*: an incomplete sentence; a sentence hanging in mid-air

[48] *heavyweights*: Trollope's monumental works

[49] *John Creasey*: (1908-73) Creasey in fact wrote over 600 novels with more than twenty pennames.

[50] *blocked*: derived from the noun phrase "writer's block"

[51] *Ruth Rendell/Barbara Vine*: (1930-2015) British woman writer of mystery and psychological crime novels, considered by some to have turned *whodunit* to *whydunit;* the slash means that these two names refer to the same person. The first part is the real name, and then the penname.

[52] *Evan Hunter/Ed McBain*: (1926-2005) American crime writer best known perhaps for his screenplay *The Birds* (1963)

Dean Koontz,[53] and Joyce Carol Oates[54]) have written easily as much as I have; some have written a good deal more.

On the other hand—the James Joyce hand—there is Harper Lee,[55] who wrote only one book (the brilliant *To Kill a Mockingbird*[56]). Any number of others, including James Agee, Malcolm Lowry, and Thomas Harris[57] (so far), wrote under five. Which is okay, but I always wonder two things about these folks: how long did it take them to write the books they *did* write, and what did they do the rest of their time? Knit afghans?[58] Organize church bazaars?[59] Deify plums?[60] I'm probably being snotty[61] here, but I am also, believe me, honestly curious. If God gives you something you can do, why in God's name wouldn't you do it?

 Note the list of authors the author apparently read up in. It is by no means coincidental that most of them are dedicated to mystery and horror. Joyce Carole Oates and Malcolm Lowry

---

53 *Dean Koontz*: (1945-) American suspense thriller and sci-fi novelist whose acknowledged breakthrough novel was *Whispers*(1980)

54 *Joyce Carol Oates*: (1938-) American novelist and essayist who has successfully produced over fifty works of fiction and the other genres while holding down a job of teaching at Princeton; her works are focused on the unsettling psychological and moral problems of contemporary American life. Among her best known novels are *A Garden of Earthly Delights* (1967), *Them* (1969), *Wonderland* (1971), etc.

55 *Harper Lee*: (1926-2016) American woman writer; see next for details.

56 *To Kill a Mockingbird*: the 1961 Pulitzer Prize-winning novel, which deals with a typical story of a black wrongly accused of raping a white woman; it was made into a highly successful film in 1962. Lee used to be Truman Capote's neighbor and was co-researching the Kansas murder case resulting in Capote's *In Cold Blood* (1966).

57 *James Agee...Thomas Harris*: respectively American, British and American writers; Thomas Harris won popularity because of his novel *The Silence of the Lambs* (1988), which was adapted for the screen and became an instant hit.

58 *Knit afghans*: Did they spend the rest of their time at home knitting carpets?

59 *Organize church bazaars*: Are they into charity activities?

60 *Deify plums*: Are they enthusiastic about making plum jellies out of them and then put them away in their cellar/basement?

61 *snotty*: impertinent, arrogant

with his stream-of-consciousness technique may be exceptions.

My own schedule is pretty clear-cut. Mornings belong to whatever is new—the current composition. Afternoons are for naps and letters. Evenings are for reading, family, Red Sox[62] games on TV, and any revisions that just cannot wait.[63] Basically, mornings are my prime writing time.

Once I start work on a project, I don't stop and I don't slow down unless I absolutely have to. If I don't write every day, the characters begin to stale off[64] in my mind—they begin to *seem* like characters instead of real people. The tale's narrative cutting edge starts to rust and I begin to lose my hold on the story's plot and pace. Worst of all, the excitement of spinning something new begins to fade. The work starts to *feel* like work,[65] and for most writers that is the smooch[66] of death. Writing is at its best—always, always, always—when it is a kind of inspired play for the writer. I can write in cold blood[67] if I have to, but I like it best when it's fresh and almost too hot to handle.

 The author demands our attention by using "always" three times in a row. The points he wishes to establish is: a) writing is compulsory fun, b) write non-stop when the inspiration is on, and c) characters should be real people and the narrative should keep its sharp cutting edge.

I used to tell interviewers that I wrote every day except for Christmas, the Fourth of July, and my birthday. That was a lie. I told them that because if you agree to an interview you have to say *something*, and it plays better[68] if it's something at least half-clever. Also, I didn't want to sound like a workaholic dweeb[69] (just a workaholic, I guess). The truth is that when

---

62 *Red Sox*: name of the baseball team of Boston

63 *cannot wait*: must be put down on paper in no time lest I forget them

64 *stale off*: lose freshness and vividness

65 *work*: burden; a bread-and-butter thing rather than fun

66 *smooch*: a slangy word for kiss

67 *in cold blood*: rationally, without inspiration

68 *it plays better*: It sounds like what the audience would love to hear when it gets broadcast.

69 *workaholic dweeb*: a stupid person who knows nothing but work

I'm writing, I write every day, workaholic dweeb or not. That *includes* Christmas, the Fourth, and my birthday (at my age you try to ignore your goddam birthday anyway[70]). And when I'm not working, I'm not working at all, although during those periods of full stop[71] I usually feel at loose ends with myself and have trouble sleeping.[72] For me, not working is the real work.[73] When I'm writing, it's all the playground, and the worst three hours I ever spent there were still pretty damned good.[74]

I used to be faster than I am now; one of my books (*The Running Man*) was written in a single week, an accomplishment John Creasey would perhaps have appreciated (although I have read that Creasey wrote several of his mysteries in *two days*). I think it was quitting smoking that slowed me down; nicotine is a great synapse[75] enhancer. The problem, of course, is that it's killing you at the same time it's helping you compose.[76] Still, I believe the first draft of a book—even a long one—should take no more than three months, the length of a season. Any longer and—for me, at least—the story begins to take on an odd foreign feel, like a dispatch from the Romanian Department of Public Affairs,[77] or something broadcast on high-band shortwave during a period of severe sunspot activity.[78]

I like to get ten pages a day, which amounts to 2,000 words. That's

---

[70] *you try...birthday anyway*: implying that he is getting on in years

[71] *full stop*: absolutely no work at all

[72] *feel at...trouble sleeping*: feel out of sorts and suffer sleeplessness

[73] *not working...real work*: a clever paradoxical statement with "not working" meaning "not writing" and "the real work" the real burden

[74] *pretty damned good*: However hard it was to write, this is the prime of my day.

[75] *synapse*: neural transmission

[76] *it's killing...you compose*: Smoking is helpful to his writing but it's also harmful to his health.

[77] *Romanian Department of Public Affairs*: a randomly chosen institution indicating the most unlikely quarters with a view to emphasizing the "foreign feel" mentioned earlier

[78] *sunspot activity*: activity known to interfere with the communication on earth with noisy static and so forth

180,000 words over a three-month span, a goodish[79] length for a book—something in which the reader can get happily lost, if the tale is done well and stays fresh. On some days those ten pages come easily; I'm up and out and doing errands by eleven-thirty in the morning,[80] perky as a rat in liverwurst.[81] More frequently, as I grow older, I find myself eating lunch at my desk and finishing the day's work around one-thirty in the afternoon. Sometimes, when the words come hard, I'm still fiddling around at teatime.[82] Either way is fine with me, but only under dire[83] circumstances do I allow myself to shut down before I get my 2,000 words.

 Note how age tells on one, writers being no exception.

The biggest aid to regular (Trollopian?)[84] production is working in a serene atmosphere. It's difficult for even the most naturally productive writer to work in an environment where alarms and excursions are the rule rather than the exception. When I'm asked for "the secret of my success" (an absurd idea, that,[85] but impossible to get away from), I sometimes say there are two: I stayed physically healthy (at least until a van knocked me down by the side of the road in the summer of 1999), and I stayed married. It's a good answer because it makes the question go away, and because there is an element of truth in it. The combination of a healthy body and a stable relationship with a self-reliant woman who takes zero shit[86] from me or

---

[79] *goodish*: tolerably or passably good

[80] *On some...the morning*: Early in the morning I had already done my designated quota of the work for the day, so I could start to do other things, doing errands like grocery shopping.

[81] *a rat in liverwurst*: Liverwurst is a German sausage; compare 如鱼得水.

[82] *at teatime*: With diminished productivity the writing session is invariably lengthened—even to 5-ish p.m.

[83] *dire*: extremely serious, urgent

[84] *regular (Trollopian?)*: The question mark shows that King is skeptical about Trollopian productivity being normal.

[85] *that*: a colloquial tag, meaning that is an absurd idea

[86] *who takes zero shit*: who is a no-nonsense woman

anyone else has made the continuity of my working life possible. And I believe the converse is also true:[87] that my writing and the pleasure I take in it has contributed to the stability of my health and my home life.

Author

Stephen King (1947-) is one of the most popular horror writers in the present-day US. He was born in Portland, Maine in 1947. His first-published novel *Carrie* was published in 1974, and King soon established his reputation as a major horror writer after the breakthrough novel

'Salem's Lot (1975). Stephen King is a highly prolific writer, and his novels, short stories, screenplays, and essays have made him one of the best-selling authors in the world. The best-known novels by King include *The Stand* (1978), *The Eyes of the Dragon* (1987), *The Dark Half* (1989), *Bag of Bones* (1998), *Dreamcatcher* (2001), and the *Dark Tower* series (1982-2012), which contains eight individual works. One of his latest novels *The Institute* was published in 2019. A number of King's stories have been adapted for the screen and made a big success: *The Shining* (1980), *Misery* (1990), *The Shawshank Redemption* (1994), and *The Green Mile* (1996), for instance.

King's enormously popular books revived the interest in horror fiction from the 1970s. His place in the modern horror fiction is comparable to that of J. R. R. Tolkien's who created the modern genre of fantasy. King's horror stories are influenced by the 19th-century Gothic tradition and by that of Edgar Allan Poe. He is adept at taking everyday situations and

[87] *the converse is also true*: cause and effect reinforcing each other

experiences and reveals their macabre and horrific potential. His characters are often found to fight against the demon of their own imagination. While his early novels tried to explore the agonies of childhood, parental neglect and abuse, from the 1980s his perspective shifted into the various pains of adulthood and the loneliness of older people.

Critical responses to King's works have been mixed. Although King is widely respected as a major force in popular fiction, his books are considered by some critics to blend the line between high art and pop culture. In 2003, when King was honored with the Lifetime Achievement Award by the National Book Awards, there was an uproar in the literary community, with literary critic Harold Bloom denouncing the choice: "He is a man who writes what used to be called penny dreadfuls. That they could believe that there is any literary value there or any aesthetic accomplishment or signs of an inventive human intelligence is simply a testimony to their own idiocy. " But the Foundation said: "Stephen King's writing is securely rooted in the great American tradition that glorifies spirit-of-place and the abiding power of narrative... This Award commemorates Mr. King's well-earned place of distinction in the wide world of readers and book lovers of all ages."

Text

This essay is taken from Stephen King's non-fiction *On Writing: A Memoir of the Craft* (2000), wherein King describes his life, his craft, and a near-fatal car accident. But most of all, the book gives down-to-earth advice for aspiring writers. "Write what you like, then imbue it with life and make it unique by blending in your own personal knowledge of life, friendship, relationships, sex and work. Especially work. People love to read about work. God knows why, but they do," King says.

In this essay, King demonstrates to the readers his compulsion to write. While George Orwell advises that when you write, you should always have in mind your purpose and audience, King believes that one writes simply because there's an urge to write. As for writing as a technique, there are at least two lessons we can learn from Stephen King:

a) A seminal idea, sometimes a fleeting one, is important. However, there is no need to stick to it. In fact, you will have to alternate, moderate, or change the plan as you write.

b) Write in a hurry with a true urge. If you really feel agonized while writing, then you are almost sure to suffer from a writer's block and better stop. Write only when you feel it fun to write.

Further Reading

On Writing, Stephen King
Misery, Stephen King
The Practice of Writing, David Lodge

Florence

by Bill Bryson

I went on the world's slowest train to Florence. It limped[1] across the landscape like a runner with a pulled[2] muscle, and it had no buffet. At first it was crowded, but as afternoon gave way to evening and evening merged into the inkiness[3] of night, there were fewer and fewer of us left, until eventually it was a businessman buried in paperwork and a guy who looked as if he was on his way to an Igor look-alike competition[4] and me. Every two or three miles the train stopped at some darkened station where no train had stopped for weeks,[5] where grass grew on the platforms and where no one got on and no one got off.

Mark the word *slowest* in the first sentence. There is no way for the author to tell whether this IS the slowest train in the world or not. The author is exaggerating and apparently prejudiced against the Italians who are noted, to do them injustice, for being lazy and inefficient. This comment applies equally to the following assertion "where no train had stopped for weeks."

---

[1] *limped*: as if moving on two uneven legs

[2] *pulled*: sprained

[3] *inkiness*: darkness; a vivid way to describe what an ellipsis like "and evening to night" would have done

[4] *an Igor look-alike competition*: a competition to see who is a more typically Igor-looking man or who looks more manly by Russian standards as Igor is a typical Russian male name. So what the author actually wants to say is that the guy looks typically Russian.

[5] *where no...for weeks*: which looked absolutely deserted, desolate; almost like a pre-modern abandoned railroad station

Sometimes the train would come to a halt in the middle of nowhere,[6] in the black countryside, and just sit.[7] It would sit for so long that you began to wonder if the driver had gone off into the surrounding fields for a pee and fallen down a well. After a time the train would roll backwards[8] for perhaps thirty yards, then stop and sit again. Then suddenly, with a mighty *whoop*[9] that made the carriage rock and the windows sound as if they were about to implode,[10] a train on the parallel line would fly past. Bright lights would flash by—you could see people in there dining and playing cards, having a wonderful time, moving across Europe at the speed of a laser[11]—and then all would be silence again and we would sit for another eternity[12] before our train gathered the energy to creep onwards to the next desolate station.

 Mark the underlined sentence, a typical example of American humor which, unlike cerebral British humor, is oftentimes associated with bodily functions and even scatological descriptions.

It was well after eleven when we reached Florence. I was starving and weary and felt that I deserved any luxury that came my way.[13] I saw with alarm, but not exactly surprise, that the restaurants around the station were all closed. One snack bar was still lighted and I hastened to it, dreaming of

---

[6] *in the middle of nowhere*: a useful expression for a place far away from where the action is. It can be translated as 前不着村，后不着店.

[7] *sit*: stay put; a pet stylistic device of personification perhaps because it is used at least three times within three lines

[8] *roll backwards*: apparently to make room for an oncoming train

[9] *whoop*: an onomatopoeic word, signifying a really loud, sudden sound

[10] *the windows…to implode*: exaggeration again

[11] *at the…a laser*: used as a contrastive frame of reference

[12] *another eternity*: exaggeration over and over again

[13] *I deserved…my way*: luxury especially in the form of food that I could lay my hands on at the earliest convenience

a pizza the size of a[14] dustbin lid, drowning in mushrooms and salami and olive oil, but the proprietor was just locking up as I reached the door.

The exaggerated description of the much craved-for pizza has an inevitable local flavor as olive oil is typically Mediterranean.

Dejected, I went to the first hotel I came to, a modern concrete box[15] half a block away. I could tell from the outside that it was going to be expensive, and it contravened[16] all my principles to patronize[17] a hotel of such exquisite ugliness,[18] especially in a city as historic as Florence, but I was tired and hungry and in serious need of a pee and a face-wash and my principles were just tapped out.[19]

It is Bryson's principle to travel without creature comforts. To him a proper traveler goes to dangerous places, engages in high-risk activities, and writes exciting notes.

The receptionist quoted me some ludicrous figure[20] for a single room, but I accepted with a surrendering wave[21] and was shown to my room by a 112-year-old porter[22] who escorted me into the world's slowest lift and from whom I learned, during the course of our two-day ascent to the fifth floor, that the dining-room was closed and there was no room service—he

---

[14] *the size of a*: an appositional phrase. Compare "a mountain of a man" for instance.

[15] *a modern concrete box*: a construction of steel and glass. This metaphor reveals the author's disaffection for the hotel at first sight. *Modern* is apparently ironic, and *box* dismissive.

[16] *contravened*: ran contrary to

[17] *to patronize*: to be a patron of, i.e., to support, trade with, or in a word, pay money to

[18] *exquisite ugliness*: extreme ugliness. It is a typical example of oxymoron, i.e., two words of entirely different natures are collocated together. Other examples are mute eloquence, bitter-sweet, etc.

[19] *tapped out*: Normally we say "to tap out the ashes in a pipe." Here it means that my principles were off-handedly put aside and given up.

[20] *ludicrous figure*: ludicrous in the sense of being inconceivably expensive

[21] *a surrendering wave*: a wave in sheer helplessness and resignation

[22] *a 112-year-old porter*: an ancient porter; a really old man

said this with a certain smack[23] of pride—but that the bar would be open for another thirty-five minutes and I might be able to get some small snack stuff there. He waggled his fingers cheerfully[24] to indicate that this was by no means a certainty.

 Note the phrases "112-year-old," "slowest," and "two-day ascent," which are typical "Brysonian" exaggerations. Yes, the author is capable of cerebral British humor. But from time to time his Americanness features in his humor, too.

 The porter betrayed his pride in confirming that there was no room service because he probably thought of room service as too fancy and modern, and it is thus unbecoming his hotel that stuck only to tradition.

I was desperate for a pee and to get to the bar before it shut, but the porter was one of those who feel they have to show you everything in the room and required me to follow him around while he demonstrated the shower and television and showed me where the cupboard was.[25] "Thank you, I would never have found that cupboard without you,"[26] I said, pressing thousand-lire[27] notes into his pocket and more or less bundling[28] him out the door. I don't like to be rude, but I felt as if I were holding back the Hoover Dam. Five more seconds and it would have been like trying to deal with a dropped fire hose. As it was I only barely made it, but oh my,[29] the relief. I washed my face, grabbed a book and hastened to the lift. I could hear it still descending.[30] I pushed the Down button and looked at my watch. Things weren't too bad. I still had twenty-five minutes till the bar closed, time enough for a beer and whatever snacks they could offer. I

---

[23] *a certain smack*: a slight trace or suggestion

[24] *cheerfully*: gleefully with what the Germans call *Schadenfreude*

[25] *demonstrated the…cupboard was*: all unnecessary except for forcing him to delay pee-peeing

[26] *I would…without you*: This sentence is one of downright sarcasm.

[27] *lire*: Lire is the plural form of lira, the basic money unit of Italy before the time of the euro.

[28] *bundling*: I almost pushed him out forcibly.

[29] *my*: an interjection, expressing great relief here

[30] *I could…still descending*: descriptive of how slow the lift was

pushed the button again and passed the time by humming the Waiting for an Elevator Song,[31] puffing my cheeks for the heck[32] of it and looking speculatively at my neck in the hallway mirror.

 Both underlined sentences on the previous page refer to his "serious need of a pee" and are overly exaggerated. The Hoover Dam is the highest dam in the US, named after the 31st US President, Herbert Hoover.

Still the elevator didn't come. I decided to take the fire stairs. I bounded down them two at a time,[33] the whole of my existence dedicated to the idea of a beer and a sandwich, and at the bottom found a padlocked door and a sign in Italian that said IF THERE IS EVER A FIRE HERE, THIS IS WHERE THE BODIES WILL PILE UP. Without pause, I bounded back up to the first floor.[34] The door there was locked, too. Through a tiny window I could see the bar, dark and cozy and still full of people. Somebody was playing a piano. What's more, there were little bowls of peanuts and pistachios on each table. I'd settle for that! I tapped on the door and scraped it[35] with my fingernails, but nobody could hear me, so I bounded up to the second floor and the door there was unlocked, thank goodness. I went straight to the lift and jabbed the Down button. An instant later the Up light dinged[36] on and the doors slid open to reveal three Japanese men in identical blue suits. I indicated to them, as best I could in my breathless state,[37] that they were going the wrong direction for me and

---

[31] *the Waiting for an Elevator Song*: a tuneless tune hummed subconsciously when one is bored or has time to kill. Note the author's use of both *lift* (British English) and *elevator* (American English).

[32] *heck*: a euphemism for hell. He was puffing his cheeks for no particular reasons, just to kill time, which hangs heavily on him.

[33] *I bounded...a time*: two steps at a time in a hurry with *down* used as a preposition

[34] *the first floor* : a Briticism meaning the second floor

[35] *scraped it*: produced a shrill jarring sound

[36] *dinged*: an onomatopoeic word

[37] *in my breathless state*: because he had been bouncing up and down the stairs

that my reluctance to join them had nothing to do with Pearl Harbor or anything like that.[38] We exchanged little bows and the door closed.

The sentence with all letters in the upper case on the previous page is a fabrication of the author. He did not know Italian and so could not possibly tell what the sign said. What he meant to say, seeing the padlock, is, if translated into English it could mean nothing but this.

The underlined sentence on the previous page means "How agreeable the bowls of peanuts and pistachios are! I wish I could have them!"

I pushed the Down button again and immediately the doors popped open to reveal the Japanese men. This was repeated four times until it dawned on me that I was somehow cancelling out their instructions to ascend,[39] so I stood back and let them go away. I waited a full two minutes; caught my breath,[40] counted my remaining traveller's cheques, hummed the Elevator Song, glanced at my watch—ten minutes till closing!—and pushed the Down button.

Four times he pushed the Down button, and four times he prevented the lift from moving. It shows what a hot-headed person the author was. And apparently an impatient American was slow in learning his lesson.

Immediately the doors opened to reveal the Japanese men still standing there. Impulsively[41] I jumped in with them. I don't know if it was the extra weight that kick-started it or what[42] but we began to rise, at the usual speed of about one foot every thirty seconds. The lift was tiny. We were close

---

[38] *that my reluctance...like that*: a far-fetched joke of American vintage meaning that I bore them no animosity

[39] *I was...to ascend*: My keeping pushing the Down button made it impossible for the lift with its Japanese riders to go upstairs.

[40] *caught my breath*: got over my breathless state

[41] *Impulsively*: by the impulse of the moment; I did not think what I was doing.

[42] *or what*: or whatever other reasons

enough together to be arrested in some countries[43] and as I was facing them, all but[44] rubbing noses, I felt compelled to utter some pleasantry.

"Businessmen?" I asked.

One of them gave a small, meaningless bow from the shoulders.[45]

"In Italy on business?" I elaborated.[46] It was a stupid question. How many people go on holiday in blue suits?[47]

The Japanese man bowed again and I realized he had no idea what I was saying.

"Do you speak English?"

"Ahhhr... no," said the second man, as if not certain, swaying just a tiny bit, and it dawned on me that they were all extremely drunk. I looked at the third man and he bowed before I could say anything.[48]

"You guys been to the bar?" A small uncomprehending bow. I was rather beginning to enjoy this one-way conversation. "You look like you've had a few,[49] if you don't mind me saying so. Hope nobody's going to be sick!" I added jauntily.[50]

The elevator crept on and eventually thudded to a halt.[51] "Well, here we are, gentlemen, eighth floor. Alight here for all stations to Iwo Jima."[52]

They turned to me in the hallway and said simultaneously, "*Buon*

---

[43] *to be arrested in some countries*: indicating that in some European countries people get arrested for violating interpersonal spatial laws

[44] *all but*: almost

[45] *from the shoulders*: not by bending the neck, showing how stiff the bowing was

[46] *elaborated*: made my question more specific

[47] *in blue suits*: indicating the formality of their apparel

[48] *he bowed...say anything*: a bow forestalling the meaningless question; I was gagged before I could phrase my question.

[49] *a few*: an understatement meaning a few glasses of beer or wine

[50] *jauntily*: cheerfully

[51] *thudded to a halt*: stopped with a thud, i.e., a deep, muffled sound

[52] *for all...Iwo Jima*: and go to hell; a reference to the site of a fierce battle in the Pacific during WWII

giorno."[53]

"And a very *buon giorno* to you," I riposted,[54] jabbing button number one anxiously.

I got to the bar two minutes before it shut, though in fact it was effectively[55] shut already. An over-zealous waiter[56] had gathered up all the little dishes of nuts and the pianist was nowhere to be seen. It didn't really matter because they didn't serve snacks there anyway. I returned to my room, rummaged[57] in the mini-bar and found two tiny foil bags containing about fourteen peanuts each. I searched again, but this was the only food among the many bottles of soft drinks and intoxicants.[58] As I stood eating the peanuts one at a time, to make the pleasure last, I idly looked at the mini-bar tariff[59] card and discovered that this pathetic little snack was costing me $4.80. Or at least it would have if I'd been foolish enough to tell anyone about it.

Author

Bill Bryson (1951-) is a contemporary best-selling America-born author of humorous books on travel, the English language and recently scientific subjects and Shakespeare. In 1973 he visited England for the first time in a round trip of Europe and decided to settle down. However, in 1995 Bryson returned to his native country with

---

[53] *Buon giorno*: a misfitting Italian greeting, meaning "good day," showing the pathetic knowledge of Italian on the part of these Japanese

[54] *riposted*: gave a quick, clever reply

[55] *effectively*: in effect, actually

[56] *An over-zealous waiter*: ironic in that the waiter was calling it a day before closing time

[57] *rummaged*: searched haphazardly and hastily

[58] *intoxicants*: liquors

[59] *tariff*: a card listing prices of the items in the mini-bar

his family. But he eventually decided that the American culture was not suitable for him and in 2003 he brought his whole family back to England again. He has been literally hopping between the two sides of the Atlantic.

Bill Bryson writes in lucid, simple English, posing few, if any, difficulties to his readers. His works are noted for an observant eye for detail and, last but not least, for a typical sense of hilarious American humor, which is marked by exaggeration and sometimes a little wordiness. However, having married a British woman and exposed himself in-depth to British culture, he is quickly acquiring British humor too. What follows is a bibliography of his works:

On Travel

- *The Palace Under the Alps and Over 200 Other Unusual, Unspoiled, and Infrequently Visited Spots in 16 European Countries* (1985)
- *The Lost Continent: Travels in Small-Town America* (1989)
- *Neither Here Nor There: Travels in Europe* (1991)
- *Notes from a Small Island* (1995)
- *A Walk in the Woods: Rediscovering America on the Appalachian Trail* (1998)
- *Notes from a Big Country* (UK) / *I'm a Stranger Here Myself: Notes on Returning to America after Twenty Years Away* (US) (1999)
- *Down Under* (UK) / *In a Sunburned Country* (US) (2000) (travels in Australia)
- *Bill Bryson's African Diary* (2002)

On Language

- *The Mother Tongue: English and How It Got That Way* (1990)
- *Made in America: An Informal History of the English Language in the United States* (1994)
- *Bryson's Dictionary of Troublesome Words* (1984)

On Science

- *A Short History of Nearly Everything* (2003)

Memoir

- *The Life and Times of the Thunderbolt Kid* (2006)

Biography

- *Shakespeare: The World as Stage* (2007)

Text

"Florence" is an excerpt from Bill Bryson's 1991 travelogue *Neither Here Nor There: Travels in Europe*. The title "Florence" is added to the excerpt by the current anthologist. This book is a collection of notes from his travel in continental Europe. The title "neither here nor there" is actually a pun that reveals Bryson's agony of feeling that he belonged nowhere as he toured around. Bryson's is a restless soul, a probing, imaginative mind ready to explore whatever is new and unknown.

Further Reading

See the bibliography of Bill Bryson's books.

Introduction to *The Art of the Personal Essay*

by Phillip Lopate

This book attempts to put forward and interpret a tradition: the personal essay. Though long spoken of as a subcategory of the essay, the personal essay has rarely been isolated and studied as such. It should certainly be celebrated, because it is one of the most approachable and diverting types of literature we possess.

The hallmark of the personal essay is its intimacy. The writer seems to be speaking directly into your ear, confiding everything from gossip to wisdom. Through sharing thoughts, memories, desires, complaints, and whimsies, the personal essayist sets up a relationship with the reader, a dialogue—a friendship, if you will,[1] based on identification,[2] understanding, testiness,[3] and companionship.

At the core of the personal essay is the supposition that there is a certain unity to human experience. As Michel de Montaigne,[4] the great innovator and patron saint of personal essayists, put it, "Every man has within himself the entire human condition." This meant that when he was telling about himself, he was talking, to some degree, about all of us. The personal essay has an implicitly democratic bent, in the value it places on

---

1 *if you will*: as it were, so to speak

2 *identification*: for the reader to identify with the essayist and relate to what is said in the essay

3 *testiness*: This "impatience or irritability" is in reference to "complaints" and "whimsies" shared by the essayist with readers.

4 *Michel de Montaigne*: (1533-92) the great French essayist known to the Chinese readers as 蒙田, the very first man to describe his work as essays, i.e., "attempts" to put his thoughts into writings

experience rather than status distinctions. "And on the loftiest throne in the world we are still sitting only on our own rump," wrote Montaigne.

The personal essay is of a democratic spirit because it is based on the belief that communication is possible exactly because every man is equally capable in terms of his/her spiritual endowment. To quote Emerson: "Trust thyself: every heart vibrates to that iron string."

Let us get certain worrisome distinctions[5] out of the way. The traditional division in the essay has been between formal and informal essays. Not being good at definitions, I will take the easy way out and quote Holman and Harmon's *A Handbook to Literature*. The formal (sometimes called impersonal) essay is characterized by "seriousness of purpose, dignity, logical organization, length... The technique of the formal essay is now practically identical with that of all factual or theoretical prose writing in which literary effect is secondary to serious purpose." The informal essay, in contrast, is characterized by "the personal element (self-revelation, individual tastes and experiences, confidential manner), humor, graceful style, rambling structure,[6] unconventionality or novelty of theme, freshness of form, freedom from stiffness and affectation, incomplete or tentative[7] treatment of topic."

Eight pairs of Chinese four-character idioms could perhaps be suggested for describing the "informal essay": 实现自我诚实坦露，细处着墨杂而有章，由远及近娓娓道来，因世感时因小见大，笔随心至收放自如，思无定器详而勿尽，引经据典妙语如珠，亦庄亦谐述而不著。

The personal essay is a subset of the informal essay, or, as *A Handbook of Literature* defines it, "a kind of informal essay, with an intimate style,

[5] *worrisome distinctions*: differentiations of essay types that are not deemed really significant or helpful by the current author

[6] *rambling structure*: casual rather than the tight "logical" organization of "the formal essay"

[7] *tentative*: inconclusive

some autobiographical content or interest, and an urbane[8] conversational manner." To make things more confusing, another subset of the informal essay is the familiar essay, which sounds rather like the personal essay. "The more personal, intimate type of informal essay. It deals lightly, often humorously, with personal experiences, opinions, and prejudices, stressing especially the unusual or novel in attitude and having to do with the varied aspects of everyday life." I have never seen a strong distinction drawn in print between the personal essay and the familiar essay, maybe they are identical twins, maybe close cousins. The difference, if there is any, is one of nuance, I suspect. The familiar essay values lightness of touch above all else; the personal essay, which need not be light, tends to put the writer's "I" or idiosyncratic angle more at center stage.

The personal essay has an open form and a drive toward candor and self-disclosure. Unlike the formal essay, it depends less on airtight reasoning than on style and personality, what Elizabeth Hardwick called "the soloist's personal signature flowing through the text."

 Though flexible in form, the personal essay urges sincerity and a tendency to reveal the author's inner world.

The Conversational Element

In its preference for a conversational approach, the personal essay shows its relationship to the dialogue, an ancient form going back to Plato. Both forms acknowledge the duality, or rather multiplicity, of selves that human beings harbor. "It is natural to enter into dialogues and disputes with others," writes the critic Stuart Hampshire, "because it is natural to enter into disputes with oneself. The mind works by contradiction." Personal essayists converse with the reader because they are already having dialogues and disputes with themselves.

 Human beings talk to themselves, a fact which seems to explain the conversational manner of the personal essay.

---

[8] *urbane*: polite, suave

Montaigne may not have been, as he claimed, the first writer to take himself as his subject, but he was perhaps the first to talk to himself convincingly on the page. Reading him, we seem to be eavesdropping on a mind in solitude. He chatters, pen in hand, and keeps putting questions to himself when the essay threatens to flag.[9]

Still, this talky manner is not entirely original. If we go back to Seneca, as Montaigne did, we see the same tendency to reproduce the give-and-take of conversation. I'm not speaking of Seneca's formal essays, which employ the full machinery of classical oratory, but his letters, which come much closer to being personal essays in the modern mode. By using the device of a letter to a friend, Seneca was able to incorporate conversational throat-clearings[10] feints,[11] rhetorical questions, and replies, talking past his alleged correspondent to the general reader.[12] He will pop in a phrase such as "This is all very well, you might say, but isn't it sometimes a lot simpler...?" Seneca examines his own doubts by placing objections in the mouth of the reader. His prose is thorny, abrupt like conversation, and it leaves a sort of dry almond taste from all those chewy aphorisms.

 Mark the interesting metaphor in the last sentence describing the effect of Seneca's aphorisms: slightly bitter, yet also a lingering taste, inviting further contemplation.

The personal essay has historically sought to puncture the stiffness of formal discourse with language that is casual, everyday, demotic, direct.

---

[9] *when the...to flag*: when the essay is in danger of becoming less interesting, energetic, or engaging

[10] *conversational throat-clearings*: immediately suggests the casual manner of Seneca's letters

[11] *feints*: meaning "mock movements intended to confuse or mislead," implies almost a fun-seeking game spirit of the author

[12] *talking past...general reader*: Though Seneca was supposed to be writing to his friend, his letters sometimes read as if they were written for the benefit of some other general readers.

William Hazlitt,[13] one of the giants of the form, took Dr. Johnson[14] to task for always using big words and Latinate syntax.[15] Hazlitt defined his own ideal, the familiar style, as the following: "To write a genuine familiar or truly English style, is to write as any one would speak in common conversation who had a thorough command and choice of words, or who could discourse with ease, force, and perspicuity,[16] setting aside all pedantic and oratorical flourishes." The conversational dynamic—the desire for contact—is ingrained in the form, and serves to establish a quick emotional intimacy with the audience.

Honesty, Confession, and Privacy

Let us say that the writer has caught the reader's attention with a frank, conversational manner. In effect, a contract between writer and reader has been drawn up: the essayist must then make good on it[17] by delivering, or discovering, as much honesty as possible.

The struggle for honesty is central to the ethos of the personal essay. "I want to be an honest man and a good writer," James Baldwin put it, in that order. Yet the personal essayist often admits that few of us can remain honest for long, since humans are incorrigibly self-deceiving, rationalizing

---

[13] *William Hazlitt*: (1778-1830) English writer best known for his humanistic essays, now considered as one of the greatest essayists and critics in the history of the English language, placed in the company of Samuel Johnson and George Orwell

[14] *Samuel Johnson*: (1709-84) often referred to as Dr. Johnson, is an English essayist, critic, poet, and lexicographer, regarded as one of the greatest figures of 18th-century life and letters. Dr. Johnson's Dictionary is considered the first truly great English dictionary with a national long-lasting influence : it had been the singularly authoritative dictionary of the English-speaking people ever since its publication in 1775 and was only replaced by the *Oxford English Dictionary* coming out around the beginning of the 19th century. Dr. Johnson is famous for his learnedness and the highly dignified scholarly style of his writings.

[15] *Latinate syntax*: sentence structures modeled on the Latin language

[16] *perspicuity*: clarity, lucidness, clear expression

[17] *the essayist...on it*: The essayist must fulfill his obligations as are noted down in the aforementioned "contract between writer and reader."

animals. Ironically, it is this skepticism that uniquely equips the personal essayist for the difficult climb into honesty. So often the "plot" of a personal essay, its drama, its suspense, consists in watching how far the essayist can drop past his or her psychic defenses toward deeper levels of honesty. One may speak of a vertical dimension in the form: if the essayist can delve further underneath, until we feel the topic has been handled as honestly, as *fairly* as possible, then at least one essential condition of a successful personal essay has been met. (The others, such as pleasurable literary style, formal shapeliness, and intellectual sustenance, still await consideration.) If, however, the essayist stays at the same flat level of self-disclosure and understanding throughout, the piece may be pleasantly smooth, but it will not awaken that shiver of self-recognition—equivalent to the frisson[18] in horror films when the monster looks at himself in the mirror—which all lovers of the personal essay await as a reward.

The personal essayist is expected to be as honest as possible. The fact that he often admits how difficult or impossible it is for any man to stay honest for long testifies exactly to his honesty. Put in another way, the personal essayist's recognition of his own fallibility as the human animal or the illusion of complete and enduring honesty qualifies him for the clamber toward the height of true honesty.

This paragraph again ends with an engaging metaphor: one expects to see at the end of a personal essay the real "self-recognition" which is bound to be awe-inspiring, if not actually hair-raising as in horror films.

There is a certain strictness, or even cruelty at times, in the impulse of the personal essayist to scrape away illusions. In "On the Pleasure of Hating," Hazlitt describes friends getting together to analyze their mutual acquaintances: "We regarded them no more in our experiments than 'mice in an air-pump': or like malefactors, they were regularly cut down and given over to the dissecting-knife. We spared neither friend nor foe. We sacrificed

18 *frisson*: shiver, shudder, as a result of deep fear

human infirmities at the shrine of truth. The skeletons of character might be seen, after the juice was extracted, dangling in the air like flies in cobwebs."

 Mark how the verbal phrase "scrape away" underlines the abrasive as well as indiscriminate "cruelty" of getting rid of illusions of all kinds.

Often the rough handling begins with oneself. "We must remove the mask," says Montaigne. For Wendell Berry, in "An Entrance to the Woods," the mask is human nature itself, and the wilderness alone can help him shed its false lendings:[19] "And so, coming here, what I have done is strip away the human façade that usually stands between me and the universe."

The spectacle of baring the naked soul is meant to awaken the sympathy of the reader, who is apt to forgive the essayist's self-absorption in return for the warmth of his or her candor. Some vulnerability is essential to the personal essay. Unproblematically self-assured, self-contained, self-satisfied types will not make good essayists. There is, of course, such a thing as a rhetoric of sincerity,[20] and the skilled essayist can fake a vulnerable tone. But if this is done too often, the skilled reader will turn away in disgust. "There is one thing the essayist cannot do—he cannot indulge himself in deceit or in concealment, for he will be found out in no time," wrote E. B. White.

 It is suggested that in being sincere, the essayist also becomes vulnerable, but this is exactly how s/he wins sympathy from the reader. It also goes without saying that faked or forced sincerity never makes worthy essays.

The personal essayist must above all be a reliable narrator; we must trust his or her core of sincerity. We must also feel secure that the essayist has done a fair amount of introspective homework already, is grounded in

[19] *lendings*: could perhaps be interpreted as various masks lent by "human nature" to the individual man. When Wendell Berry walks into the woods, he is able to put down all the human masks ("the human facade") and face the universe with his naked self/soul.

[20] *a rhetoric of sincerity*: using sincerity as a device in writing, which inevitably renders this sort of "sincerity" artificial, forced, too calculated to be truly sincere

reality, and is trying to give us the maximum understanding and intelligence of which he or she is capable. A dunderhead and a psychotic killer may be sincere, but that would not sufficiently recommend them for the genre.

 For the essayist to be "a reliable narrator," sincerity alone is not enough. S/he also needs to be someone capable of "the maximum understanding and intelligence," as well as ample sound self-knowledge based on regular introspection.

Part of our trust in good personal essayists issues, paradoxically, from their exposure of their own betrayals, uncertainties, and self-mistrust. Their sincerity issues from an awareness of their potential for insincerity—see Max Beerbohm's telling aside, "But (it seems that I must begin every paragraph by questioning the sincerity of what I have just said)"—and it gives them a doubled authority.

 The reader finds good essayists trustworthy because of the confessions they make, including their suspicion of their own sincerity.

In focusing on the honesty of personal essayists, I do not mean to imply that they are relentlessly exposing dark secrets about themselves. We learn more about their habits of thought than about the sorts of abuses and crimes that spice our afternoon TV talk shows: incest, date-rape, addictions. The sins that make these essayists cringe in retrospect usually turn out to be an insensitivity that wounded another, a lack of empathy, or the callowness of youth.

 It's not surprising that the essayist would be sensitive enough to feel guilty about any number of insensitivity towards others.

Is it a paradox that personal essayists are often excruciatingly frank, yet protective of their privacy? Richard Rodriguez, for instance, is a master of the confessional tone, yet he tells us that his family calls him "Mr. Secrets," and he plays a hide-and-seek game of revealing himself. We learn very little about the actual circumstances of Max Beerbohm's life from his writings. How he managed to make ends meet, with whom he had affairs, whether his was a difficult or an easy marriage—these celebrity tidbits are never volunteered by the gentlemanly Max. Yet few writers have limned[21] so quirky[22] and recognizable a self-portrait. Chronic Beerbohm readers come to feel as close to him as if they were behind the wheel of a video arcade game, seeing how the world comes at him and recognizing the exact moment at which his tenderness is likely to swerve into mischief.

 Confession is not to be confused with exposure of personal affairs. Those who are more interested in nosing about in the celebrity's closet might as well turn to tabloids and talk shows.

How the world comes at another person, the irritations, jubilations, aches and pains, humorous flashes—these are the classic building materials of the personal essay. We learn the rhythm by which the essayist receives, digests, and spits out the world, and we learn the shape of his or her privacy. "If you wish to preserve your secret," wrote Alexander Smith of Montaigne, "wrap it up in frankness."* Note it is what the essayist experiences in the inner world, as a response to what is or occurs in the "real" world, that truly matters as "the classic building materials of the personal essay." This uniquely personal response to the usually familiar and ordinary everyday objects or experiences marks another feature of personal essays, which is to be dealt with in the following part.

The Contractions and Expansions of the Self

Personal essayists are adept at interrogating their ignorance. Just as often as they tell us what they know, they ask at the beginning of an exploration of a problem what it is they don't know—and why. They follow the clue of their ignorance through the maze. Intrigued with their limitations, both physical and mental, they are attracted to cul-de-sac:[23] what one doesn't understand, or can't do, is as good a place as any to start investigating the

---

21 *limned*: drawed, portrayed in words

22 *quirky*: odd, eccentric, peculiar

23 *cul-de-sac*: a dead end

borders of the self. So Natalia Ginzburg tells us that she can never remember the names of even the most famous actors; Charles Lamb confides that he has no musical ear; Max Beerbohm analyzes his failure to grasp philosophy.

Also common to the genre is a taste for littleness. This includes self-belittlement.[24] In "Of Greatness," Abraham Cowley, after quoting Horace's "The gods have done well in making me a humble and small-spirited fellow," goes on to say slyly, "I confess I love littleness almost in all things. A little convenient estate, a little cheerful house, a little company, and a very little feast; and, if I were to fall in love again (which is a great passion, and therefore, I hope, I have done with it), it would be, I think, with prettiness, rather than with majestical beauty."

Natalia Ginzburg's collection of essays is entitled *The Little Virtues.* We see operating here a form of inverse boasting: in exchange for lack of stature or power in the world, the personal essayist claims unique access to the small, humble things in life. And this taste for the miniature becomes a strong suit[25] of the form: the ability to turn anything close at hand (Charles Lamb's cars, Virginia Woolf's moth, Samuel Johnson's boarding house) into a grand meditational adventure.

 Personal essayists find meanings and values in"the small, humble things in life" instead of "stature or power in the world." That is why it's termed "a form of inverse boasting": to take pride in what is seemingly so lusterless and negligible. It's worth noting that stature and power in the worldly sense are indeed what most writers do "lack."

 The contrast between "small" and "grand" points exactly to the magic of the personal essays: the objects cannot be more common, yet they still can be possessed in a most rare, or literally "unique" way.

Just as the personal essayist is able to make the small loom large, so he or she simultaneously contracts and expands the self. This is done first by finding the borders, limits, defects, and disabilities of the particular

---

24 *self-belittlement*: Personal essayists apparently don't mind poking fun at themselves.

25 *a strong suit*: an excellent quality

human package one owns, then by pointing them out, which implies at least a partial surmounting through detachment. The personal essay is the reverse of that set of Chinese boxes[26] that you keep opening, only to find a smaller one within. Here you start with the small—the package of flaws and limits—and suddenly find a slightly larger container, insinuated by the essay's successful articulation and the writer's self-knowledge. The personal essayist is a Houdini who, having confessed his sins and peccadilloes[27] and submitted voluntarily to the reader's censuring handcuffs, suddenly slips them off with malicious ease by claiming, *I am more than the perpetrator of that shameful act; I am the knower and commentator as well.*

Mark how "make the small loom large" and "simultaneously contracts and expands the self" both highlight the essayist's magician-like abilities. Like Houdini (1874-1926), the American stunt performer noted especially for his miraculous escape acts, the essayist always manages to escape the confinement of various personal faults and limits via self-knowledge, a clear-minded understanding of all that is contained in "the particular human package one owns."

If tragedy is said to ennoble people and comedy to cut people down to size,[28] then the personal essay, with its ironic deflations, its insistence on human frailty, tilts toward[29] the comic. Montaigne (like his predecessor and fellow humanist Erasmus) was at pains to show *Homo sapiens*[30] as a fickle[31] conceited fool whose vanity needed pulling down. However, by drawing attention to so many strands of inconsistency in human behavior, he could not help but create the opposite impression: a humanity enlarged

---

[26] *Chinese boxes*: similar to Russian dolls, with always a smaller one contained in the next larger one

[27] *peccadilloes*: petty sins or trifling faults

[28] *cut people...to size*: to minimize or belittle men in general

[29] *tilts toward*: inclines to, is closer to

[30] *Homo sapiens*: a new Latin word for the modern species of humans

[31] *fickle*: capricious, changeable in affections, the very equivalent to "喜怒无常"

by complexity. The fulsome[32] confession of limit carries the secret promise of an almost infinite opening-out.

 The paradox of Montaigne's success as an essayist lies in that through his efforts in exposing human follies and vanities, he throws light on the very complexity of human nature and points to unlimited possibilities in its unfolding.

Personal essayists from Montaigne on have been fascinated with <u>the changeableness and plasticity of the materials of human personality.</u> Starting with self-description, they have realized they can never render[33] all at once the entire complexity of a personality. So they have elected to follow an additive strategy, offering incomplete shards,[34] one mask or persona after another: the eager, skeptical, amiable, tender, curmudgeonly, antic,[35] somber. If "we must remove the mask," it is only to substitute another mask. The hope is that in the end, when an essayist's lifework has been accumulated, all these personae will add up to a genuine unmasking.

 Mark how "the changeability and plasticity of the materials of the human personality" corresponds to "the contractions and expansions of the self." While the former denotes the natural state of the human personality in general, the latter clearly suggests the personal essayist's deliberation in shaping the self with ink.

In the meantime, the personal essayist tries to make his many partial selves dance to the same beat—to unite, through force of voice and style, these discordant, fragmentary personae so that the reader can accept them as issuing from one coherent self. Sometimes a persona is literally artificial, as in Charles Lamb's "Elia," a lightly fictionalized stand-in for himself. Lamb comically exploits the supposed differences between his narrator and

---

32 *fulsome*: should be taken to mean "comprehensive, encompassing all aspects" rather than "excessive and insincere."

33 *render*: depict, portray

34 *shards*: broken pieces, fragments

35 *antic*: ludicrous, funny

himself while getting away with a fair amount of autobiography.[36] Unless the essayist forces the issue,[37] the reader is often not aware of the discontinuities among his personae, so strong is the illusion of cohesive self-hood in the voice of a writer we admire.

 The good essayist knows how to give a coherent voice in spite of the many different personae s/he possesses. Unless the essayist allows it, the reader is not likely to detect any inevitable self-contradiction in one single piece of essay.

The harvesting of self-contradiction is an intrinsic part of the personal essay form. Often, seeing two samples of an essayist's work allows us to grasp this principle of multiple personae in action. The Edward Hoagland we meet in "The Courage of Turtles," a gentle naturalist stroking a turtle's belly, is both contradicted and extended by Hoagland's confession of spanking women in "The Threshold and the Jolt of Pain." If some readers are repelled by a writer's behavioral contradictions, this is quite all right, because the personal essayist is not necessarily out to win the audience's unqualified[38] love but to present the complex portrait of a human being.

This spectacle is offered up in sections, which makes autobiographies and personal essays, for all their overlapping aspects, fundamentally different. A memoirist is entitled to move in a linear direction, accruing extra points of psychological or social shading from initial set-ups, like a novelist, the deeper he or she moves in the narrative. There is no need to keep explaining who the narrator or the narrator's father or mother are at the beginning of each chapter. The personal essayist, though, cannot assume that the reader will ever have read anything by him or her before, and so must reestablish a persona each time and embed it in a context by providing sufficient autobiographical background. This usually means having to repeat basic circumstances of his life materials over and over—a

---

36 *getting away...of autobiography*: The fictional narrator in Lamb's essay is actually one of his "partial selves," but no one seems to suspect his being distinct from the author himself.

37 *forces the issue*: deliberately calls the reader's attention to this

38 *unqualified*: absolute, complete, not modified

wildly wasteful procedure, from the standpoint of narrative economy. Far better, you would think, for the essayist to get it over with once and for all and simply write his life story in a linear fashion. But for one thing, he may, in a fit of modesty, feel that his life story is not worth telling in toto,[39] even if a portion of it seems to be. And for another, the essay form allows the writer to circle around one particular autobiographical piece, squeezing all possible meaning out of it, while leaving the greater part of his life story available for later milking.[40] It may even be that the personal essayist is more temperamentally suited to this circling procedure, diving into the volcano of self and extracting a single hot cola to consider and shape, either because of laziness or because of an aesthetic impulse to control a smaller frame.

 "This spectacle" refers to the essayist's endeavor to "present the complex portrait of a human being." And yet this portrait is done "in sections" as it is the essayist's rather than the autobiographer's work. The latter tells his life story as a whole, while the former always goes for just a portion of his.

The Role of Contrariety

It is often the case that personal essayists intentionally go against the grain of popular opinion. They raise the ante,[41] as it were, making it more difficult for the reader to identify frictionlessly with the writer. The need to assert a quite specific temperament frequently leads the essayist into playing the curmudgeon,[42] for there is no quicker way to demonstrate idiosyncrasy and independence than to stand a platitude on its head[43] (see Dr. Johnson

---

39 *in toto*: totally, entirely

40 *for later milking*: For the essayist to milk his life story means for him to find in it something meaningful enough to be worth writing about. The word "milking" echoes "squeezing" in the preceding phrase.

41 *Raise the ante*: increase the level of difficulty, make it more demanding

42 *curmudgeon*: a bad-tempered person

43 *to stand...its head*: to turn a cliché phrase upside down, for example, to completely reverse its meaning or usage

on solitude in the country), to show a prickly[44] opposition to what the rest of humanity views as patently[45] wholesome (Beerbohm, on "Going Out for a Walk"), or to find merits in what the community regards as loathsome (Hazlitt's "On the Pleasure of Hating"). The touchy sensibility of a Hazlitt, Beerbohm, or Cioran, ever on the alert for an opportunity to bristle,[46] makes us follow them with amused suspense: what will they think to object to next?

Personal essayists see platitudes and clichés as natural enemies. To the reader's amusement, they sometimes even contradict seemingly commonsensical opinions on purpose.

Behind these contrarieties is a fear of staleness and cliché, or, to put the matter more positively, a compulsion toward fresh expression. To assert that all men are brothers, that prejudice and racism are bad, and that nature should not be despoiled may win a writer points in heaven, but it is doubtful that these pronouncements will quicken the reader's pulse. The novice essayist often errs by taking a strong moralistic stand and running it into the ground,[47] with nowhere to go after two paragraphs. Here the personal essayist will open up a new flank, locating a tension between two valid, opposing goals, or a partial virtue in some apparent ill, or an ambivalence in his own belief-system. I am not saying that an essayist should become an immoralist just for the sake of originality, but that he should be alert for contradictions that open up new ways of looking at old subjects.

"may win a writer points in heaven": this is because the listed assertions are all in accordance with traditional Christian moral codes and thus "eternally" right. But they are not likely to "quicken the reader's pulse," i.e., excite and interest him.

---

[44] *prickly*: thorny, sarcastic

[45] *patently*: obviously, apparently

[46] *to bristle*: to suddenly become very annoyed or offended

[47] *running it...the ground*: going overboard with it, being too serious about it

 Contrariety is an effective antidoteto triteness and banality. It challenges absolute moralistic stands and raises questions that are not readily answerable. It's not originality for its' own sake. It's the essayist's never-ending battle against clichés.

The enemy of the personal essay is self-righteousness, not just because it is tiresome and ugly in itself, but because it slows down the dialectic of self-questioning. What Cioran calls "thinking against oneself." Of course, personal essayists may write from powerful moral or political conviction, so long as they are also willing to render a frank, shaded account of their own feelings. Mary McCarthy, describing in "My Confession" how she became a staunch anti-Stalinist, is unafraid to tell the less than noble part that vanity, laziness, and stubbornness played in this conversion. George Orwell uncovers the proper little fascist in himself as a schoolboy in "Such, Such Were the Joys...."And elsewhere (*The Road to Wigan Pier*) is honest enough to admit that he sometimes found himself recoiling at the smell of the workers he was otherwise so keen to defend. James Baldwin's moral passion is all the more credible once we know about his struggles with his father and his admissions of irrational rage and opportunism.

 Self-righteousness is another enemy of the personal essay because it cancels out contrariety: a self-righteous person hardly thinks "against" himself. The examples show us how hard these essayists are on themselves in revealing the dark side of their personalities.

The conscience of the personal essay arises from the author's examination of his or her prejudices. Essayists must be able to pass judgment, or else their work will be toothless;[48] but this right should extend from an awareness of their own potential culpability,[49] if only through mental temptation. The idea is to implicate first oneself and then the reader in a fault that seems initially to belong safely elsewhere. The essayist is someone who lives with the guilty knowledge that he is "prejudiced." Mencken called his essay collections

48 *toothless*: weak, insipid

49 *culpability*: blameworthiness, criminality

Prejudices and has a strong predisposition for or against certain everyday phenomena. It then becomes his business to attend to these inner signals, these stomach growls, these seemingly indefensible intuitions, and try to analyze what lies underneath them, the better to judge them. As Georg Lukacs wrote, "The essay is a judgment, but the essential, the value-determining thing about it is not the verdict (as is the case with the system) but the process of judging."

In passing judgment on certain faults and ills, the essayist has to be clear that no one is safe, i.e., both he and the reader are equally capable of what is being criticized or condemned. And for essays, how any judgment is reached matters more than what final verdict it leads to.

The Problem of Egotism

Thoreau justifies his use of "I" on the opening page of *Walden*: "In most books the *I*, or first person, is omitted; in this it will be retained; that, in respect to egotism, is the main difference. We commonly do not remember that it is, after all, always the first person that is speaking." Still, it takes a fair amount of ego to discourse on one's private affairs and offer judgments about life. This can make the writer, let alone the reader, uneasy. Most people are brought up to think it is impolite to talk much about themselves; in academic papers, scholars are discouraged from using the first person singular. Surely one of the reasons for the self-deprecating air that many personal essayists adopt is to ward off potential charges of vanity or self-absorption.

E. B. White confronted this problem head-on[50] when he wrote:

I think some people find the essay the last resort of the egoist, a much too self-conscious and self-serving form for their taste;[51] *they feel that it is presumptuous of a writer to assume that his little excursions or his small observations will interest the reader. There is some justice*

---

[50] *head-on*: directly, face-to-face

[51] *for their taste*: As far as they're concerned, the essay form is too self-conscious and self-serving.

in their complaint. I have always been aware that I am by nature self-absorbed and egoistical; to write of myself to the extent I have done indicates a too great attention to my own life, not enough to the lives of others. I have worn many shirts, and not all of them have been a good fit. But when I am discouraged or downcast I need only fling open the door of my closet, and there, hidden behind everything else, hangs the mantle of Michel de Montaigne, smelling slightly of camphor.[52]

It's interesting to note that while White admits how he's always been aware of his egotism, the fully egotistical personality doesn't seem to be capable of a similar awareness at all. "The mantle of Michel de Montaigne" is a metaphor for the personal essay, suggesting that after all this is the writing form that fits White the most. It even serves to cheer him up and bring his confidence back.

Since White was one of the most self-effacing personal essayists, it is interesting that even he was stung with guilt about egotism. His temporary solution—wrapping himself in the mantle of Montaigne—is also interesting, as though only the personal essay tradition could validate his self-involvement.

The nineteenth-century English writer Alexander Smith drew some helpful distinctions between pleasurable and irritating egotism in essayists: "The speaking about oneself is not necessarily offensive. A modest, truthful man speaks better about himself than about anything else, and on that subject his speech is likely to be most profitable to his hearers.... If he be without taint of boastfulness, of self-sufficiency, of hungry vanity, the world will not press the charge home.[53] If a man discourses continually of his wines, his plate, his titled acquaintances,[54] the number and quality

---

[52] *camphor*: 樟脑丸

[53] *press the charge home*: insist on charging the essayist with "boastfulness," "self-sufficiency" and "vanity." If the essayist simply shows no sign of irritating egotism, there is no danger of his being labeled an egotist.

[54] *titled acquaintances*: acquaintances belonging to the aristocracy, or having high ranks in society

of his horses, his men-servants and maid-servants, he must discourse very skillfully indeed if he escapes being called a coxcomb."[55]

Smith reassures us that "it is this egotism, this perpetual reference to self, in which the charm of the essayist resides. If a man is worth knowing at all, he is worth knowing well." In a similar vein, Logan Pearsall Smith wrote that "the amused observation of one's own self is a veritable[56] gold mine whose surface has hardly yet been scratched." While personal essayists as a rule share that conviction, all have occasionally had to wrestle with what might be called the stench of ego. A person can write about himself from angles that are charmed, fond, delightfully nervy;[57] alter the lens just a little and he crosses over into gloating,[58] pettiness, defensiveness, score settling[59] (which includes self-hate), or whining about his victimization. The trick is to realize that one is not important, except insofar as one's example can serve to elucidate a more widespread human trait and make readers feel a little less lonely and freakish.

"To realize that one is not important" seems to be not only the trick for fending off "the stench of ego," but also a golden piece of advice for truly enjoying life since self-importance entails only "gloating, pettiness, defensiveness, score settling..."

Cheek and Irony

Closely allied to these seesaws of modesty and egotism, universality and touchy eccentricity, is the penchant[60] of the personal essayist for outbreaks of mischievous impudence. The conversational address to the reader is frequently the signal for such cheeky liberties, as though the rebellious,

---

55 *a coxcomb*: a dandy, a playboy, a shallow show-off man

56 *veritable*: real, authentic

57 *nervy*: uptight, emotional, daring

58 *gloating*: complacency, self-satisfaction, smugness

59 *score settling*: account settling, squaring up with somebody or oneself. It suggests a grudging attitude and trivial-mindedness.

60 *penchant*: strong inclination

clever servant-author were tweaking the nose[61] of the dull-witted master-reader. Cheekiness is a way of keeping readers alert. It cuts through the pious and commonplace.

Such cool impertinence[62] often takes the form of a self-reflexive moment, which punctures[63] the argument by drawing attention to the stage machinery of essayistic discourse. Montaigne launched this habit by impishly[64] and preemptively criticizing his essays[65] ("some excrements of an aged mind"). Beerbohm's "Laughter" begins, "M. Bergson, in his well-known essay on the theme, says... well, he says many things; but none of these, though I have just read them, do I clearly remember, nor am I sure that in the act of reading I understand any of them." This is an example of how the facetiously self-reflective confession of an inadequacy can have the perverse effect of cheek. When Walter Benjamin ends "Unpacking My Library" by saying about the true collector, "So I have erected one of his dwellings, with books as the building stones, before you, and now he is going to disappear inside, as is only fitting," he is both parodying the solemnity of the learned essay and treating the reading audience like children at a puppet show.

When the essayist appears cheeky and mischievous, the reader is often reminded that essay also offers a stage for performance.

Part of what gives personal essayists the license to be so cheeky is their suspicion that they are not performing in the central ring of the literary circus. "The essayist, unlike the novelist, the poet, and the playwright, must be content in his self-imposed role of second-class citizen," wrote E. B. White. "A writer who has his sights trained on the Nobel Prize or other

[61] *tweaking the nose*: pinching or plucking the nose, as a way of teasing somebody
[62] *impertinence*: insolence, rudeness
[63] *punctures*: pierces, breaks
[64] *impishly*: mischievously
[65] *preemptively criticizing his essays*: Montaigne criticized his own essays before anyone else did it, so as to prevent some anticipated unpleasant responses from others.

earthly triumphs had best write a novel, a poem, or a play, and leave the essayist to ramble about, content with living a free life and enjoying the satisfactions of a somewhat undisciplined existence."

 The essayist knows that he could never compete with poets or novelists for literary importance or influence. And because of this, he thinks he is entitled to being cheeky or impervious.

Georg Lukacs, in "On the Nature and Form of the Essay," specifically linked the essayist's cheeky humor and the status of the genre. Referring to "that humor and that irony which we find in the writings of every truly great essayist," he observed that the "essayist dismisses his own proud hopes which sometimes lead him to believe that he has come close to the ultimate: he has, after all, no more to offer than explanations of the poems of others, or at best his own ideas. But he ironically adapts himself to this smallness—the eternal smallness of the most profound work of the intellect in the face of life—and even emphasizes it with ironic modesty."

 It is "ironic modesty" because the essayist is also likely to harbor the illusion that "he has come close to the ultimate." Nevertheless Lukacs obviously had a very high opinion of essay writing, describing it as "the most profound work of the intellect in the face of life."

The Idler Figure

As part of their ironic modesty, personal essayists frequently represent themselves as loafers[66] or retirees,[67] inactive and tangential to the marketplace.[68] The shiftless marginality of the essayist's persona is underscored[69] by the titles of some of the most famous essay series: *The Idler, The Rambler* (Samuel Johnson), *The Spectator, The Tatler* (Addison and Steele). Perhaps by affecting the role of lazy scribblers, essayists make

---

66 *loafer*: habitual idler

67 *retiree*: one who retires from active work

68 *tangential to the marketplace*: not seriously involved in any economical activities

69 *underscored*: underlined, stressed, reinforced

themselves out to be harmless,[70] thereby able to poke fun at will.[71]

Asian literature has a long tradition of the retired scholar—sometimes forced into premature exile by falling into political disfavor, like the Chinese essayist Ou-yang Hsiu—who uses his leisure to contemplate the beauties of nature and the poetic transience of life. The Japanese monk Kenko, having withdrawn from the world for spiritual purposes, wrote a book of stream-of-consciousness mini-essays called *Essays in Idleness*. Seneca penned his letters during enforced idleness and exile. Montaigne also portrayed himself as a retired country gentleman, given over to his library and idle thoughts, when in fact he still carried on important diplomatic missions during the religious wars.

Joseph Addison wrote in his *Spectator*, "I live in the World rather as a Spectator of Mankind, than as one of the species... I have acted in all the Parts of my Life as a looker-on, which is the Character I intend to preserve in this Paper." The use of the term "Character," a popular eighteenth-century literary form which broke mankind down into types, alerts us that we are getting from Addison a stylized essayistic persona rather than realistic autobiography. Addison's partner, Sir Richard Steele, similarly offers us a detached narrator, cheerfully outside the net of economic productivity. In "Twenty-four Hours in London," he follows the crowd around for a day: "It is an inexpressible Pleasure to know a little of the World, and be of no Character or Significancy in it. To be ever unconcerned, and ever looking on new Objects with an endless Curiosity, is a Delight known only to those who are turned for Speculation: Nay, they who enjoy it, must value things only as they are the Objects of Speculation, without drawing any worldly Advantage to themselves from them, but just as they are what they contribute to their Amusement, or the Improvement of the Mind."

 Mark that in 18th-century English writing, nouns were still mostly capitalized, just as in the German language.

---

[70] *make themselves...be harmless*: cut an image of harmless outsiders for themselves

[71] *to poke...at will*: to make jokes freely

Addison made it clear that the figure of himself as "a Spectator of Mankind" is actually a "Character" he invented for his essays to preserve. While the mental state of such a spectator as was delineated in Steele's passage easily reminds one of the aesthete of the 19th century: both transcend the concern for the immediately useful or any perceivable worldly interest.

Here the idler begins to defend himself, even to adapt a tone of superiority toward the breadwinner. Robert Louis Stevenson, in his essay "An Apology for Idlers," advances this line of argument.

> *Extreme busyness... is a symptom of deficient vitality; and a faculty for idleness implies a catholic*[72] *appetite and a strong sense of personal identity. There is a sort of dead-alive, hackneyed people about, who are scarcely conscious of living except in the exercise of some conventional occupation. Bring these fellows into the country, or set them aboard ship, and you will see how they pine for their desk or their study. They have no curiosity; they cannot give themselves to random provocations; they do not take pleasure in the exercise of their faculties for its own sake... they cannot be idle, their nature is not generous enough; and they pass those hours in a sort of coma, which are not dedicated to furious moiling*[73] *in the gold-mill.*[74]

Substitute "essayist" for "idler" in Stevenson's passage, and you have a catalogue of the genre's virtues: curiosity; openness; appetite for pleasure; willingness to reflect, to give oneself to "random provocations," nature, beauty. All this adds up to the capacity for perception. The essayist is fascinated with perception, which provides a never-ending source of speculative material. The art of vision can take place under normal circumstances (as in Woolf's "Street Haunting") or be heightened by

---

[72] *catholic*: comprehensive, universal

[73] *moiling*: working hard, toiling

[74] *furious moiling...the gold-mill*: metaphor for laboring hard for money

drugs (Benjamin's "Hashish in Marseilles"), hunger (Soyinka's "Why Do I Fast?"), ecstatic nature mysticism (Dillard's "Seeing"), or illness (Lu Hsun's "Death"[75]).

By Stevenson's logic, only the idle person is able to practice *seeing*—to perceive the little, uncommercial miracles in life. The essayist here aligns himself with what is traditionally considered a female perspective, in its appreciation of sentiment, dailiness, and the domestic. Indeed, the male personal essayist, quick to label himself an idler, also volunteers that he is something less than a virile patriarch. A somewhat celibate bachelorhood seems to hover around the Spectator, Idler, Rambler, and other stylized essayistic personae. Lamb describes his first-person surrogate, Elia, with a shrewd bit of self-analysis: "He was too much of the boy-man. The *togavirilis* never sate gracefully on his shoulders. The impressions of infancy had burnt into him, and he resented the impertinence of manhood." Stevenson, who did marry, was still chiefly known for his boys' stories and essays like "The Lantern-Bearers," which dwell lovingly on this preadult stage of life. Walter Benjamin portrayed himself as a bookworm, a nerd, a schlemiel[76] who could never quite grow up and enter the adult world of making a living.

One might even say that the quintessential essayist is the archetype of modern-day feminist. After all a "boy-man" is more likely to retain the innocence of the "preadult stage of life" as well as disinterested idolizing of the motherly.

I must reiterate, of course, that some of this self-portraiture has a fictional slant. Many personal essayists have enjoyed alternately stripping themselves bare[77] and creating a slightly distorted, even shabbier version of themselves, the way the comedian Jack Benny made himself out to be much stingier than he was, just for the joke of it. While the personal essayist is such a trustworthy witness, at times no one works closer to "unreliable

---

[75] *Lu Hsun's "Death"*: that is, 鲁迅名篇《死》(1936)

[76] *schlemiel*: a stupid, awkward and often unlucky person

[77] *stripping themselves bare*: completely revealing themselves

narrator" territory. Certain high-pitched tones of Lamb, Hazlitt, Beerbohm, and others stir up unmistakable echoes of Dostoevsky's Underground Man, Ford Madox Ford's Good Soldier, and other unreliable narrators. How to account for this paradox? We should recall that the novel and the essay rose together and fed off each other as literary forms; fiction's "unreliable narrator" may have even derived initially, in part, from the mischievous candor and first-person expressiveness unleashed in personal essays.

 It's such a paradox that while the very true value of personal essays is trustworthiness or sincerity, the essayist could actually be an "unreliable narrator." But the current author also reminds us how the fictional first-person narrator may have even originated from the narrative pattern of essays.

The Past, the Local, and the Melancholy

The past is frequently and often lyrically visited by personal essayists. The retrospective glance comes naturally to the essayist: the past is an Aladdin's lamp which he or she never tires of rubbing. As Hazlitt said about his friend Lamb, "Mr. Lamb has a distaste to new faces, to new books, to new buildings, to new customs.... He evades the present, he mocks the future. His affections revert to, and settle on, the past, but then, even this must have something personal and local in it to interest him deeply and thoroughly."

 The personal is essentially defined by one's past and what is local and familiar to you.

Beerbohm, who took up Lamb's mantle a century later, also showed a fastidious, unjournalistic distaste for the topical. "Sir Max Beerbohm seems to bring with him the aroma of an age that is just past: his writings always were like that and they always will be; just not quite up to date," wrote Bonamy Dobrée, "and so, one guesses, enduring."

 Hopefully, reading good essays would help lift us above the fallacy of what C. S. Lewis called "chronological snobbery."

Another fine sifter of the past, the contemporary Irish essayist Hubert

Butler, now in his nineties, remarked in "Beside the Nore," "I have always believed that local history is more important than national history." In Butler, the personal essayist's loyalty to the local and near-at-hand are intermixed with an amateur archeologist's search for traces of history. "The past comes close in disconnected fragments and I was thinking of the days when we were children and had dancing classes with the young Tighes at the Noreview Hotel in Thomastown; their mother, with my Aunt Harriet, used to run a Christian Science Reading Room opposite the Castle in Killkenny, two spiders into whose web no fly ever came." Though Butler traveled widely, in Russia, Egypt, China, and the United States, and got swept up in the political events of his time, he wrote, "I am more inclined to apologize for writing about great events, which touched me not at all, than for tracing again the tiny snail track which I made myself." This "snail track" might be the insignia of the personal essay genre.

There is a melancholy tone in much of Butler's work, which also crops up in Montaigne, Lamb, Hazlitt, Lu Hsun, Gore Vidal, and so on. It might be called "the voice of middle age." If the personal essay frequently presents a middle-aged point of view, it may be because it is the fruit of ripened experience, which naturally brings with it some worldly disenchantment, or at least realism. With middle age also comes a taste for equilibrium; hence, that stubborn, almost unnerving calm that so often pervades the personal essay. Montaigne exemplified the melancholy, stoical balance of middle age ("I have seen the grass, the flower, and the fruit; now I see the dryness—happily since it is naturally"), which is, for better or worse, the by-product of a developed sense of selfhood.

📖 The typical melancholy tone of personal essays points to a disenchanted, realistic outlook of middle age.

F. Scott Fitzgerald starts "The Crack-Up" by sounding the quintessential note of middle-aged experience: "Of course all life is a process of breaking down, but the blows that do the dramatic side of the work—the big sudden blows that come, or seem to come, from outside—the ones you remember and blame things on and, in moments of weakness, tell your friends about, don't show their effect all at once. There is another sort of blow that comes from within—that you don't feel until it's too late to do anything about it, until you realize with finality that in some regard you will never be as good a man again."

 What's really tragic about middle age in general is a growing sense of nonchalance towards even the realization that "you will never be as good a man again." One simply takes this for granted and lives with those blows within or without.

While young people excel at lyrical poetry and mathematics, it is hard to think of anyone who made a mark on the personal essay form in his or her youth. The closest candidates might be James Baldwin and Joan Didion, and both adopted precociously world-weary personae while still in their twenties. Baldwin had no sooner left his brutal Harlem adolescence than he began describing it, with rueful ache and Jamesian distance, like a lost kingdom. Didion's elegiac "Goodbye to All That," written at thirty-four, is already saturated with her trademark disenchantment.

 Both James Baldwin's *Notes of a Native Son* and Joan Didion's *The White Album* are must-reads for anyone with the least interest in contemporary American essays.

It is difficult to write analytically from the middle of confusion, and youth is a confusion in which the self and its desires have not yet sorted themselves out. A young person still thinks it is possible—there is time enough—to become all things: athlete and aesthete, soldier and pacifist, anchorite and debauchee. Later, knowing one's fate and accepting the responsibility of that uninnocent knowledge define the perspective of the form. The personal essayist looks back at the choices that were made, the roads not taken, the limiting familial and historic circumstances, and what might be called the catastrophe of personality.[78] In literature, noted Gore Vidal, "the true confessors have been aware that not only is life mostly

---

78 *the catastrophe of personality*: It may well be rendered as "性格悲剧."

failure, but that in one's failure or pettiness or wrongness exists the living drama of the self." The wonder is that the personal essay can make this bitter awareness appetizing and even amusing to the reader.

 The personal essay genre is for writers with a clear-minded knowledge of one's fate, or the so-called "catastrophe of personality" and a readiness to take the responsibility that comes with that knowledge.

Questions of Form and Style

The essay is a notoriously flexible and adaptable form. It possesses the freedom to move anywhere, in all directions. It acts as if all objects were equally near the center and as if "all subjects are linked to each other" (Montaigne) by free association. This freedom can be daunting, not only for the novice essayist confronting such latitude but for the critic attempting to pin down its formal properties.

The essay challenges formal analysis by what Walter Pater called its "unmethodical method," open to digression and promiscuous meanderings. Dr. Johnson described the essay as "a loose sally of the mind" and "an irregular, undigested piece"—which did not prevent him from undertaking a substantial involvement in the form, suggesting at least a hope that it would bring him aesthetic dividends. I take with a grain of salt[79] those claims, by slumming lovers of the essay,[80] that it is not really an art form, and somehow better off for being what the Spanish philosopher Eduardo Nicol called "*almost* literature and *almost* philosophy." From my perspective, there is no *almost* about it: good essays are works of literary art. Their supposed formlessness is more a strategy to disarm the reader with the appearance of unstudied spontaneity than a reality of composition.

 The essay only appears to be formless. It's the essayist's strategy to convince the reader that the whole piece writes itself without being planned or devised in any way.

---

79 *with a...of salt*: with a skeptical attitude

80 *slumming lovers...the essay*: those who love the essay only out of curiosity or for amusement. It implies that those claims about the essay being formless or unmethodical are unreliable.

Formally personal essays have, in one sense, a head start[81] over other essay types, being already unified by a strong "I" perspective (either an actual first-person narrator or an implied one). Still, there is no guarantee that the personal essay will attain a shapeliness or a sense of aesthetic inevitability. The well-made short story has a recognizable arc that seems to follow a more intuitive, groping path. The writer of the poorest sonnet is assured that in the end there will be a fourteen-line poem, whereas the essayist may be left with nothing more than a set of fragmentary notes.

The essayist attempts to surround a something—a subject, a mood, a problematic irritation—by coming at it from all angles, wheeling and diving like a hawk, each seemingly digressive spiral actually taking us closer to the heart of the matter. In a well-wrought essay, while the search appears to be widening, even losing its way, it is actually eliminating false hypotheses, narrowing its emotional target and zeroing in on it.

The essayist must be a good storyteller. This is a point rarely made, perhaps because of the classifying urge to keep the two genres neatly fenced off. True, the essayist happily violates the number-one rule of short story workshops, "Show, don't tell;" the glory of the essayist is to tell, once and for all, everything that he or she thinks, knows, and understands. Yet often it happens that a personal essay starts out in a seemingly directionless or at least open manner, with all the time in the world, only to hop onto a narrative possibility and let the storytelling momentum take it home. Addison and Steele often walk a thin line between the reflective essay and the anecdotal vignette, crossing over when it suits them; Hazlitt's "The Fight" and Lamb's "Dream Children: A Reverie" are both hybrids of essay and fictional technique; Virginia Woolf's "Street Haunting" follows a single character, the narrator, around for an evening; Turgenev organizes "The Execution of Tropmann" around his reactions to a single dramatic event; Orwell's "Such, such Were the Joys..." performs in many ways like

[81] *have a head start*: In Chinese we say "赢在起跑线上." According to the author, personal essays have an advantage over other essay types in form because of "a strong 'I' perspective." Though this by no means guarantee a shapeliness for personal essays.

an autobiographical novella; Baldwin's personal essays push at the frontier between fiction and reportage. All good essayists make use at times of storytelling devices: descriptions of character and place, incident, dialogue, conflict. They needn't narrate some actual event to produce a narrative. Even a "pure" meditation, the track of one's thoughts, has to be shaped, given a kind of plot or urgency, if it is to communicate.

The contemporary neo-journalism or nonfiction writing could perhaps be seen as the full-fledged outcome of mingling essay with storytelling devices. Mark the development from Addison and Steele's "anecdotal vignette," to Hazlitt and Lamb's "fictional technique," down to the dramatic elements employed by Woolf and Turgenev, and finally to experimenting with typical nonfiction literature such as autobiography and reportage in the essay form by Orwell and Baldwin.

About Hazlitt's style, Ronald Blythe wrote, "Each essay shows the build-up of numerous small climaxes, such as are sometimes employed in the novel. Excitement and expectation mount." Hazlitt, trained in philosophy, tended to stay closer to a line of argument than other personal essayists do. But even when writers have deliberately shied away from developing a single thesis or line of attack, usually we can locate in their essays a buried argument. The stated subject or title of a piece may be only its pretext. Montaigne's "Of Coaches" works its way round from modes of conveyance to a ringing denunciation of European settlers' treatment of Indians in the New World. E. B. White's "The Ring of Time" begins as a description of a small circus and veers off into a commentary on racial integration. White would probably have been embarrassed to preach integration head-on, but he was less hesitant to back into it casually.

Many times the personal essayist will start to explore a subject, then set up a countertheme, and eventually braid the two.[82] Sara Suleri's "Meatless Days," for instance, begins as an almost facetious treatment of certain organ meats, but along the way this theme is thickened with family history, cultural conflicts, gender, and grief. The personal essayist is like a

---

[82] *braid the two*: mingle the two countering ideas

cook who learns through trial and error just when to add another spice or countertaste to the stew.

Here the art of elaboration enters in. Much of what characterizes true essayists is the ability to draw out a point through example, list, simile, small variation, hyperbolic exaggeration, whatever. The great essayists have all had this gusto in fleshing out an idea,[83] which becomes not a chore but an opportunity. An example is the opening of Charles Lamb's essay "A Chapter on Ears."

> *I have no ear.—*
> *Mistake me not, reader—nor imagine that I am by nature destitute of those exterior twin appendages, hanging ornaments, and (architecturally speaking) handsome volutes to the human capital. Better my mother had never borne me.—I am, I think, rather delicately than copiously provided with those conduits; and I feel no disposition to envy the mule for his plenty, or the mole for her exactness, in those ingenious labyrinthine inlets—those indispensable side-intelligencers.*
> *Neither have I incurred, or done anything to incur, with Defoe, that hideous disfigurement, which constrained him to draw upon assurance—to feel "quite unabashed," and at ease upon that article. I was never, I thank my stars, in the pillory; nor, if I read them aright, is it within the compass of my destiny, that I ever should be.*
> *When therefore I say that I have no ear, you will understand me to mean—*for music.

By this time, the reader will want either to strangle the author or, if he has a taste for Lamb, to laugh. The mock-solemnity with which this slender idea is elaborated, the piling-up of mules and architecture, inlets and punitive instruments and "side-intelligencers," always makes me smile. Part of the humor rests in the peculiar dictional spin Lamb puts on words. Today's readers may miss the joke, but his contemporaries knew how

---

83 *flesh out an idea*: expand an idea, make it substantial

absurdly dusty his vocabulary was, even for the early nineteenth century. A runaway antiquarianism[84] is one of Lamb's standard comic techniques. Another is the pretended fussy sense of dignity ("rather delicately than copiously provided"). The elegant care with which Lamb's sentences are written, the humor in his wry linguistic touches, make him a writer to savor.

Another technique of the personal essay that serves both structural and comic functions is the digression. The chief role of the digression is to amass all the dimensions of understanding that the essayist can accumulate by bringing in as many contexts as a problem or insight can sustain without overburdening it. The digression must wander off the point only to fulfill it. A kind of elaboration, it scoops up subordinate themes in passing. Some of the essayist's comic irony derives from a self-consciousness about digression, the joke being, as in *Tristram Shandy*, that the writer cannot stay on the point but must garrulously blab about everything.

Another formal technique employed by the personal essayist is the movement from individual to universal. The concrete details of personal experience earn the generalization (often an aphorism), and the generalization sends the author back for more particulars. Sometimes this spiral is aided by a modulation in pronouns: "I,""one,""we," and "you." The jump from "I" to "we" or "you" can seem presumptuous if taken too quickly (as the joke goes, "What do you mean 'we,' masked man?"). It requires preparation and timing; personal essayists must always watch their pronouns carefully.

William Hazlitt, for all his brusque lack of diplomacy, was a master of this pronominal tact. At the beginning of "On Going a Journey," he establishes a highly individuated first-person voice, proudly refusing to sue for reader empathy: "One of the pleasantest things in the world is going a journey; but I like to go by myself. I can enjoy society in a room; but out of doors, nature is company enough for me." In each of these sentences,

[84] *runaway antiquarianism*: antiquarianism that gets out of control, referring to Lamb's "absurdly dusty vocabulary"

Hazlitt's jaunty rhythms suggest a hiker swinging his arms, entirely self-sufficient: the first clause invites us in, the semicolon stops us, the second clause pushes us away. The author is celebrating his solitude: the rest of us, stay out. Yet midway down the first page, he is already declaring, "The soul of a journey is liberty, perfect liberty, to think, feel, do, just as one pleases. We go a journey chiefly to be free of all impediments and of all inconveniences; to leave ourselves behind, much more to get rid of others. It is because I want a little breathing-space..." and so on. In four sentences he has moved from the eccentric "I" to the mildly generalizing "one," which forms a tactical bridge to the "we" of aphorism and sweeping pronouncement; then back to "I" for more evidence-gathering based on personal experience. "You" comes in a few sentences later, at first as the actual reader who is being addressed ("if I were to explain to you"), then as a substitute for "I," which furthers the symbiosis between author and audience.

 To sum up, personal essayists are all masters of "a reality of composition" beneath "the appearance of unstudied spontaneity." They know the secret recipe of giving shape to pure meditations, or how to send words on some peculiar linguistics pin and move freely between the personal and the universal with the right pronominal tact.

The Personal Essay as Mode of Thinking and Being

The essay form as a whole has long been associated with an experimental method. This idea goes back to Montaigne and his endlessly suggestive use of the term *essai* for his writings. To essay is to attempt, to test, to make a run at something without knowing whether you are going to succeed. The experimental association also derives from the other fountainhead of the essay, Francis Bacon, and his stress on the empirical inductive method, so useful to the development of the physical sciences.

 Essays have a humble root indeed, as Montaigne called his writings essai in order to suggest that he was merely attempting to set his thoughts to paper. While in Bacon's hands, the "essaying form" acquired its "experimental spirit" with a new emphasis on trials and empirical methods.

There is something heroic in the essayist's gesture of striking out toward the unknown, not only without a map but without certainty that there is anything worthy to be found. One would like to think that the personal essay represents a kind of basic research on the self, in ways that are allied with science and philosophy. Montaigne called himself a new type, an "accidental philosopher," expressing the mocking hope that his impromptu approach—seemingly the opposite to that of traditional philosophers, with their patient construction of logical systems—might almost by chance add up to a philosophy. In the end he got his wish; it would not be inappropriate to teach Montaigne in a moral philosophy course. But what of other personal essayists, and the essay form in general?

 The author seems to be suggesting that there is something modernistic in the personal essay from the very beginning, opposite to classicism.

The modern German philosopher Theodor Adorno saw rich, subversive possibilities in precisely the "anti-systematic" properties of the essay. In our century, when the grand philosophical systems seem to have collapsed under their own weight and authoritarian taint, the light-footed, freewheeling essay suddenly steps forward as an attractive way to open up philosophical discourse. As Adorno put it, "Luck and play are what are essential to the essay. It does not begin with Adam and Eve but with what it wants to discuss; it says what is at issue and stops where it feels itself complete—not where nothing is left to say.... The essay does not strive for closed, deductive or inductive construction. It revolts above all against the doctrine—deeply rooted since Plato—that the changing and ephemeral is unworthy of philosophy, against the ancient injustice toward the transitory."

 Adorno's quotation actually highlights the modernistic properties of the essay. It probes into exactly the significance of the individual, which by tradition has long been deemed insignificant because of its limitedness and temporality.

Adorno's approving statement that "the essay shies away from the violence of dogma" echoes Robert Louis Stevenson's about the idler (read:

essayist): "He will not be heard among the dogmatists. He will have a great and cool allowance for all sorts of people and opinions. If he finds no out-of-the-way truths, he will identify himself with no very burning falsehood." When Beerbohm apologizes in "Laughter" for never being able to retain abstract philosophy, he is also inversely speaking out for another way of thinking, taking sides in what R. Lane Kauffmann calls "the historical conflict between fragmentary and totalizing modes of thought—between essay and system."

 Apparently essay stands for the fragmentary mode of thought as opposed to system, the totalizing mode of thought.

Recent essayists, such as Roland Barthes, Joan Didion, and Richard Rodriguez, have made a virtue of fragmentation, offering it as a mirror to the unconnectable, archipelago-like nature of modern life. "The usual reproach against the essay," wrote Adorno, "that it is fragmentary and random, itself assumes the givenness of totality[85] and... suggests that man is in control of totality. But the desire of the essay is not to seek and filter the eternal out of the transitory; it wants, rather, to make the transitory eternal."

Roland Barthes said toward the end of his life that he had produced "only essays, an ambiguous genre in which analysis vies with writing." The rueful tone of this statement should not distract us from its pride. In Europe, the essay has provided those with philosophic minds, such as Barthes, Benjamin, Adorno, Cioran, Simone Weil, and Jurgen Habermas, the chance to be writers as well.

The unashamed subjectivity of the personal essay makes it less suspect in a mental climate in which people have learned to mistrust the "value-free, objective" claims of scholarship and science. Another intriguing feature of the form for contemporary theorists and advocates of "process" writing is that it seems to lay bare its process as it goes along. I say "seems" because there is still a good deal of selection and art in this appearance of spontaneous process. Still, as Alexander Smith noted, "The essayist gives

[85] *the givenness of totality*: the indisputability of totality; that totality is simply taken for granted.

you his thoughts, and lets you know, in addition, how he came by them." This honoring of the thought as it pops up lends a watercolorist's freshness to the form.

Naturally, essayists who honor the flow of their thoughts may often end up contradicting themselves. But what would be a flaw in the systems-building philosopher may be an essential step for the essayist. As F. Scott Fitzgerald said, paraphrasing Keats' idea of negative capability, "The test of a first-rate intelligence is the ability to hold two opposed ideas in the mind at the same time, and still retain the ability to function." The essay's capacity for processing doubt is part of what makes it so stimulating and tonic.

This tolerance for contradiction also puts an added pressure on the essayist, according to Adorno: "The slightly yielding quality of the essayist's thought forces him to greater intensity than discursive thought can offer; for the essay, unlike discursive thought, does not proceed blindly, automatically, but at every moment it must reflect on itself." Here, O. B. Hardison, Jr.'s definition of the essay seems particularly apt: "The essay is the enactment of a process by which the soul realizes itself even as it is passing from day to day and from moment to moment."

The self-consciousness and self-reflection that essay writing demands cannot help but have an influence on the personal essayist's life. Montaigne confessed at one point that "in modeling this figure upon myself, I have had to fashion and compose myself so often to bring myself out, that the model itself has to some extent grown firm and taken shape. Painting myself for others, I have painted my inward self with colors clearer than my original ones. I have no more made my book than my book has made me." Thus the writing of personal essays not only monitors the self but helps it gel.[86] The essay is an enactment of the creation of the self.

Whether as an enactment of self-realization or creation, the personal essay offers yet another means for the modern man to carry on with his eternal quest of the self: to know thyself and be true to thyself.

---

86 *helps it gel*: helps it take shape or become clear

"I write what I please," stated George Orwell. Whether entirely true or not, this represents the ideal mental condition of the personal essayist, the same one enunciated by Hazlitt when he wrote, "No one has said to me, *Believe this, do that, say what we would have you*; no one has come between me and my free-will; I have breathed the very air of truth and independence."

In the final analysis, the personal essay represents a mode of being. It points a way for the self to function with relative freedom in an uncertain world. Skeptical yet gyroscopically poised, undeceived but finally tolerant of flaws and inconsistencies, this mode of being suits the modern existential situation, which Montaigne first diagnosed. His recognition that human beings were surrounded by darkness, with nothing particularly solid to cling to, led to a philosophical acceptance that one had to make oneself up from moment to moment.

 To make oneself up is to find meanings for one's own existence.

Still, we must not make excessive claims. The essay is not, for the most part, philosophy; nor is it yet science. How seriously ought we to take its claims of being experimental? It lacks the rigor of a laboratory experiment; it does not hold on to its hypotheses long enough to prove them. But it is what it is: a mode of inquiry, another way of getting at the truth.

 So the givenness of "the truth" is assumed here after all.

As one pedagogic champion of the personal essay, William Zeiger, put it,

> *The practice of experimenting, or trying something out, is expressed in the now uncommon sense of the verb to* prove*—the sense of "testing" rather than of "demonstrating validity." Montaigne "proved" his ideas in that he tried them out in his essays. He spun out their implications, sampled their suggestions. He did not argue or try to persuade. He had no investment in winning over his audience to his opinion; accordingly,*

he had no fear of being refuted. On the contrary, he expected that some of the ideas he expressed would change, as they did in later essays. Refutation represented not a personal defeat but an advance toward truth as valuable as confirmation. To "prove" an idea, for Montaigne, was to examine it in order to find out how true it was.

Author

Phillip Lopate (1943-), an American writer, considered as one of America's best personal essayists. He was especially noted as editor of the celebrated anthology *The Art of the Personal Essay* (1994). His name is almost synonymous with the form of the modern personal essay for contemporary Americans.

Text

This piece is Lopate's famous introduction written for *The Art of the Personal Essay*, the first anthology of this particular essay genre. More than 75 personal essays are included, either influential in history or acclaimed the finest in the modern world. In the chapter "Other Cultures, Other Continents," Lopate even introduces Lu Xun's essays and calls him the greatest modern Chinese writer.

This introduction offers a lengthy account of the history of personal essay-writing through exploring its essential properties. It also offers a valuable survey of important essayists over the past 2,000 years. Lopate's demonstrates what one might call "autological essay-writing" in this piece as it is one of the best of its own kind.

Further Reading

The Art of the Personal Essay, Phillip Lopate
Notes of a Native Son, James Baldwin

Extensive Reading

Rivalry

by E. V. Lucas

From Mrs. Horace Spong to the Rev.[1] Samson Spong

Dear Samson,—I was so glad to hear from Lydia that you are better. We have been rather nervous about you, for a cold at this time of year is often difficult to throw off. Horace is better too, and we are making our plans for Mentone as usual. I don't pretend to care much for this annual exile[2] from home, but Horace counts on it.

I am,

Your affectionate Sister,

Grace Spong

The Rev. Samson Spong to Mrs. Horace Spong

Dear Grace,—I can't think what Lydia was about, to tell you that I am better. I am not better. If anything I am worse. Indeed it is within the bounds of probability that I shall never be anything but a wreck,[3] for this cold is the most malignant that I've ever had and gives me no peace. I am miserable all day and at night unable to sleep. Either I am coughing or I have the feeling of being smothered.

Tell Horace that I envy him his recovery: he was always so much stronger than I. In fact, our dead mother often expressed surprise that as an infant I survived at all.

You are fortunate in being able to get to the south of France and avoid

---

[1] *Rev.*: Reverend, used as a title and form of address for certain clerics in many Christian churches

[2] *exile*: self-imposed absence from one's living place. Note the pretentious self-mockery in the tone.

[3] *wreck*: a person who is physically worn out

this terrible climate. I should like nothing better, but I dread the journey too much; nor would my straitened means, much deplenished[4] by excessive taxation, permit it. Horace has always been so richly blessed in worldly goods.

Your affectionate Brother,
Samson Spong

Mrs. Samson Spong to Mrs. Horace Spong

My Dear Grace,—Please don't write to Samson again about his condition. He much resented my telling you that he was better, although as a matter of fact he is—much better. He eats better, is more cheerful, except when he recollects that he is an invalid,[5] and sleeps well. He may not always sleep right through the night, but like all men, if he is awake five minutes he thinks it is two hours.

Yours,
Lydia

Mr. Horace Spong to the Rev. Samson Spong

Dear Samson,—Grace has given me your message about my recovery. I only wish I had earned it; but, alas! I feel anything but a convalescent. In fact, in confidence,[6] for I should not like every one to know, I am conscious of increasing weakness daily, I have even kept it a secret from Grace. There are some colds that seem to strike deeper the more you nurse them, and mine is one of them.

I am sorry for the pessimistic tone of your letter, but I feel sure that things are not so bad with you as you say. It is possible to take too gloomy a view of oneself, especially when one is weak, and I have discounted your remarks in consequence. You are a stronger man *au fond*[7] and you will shake this off very soon. I am convinced.

---

[4] *deplenished*: reduced the number or quantity of, depleted

[5] *invalid*: a person made weak or disabled by illness or injury

[6] *in confidence*: secretly, between you and me

[7] *au fond*: in essence, fundamentally

We are off to Mentone next week. It is a dreary business, but Grace likes it there, and what she likes is law with me.

Yours,

Horace

The Rev. Samson Spong to Mr. Horace Spong

Dear Horace,—I wish you wouldn't write nonsense about my being strong. I am not strong and never was. I was always delicate,[8] even before cold after cold enfeebled me, and now I am a wreck. Surely I am the best judge as to how ill I am! Now you, I consider, really are stronger, though you may not look it. Only a strong man could undertake a journey to Mentone at this time of year.

I will say good-bye, my dear brother, as it is exceedingly unlikely that you will find me here when you return in the spring.

Yours,

Samson

Miss Hilda Spong to the Rev. Samson Spong

Dear Uncle Samson,—I was very glad to hear the other day from mother that you are better. I send you a little present now as at Christmas I shall be far away in Switzerland with a Winter Sports Party. We are going to some place thousands of feet up, where skating and skiing and bob-sleighing[9] are a cert.[10] I will send you a card from there.

Your affectionate Niece,

Hilda

The Rev. Samson Spong to Mrs. Horace Spong

Dear Grace,—If you are writing to Hilda you might give her a hint that it would be kinder not to send me a card as she has undertaken to do. I feel sure it would suggest snow and be harmful to me in my present delicate

---

[8] *delicate*: frail in constitution or health

[9] *bob-sleighing*: Bob-sleigh is a vehicle with long thin strips of metal fixed to the bottom, which is used for racing downhill on ice.

[10] *cert*: an event regarded as inevitable or a certainty

state. She is a dear girl, but her letter about those Alpine heights, although meant, I am sure, in all good faith, gave me a severe shock. I have just now to be very, very careful.

Your affectionate Brother,
Samson

P.S.—Tell Horace that what he wants is more employment. It is when one is idle that one broods on one's health.[11] He should take up some hobby.

Mr. Horace Spong to the Rev. Samson Spong

My dear Samson,—I really must protest against the suggestion in your letter to Grace that I am a *malade imaginaire.*[12] Fortunately Grace and I understand one another and there is no fear of any mishap; but I can believe that there are households which might be undermined by such insinuations. So far from being idle, as you put it, I am continually busy. There is not a penny spent in this establishment,[13] indoors or out, that I am unaware of; I see all the tradesmen's books; I know exactly how much petrol the car uses from day to day; in fact, I am constantly vigilant and interested. Please do not again refer to the matter.

While on this subject, let me say that it is increasingly borne in upon[14] me that you made a terrible mistake when you gave up your living. You were far less faddy[15] about yourself when you had your duties to perform. You were also more considerate for others. Your very gloomy reference in your last letter to your imminent decease might have caused me a really serious relapse, had I not just run into Corder in our London hotel and had a talk with him about you. But from what he says you are getting along famously.

---

[11] *It is...one's health*: Cf. Mr. Horace Spong's remark in his letter to the Rev. Samson Spong: "It is possible to take too gloomy a view of oneself, especially when one is weak..."

[12] *malade imaginaire*: a person who imagines him/herself to be ill

[13] *establishment*: household hyperbolically

[14] *(be) borne in upon*: come to be realized by

[15] *faddy*: having many arbitrary and often unusual likes, fussy

My love to Lydia.

Yours,

Horace

***The Rev. Samson Spong to Richard Corder, MD*[16]**

Dear Corder,—I am sorry that after all these years we should have to part, but I must ask you for your account.[17] I cannot continue with a medical man who gossips about his patient. I was much distressed this morning to learn from my brother that you had told him I was better. Apart from the fact that I am not, I hold that a doctor's first duty is not to tell. You have greatly shaken[18] me.

I am,

Yours sincerely,

Samson Spong

Author

Edward Verrall Lucas (1868-1938) was born at Eltham and educated at University College in London. A famous journalist, Lucas contributed to many prestigious magazines such as *The Globe* and *Punch*. He held the position of assistant editor of *Punch* for years. After serving on the Board of Methuen & Company, Ltd. as an editorial adviser for some time, he became Chairman of the Company in 1925. Lucas was a celebrated versatile writer, but was chiefly renowned for his witty essays. His works include volumes of collected essays: *Fireside and Sunshine* (1906), *Old Lamps for New* (1911), *Adventures and Enthusiasms* (1920), *A Fronded Isle and Other Essays* (1927), and *Traveller's Luck* (1930).

16 *MD*: Doctor of Medicine

17 *I must...your account*: I must hold you accountable for it.

18 *shaken*: extremely upset, astonished

Seeing People Off

by Max Beerbohm

I am not good at it. To do it well seems to me one of the most difficult things in the world, and probably seems so to you, too.

To see a friend off from Waterloo to Vauxhall were easy enough. But we are never called on to perform that small feat.[1] It is only when a friend is going on a longish journey, and will be absent for a longish time, that we turn up at the railway station. The dearer the friend, and the longer the journey, and the longer the likely absence, the earlier do we turn up, and the more lamentably do we fail. Our failure is in exact ratio to the seriousness of the occasion, and to the depth of our feeling.

In a room or even on a door step, we can make the farewell quite worthily. We can express in our faces the genuine sorrow we feel. Nor do words fail us. There is no awkwardness, no restraint on either side. The thread of our intimacy has not been snapped.[2] The leave-taking is an ideal one. Why not, then leave the leave-taking at that? Always, departing friends implore us not to bother to come to the railway station next morning. Always, we are deaf to these entreaties, knowing them to be not quite sincere. The departing friends would think it very odd of us if we took them at their word.[3] Besides, they really do want to see us again. And that wish is heartily reciprocated. We duly[4] turn up. And then, oh then, what a gulf yawns![5] We stretch our arms vainly across it. We have utterly lost touch.

---

[1] *feat*: a notable act or deed, especially an act of courage, an exploit. Note the irony in the collocation "small feat."

[2] *snapped*: broken

[3] *took them at their word*: took their word at face value, believe their word

[4] *duly*: properly and in due time

[5] *yawns*: opens wide, gapes

We have nothing at all to say. We gaze at each other as dumb animals gaze at human beings. We make conversation[6]—and such conversation! We know that these friends are the friends from whom we parted overnight. They know that we have not altered. Yet, on the surface, everything is different; and the tension is such that we only long for the guard to blow his whistle and put an end to the farce.

On a cold grey morning of last week I duly turned up at Euston, to see off an old friend who was starting for America. Overnight, we had given him a farewell dinner, in which sadness was well mingled with festivity. Years probably would elapse before his return. Some of us might never see him again. Not ignoring the shadow of the future, we gaily celebrated the past. We were as thankful to have known our guest as we were grieved to lose him; and both these emotions were made manifest. It was a perfect farewell.

And now, here we were, stiff and self-conscious on the platform; and framed in the window of the railway-carriage was the face of our friend; but it was as the face of a stranger—a stranger anxious to please, an appealing[7] stranger, an awkward stranger. "Have you got everything?" asked one of us, breaking a silence. "Yes, everything," said our friend, with a pleasant nod. "Everything," he repeated, with the emphasis of an empty brain. "You'll be able to lunch on the train," said I, though the prophecy[8] had already been made more than once. "Oh, yes," he said with conviction. He added that the train went straight through to Liverpool. This fact seemed to strike us as rather odd. We exchanged glances. "Doesn't it stop at Crewe?" asked one of us. "No," said our friend, briefly. He seemed almost disagreeable.[9] There was a long pause. One of us, with a nod and a forced[10] smile at the traveller, said "Well!" The nod, the smile and the unmeaning

---

[6] *make conversation*: laboriously make small talk to avoid embarrassing silence

[7] *appealing*: pleading, begging, solicitous

[8] *prophecy*: prediction. Pay attention to the sarcasm in the tone.

[9] *disagreeable*: bad-tempered, grumpy, cranky

[10] *forced*: not spontaneous, produced under the strain of the occasion

monosyllable were returned conscientiously.[11] Another pause was broken by one of us with a fit of coughing. It was an obviously assumed[12] fit, but it served to pass the time. The bustle[13] of the platform was unabated.[14] There was no sign of the train's departure. Release[15]—ours, and our friend's,—was not yet.

My wandering eye alighted[16] on a rather portly[17] middle-aged man who was talking earnestly from the platform to a young lady at the next window but one to ours. His fine profile was vaguely[18] familiar to me. The young lady was evidently American, and he was evidently English; otherwise I should have guessed from his impressive air[19] that he was her father. I wished I could hear what he was saying. I was sure he was giving the very best advice; and the strong tenderness of his gaze was really beautiful. He seemed magnetic,[20] as he poured out his final injunctions. I could feel something of his magnetism even where I stood. And the magnetism like the profile, was vaguely familiar to me. Where had I experienced it?

In a flash[21] I remembered. The man was Hubert Le Ros. But how changed since last I saw him! That was seven or eight years ago, in the Strand. He was then as usual out of an engagement, and borrowed half a crown. It seemed a privilege to lend anything to him. He was always magnetic. And why his magnetism had never made him successful on the London stage was always a mystery to me. He was an excellent actor, and a man of sober[22] habit. But, like many others of his kind, Hubert Le

---

[11] *conscientiously*: carefully as if fulfilling a duty

[12] *assumed*: pretended, affected

[13] *bustle*: noisy activity

[14] *unabated*: sustaining original intensity or maintaining full force with no decrease

[15] *release*: liberation (from the embarrassment of having nothing more to say)

[16] *alighted*: landed, descended

[17] *portly*: rather fat, stout, corpulent

[18] *vaguely*: dimly, slightly

[19] *air*: personal bearing, manner, or mien

[20] *magnetic*: very attractive or alluring

[21] *in a flash*: all of a sudden, suddenly

[22] *sober*: not affected by alcohol, not drunk, abstinent

Ros (I do not, of course, give the actual name by which he was known) drifted speedily away into the provinces; and I, like every one else, ceased to remember him.

It was strange to see him, after all these years, here on the platform of Euston, looking so prosperous[23] and solid.[24] It was not only the flesh that he had put on, but also the clothes, that made him hard to recognize. In the old days, an imitation[25] fur coat had seemed to be as integral a part of him as were his ill-shorn lantern jaws.[26] But now his costume was a model of rich and sombre[27] moderation, drawing, not calling attention to[28] itself. He looked like a banker. Any one would have been proud to be seen off by him.

"Stand back, please!" The train was about to start, and I waved farewell to my friend. Le Ros did not stand back. He stood clasping in both hands the hands of the young American. "Stand back, sir, please!" He obeyed, but quickly darted[29] forward again to whisper some final word. I think there were tears in her eyes. There certainly were tears in his when, at length, having watched the train out of sight, he turned round. He seemed, nevertheless, delighted to see me. He asked me where I had been hiding all these years; and simultaneously repaid me the half-crown as though it had been borrowed yesterday. He linked his arm in mine, and walked with me slowly along the platform, saying with what pleasure he read my dramatic criticisms every Saturday.

I told him, in return, how much he was missed on the stage. "Ah, yes,"

---

[23] *prosperous*: well-off, successful

[24] *solid*: physically strong, dependable

[25] *imitation*: not real, artificial, synthetic

[26] *lantern jaws*: long, thin jaws, with sunken cheeks, that give the face a lean, gaunt appearance

[27] *sombre*: dark in color, conveying a feeling of deep seriousness

[28] *drawing, not calling attention to*: Pay attention to the nuance between the two verbs *draw* and *call* (attention). The word *draw* emphasizes the intrinsic attractiveness of the subject, while *call* implies the subject's demand for attention.

[29] *darted*: moved suddenly and rapidly

he said, "I never act on the stage nowadays." He laid some emphasis on the "stage," and I asked him where, then, he did act. "On the platform," he answered. "You mean," said I, "that you recite at concerts?" He smiled. "This," he whispered, striking his stick on the ground, "is the platform I mean." Had his mysterious prosperity unhinged[30] him? He looked quite sane. I begged him to be more explicit.

"I suppose," he said presently, giving me a light for the cigar which he had offered me, "you have been seeing a friend off?" I assented. He asked me what I supposed he had been doing. I said that I had watched him doing the same thing. "No," he said gravely. "That lady was not a friend of mine. I met her for the first time this morning, less than half an hour ago, here," and again he struck the platform with his stick.

I confessed that I was bewildered. He smiled. "You may," he said, "have heard of the Anglo-American Social Bureau?" I had not. He explained to me that of the thousands of Americans who annually pass through England there are many hundreds who have no English friends. In the old days they used to bring letters of introduction. But the English are so inhospitable that these letters are hardly worth the paper they are written on. "Thus," said Le Ros, "The A.A.S.B. supplies a long-felt want. Americans are a sociable people, and most of them have plenty of money to spend. The A.A.S.B. supplies them with English friends. Fifty per cent of the fees is paid over to the friends. The other fifty is retained by the A.A.S.B. I am not, alas! a director. If I were, I should be a very rich man indeed. I am only an employee. But even so I do very well. I am one of the seers-off."

Again I asked for enlightenment.[31] "Many Americans," he said, "cannot afford to keep friends in England. But they can all afford to be seen off. The fee is only five pounds (twenty-five dollars) for a single traveller; and eight

---

[30] *unhinged*: unbalanced, deranged

[31] *enlightenment*: explanation, illumination. The Enlightenment refers to a philosophical movement of the 18th century that emphasized the use of reason to reflect on previously accepted doctrines and traditions and that inspired many humanitarian reforms.

pounds (forty dollars) for a party of two or more. They send that in to the Bureau, giving the date of their departure and a description by which the seer-off can identify them on the platform. And then—well, then they are seen off."

"But is it worth it?" I exclaimed. "Of course it is worth it," said Le Ros. "It prevents them from feeling 'out of it.'[32] It earns them the respect of the guard. It saves them from being despised by their fellow-passengers—the people who are going to be on the boat. It gives them a footing for the whole voyage. Besides, it is a great pleasure in itself. You saw me seeing that young lady off. Didn't you think I did it beautifully?" "Beautifully," I admitted. "I envied you. There was I—" "Yes, I can imagine. There were you, shuffling[33] from head to foot, staring blankly at your friend, trying to make conversation. I know. That's how I used to be myself, before I studied, and went into the thing professionally. I don't say I'm perfect yet. I'm still a martyr to platform fright.[34] A railway station is the most difficult of all places to act in, as you have discovered for yourself." "But," I said with resentment, "I wasn't trying to act. I really felt!" "So did I, my boy," said Le Ros, "You can't act without feeling. What's—his—name, the Frenchman—Diderot,[35] yes—said you could; but what did he know about it? Didn't you see those tears in my eyes when the train started? I hadn't forced them. I tell you I was moved. So were you, I dare say. But you couldn't have pumped up a tear to prove it. You can't express your feelings. In other words, you can't act. At any rate," he added kindly, "not in a railway station." "Teach me!" I cried. He looked thoughtfully at me. "Well," he said at length, "the seeing-off season is practically over. Yes, I'll give you a course. I have a good many pupils on hand already; but yes," he said, consulting an ornate notebook, "I could give you an hour on Tuesdays and Fridays."

---

32 *out of it*: being left out in the cold, lonely

33 *shuffling*: shifting position because of nervousness or embarrassment

34 *I'm still...platform fright*: I still suffer from my fright of the platform. Cf. stage fright.

35 *Diderot*: (1713-84) French philosopher and writer whose major accomplishment was his work on the *Encyclopédie*, which epitomized the spirit of Enlightenment thought

His terms, I confess, are rather high.[36] But I don't grudge[37] the investment.

Author

Max Beerbohm (1872-1956), equally admired as an English essayist and caricaturist, is noted for his elegantly mannered prose, as well as the stylized humor of his drawings. He was educated at Charterhouse School and Merton College, Oxford. His works are often keenly satirical about the fraudulent and ostentatious. A contemporary of such great writers as Shaw, Wilde, and Kipling, Beerbohm was a connoisseur of the social and literary life of his time. His works include one full-length novel entitled *Zuleika Dobson* (1911); *A Christmas Garland* (1912), which was a famous work of parody; anthologies of his fine essays *Severn Men* (1919); and *And Even Now* (1920).

---

[36] *His terms,...rather high*: I confess that he charges much money for the course he gives.

[37] *grudge*: be unwilling to give or pay

Education and Discipline

by Bertrand Russell

Any serious educational theory must consist of two parts: a conception of the ends of life,[1] and a science of psychological dynamics, i.e., of the laws of mental change. Two men who differ as to the ends of life[2] cannot hope to agree about education. The educational machine, throughout Western civilization, is dominated by two ethical theories: that of Christianity, and that of nationalism. These two, when taken seriously, are incompatible, as is becoming evident in Germany. For my part, I hold that, where they differ, Christianity is preferable, but where they agree, both are mistaken. The conception which I should substitute as the purpose of education is civilization, a term which, as I meant it, has a definition which is partly individual, partly social. It consists, in the individual, of both intellectual and moral qualities: intellectually, a certain minimum of general knowledge, technical skill in one's own profession, and a habit of forming opinions on evidence; morally, of impartiality, kindliness, and a modicum of[3] self-control. I should add a quality which is neither moral nor intellectual, but perhaps physiological:[4] zest and joy of life. In communities,[5] civilization demands respect for law, justice as between man and man, purposes not involving permanent injury to any section of the human race, and intelligent adaptation of means to ends.

If these are to be the purpose of education, it is a question for the science of psychology to consider what can be done towards realising them,

---

[1] *the ends of life*: the goals of life, what one seeks to achieve in life

[2] *Two men...of life*: two men who hold different opinions about the ends of life

[3] *a modicum of*: a small quantity of (especially something desirable)

[4] *physiological*: of the body, usually as opposed to psychological

[5] *in communities*: from the social perspective

and, in particular, what degree of freedom is likely to prove most effective.

On the question of freedom in education there are at present three main schools of thought, deriving partly from differences as to ends and partly from differences in psychological theory. There are those who say that children should be completely free, however bad they may be; there are those who say they should be completely subject to authority, however good they may be; and there are those who say they should be free, but in spite of freedom they should be always good. This last party is larger than it has any logical right to be; children, like adults, will not all be virtuous if they are all free. The belief that liberty will ensure moral perfection is a relic[6] of Rousseauism, and would not survive a study of animals and babies. Those who hold this belief think that education should have no positive purpose, but should merely offer an environment suitable for spontaneous development. I cannot agree with this school, which seems to me too individualistic, and unduly[7] indifferent to the importance of knowledge. We live in communities which require cooperation, and it would be utopian[8] to expect all the necessary cooperation to result from spontaneous impulse. The existence of a large population on a limited area is only possible owing to science and technique; education must, therefore, hand on[9] the necessary minimum of these. The educators who allow most freedom are men whose success depends upon a degree of benevolence,[10] self-control, and trained intelligence which can hardly be generated where every impulse is left unchecked;[11] their merits, therefore, are not likely to be perpetuated if their methods are undiluted.[12] Education, viewed from a social standpoint,

6 *relic*: a belief that has survived from an earlier time but is now outmoded

7 *unduly*: inappropriately, excessively, overly

8 *utopian*: The word *Utopia* was first used in the book *Utopia* (1516) by Sir Thomas More. It refers to an imagined land where everything is perfect, and everyone exists in complete harmony with one another. To be utopian is to be idealistic or simply downright impractical.

9 *hand on*: pass on, impart

10 *benevolence*: goodness, kindness, generosity, compassion

11 *unchecked*: unrestrained, uncontrolled

12 *undiluted*: not moderated, not mitigated

must be something more positive than a mere opportunity for growth. It must, of course, provide this,[13] but it must also provide a mental and moral equipment which children cannot acquire entirely for themselves.

The arguments in favor of a great degree of freedom in education are derived not from man's natural goodness, but from the effects of authority, both on those who suffer it and on those who exercise it. Those who are subject to authority become either submissive[14] or rebellious, and each attitude has its drawbacks.

The submissive lose initiative,[15] both in thought and action; moreover, the anger generated by the feeling of being thwarted tends to find an outlet[16] in bullying[17] those who are weaker. That is why tyrannical institutions are self-perpetuating: what a man has suffered from his father he inflicts upon his son, and the humiliations which he remembers having endured at his public school he passes on to "natives"[18] when he becomes an empire-builder. Thus an unduly authoritative education turns the pupils into timid tyrants, incapable of either claiming or tolerating originality[19] in word or deed. The effect upon the educators is even worse: they tend to become sadistic disciplinarians, glad to inspire terror, and content to inspire nothing else. As these men represent knowledge, the pupils acquire a horror of knowledge, which, among the English upper class, is supposed to be part of human nature, but is really part of the well-grounded[20] hatred of the authoritarian pedagogue.[21]

---

[13] *this*: the opportunity for growth

[14] *submissive*: meekly obedient, passive, ready to say "yes" to the authority

[15] *lose initiative*: lose the ability to think and act using one's own judgment rather than relying on other people's orders or instructions

[16] *find an outlet*: find a way of releasing (negative) emotions

[17] *bullying*: tormenting, persecuting

[18] *natives*: citizens other than the British; local inhabitants of what used to be part of the British Empire

[19] *either claiming or tolerating originality*: either being original himself or accepting originality in others

[20] *well-grounded*: well-founded, justified

[21] *pedagogue*: a teacher, especially a strict or pedantic one

Rebels,[22] on the other hand, though they may be necessary, can hardly be just to[23] what exists. Moreover, there are many ways of rebelling, and only a small minority of these are wise. Galileo was a rebel and was wise; believers in the flat-earth theory are equally rebels, but are foolish. There is a great danger in the tendency to suppose that opposition to authority is essentially meritorious and that unconventional opinions are bound to be correct: no useful purpose is served by smashing lamp-posts or maintaining Shakespeare to be no poet.[24] Yet this excessive rebelliousness is often the effect that too much authority has on spirited pupils.[25] And when rebels become educators, they sometimes encourage defiance[26] in their pupils, for whom at the same time they are trying to produce a perfect environment, although these two aims are scarcely compatible.

What is wanted is neither submissiveness nor rebellion, but good nature, and general friendliness both to people and to new ideas. These qualities are due in part to physical causes, to which old-fashioned educators paid too little attention; but they are due still more to freedom from the feeling of baffled impotence[27] which arises when vital impulses are thwarted. If the young are to grow into friendly adults, it is necessary, in most cases, that they should feel their environment friendly. This requires that there should be a certain sympathy with the child's important desires, and not merely an attempt to use him for some abstract end such as the

---

[22] *rebels*: the rebellious ones, those who resist authority

[23] *be just to*: have an unbiased attitude

[24] *no useful...no poet*: Breaking lamp-posts and insisting that Shakespeare is not a poet are equally "rebellious" or "unconventional" in a way, but neither makes any real sense or is less foolish than the flat-earth theory believers.

[25] *spirited pupils*: vigorous pupils, those who are full of life and easy to become overly rebellious under too much authority

[26] *defiance*: resistance, opposition, confrontation

[27] *freedom from...baffled impotence*: If a child is freed from the confused feeling of weakness and worthlessness, he is lucky enough to acquire the qualities like "good nature" and "general friendliness both to people and to new ideas."

glory of God or the greatness of one's country. And, in teaching, every attempt should be made to cause the pupil to feel that it is worth his while to know what is being taught—at least when this is true. When the pupil cooperates willingly, he learns twice as fast and with half the fatigue. All these are valid[28] reasons for a very great degree of freedom.

It is easy, however, to carry the argument too far.[29] It is not desirable that children, in avoiding the vices[30] of the slave, should acquire those of the aristocrat. Consideration for others, not only in great matters, but also in little everyday things, is an essential element in civilization, without which social life would be intolerable. I am not thinking of mere forms of politeness, such as saying "please" and "thank you": formal manners are most fully developed among barbarians, and diminish with every advance in culture. I am thinking rather of willingness to take a fair share of necessary work, to be obliging[31] in small ways that save trouble on the balance.[32] Sanity itself is a form of politeness and it is not desirable to give a child a sense of omnipotence, or a belief that adults exist only to minister to[33] the pleasures of the young. And those who disapprove of the existence of the idle rich are hardly consistent if they bring up their children without any sense that work is necessary, and without the habits that make continuous application[34] possible.

There is another consideration to which some advocates of freedom attach too little importance. In a community of children which is left without adult interference there is a tyranny of the stronger, which is likely to be far more brutal than most adult tyranny. If two children of two or three years old are left to play together, they will, after a few fights, discover which is

---

28 *valid*: well-grounded, justifiable

29 *to carry...too far*: to overstrain the argument, to push the argument to extremes

30 *vices*: serious moral faults

31 *obliging*: willing and eager to be helpful

32 *on the balance*: on the whole

33 *minister to*: attend to (the needs of another), answer, serve

34 *continuous application*: continuous hard work, sustained effort

bound to be the victor,[35] and the other will then become a slave. Where the number of children is larger, one or two acquire complete mastery, and the others have far less liberty than they would have if the adults interfered to protect the weaker and less pugnacious. Consideration for others does not, with most children, arise spontaneously, but has to be taught, and can hardly be taught except by the exercise of authority. This is perhaps the most important argument against the abdication of the adults.[36]

I do not think that educators have yet solved the problem of combining the desirable forms of freedom with the necessary minimum of moral training. The right solution, it must be admitted, is often made impossible by parents before the child is brought to an enlightened school.[37] Just as psychoanalysts, from their clinical experience, conclude that we are all mad, so the authorities in modern schools, from their contact with pupils whose parents have made them unmanageable, are disposed to[38] conclude that all children are "difficult" and all parents utterly foolish. Children who have been driven wild by parental tyranny (which often takes the form of solicitous affection) may require a longer or shorter period of complete liberty before they can view any adult without suspicion. But children who have been sensibly handled at home can bear to be checked in minor ways, so long as they feel that they are being helped in the ways that they themselves regard as important. Adults who like children, and are not reduced to a condition of nervous exhaustion by their company, can achieve a great deal in the way of discipline without ceasing to be regarded with friendly feelings by their pupils.

I think modern educational theorists are inclined to attach too much importance to the negative virtue of not interfering with children, and too little to the positive merit of enjoying their company. If you have the sort of liking for children that many people have for horses or dogs, they will

---

35 *victor*: winner, conqueror

36 *the abdication of the adults*: the refusal of adults to take the responsibility or to wield the power

37 *an enlightened school*: a school having a rational, modern, and well-informed outlook

38 *are disposed to*: are inclined to, tend to

be apt to respond to your suggestions, and to accept prohibitions, perhaps with some good-humoured[39] grumbling,[40] but without resentment.[41] It is no use to have the sort of liking that consists in regarding them as a field for valuable social endeavour,[42] or—what amounts to the same thing—as an outlet for power-impulses. No child will be grateful for an interest in him that springs from the thought that he will have a vote to be secured for your party[43] or a body to be sacrificed to king and country. The desirable sort of interest is that which consists in spontaneous pleasure in the presence of children, without any ulterior purpose.[44] Teachers who have this quality will seldom need to interfere with children's freedom, but will be able to do so, when necessary, without causing psychological damage.

Unfortunately, it is utterly impossible for overworked teachers to preserve an instinctive liking for children; they are bound to come to feel towards them as the proverbial[45] confectioner's apprentice[46] does toward macaroons.[47] I do not think that education ought to be any one's whole profession: it should be undertaken for at most two hours a day by people whose remaining hours are spent away with children. The society of the young is fatiguing, especially when strict discipline is avoided. Fatigue, in the end, produces irritation, which is likely to express itself somehow,[48] whatever

---

[39] *good-humoured*: good-tempered, genial

[40] *grumbling*: complaining, whining

[41] *resentment*: bitterness, indignation

[42] *valuable social endeavour*: This refers to the above-mentioned "abstract end such as the glory of God or the greatness of one's country."

[43] *he will...your party*: He will be made to vote for your party.

[44] *ulterior purpose*: purpose beyond what is obvious, concealed purpose, usually rather selfish or dishonest

[45] *proverbial*: well-known to a lot of people

[46] *confectioner's apprentice*: 糖果店学徒工

[47] *macaroons*: 杏仁饼干

[48] *to express itself somehow*: to find an outlet in this or that way

theories the harassed[49] teacher may have taught himself or herself to believe. The necessary friendliness cannot be preserved by self-control alone. But where it exists, it should be unnecessary to have rules in advance as to how "naughty" children are to be treated, since impulse is likely to lead to the right decision, and almost any decision will be right if the child feels that you like him. No rules, however wise, are a substitute for affection and tact.[50]

Author

Bertrand Russell (1872-1970) is a world-famous British philosopher, logician, and writer. He wrote voluminously on philosophy, logic, ethics, and politics and was awarded the Nobel Prize in literature in 1950.

The crisis of the First World War turned his attention from philosophy to ethics and politics, and much of his later writing deals exclusively, and often controversially, with social problems. His social criticism is always constructive, though it is often combined with a challenging wit and humour. From 1927 to 1932 he and his second wife, Dora Winifred Black, ran an experimental school for children, and Russell's views on education are put forward in *On Education* (1926) and *Education and the Social Order* (1932).

[49] *harassed*: stressed, hard-pressed, careworn

[50] *tact*: skill and sensitivity in dealing with others or with difficult issues

Notes on the English Character

by E. M. Forster

First note. I had better let the cat out of the bag[1] at once and record my opinion that the character of the English is essentially middle class. There is a sound historical reason for this, for, since the end of the eighteenth century, the middle classes have been the dominant force in our community. They gained wealth by the Industrial Revolution, political power by the Reform Bill of 1832;[2] they are connected with the rise and organisation of the British Empire; they are responsible for the literature of the nineteenth century. Solidity,[3] caution, integrity, efficiency. Lack of imagination, hypocrisy. These qualities characterise the middle classes in every country, but in England they are national characteristics also, because only in England have the middle classes been in power for one hundred and fifty years. Napoleon, in his rude way, called us "a nation of shopkeepers." We prefer to call ourselves "a great commercial nation"—it sounds more dignified—but the two phrases amount to the same. Of course there are other classes: there is an aristocracy, there are the poor. But it is on the middle classes that the eye of the critic rests—just as it rests on the poor in Russia and on the aristocracy in Japan. Russia is symbolised by the peasant or by the factory worker; Japan by the samurai;[4] the national figure of England is Mr. Bull[5]

---

1 *let the...the bag*: reveal the secret, come straight to the point

2 *the Reform Bill of 1832*: 1st of a series of 19th and 20th century enactments of the British Parliament restricting the power of the House of Lords and redistributing lawmakers' seats

3 *solidity*: soundness of finances

4 *samurai*: the Japanese feudal military aristocracy

5 *Mr. Bull*: a character created by Dr. John Arbuthnot in 1712 to represent Englishness

with his top hat,[6] his comfortable clothes, his substantial stomach, and his substantial balance at the bank. Saint George may caper[7] on banners and in the speeches of politicians,[8] but it is John Bull who delivers the goods. And even Saint George—if Gibbon[9] is correct—wore a top hat once; he was an army contractor and supplied indifferent[10] bacon. It all amounts to the same in the end.

Second Note. Just as the heart of England is the middle classes, so the heart of the middle classes is the public school system. This extraordinary institution is local. It does not even exist all over the British Isles. It is unknown in Ireland, almost unknown in Scotland (countries excluded from my survey), and though it may inspire other great institutions—Aligarh,[11] for example, and some of the schools in the United States—it remains unique, because it was created by the Anglo-Saxon middle classes, and can flourish only where they flourish. How perfectly it expresses their character—far better for instance, than does the university, into which social and spiritual complexities have already entered. With its boarding-houses, its compulsory games, its system of prefects[12] and fagging,[13] its insistence on good form and on *esprit de corps*,[14] it produces a type whose

---

[6] *top hat*: a man's hat having a narrow brim and a tall cylindrical crown, usually made of silk; symbol of wealth

[7] *caper*: skip or dance about in a lively or playful way

[8] *Saint George...of politicians*: Saint George may seem to be the image that figures more prominently in festive or political contexts.

[9] *Gibbon*: Edward (1737-94) British historian, renowned for his classic work *The History of the Decline and Fall of the Roman Empire* (1776-88)

[10] *indifferent*: neither good nor bad, mediocre

[11] *Aligarh*: a city in north-central India, noted for its university, which was established in 1875 as Anglo-Oriental College

[12] *prefects*: senior pupils who are authorized to enforce discipline

[13] *fagging*: (a boy at a British public school) performing menial tasks for an older boy

[14] *esprit de corps*: a common spirit of pride and mutual loyalty shared by members of a group; team spirit

weight is out of all proportion to its numbers.[15]

On leaving his school, the boy either sets to work at once—goes into the army or into business, or emigrates—or else proceeds to the university, and after three or four years there enters some other profession—becomes a barrister, doctor, civil servant, schoolmaster, or journalist. (If through some mishap he does not become a manual worker or an artist.) In all these careers his education, or the absence of it, influences him. Its memories influence him also. Many men look back on their school days as the happiest of their lives. They remember with regret that golden time when life, though hard, was not yet complex, when they all worked together and played together and thought together, so far as they thought at all; when they were taught that school is the world in miniature[16] and believed that no one can love his country who does not love his school. And they prolong that time as best they can by joining their Old Boys' society:[17] indeed, some of them remain Old Boys and nothing else for the rest of their lives. They attribute all good to the school. They worship it. They quote the remark that "The battle of Waterloo was won on the playing fields of Eton."[18] It is nothing to them that the remark is inapplicable historically and was never made by the Duke of Wellington, and that the Duke of Wellington was an Irishman. They go on quoting it because it expresses their sentiments; they feel that if the Duke of Wellington didn't make it he ought to have, and if he wasn't an Englishman he ought to have been. And they go forth into a world that is not entirely composed of public-school men or even of Anglo-Saxons, but of men who are as various as the sands of the sea; into a world of whose richness and subtlety they have no conception. They go forth into it with well-developed bodies, fairly developed minds, and undeveloped

---

[15] *it produces...its numbers*: Though the public school is small in number, the students it produces are disproportionately influential in England.

[16] *in miniature*: in a small scale, in epitome

[17] *Old Boys' society*: an informal network through which people often use their positions of influence to help others who went to the same school as they did

[18] *Eton*: the largest and most famous of England's public schools, founded by Henry VI in 1440

hearts. And it is this undeveloped heart that is largely responsible for the difficulties of Englishmen abroad. An undeveloped heart—not a cold one. The difference is important, and on it my next note will be based.

For it is not that the Englishman can't feel—it is that he is afraid to feel. He has been taught at his public school that feeling is bad form. He must not express great joy or sorrow, or even open his mouth too wide when he talks—his pipe might fall out if he did. He must bottle up[19] his emotions, or let them out only on a very special occasion.

Once upon a time (this is an anecdote) I went for a week's holiday on the Continent with an Indian friend. We both enjoyed ourselves and were sorry when the week was over, but on parting our behaviour was absolutely different. He was plunged[20] in despair.

He felt that because the holiday was over all happiness was over until the world ended. He could not express his sorrow too much. But in me the Englishman came out strong. I reflected that we should meet again in a month or two, and could write in the interval if we had anything to say; and under these circumstances I could not see what there was to make a fuss about. It wasn't as if we were parting forever or dying. "Buck up,"[21] I said, "do buck up." He refused to buck up, and I left him plunged in gloom.

The conclusion of the anecdote is even more instructive. For when we met the next month our conversation threw a good deal of light on the English character. I began by scolding my friend. I told him that he had been wrong to feel and display so much emotion upon so slight an occasion; that it was inappropriate. The word "inappropriate" roused him to fury. "What?" he cried. "Do you measure out your emotions as if they were potatoes?" I did not like the simile of the potatoes, but after a moment's reflection I said: "Yes, I do; and what's more, I think I ought to. A small occasion demands a little emotion just as a large occasion demands a great one. I would like my emotions to be appropriate. This may be measuring

---

[19] *bottle up*: repress or conceal, not let out

[20] *plunged*: thrown suddenly, violently, or deeply into a specified state or situation

[21] *Buck up*: Cheer up

them like potatoes, but it is better than slopping them about like water from a pail, which is what you did." He did not like the simile of the pail. "If those are your opinions, they part us forever," he cried, and left the room. Returning immediately, he added: "No—but your whole attitude toward emotion is wrong. Emotion has nothing to do with appropriateness. It matters only that it shall be sincere. I happened to feel deeply. I showed it. It doesn't matter whether I ought to have felt deeply or not."

This remark impressed me very much. Yet I could not agree with it, and said that I valued emotion as much as he did, but used it differently; if I poured it out on small occasions I was afraid of having none left for the great ones, and of being bankrupt at the crises of life. Note the word "bankrupt." I spoke as a member of a prudent middle-class nation, always anxious to meet my liabilities,[22] but my friend spoke as an Oriental, and the Oriental has behind him a tradition, not of middle-class prudence but of kingly munificence and splendour. He feels his resources are endless, just as John Bull feels his are finite. As regards material resources, the Oriental is clearly unwise. Money isn't endless. If we spend or give away all the money we have, we haven't any more, and must take the consequences,[23] which are frequently unpleasant. But, as regards the resources of the spirit, he may be right. The emotions may be endless. The more we express them, the more we may have to express.

True love in this differs from gold and clay,
That to divide is not to take away.

Says Shelley. Shelley, at all events, believes that the wealth of the spirit is endless; that we may express it copiously, passionately, and always; that we can never feel sorrow or joy too acutely.

In the above anecdote, I have figured as a typical Englishman. I will now descend from that dizzy and somewhat unfamiliar height, and return to my business of note-taking. A note on the slowness of the English

---

22 *liabilities*: the financial obligations entered in the balance sheet of a business enterprise

23 *take the consequences*: take the responsibilities; reap as what one has sown

character. The Englishman appears to be cold and unemotional because he is really slow. When an event happens, he may understand it quickly enough with his mind, but he takes quite a while to feel it. Once upon a time a coach,[24] containing some Englishmen and some Frenchmen, was driving over the Alps. The horses ran away, and as they were dashing across a bridge the coach caught on the stonework, tottered, and nearly fell into the ravine below. The Frenchmen were frantic with terror: they screamed and gesticulated and flung themselves about, as Frenchmen would. The Englishmen sat quite calm. An hour later, the coach drew up[25] at an inn to change horses, and by that time the situations were exactly reversed. The Frenchmen had forgotten all about the danger, and were chattering gaily; the Englishmen had just begun to feel it, and one had a nervous breakdown and was obliged to go to bed. We have here a clear physical difference between the two races—a difference that goes deep into character. The Frenchmen responded at once; the Englishmen responded in time. They were slow and they were also practical. Their instinct forbade them to throw themselves about in the coach, because it was more likely to tip over if they did. They had this extraordinary appreciation of fact that we shall notice again and again. When a disaster comes, the English instinct is to do what can be done first, and to postpone the feeling as long as possible. Hence they are splendid at emergencies. No doubt they are brave—no one will deny that—bravery is partly an affair of the nerves, and the English nervous system is well equipped for meeting physical emergency.

It acts promptly and feels slowly. Such a combination is fruitful, and anyone who possesses it has gone a long way toward being brave. And when the action is over, then the Englishman can feel.

There is one more consideration—a most important one. If the English nature is cold, how is it that it has produced a great literature and a literature that is particularly great in poetry? Judged by its prose, English literature would not stand in the first rank. It is its poetry that raises it to the level

---

[24] *coach*: a large, closed, four-wheeled carriage

[25] *draw up*: stop, pull over

of Greek, Persian, or French. And yet the English are supposed to be so unpoetical. How is this? The nation that produced the Elizabethan drama and the Lake Poets[26] cannot be a cold, unpoetical nation. We can't get fire out of ice. Since literature always rests upon national character, there must be in the English nature hidden springs of fire to produce the fire we see. The warm sympathy, the romance, the imagination, that we look for in Englishmen whom we meet, and too often vainly look for, must exist in the nation as a whole, or we could not have this outburst[27] of national song. An undeveloped heart—not a cold one.

The trouble is that the English nature is not at all easy to understand. It has a great air of simplicity, it advertises itself as simple, but the more we consider it, the greater the problems we shall encounter. People talk of the mysterious East, but the West also is mysterious. It has depths that do not reveal themselves at the first gaze. We know what the sea looks like from a distance: it is of one colour, and level, and obviously cannot contain such creatures as fish. But if we look into the sea over the edge of a boat, we see a dozen colours, and depth below depth, and fish swimming in them. That sea is the English character—apparently imperturbable and even. These depths and the colours are the English romanticism and the English sensitiveness—we do not expect to find such things, but they exist. And—to continue my metaphor—the fish are the English emotions, which are always trying to get up to the surface, but don't quite know how. For the most part we see them moving far below, distorted and obscure. Now and then they succeed and we exclaim, "Why, the Englishman has emotions! He actually can feel!" And occasionally we see that beautiful creature the flying fish, which rises out of the water altogether into the air and the sunlight. English literature is a flying fish. It is a sample of the life that goes on day after day beneath the surface; it is a proof that beauty and emotion exist in the salt, inhospitable sea.

---

26 *Lake Poets*: also Lake School, the poets, i.e., Samuel Taylor Coleridge, Robert Southey, and William Wordsworth, who lived in and were inspired by the Lake District

27 *outburst*: a sudden, violent display of emotion

And now let's get back to *terra firma*.[28] The Englishman's attitude toward criticism will give us another starting point. He is not annoyed by criticism. He listens or not as the case may be, smiles and passes on, saying, "Oh, the fellow's jealous;" "Oh, I'm used to Bernard Shaw;[29] monkey tricks[30] don't hurt me." It never occurs to him that the fellow may be accurate as well as jealous, and that he might do well to take the criticism to heart and profit by it. It never strikes him—except as a form of words—that he is capable of improvement; his self-complacency is abysmal. Other nations, both Oriental and European, have an uneasy feeling that they are not quite perfect. In consequence they resent criticism. It hurts them; and their snappy answers often mask a determination to improve themselves. Not so the Englishman. He has no uneasy feeling. Let the critics bark. And the "tolerant humourous attitude" with which he confronts them is not really humourous, because it is bounded by the titter[31] and the guffaw.[32]

Turn over the pages of *Punch*.[33] There is neither wit, laughter, nor satire[34] in our national jester—only the snigger[35] of a suburban householder who can understand nothing that does not resemble himself. Week after week, under Mr. Punch's supervision, a man falls off his horse, or a colonel misses a golf ball, or a little girl makes a mistake in her prayers. Week after week ladies show not too much of their legs, foreigners are deprecated, originality condemned. Week after week a bricklayer does not do as much work as he ought and a futurist does more than he need. It is all supposed to be so good-tempered and clean; it is also supposed to be funny. It is actually

28 *terra firma*: solid ground

29 *Bernard Shaw*: George (1856-1950), Irish dramatist and writer. His best-known plays combine comedy with a questioning of conventional morality and thought; they include *Man and Superman* (1903), *Pygmalion* (1913), and *St. Joan* (1924). Shaw was also an active member of the Fabian Society. He won the Nobel Prize in literature in 1925.

30 *monkey tricks*: mischievous behavior

31 *titter*: laughter in a restrained way, giggle

32 *guffaw*: a hearty, boisterous burst of laughter

33 *Punch*: a famous magazine established in England in 1841, now defunct

34 *satire*: irony or sarcasm used to attack or expose folly, vice, or stupidity

35 *snigger*: laugh in a half-suppressed, typically scornful way

an outstanding example of our attitude toward criticism: the middle-class Englishman, with a smile on his clean-shaven lips, is engaged in admiring himself and ignoring the rest of mankind. If, in those colourless pages, he came across anything that really was funny—a drawing by Max Beerbohm,[36] for instance—his smile would disappear, and he would say to himself, "The fellow's a bit of a crank,"[37] and pass on.

This particular attitude reveals such insensitiveness as to suggest a more serious charge: is the Englishman altogether indifferent to the things of the spirit? Let us glance for a moment at his religion—not, indeed, at his theology, which would not merit[38] inspection, but at the action on his daily life of his belief in the unseen. Here again his attitude is practical. But an innate decency comes out: he is thinking of others rather than of himself. Right conduct is his aim. He asks of his religion that it shall make him a better man in daily life: that he shall be more kind, more just, more merciful, more desirous to fight what is evil and to protect what is good. No one could call this a low conception. It is, as far as it goes, a spiritual one. Yet—and this seems to be typical of the race—it is only half the religious idea. Religion is more than an ethical code with a divine sanction.[39] It is also a means through which man may get into direct connection with the divine, and, judging by history, few Englishmen have succeeded in doing this. We have produced no series of prophets, as has Judaism or Islam. We have not even produced a Joan of Arc,[40] or a Savonarola.[41] We have produced few saints. In Germany the Reformation was due to the passionate

---

[36] *Max Beerbohm*: See the essay "Seeing People Off."

[37] *crank*: a strange, bad-tempered person

[38] *merit*: deserve, warrant

[39] *sanction*: a consideration, an influence, or a principle that dictates an ethical choice

[40] *Joan of Arc*: (1412-31) French military leader and heroine. Inspired and directed by religious visions, she organized the French resistance that forced the English to end their siege of Orléans (1429). Captured and sold to the English by the Burgundians (1430), she was later tried for heresy and sorcery and was burned at the stake in Rouen. She was canonized in 1920.

[41] *Savonarola*: Girolamo (1452-98), Italian reformer. A Dominican friar, he gained a vast popular following and drove the Medici family out of Florence in 1494. He was later excommunicated and executed for criticizing Pope Alexander VI.

conviction of Luther. In England it was due to palace intrigue. We can show a steady level of piety, a fixed determination to live decently according to our lights—little more.

Well, it is something. It clears us of the charge of being an unspiritual nation. That facile contrast between the spiritual East and the materialistic West can be pushed too far. The West also is spiritual. Only it expresses its belief, not in fasting[42] and visions, not in prophetic rapture, but in the daily round, the common task. An incomplete expression, if you like. I agree. But the argument underlying these scattered notes is that the Englishman is an incomplete person. Not a cold or an unspiritual one. But undeveloped, incomplete.

I have suggested earlier that the English are sometimes hypocrites, and it is not my duty to develop this rather painful subject. Hypocrisy is the prime charge that is always brought against us. The Germans are called brutal, the Spanish cruel, the Americans superficial, and so on; but we are *perfide Albion*,[43] the island of hypocrites, the people who have built up an Empire with a Bible in one hand, a pistol in the other and financial concessions[44] in both pockets. Is the charge true? I think it is; but what we mean by hypocrisy? Do we mean conscious deceit? Well, the English are comparatively guiltless of this; they have little of the Renaissance villain about them. Do we mean unconscious deceit? Muddle-headedness? Of this I believe them to be guilty. When an Englishman has been led into a course of wrong action, he has nearly always begun by muddling himself. A public-school education does not make for mental clearness, and he possesses to a very high degree the power of confusing his own mind. How does it work in the domain of conduct?

Jane Austen[45] may seem an odd authority to cite, but Jane Austen has,

---

[42] *fasting*: abstaining from all or some kinds of food or drink

[43] *perfide Albion*: Latin name for "treacherous England," often used poetically

[44] *concessions*: the privileges of exercising jurisdiction or maintaining a subsidiary business within certain premises

[45] *Jane Austen*: see Page 8, Note 44

within her limits, a marvelous insight into the English mind. Her range is limited, her characters never attempt any of the more scarlet[46] sins. But she has a merciless eye for questions of conduct, and the classical example of two English people muddling themselves before they embark upon a wrong course of action is to be found in the opening chapters of *Sense and Sensibility*. Old Mr. Dashwood has just died. He has been twice married. By his first marriage he has a son, John; by his second marriage three daughters. The son is well off; the young ladies and their mother—for Mr. Dashwood's second wife survives him—are badly off. He has called his son to his death-bed and has solemnly adjured[47] him to provide for the second family. Much moved, the young man promises, and mentally decides to give each of his sisters a thousand pounds: and then the comedy begins. For he announces his generous intention to his wife, and Mrs. John Dashwood by no means approves of depriving their own little boy of so large a sum. The thousand pounds are accordingly reduced to five hundred. But even this seems rather much. Might not an annuity[48] to the stepmother be less of a wrench?[49] Yes—but though less of a wrench it might be more of a drain, for "she is very stout[50] and healthy, and scarcely forty." An occasional present of fifty pounds will be better, "and will, I think, be amply discharging my promise to my father." Or, better still, an occasional present of fish. And in the end nothing is done, nothing; the four impecunious ladies are not even helped in the moving of their furniture.

Well, are the John Dashwoods hypocrites? It depends upon our definition of hypocrisy. The young man could not see his evil impulses as they gathered force and gained on him.[51] And even his wife, though a worse character, is also self-deceived. She reflects that old Mr. Dashwood may have

---

[46] *scarlet*: flagrantly immoral or unchaste

[47] *adjured*: appealed to, entreated earnestly

[48] *annuity*: the annual payment of an allowance or income

[49] *wrench*: a distortion, a feeling of unhappiness or distress

[50] *stout*: strong in body, sturdy

[51] *gained on him*: took the upper hand of him, gripped him

been out of his mind at his death. She thinks of her own little boy—and surely a mother ought to think of her own child. She has muddled herself so completely that in one sentence she can refuse the ladies the income that would enable them to keep a carriage and in the next can say that they will not be keeping a carriage and so will have no expenses. No doubt men and women in other lands can muddle themselves, too, yet the state of mind of Mr. and Mrs. John Dashwood seems to me typical of England. They are slow—they take time even to do wrong; whereas people in other lands do wrong quickly.

There are national faults as there are national diseases, and perhaps one can draw a parallel between them. It has always impressed me that the national diseases of England should be cancer and consumption—slow, insidious, pretending to be something else; while the diseases proper to the South[52] should be cholera and plague, which strike at a man when he is perfectly well and may leave him a corpse by evening. Mr. and Mrs. John Dashwood are moral consumptives. They collapse gradually without realising what the disease is. There is nothing dramatic or violent about their sin. You cannot call them villains.

Here is the place to glance at some of the other charges that have been brought against the English as a nation. They have, for instance, been accused of treachery, cruelty, and fanaticism. In these charges I have never been able to see the least point, because treachery and cruelty are conscious sins. The man knows he is doing wrong, and does it deliberately, like Tartuffe[53] or Iago.[54] He betrays his friend because he wishes to. He tortures his prisoners because he enjoys seeing the blood flow. He worships the Devil because he prefers evil to good. From villainies such as these the average Englishman is free.[55] His character, which prevents his rising to certain heights, also

---

[52] *the South*: the Southern Hemisphere

[53] *Tartuffe*: the name of the protagonist, a religious hypocrite, in Molière's *Tartuffe* (1664)

[54] *Iago*: the name of the evil character in Shakespeare's tragedy *Othello*

[55] *From villainies...is free*: The average Englishman should not be charged with villainies such as these.

prevents him from sinking to these depths. Because he doesn't produce mystics[56] he doesn't produce villains either; he gives the world no prophets, but no anarchists, no fanatics—religious or political.

Of course there are cruel and treacherous people in England—one has only to look at the police courts—and examples of public infamy can be found, such as the Amritsar massacre.[57] But one does not look at the police courts or the military mind to find the soul of any nation; and the more English people one meets the more convinced one becomes that the charges as a whole are untrue. Yet foreign critics often make them. Why? Partly because they are annoyed with certain genuine defects in the English character, and in their irritation throw in cruelty in order to make the problem simpler. Moral indignation is always agreeable, but nearly always misplaced. It is indulged in both by the English and by the critics of the English. They all find it great fun. The drawback is that while they are amusing themselves the world becomes neither wiser nor better.

The main point of these notes is that the English character is incomplete. No national character is complete. We have to look for some qualities in one part of the world and others in another. But the English character is incomplete in a way that is particularly annoying to the foreign observer. It has a bad surface—self-complacent, unsympathetic, and reserved. There is plenty of emotion further down, but it never gets used. There is plenty of brain power, but it is more often used to confirm prejudices than to dispel them.[58] With such an equipment[59] the Englishman cannot be popular. Only I would repeat: there is little vice in him and no real coldness. It is the machinery[60] that is wrong.

---

[56] *mystic*: a person who practices or believes in mysticism or a given form of mysticism

[57] *the Amritsar massacre*: Amritsar is a city in northwest India near the Pakistan border. In the Amritsar massacre on April 13, 1919, hundreds of Indian nationalists were killed by British-led troops.

[58] *dispel them*: remove the prejudices

[59] *equipment*: the qualities or traits that make up the mental and emotional resources of an individual

[60] *machinery*: mechanism, workings of the structure of the social and educational systems

I hope and believe myself that in the next twenty years we shall see a great change, and that the national character will alter into something that is less unique but more lovable. The supremacy of the middle classes is probably ending. What new element the working classes will introduce one cannot say, but at all events they will not have been educated at public schools. And whether these notes praise or blame the English character—that is only incidental. They are the notes of a student who is trying to get at the truth and would value the assistance of others. I believe myself that the truth is great and that it shall prevail.[61] I have no faith in official caution and reticence. The cats are all out of their bags, and diplomacy cannot recall them. The nations must understand one another and quickly; and without the interposition of their governments, for the shrinkage of the globe is throwing them into one another's arms. To that understanding these notes are a feeble contribution—notes on the English character as it has struck a novelist.

Author

Edward Morgan Forster (1879-1970), English modern writer most renowned for his novels. Forster was born in London and educated at Tonbridge School, which he attended as a day boy, and King's College, Cambridge. His most celebrated novels include: *Where Angels Fear to Tread* (1905), *The Longest Journey* (1907), *A Room with a View* (1908), *Howards End* (1910), and *A Passage to India* (1924). His last novel *Maurice*, a study of a homosexual's self-discovery, was published posthumously in 1971. In his later writing career, Forster devoted himself largely to essays and broadcasts. *Aspects of the Novel*

[61] *prevail*: be greater in strength or influence, triumph

(1927) is Forster's work of literary criticism. Forster is adept at portraying middle-class English people, with all their ingrained attitudes and prejudices, in settings where their businesslike expedients may prove particularly inadequate to deal with the depths of a human situation. Forster is noted for his understated style when commenting on society, but at his best, his works scintillate with irony, humor and shrewdness.

Once More to the Lake

by E. B. White

One summer, along about 1904, my father rented a camp on a lake in Maine[1] and took us all there for the month of August. We all got ringworm from some kittens and had to rub Pond's Extract[2] on our arms and legs night and morning, and my father rolled over in a canoe with all his clothes on; but outside of that[3] the vacation was a success and from then on none of us ever thought there was any place in the world like that lake in Maine. We returned summer after summer—always on August 1st for one month. I have since become a salt-water man,[4] but sometimes in summer there are days when the restlessness of the tides and the fearful cold of the sea water and the incessant wind which blows across the afternoon and into the evening make me wish for the placidity of a lake in the woods. A few weeks ago this feeling got so strong I bought myself a couple of bass hooks and a spinner and returned to the lake where we used to go, for a week's fishing and to revisit old haunts.

I took along my son, who had never had any fresh water up his nose and who had seen lily pads only from train windows. On the journey over to the lake I began to wonder what it would be like. I wondered how time would have marred this unique, this holy spot—the coves and streams, the hills that the sun set behind, the camps and the paths behind the camps. I was sure that the tarred road would have found it out and I wondered in what other ways it would be desolated. It is strange how much you can remember about places like that once you allow your mind to return into

---

1 *Maine*: a state in the northeast of the US

2 *Pond's Extract*: a product of Pond's company that could heal small cuts and other ailments

3 *outside of that*: except for that

4 *a salt-water man*: a person related to, or located near salty water or the sea

the grooves which lead back. You remember one thing, and that suddenly reminds you of another thing. I guess I remembered clearest of all the early mornings, when the lake was cool and motionless, remembered how the bedroom smelled of the lumber it was made of and of the wet woods whose scent entered through the screen. The partitions in the camp were thin and did not extend clear to the top of the rooms, and as I was always the first up I would dress softly so as not to wake the others, and sneak out into the sweet outdoors and start out in the canoe, keeping close along the shore in the long shadows of the pines. I remembered being very careful never to rub my paddle against the gunwale for fear of disturbing the stillness of the cathedral.

The lake had never been what you would call a wild lake. There were cottages sprinkled around the shores, and it was in farming although the shores of the lake were quite heavily wooded. Some of the cottages were owned by nearby farmers, and you would live at the shore and eat your meals at the farmhouse. That's what our family did. But although it wasn't wild, it was a fairly large and undisturbed lake and there were places in it which, to a child at least, seemed infinitely remote and primeval.[5]

I was right about the tar: it led to within half a mile of the shore. But when I got back there, with my boy, and we settled into a camp near a farmhouse and into the kind of summertime I had known, I could tell that it was going to be pretty much the same as it had been before—I knew it, lying in bed the first morning, smelling the bedroom, and hearing the boy sneak quietly out and go off along the shore in a boat. I began to sustain the illusion that he was I,[6] and therefore, by simple transposition, that I was my father. This sensation persisted, kept cropping up[7] all the time we were there. It was not an entirely new feeling, but in this setting it grew much stronger. I seemed to be living a dual existence. I would be in the middle of some simple act, I would be picking up a bait box or laying down a table

---

5 *primeval*: very ancient

6 *I*: Today, people are more likely to use "me" instead.

7 *cropping up*: happening or appearing unexpectedly

fork, or I would be saying something, and suddenly it would be not I but my father who was saying the words or making the gesture. It gave me a creepy[8] sensation.

We went fishing the first morning. I felt the same damp moss covering the worms in the bait can, and saw the dragonfly alight on the tip of my rod as it hovered a few inches from the surface of the water. It was the arrival of this fly that convinced me beyond any doubt that everything was as it always had been, that the years were a mirage and there had been no years. The small waves were the same, chucking the rowboat under the chin[9] as we fished at anchor,[10] and the boat was the same boat, the same color green and the ribs broken in the same places, and under the floor-boards the same freshwater leavings and debris—the dead hellgrammite, the wisps of moss, the rusty discarded fishhook, the dried blood from yesterday's catch.[11] We stared silently at the tips of our rods, at the dragonflies that came and went. I lowered the tip of mine into the water, tentatively, pensively dislodging the fly, which darted two feet away, poised, darted two feet back, and came to rest again a little farther up the rod. There had been no years between the ducking[12] of this dragonfly and the other one—the one that was part of memory. I looked at the boy, who was silently watching his fly, and it was my hands that held his rod, my eyes watching. I felt dizzy and didn't know which rod I was at the end of.

We caught two bass, hauling them in briskly as though they were mackerel, pulling them over the side of the boat in a businesslike manner without any landing net, and stunning them with a blow on the back of the head. When we got back for a swim before lunch, the lake was exactly where we had left it, the same number of inches from the dock, and there was only the merest suggestion of a breeze. This seemed an utterly enchanted sea,

---

8 *creepy*: making you feel nervous and scared

9 *chucking the...the chin*: touching or stroking the rowboat lovingly or playfully

10 *at anchor*: where the rowboat was moored by the anchor

11 *catch*: the fish that were caught

12 *ducking*: moving in order to evade

this lake you could leave to its own devices[13] for a few hours and come back to, and find that it had not stirred, this constant and trustworthy body of water. In the shallows, the dark, water-soaked sticks and twigs, smooth and old, were undulating in clusters on the bottom against the clean ribbed sand, and the track of the mussel was plain. A school of minnows swam by, each minnow with its small, individual shadow, doubling the attendance,[14] so clear and sharp in the sunlight. Some of the other campers were in swimming, along the shore, one of them with a cake of soap, and the water felt thin and clear and unsubstantial.[15] Over the years there had been this person with the cake of soap, this cultist, and here he was. There had been no years.

Up to the farmhouse to dinner through the teeming, dusty field, the road under our sneakers was only a two-track road. The middle track was missing, the one with the marks of the hooves and the splotches of dried, flaky manure. There had always been three tracks to choose from in choosing which track to walk in; now the choice was narrowed down to two. For a moment I missed terribly the middle alternative. But the way led past the tennis court, and something about the way it lay there in the sun reassured me; the tape had loosened along the backline, the alleys were green with plantains[16] and other weeds, and the net (installed in June and removed in September) sagged[17] in the dry noon, and the whole place steamed with midday heat and hunger and emptiness. There was a choice of pie for dessert, and one was blueberry and one was apple, and the waitresses were the same country girls, there having been no passage of time, only the illusion of it as in a dropped curtain—the waitresses were still fifteen; their hair had been washed, that was the only difference—they had been to the movies and seen the pretty girls with the clean hair.

---

[13] *this lake...own devices*: this lake you could leave alone

[14] *doubling the attendance*: making it look like two with its shadow

[15] *the water...and insubstantial*: 水感清浅，拂身如无

[16] *plantains*: a common wild plant with small green flowers and wide leaves

[17] *sagged*: hung loosely instead of tautly

Summertime, oh summertime, pattern of life indelible, the fade-proof lake, the woods unshatterable, the pasture with the sweet fern and the juniper forever and ever, summer without end; this was the background, and the life along the shore was the design, the cottages with their innocent and tranquil design, their tiny docks with the flagpole and the American flag floating against the white clouds in the blue sky, the little paths over the roots of the trees leading from camp to camp and the paths leading back to the outhouses and the can of lime for sprinkling, and at the souvenir counters at the store the miniature birch-bark canoes and the postcards that showed things looking a little better than they looked. This was the American family at play, escaping the city heat, wondering whether the newcomers at the camp at the head of the cove were "common" or "nice," wondering whether it was true that the people who drove up for Sunday dinner at the farmhouse were turned away because there wasn't enough chicken.

It seemed to me, as I kept remembering all this, that those times and those summers had been infinitely precious and worth saving. There had been jollity and peace and goodness. The arriving (at the beginning of August) had been so big a business in itself, at the railway station the farm wagon drawn up, the first smell of the pine-laden air, the first glimpse of the smiling farmer, and the great importance of the trunks and your father's enormous authority in such matters, and the feel of the wagon under you for the long ten-mile haul, and at the top of the last long hill catching the first view of the lake after eleven months of not seeing this cherished body of water. The shouts and cries of the other campers when they saw you, and the trunks to be unpacked, to give up their rich burden. (Arriving was less exciting nowadays, when you sneaked up in your car and parked it under a tree near the camp and took out the bags and in five minutes it was all over, no fuss, no loud wonderful fuss about trunks.)

Peace and goodness and jollity. The only thing that was wrong now, really, was the sound of the place, an unfamiliar nervous sound of the outboard motors. This was the note that jarred,[18] the one thing that would sometimes break the illusion and set the years moving. In those other summertimes, all motors were inboard; and when they were at a little distance, the noise they made was a sedative, an ingredient of summer sleep. They were one-cylinder[19] and two-cylinder engines, and some were make-and-break[20] and some were jump-spark,[21] but they all made a sleepy sound across the lake. The one-lungers[22] throbbed[23] and fluttered, and the twin-cylinder ones purred and purred, and that was a quiet sound too. But now the campers all had outboards. In the daytime, in the hot mornings, these motors made a petulant, irritable sound; at night, in the still evening when the afterglow lit the water, they whined about one's ears like mosquitoes. My boy loved our rented outboard, and his great desire was to achieve single-handed mastery over it, and authority, and he soon learned the trick of choking[24] it a little (but not too much), and the adjustment of the needle valve. Watching him I would remember the things you could do with the old one-cylinder engine with the heavy flywheel, how you could have it eating out of your hand if you got really close to it spiritually. Motor boats in those days didn't have clutches, and you would make a landing by shutting off the motor at the proper time and coasting in with a dead rudder. But there was a way of reversing them, if you learned the trick, by cutting the switch and putting it on again exactly on the final dying revolution of the flywheel, so that it would kick back against compression and begin reversing. Approaching a dock in a strong following breeze, it was difficult to slow up sufficiently by the ordinary coasting method, and if

---

[18] *jarred*: had a harsh or an unpleasant effect

[19] *cylinder*: the tube within which a piston moves forwards and backwards in an engine 汽缸

[20] *make-and-break*: with apparatus for making and breaking an electric circuit

[21] *jump-spark*: with electricity jumping across a gap and producing sparks

[22] *one-lungers*: one-cylinder engines 单缸发动机

[23] *throbbed*: vibrated or sounded with a persistent rhythm

[24] *choking*: checking, controlling or restraining the activity of something

a boy felt he had complete mastery over his motor, he was tempted to keep it running beyond its time and then reverse it a few feet from the dock. It took a cool nerve,[25] because if you threw the switch a twentieth of a second too soon you would catch the flywheel when it still had speed enough to go up past center, and the boat would leap ahead, charging bull-fashion at the dock.

We had a good week at the camp. The bass were biting well and the sun shone endlessly, day after day. We would be tired at night and lie down in the accumulated heat of the little bedrooms after the long hot day and the breeze would stir almost imperceptibly outside and the smell of the swamp drift in through the rusty screens. Sleep would come easily and in the morning the red squirrel would be on the roof, tapping out his gay[26] routine. I kept remembering everything, lying in bed in the mornings—the small steamboat that had a long rounded stern like the lip of a Ubangi,[27] and how quietly she ran on the moonlight sails, when the older boys played their mandolins and the girls sang and we ate doughnuts dipped in sugar, and how sweet the music was on the water in the shining night, and what it had felt like to think about girls then. After breakfast we would go up to the store and the things were in the same place—the minnows in a bottle, the plugs and spinners disarranged and pawed over[28] by the youngsters from the boys' camp, the fig newtons[29] and the Beeman's gum.[30] Outside, the road was tarred and cars stood in front of the store. Inside, all was just as it had always been, except there was more Coca-Cola and not so much

---

[25] *a cool nerve*: the ability to stay calm and behave in a reasonable way in difficult situations

[26] *gay*: happy and full of fun

[27] *Ubangi*: a woman of the district of Kyabé village in Chad with lips pierced and distended to unusual dimensions with wooden disks

[28] *pawed over*: touched roughly and made in disorder

[29] *fig newtons*: a brand of fig bar (in Europe, fig roll), pastry filled with fig jam

[30] *the Beeman's gum*: a chewing gum in the late 19th century as an aid to digestion

Moxie[31] and root beer[32] and birch beer[33] and sarsaparilla.[34] We would walk out with a bottle of pop[35] apiece[36] and sometimes the pop would backfire[37] up our noses and hurt. We explored the streams, quietly, where the turtles slid off the sunny logs and dug their way into the soft bottom; and we lay on the town wharf and fed worms to the tame bass. Everywhere we went I had trouble making out which was I, the one walking at my side, the one walking in my pants.

One afternoon while we were there at that lake a thunderstorm came up. It was like the revival of an old melodrama[38] that I had seen long ago with childish awe. The second-act climax of the drama of the electrical disturbance over a lake in America had not changed in any important respect. This was the big scene, still the big scene. The whole thing was so familiar, the first feeling of oppression and heat and a general air around camp of not wanting to go very far away. In midafternoon (it was all the same) a curious darkening of the sky, and a lull in everything that had made life tick;[39] and then the way the boats suddenly swung the other way at their moorings with the coming of a breeze out of the new quarter, and the premonitory rumble. Then the kettle drum, then the snare, then the bass drum and cymbals, then crackling light against the dark, and the gods grinning and licking their chops in the hills. Afterward the calm, the rain steadily rustling in the calm lake, the return of light and hope and spirits, and the campers running out in joy and relief to go swimming in the rain, their bright cries perpetuating the deathless joke about how they were

---

[31] *Moxie*: a regionally popular carbonated beverage in America

[32] *root beer*: a carbonated soft drink made from extracts of certain plant roots and herbs

[33] *birch beer*: a carbonated soft drink made from herbal extracts, usually from birch bark

[34] *sarsaparilla*: a sweet drink without alcohol, made from the root of the sassafras plant

[35] *pop*: (esp. non-alcoholic) fizzy drink

[36] *apiece*: to, for or by each one of a group

[37] *backfire*: have the reverse of the desired or expected effect

[38] *melodrama*: events, behavior, language, etc. resembling a drama of this kind

[39] *tick*: (of a clock, etc.) make a series of ticking sounds

getting simply drenched, and the children screaming with delight at the new sensation of bathing in the rain, and the joke about getting drenched linking the generations in a strong indestructible chain. And the comedian[40] who waded in carrying an umbrella.

When the others went swimming my son said he was going in too. He pulled his dripping trunks[41] from the line where they had hung all through the shower, and wrung them out. Languidly, and with no thought of going in, I watched him, his hard little body, skinny and bare, saw him wince slightly as he pulled up around his vitals[42] the small, soggy,[43] icy garment. As he buckled the swollen belt suddenly my groin felt the chill of death.

Author

Elwyn Brooks White (1899-1985) was an American writer, best known as the author of children's books *Charlotte's Web* (1952) and *Stuart Little* (1945). He is also a witty, satiric observer of contemporary society, whose influence was profound particularly in the popular essay. Best recognized for his essays and unsigned "Notes and Comment" pieces, he was the most important contributor to *The New Yorker* at a time. White edited and updated *The Elements of Style* (1959), a handbook of grammatical and stylistic dos and don'ts for writers of American English by William Strunk, Jr., and it was widely used in college English courses. In 1978, White won an honorary Pulitzer Prize.

---

[40] *comedian*: person who is always behaving comically

[41] *trunks*: shorts worn by men or boys for swimming, boxing, etc.

[42] *vitals*: the parts of your body that are necessary to keep you alive

[43] *soggy*: unpleasantly wet

College Pressures

by William Zinsser

Dear Carlos: I desperately need a dean's excuse for my chem midterm[1] which will begin in about 1 hour. All I can say is that I totally blew it[2] this week. I've fallen incredibly, inconceivably behind.

Carlos: Help! I'm anxious to hear from you. I'll be in my room and won't leave it until I hear from you. Tomorrow is the last day for...

Carlos: I left town because I started bugging out[3] again. I stayed up all night to finish a take-home make-up exam & am typing it to hand in on the 10th. It was due on the 5th. P.S. I'm going to the dentist. Pain is pretty bad.

Carlos: Probably by Friday I'll be able to get back to my studies. Right now I'm going to take a long walk. This whole thing has taken a lot out of me.

Carlos: I'm really up the proverbial creek.[4] The problem is I really *bombed*[5] the history final. Since I need that course for my major I...

Carlos: Here follows a tale of woe. I went home this weekend, had to help my Mom, & caught a fever so didn't have much time to study. My professor...

Carlos: Aargh![6] Trouble. Nothing original but everything's piling up at once. To be brief, my job interview...

Hey Carlos, good news! I've got mononucleosis.[7]

---

1 *chem midterm*: chemistry midterm exam

2 *blew it*: spoiled it, bungled it

3 *started bugging out*: started chickening out in anticipation of sth. threatening

4 *I'm really...proverbial creek*: "[B]e up the creek" means "be in a difficult situation." "Proverbial" is added for the sake of emphasis as if everybody knows about the phrase.

5 *bombed*: failed badly

6 *Aargh!*: used as an expression of anguish, disgust, horror, rage, or other strong emotion, often with humorous intent

7 *mononucleosis*: 单核细胞增多症

Who are these wretched supplicants, scribbling notes so laden with anxiety, seeking such miracles of postponement and balm?[8] They are men and women who belong to Branford College, one of the twelve residential colleges[9] at Yale University, and the messages are just a few of the hundreds that they left for their dean, Carlos Hortas—often slipped under his door at 4 am—last year.

But students like the ones who wrote those notes can also be found on campuses from coast to coast—especially in New England and at many other private colleges across the country that have high academic standards and highly motivated students. Nobody could doubt that the notes are real. In their urgency and their gallows humor[10] they are authentic voices of a generation that is panicky to succeed.

My own connection with the message writers is that I am master of Branford College. I live in its Gothic quadrangle[11] and know the students well. (We have 485 of them.) I am privy to[12] their hopes and fears—and also to their stereo music and their piercing cries in the dead of night ("Does anybody *ca-a-are*?"). If they went to Carlos to ask how to get through tomorrow, they come to me to ask how to get through the rest of their lives.

Mainly I try to remind them that the road ahead is a long one and that it will have more unexpected turns than they think. There will be plenty of time to change jobs, change careers, change whole attitudes and approaches. They don't want to hear such liberating news. They want a map—right now—that they can follow unswervingly to career security, financial security, Social Security and, presumably, a prepaid grave.

What I wish for all students is some release from the clammy grip of the future. I wish them a chance to savor[13] each segment of their education

---

8 *balm*: anything which is comforting or soothing

9 *residential colleges*: boarding colleges

10 *gallows humor*: grim and ironical humor in a desperate or helpless situation

11 *Gothic quadrangle*: 哥特式四方院落

12 *I am privy to*: I am sharing the knowledge of

13 *savor*: enjoy and appreciate

as an experience in itself and not as a grim preparation for the next step. I wish them the right to experiment, to trip[14] and fall, to learn that defeat is as instructive as victory and is not the end of the world.

My wish, of course, is naive. One of the few rights that America does not proclaim is the right to fail. Achievement is the national god, venerated in our media—the million-dollar athlete, the wealthy executive—and glorified in our praise of possessions. In the presence of such a potent[15] state religion, the young are growing up old.

I see four kinds of pressure working on college students today: economic pressure, parental pressure, peer pressure,[16] and self-induced pressure.[17] It is easy to look around for villains—to blame the colleges for charging too much money, the professors for assigning too much work, the parents for pushing their children too far, the students for driving themselves too hard. But there are no villains; only victims.

"In the late 1960s," one dean told me, "the typical question that I got from students was 'Why is there so much suffering in the world?' or 'How can I make a contribution?' Today it's 'Do you think it would look better for getting into law school if I did a double major in history and political science, or just majored in one of them?'" Many other deans confirmed this pattern. One said: "they're trying to find an edge[18]—the intangible something that will look better on paper if two students are about equal."

Note the emphasis on looking better. The transcript has become a sacred document, the passport to security. How one appears on paper is more important than how one appears in person. A is for Admirable and B is for Borderline,[19] even though, in Yale's official system of grading, A

---

[14] *trip*: stumble and fall

[15] *potent*: influential, forceful

[16] *peer pressure*: pressure from one's fellow schoolmates

[17] *self-induced pressure*: self-imposed pressure, pressure brought on by oneself

[18] *edge*: a quality that gives one superiority over close rivals

[19] *[b]orderline*: barely acceptable in quality

means "excellent" and B means "very good." Today, looking very good is no longer good enough, especially for students who hope to go on to law school or medical school. They know that entrance into the better schools will be an entrance into the better law firms and better medical practices where they will make a lot of money. They also know that the odds[20] are harsh. Yale Law School, for instance, matriculates 170 students from an applicant pool of 3,700; Harvard enrolls 550 from a pool of 7,000.

It's all very well for those of us who write letters of recommendation for our students to stress the qualities of humanity that will make them good lawyers or doctors. And it's nice to think that admission officers are really reading our letters and looking for the extra dimension of commitment or concern.[21] Still, it would be hard for a student not to visualize these officers shuffling[22] so many transcripts studded with As that they regard a B as positively[23] shameful.

The pressure is almost as heavy on students who just want to graduate and get a job. Long gone are the days of the "gentleman's C," when students journeyed through college with a certain relaxation, sampling[24] a wide variety of courses—music, art, philosophy, classics, anthropology, poetry, religion—that would send them out as liberally educated men and women. If I were an employer I would rather employ graduates who have this range and curiosity than those who narrowly pursued safe subjects and high grades. I know countless students whose inquiring minds exhilarate me. I like to hear the play of their ideas. I don't know if they are getting As or Cs, and I don't care. I also like them as people. The country needs them, and they will find satisfying jobs. I tell them to relax. They can't.

Nor can I blame them. They live in a brutal economy. Tuition, room and board at most private colleges now comes to at least $7,000, not counting

---

[20] *the odds*: the chances or likelihood

[21] *the extra...or concern*: the quality of being responsible besides good academic performance

[22] *shuffling*: sorting or looking through hurriedly

[23] *positively*: certainly, definitely

[24] *sampling*: trying out, experimenting with

books and fees. This might seem to suggest that the colleges are getting rich. But they are equally battered[25] by inflation. Tuition covers only 60 percent of what it costs to educate a student, and ordinarily the remainder comes from what colleges receive in endowments,[26] grants, and gifts. Now the remainder keeps being swallowed by the cruel costs—higher every year—of just opening the doors.[27] Heating oil is up. Insurance is up. Postage is up. Health-premium[28] costs are up. Everything is up. Deficits are up. We are witnessing in America the creation of a brotherhood of paupers—colleges, parents, and students, joined by the common bond of debt.

Today it is not unusual for a student, even if he works part-time at college and full-time during the summer, to accrue[29] $5,000 in loans after four years—loans that he must start to repay within one year after graduation. Exhorted at commencement to go forth into the world, he is already behind as he goes forth. How could he not feel under pressure throughout college to prepare for this day of reckoning?[30] I have used "he," incidentally, only for brevity. Women at Yale are under no less pressure to justify their expensive education to themselves, their parents, and society. In fact, they are probably under more pressure. For although they leave college superbly equipped to bring fresh leadership to traditionally male jobs, society hasn't yet caught up with this fact.[31]

Along with economic pressure goes parental pressure. Inevitably, the

---

[25] *battered*: stricken repeatedly with hard blows

[26] *endowments*: gifts of money that are made to the colleges in order to provide them with an annual income

[27] *opening the doors*: literally it means opening the doors of the college, i.e., running the school

[28] *health-premium*: 医疗保险费

[29] *accrue*: gradually increase in amount over a period of time

[30] *this day of reckoning*: the time when you pay or are punished for things that you have done wrong; here it refers to the day of paying off one's loans.

[31] *society hasn't...this fact*: society hasn't come to see the fact; society hasn't been ready to accept this fact

two are deeply intertwined.[32]

I see many students taking pre-medical courses with joyless tenacity. They go off to their labs as if they were going to the dentist. It saddens me because I know them in other corners of their life as cheerful people.

"Do you want to go to medical school?" I ask them.

"I guess so," they say, without conviction, or "Not really."

"Then why are you going?"

"Well, my parents want me to be a doctor. They're paying all this money and..."

Poor students, poor parents. They are caught in one of the oldest webs of love and duty and guilt. The parents mean well; they are trying to steer[33] their sons and daughters toward a secure future. But the sons and daughters want to major in history or classics or philosophy—subjects with no "practical" value. Where's the payoff on the humanities? It's not easy to persuade such loving parents that the humanities do indeed pay off. The intellectual faculties developed by studying subjects like history and classics—an ability to synthesize and relate, to weigh cause and effect, to see events in perspective[34]—are just the faculties that make creative leaders in business or almost any general field. Still, many fathers would rather put their money on courses that point toward a specific profession—courses that are pre-law, pre-medical, pre-business, or, as I sometimes heard it put, "pre-rich."

But the pressure on students is severe. They are truly torn. One part of them feels obligated to fulfill their parents' expectations; after all, their parents are older and presumably wiser. Another part tells them that the expectations that are right for their parents are not right for them.

I know a student who wants to be an artist. She is very obviously an artist and will be a good one—she has already had several modest local

[32] *intertwined*: twisted or twined together, closely connected

[33] *steer*: guide

[34] *to see events in perspective*: to think about events sensibly and consider them in relation to everything else

exhibits. Meanwhile she is growing as a well-rounded person[35] and taking humanistic subjects that will enrich the inner resources out of which her art will grow. But her father is strongly opposed. He thinks that an artist is a "dumb" thing to be. The student vacillates and tries to please everybody. She keeps up with her art somewhat furtively and takes some of the "dumb" courses her father wants her to take—at least they are dumb courses for her. She is a free spirit on a campus of tense students—no small achievement in itself—and she deserves to follow her muse.[36]

Peer pressure and self-induced pressure are also intertwined, and they begin almost at the beginning of freshman year.

"I had a freshman student I'll call Linda," one dean told me, "who came in and said she was under terrible pressure because her roommate, Barbara, was much brighter and studied all the time. I couldn't tell her that Barbara had come in two hours earlier to say the same thing about Linda."

The story is almost funny—except that it's not. It's symptomatic of all the pressures put together. When every student thinks every other student is working harder and doing better, the only solution is to study harder still. I see students going off to the library every night after dinner and coming back when it closes at midnight. I wish they would sometimes forget about their peers and go to a movie. I hear the clacking of typewriters in the hours before dawn. I see the tension in their eyes when exams are approaching and papers are due: "*Will I get everything done?*"

Probably they won't. They will get sick. They will get "blocked."[37] They will sleep. They will oversleep. They will bug out. *Hey Carlos, help!*

Part of the problem is that they do more than they are expected to do. A professor will assign five-page papers. Several students will start writing

---

[35] *a well-rounded person*: a person with a personality that is fully developed in all aspects

[36] *follow her muse*: a muse is the source of inspiration for artists; to follow one's muse is to follow one's inspiration or to be a creative artist.

[37] *They will get "blocked"*: They will undergo a short period during which their brain or memory stops functioning normally.

ten-page papers to impress him. Then more students will write ten-page papers, and a few will raise the ante[38] to fifteen. Pity the poor student who is still just doing the assignment.

"Once you have twenty or thirty percent of the student population deliberately overexerting,"[39] one dean points out, "it's bad for everybody. When a teacher gets more and more effort from his class, the student who is doing normal work can be perceived as not doing well. The tactic works, psychologically."

Why can't the professor just cut back and not accept longer papers? He can, and he probably will. But by then the term will be half over and the damage done. Grade fever is highly contagious and not easily reversed. Besides, the professor's main concern is with his course. He knows his students only in relation to the course and doesn't know that they are also overexerting in their other courses. Nor is it really his business. He didn't sign up for dealing with the student as a whole person and with all the emotional baggage[40] the student brought along from home. That's what deans, masters, chaplains,[41] and psychiatrists are for.

To some extent this is nothing new: a certain number of professors have always been self-contained[42] islands of scholarship and shyness, more comfortable with books than with people. But the new pauperism[43] has widened the gap still further, for professors who actually like to spend time with students don't have as much time to spend. They also are overexerting. If they are young, they are busy trying to publish in order not to perish,[44]

---

[38] *raise the ante*: Literally it means to increase the value of the stake in a gambling game. Here what the students expand is the length of their papers.

[39] *overexerting*: engaging in too much or too strenuous exertion, making excessive efforts

[40] *emotional baggage*: past experiences or long-held attitudes, usually perceived as emotional burdens

[41] *chaplains*: school chaplains, members of the Christian clergy who do religious work in the college

[42] *self-contained*: complete and separate, needing no help from outside

[43] *pauperism*: the state of being very poor, penury, impoverishment

[44] *to publish...to perish*: to publish articles in journals or write books so as to survive in the academia

hanging by their finger nails onto a shrinking profession.[45] If they are old and tenured,[46] they are buried under the duties of administering departments—as departmental chairmen or members of committees—that have been thinned out[47] by the budgetary axe.

Ultimately it will be the students' own business to break the circles in which they are trapped. They are too young to be prisoners of their parents' dreams and their classmates' fears. They must be jolted into[48] believing in themselves as unique men and women who have the power to shape their own future.

"Violence is being done to the undergraduate experience," says Carlos Hortas. "College should be open-ended: at the end it should open many, many roads. Instead, students are choosing their goal in advance, and their choices narrow as they go along. It's almost as if they think that the country has been codified in the type of jobs that exist—that they've got to fit into certain slots. Therefore, fit into the best-paying slot.

"They ought to take chances. Not taking chances will lead to a life of colorless mediocrity.[49] They'll be comfortable. But something in the spirit will be missing."

I have painted too drab[50] a portrait of today's students, making them seem a solemn lot.[51] That is only half of their story; if they were so dreary I wouldn't so thoroughly enjoy their company. The other half is that they are easy to like. They are quick to laugh and to offer friendship. They are

---

45 *hanging by...shrinking profession*: trying desperately to cling onto the declining profession as academics

46 *tenured*: given a permanent post as a professor

47 *have been thinned out*: have been made smaller in number or size

48 *be jolted into*: To jolt somebody is to give him a shock in order to make him act or change (usually for the better).

49 *mediocrity*: the quality of being so-so or even inferior, lack of inspiration and originality

50 *drab*: colorless, dull, lacklustre

51 *a solemn lot*: a group of solemn, serious people

not introverts. They are unusually kind and are more considerate of one another than any student generation I have known.

Nor are they so obsessed with their studies that they avoid sports and extracurricular activities. On the contrary, they juggle[52] their crowded hours to play on a variety of teams, perform with musical and dramatic groups, and write for campus publications. But this in turn is one more cause of anxiety. There are too many choices. Academically, they have 1,300 courses to select from; outside class they have to decide how much spare time they can spare and how to spend it.

This means that they engage in fewer extracurricular pursuits than their predecessors did. If they want to row on the crew[53] and play in the symphony they will eliminate one; in the '60s they would have done both. They also tend to choose activities that are self-limiting.[54] Drama, for instance, is flourishing in all twelve of Yale's residential colleges as it never has before. Students hurl themselves into these productions—as actors, directors, carpenters, and technicians—with a dedication to create the best possible play, knowing that the day will come when the run will end and they can get back to their studies.

They also can't afford to be the willing slave of organizations like the *Yale Daily News*. Last spring at the one-hundredth anniversary banquet of that paper—whose past chairmen include such once and future kings as Potter Stewart, Kingman Brewster, and William F. Buckley, Jr.—much was made of the fact that the editorial staff used to be small and totally committed and that "newsies"[55] routinely worked fifty hours a week. In effect they belonged to a club; Newsies is how they defined themselves at Yale. Today's student will write one or two articles a week, when he

---

[52] *juggle*: arrange...in the most effective way often with difficulty

[53] *row on the crew*: be a rower, a member in the rowing crew, row a boat as a sport

[54] *self-limiting*: limited in itself, self-restraining

[55] *newsies*: A newsy/newsie is a reporter or a newsboy in the Yale jargon.

can, and he defines himself as a student. I've never heard the word Newsie except at the banquet.

If I have described the modern undergraduate primarily as a driven creature who is largely ignoring the blithe spirit inside who keeps trying to come out and play, it's because that's where the crunch[56] is, not only at Yale but throughout American education. It's why I think we should all be worried about the values that are nurturing a generation so fearful of risk and so goal-obsessed at such an early age.

I tell students that there is no one "right" way to get ahead—that each of them is a different person, starting from a different point and bound for a different destination. I tell them that change is a tonic[57] and that all the slots are not codified nor the frontiers closed. One of my ways of telling them is to invite men and women who have achieved success outside the academic world to come and talk informally with my students during the year. They are heads of companies or ad agencies, editors of magazines, politicians, public officials, television magnates,[58] labor leaders, business executives, Broadway producers, artists, writers, economists, photographers, scientists, historians—a mixed bag of achievers.

I ask them to say a few words about how they got started. The students assume that they started in their present profession and knew all along that it was what they wanted to do. Luckily for me, most of them got into their field by a circuitous route, to their surprise, after many detours.[59] The students are startled. They can hardly conceive of a career that was not pre-planned. They can hardly imagine allowing the hand of God or chance to nudge[60] them down some unforeseen trail.

---

56 *the crunch*: the most important and difficult part of a situation or problem

57 *tonic*: a medicine that makes you feel stronger, healthier, and less tired; 补药

58 *magnates*: tycoons, entrepreneurs

59 *detours*: a circuitous, longer route

60 *nudge*: push gently in a particular direction with the intent of urging

Author

William Knowlton Zinsser (1922-2015) is a writer, editor, and teacher. He began his career as a journalist for *the New York Herald Tribune*, and had been a longtime contributor to leading magazines. Throughout the 1970s, Zinsser taught writing at Yale University. He had lived in New York City after teaching at the Columbia University Graduate School of Journalism.

On Flying

by Gore Vidal

I was twice footnote to the history of aviation. On July 7, 1929, still on the sunny side of four years old, I flew in the first commercially scheduled airliner (a Ford trimotor) across the United States, from New York to Los Angeles in forty-eight hours. Aviation was now so safe that even a little child could fly in comfort. I remember only two things about the flight: the lurid[1] flames from the exhaust[2] through the window; then a sudden loss of altitude[3] over Los Angeles, during which my eardrums burst. Always the trouper,[4] I was later posed, smiling, for the rotogravure[5] sections of the newspapers, blood tickling from tiny lobes.[6] Among my supporting cast that day were my father, the assistant general manager of the company (Transcontinental Air Transport), his great and good friend, as the never great, never good *Time* magazine would say, Amelia Earhart, as well as Anne Morrow Lindbergh, whose husband Charles was my pilot.* Both Lindbergh and Amelia had been hired by the line's promoter, one C. M. Keys (not even a footnote now[7] but then known as the czar[8] of aviation), to publicize TAT,[9] popularly known as "The Lindbergh Line."

* A recent investigation of a certain newspaper of record shows that, contrary to family tradition, I was not on the first flight. I made my first

---

[1] *lurid*: too brightly colored

[2] *exhaust*: a pipe on a vehicle that waste gases pass through

[3] *loss of altitude*: descent

[4] *trouper*: someone who works hard and keeps trying, even when the going is tough

[5] *rotogravure*: 轮转凹版图片

[6] *lobes*: 耳垂

[7] *not even a footnote now*: forgotten by the public

[8] *czar*: someone who is very powerful in a particular job or activity

[9] *TAT*: Transcontinental Air Transport

cross-country flight a few months later, at the age of four. In any case, I am still a triumphant footnote: the first child ever to cross the country by air-rail.

My second moment of footnotehood[10] occurred in the spring of 1936, when I was—significantly—on the sunny side of eleven. I was picked up at St. Albans School in Washington, D.C., by my father, Eugene L. Vidal, director of the Bureau of Air Commerce (an appointee of one Franklin D. Roosevelt,[11] himself mere tinkling prelude[12] to Reagan's heavenly choir).[13] FDR[14] wanted to have a ministry of aviation like the European powers; and so the Bureau of Air Commerce was created.

On hot spring mornings Washington's streets smelled of melting asphalt[15] and everything was a dull tropical green. The city was more like a Virginia county seat than a world capital. Instead of air conditioning, people used palmetto fans.[16] As we got into my implausibly[17] handsome father's plausible Plymouth,[18] he was mysterious, while I was delighted to be liberated from school. I wore short trousers and polo shirt, the standard costume of those obliged to pretend that they were children a half-century ago. What was up? I asked. My father said, you'll see. Since we were now on the familiar road to Bolling Field, I knew that whatever was up, it was

---

[10] *footnotehood*: the state of being a footnote to the history of aviation

[11] *Franklin D. Roosevelt*: D standing for Delano (1882–1945), 32nd president of the United States (1933-45)

[12] *prelude*: action or event that happens before another larger or more important one and forms an introduction to it

[13] *heavenly choir*: originally by angels; here the phrase is an ironic reference to the Star Wars.

[14] *FDR*: Franklin D. Roosevelt

[15] *asphalt*: 沥青

[16] *palmetto fans*: 芭蕉扇

[17] *implausibly*: unbelievably

[18] *Plymouth*: a Chrysler car

probably going to be us.[19] Ever since my father—known to all as Gene—had become director in 1933, we used to fly together nearly every weekend in the director's Stinson monoplane.[20] Occasionally he'd let me take the controls. Otherwise, I was navigator.[21] With a filling-station road map[22] on my bony knees, I would look out the window for familiar landmarks. When in doubt, you followed a railroad line or a main highway. Period joke: A dumb pilot was told to follow the Super Chief [23] no matter what; when the train entered a tunnel, so did the pilot. End of joke.

At Bolling Field, I recognized the so-called Hammond flivver[24] plane. Gene had recently told the press that a plane had been developed so safe that anyone could fly it and so practical that anyone who could afford a flivver car could buy it—in mass production, that is. At present, there was only the prototype. But it was my father's dream to put everyone in the air, just as Henry Ford had put everyone on the road. Since 1933, miles of newsprint and celluloid[25] had been devoted to Gene Vidal's dream—or was it folly?[26]

We had been up in the Hammond plane before, and I suppose it really was almost "foolproof,"[27] as my father claimed. I forget the plane's range and speed but the speed was probably less than a hundred miles an hour. (One pleasure of flying then: sliding the window open and sticking out your hand, and feeling the wind smash against it.) As a boy, the actual flying of a

---

[19] *it was...be us*: Probably we were going to take a flight.

[20] *monoplane*: 单翼机

[21] *navigator*: the one who directs the way in a vehicle

[22] *a filling-station road map*: a road map usually sold at a filling station for drivers

[23] *Super Chief*: a passenger train

[24] *flivver*: cheap and usually old

[25] *celluloid*: a plastic substance made mainly from cellulose that was used in the past to make photographic film and other objects

[26] *folly*: a very stupid thing to do, especially one that is likely to have serious results

[27] *foolproof*: very easy (even for a fool) to operate

plane was a lot simpler for me than building one of those model planes that the other lads were so adept at[28] making and I all thumbs[29] in the presence of balsa[30] wood, paper, and glue—the Dionysiac[31] properties of glue were hardly known then. But those were Depression years, and we Americans a serious people. That is how we beat Hitler, Mussolini, and Tojo.[32]

Next to the Hammond, there was a Pathé newsreel[33] crew,[34] presided over by the familiar figure of Floyd Gibbons,[35] a dark patch covering the vacancy in his florid[36] face where once there had been an eye that he had lost—it was rumored—as a correspondent in the war to make the world safe for democracy, and now for a flivver aircraft in every garage.[37] Since my father appeared regularly in newsreels and *The March of Time*,[38] a newsreel crew was no novelty. At age seven, when asked what my father did, I said, He's in the newsreels. But now, since I had been taken so mysteriously out of class,[39] could it be...? I felt a premonitory[40] chill.

As we drove on to the runway (no nonsense in those days when the director came calling), Gene said, "Well, you want to be a movie actor. So here's your chance." He was, if nothing else, a superb salesman. Jaded[41]

---

28 *adept at*: good at doing something that needs care and skill

29 *all thumbs*: unable to do something in which you have to make small careful movements with your fingers, very clumsy

30 *balsa*: lightweight wood used for making models

31 *Dionysiac*: intoxicating

32 *Tojo*: Hideki (1884-1948), Japanese prime minister during World War II 东条英机

33 *newsreel*: a short film of news that used to be shown in cinemas

34 *crew*: group of people working together

35 *Floyd Gibbons*: Floyd Phillips Gibbons (1887-1939), the war correspondent for the *Chicago Tribune* during World War I

36 *florid*: red in color

37 *for a...every garage*: for promoting aircraft industry

38 *The March of Time*: a newsreel series that was shown in movie theaters from 1935 to 1951

39 *out of class*: from school

40 *premonitory*: giving a warning that something unpleasant is going to happen

41 *Jaded*: tired and lacking zest

when it came to flying, I was overwhelmed by the movies. Ever since Mickey Rooney[42] played Puck in *A Midsummer Night's Dream*,[43] I had wanted to be a star, too. What could Rooney do that I couldn't? Why was I at St. Albans, starting Latin, when I might be darting about the world,[44] unconfined by either gravity or the director's Stinson? "I'll put a girdle round about the earth in forty minutes!" Rooney had croaked. Now I was about to do the same.

As we parked, Gene explained that I was to take off, circle the field once, and land. After I got out of the plane, I would have to do some acting. Floyd Gibbons would ask me what it was like to fly the flivver plane, and I was to say it was just like driving a flivver car. The fact that I had never even tried to drive a car seemed to my father and me irrelevant as we prepared for my screen debut.[45] As it turned out, I didn't learn to drive until I was twenty-five years old.

[...]

Recently, I saw some footage[46] from the newsreel. As I fasten my seat belt, I stare serenely off into space, not unlike Lindbergh-Earhart.[47] I even looked a bit like the god and goddess of flight who, in turn, looked spookily[48] like each other. I start up the engine. I am still serene. But as I watched the ancient footage, I recalled suddenly the terror that I was actually feeling. Terror not of flying but of the camera. This was my big chance to replace Mickey Rooney. But where was my script? My director? My talent? Thinking only of stardom, I took off. With Geisse behind me

---

[42] *Mickey Rooney*: (1920-2014) Joseph Yule, Jr., better known as Mickey Rooney, is an American film actor.

[43] *A Midsummer Night's Dream*: a romantic comedy by Shakespeare

[44] *darting about the world*: exploring the world with gusto

[45] *my screen debut*: my first appearance in a film

[46] *footage*: part of a film showing a particular event

[47] *Lindbergh-Earhart*: Charles Augustus Lindbergh (1902-74) and Amelia Earhart (1897-1937) were famous American man and woman pilots.

[48] *spookily*: like ghosts

kindly suggesting that I keep into the wind (that is, opposite to the way that the lady's stocking on the flagpole was blowing), I circled the field not once but twice and landed with the sort of jolt that one of today's jet cowboys[49] likes to bring to earth his DC-10.[50]

The real terror began when I got out of the plane and stood, one hand on the door knob, staring into the camera. Gibbons asked me about the flight. I said, Oh, it wasn't much, and it wasn't, either. But I was now suffering from terminal stage fright. As my voice box began to shut down,[51] the fingers on the door knob appeared to have a life of their own. I stammered incoherently. Finally, I gave what I thought was a puckish Rooneyesque grin which exploded on to the screen with all the sinister force of Peter Lorre's *M*.[52] In that final ghastly frame, suddenly broken off as if edited by someone's teeth in the cutting room,[53] my career as boy film star ended and my career as boy aviator was launched. I watched the newsreel twice in the Belasco Theater, built on the site of William Seward's[54] Old Club House. Each time, I shuddered with horror at that demented[55] leer[56] which had cost me stardom. Yet, leer notwithstanding, I was summer[57] famous; and my contemporaries knew loathing.[58] The young Streckfus Persons (a.k.a.[59] Truman Capote)[60] knew of my exploit.[61] "Among other things," Harper

---

[49] *jet cowboys*: bold pilots

[50] *DC-10*: a McDonnell Douglas plane

[51] *my voice...shut down*: I stopped speaking

[52] *Peter Lorre's M*: Lorre (1904-64), American actor typecast as a sinister foreigner; *M* was his 1931 film.

[53] *cutting room*: 剪辑室

[54] *William Seward*: (1801-72) American statesman, secretary of state (1861-69)

[55] *demented*: behaving in a crazy way because you are extremely upset or worried

[56] *leer*: sly unpleasant look suggesting lust or ill will

[57] *summer*: in that summer

[58] *knew loathing*: were envious

[59] *a.k.a.*: also known as

[60] *Truman Capote*: (1924-84) American writer, the author of *Breakfast at Tiffany's* (1958)

[61] *exploit*: feat

Lee[62] writes of the boy she based on Capote, "he had been up in a mail plane seventeen times, he had been to Nova Scotia[63], he had seen an elephant, etc." In the sixties, when I introduced Norman Mailer[64] to my father, I was amazed how much Mailer knew of Gene's pioneering.

It was not until Orville Wright[65] flew a plane at Fort Myer outside Washington in the presence of five thousand people that the world realized that man had indeed kicked[66] gravity and that the sky was only the beginning of no known limit. Like so many of the early airship makers, the Wright brothers were bicycle mechanics. But then the bicycle itself had been a revolutionary machine, adding an inch or two to the world's population by making it possible for boys to wheel over to faraway villages where taller (or shorter) girls might be found. At least in the days when eugenics[67] was a science that was the story. Other bicycle manufacturers soon got into the act, notably Glenn H. Curtiss,[68] who was to be a major manufacturer of aircraft.

Although the first generation of flyers believed that airplanes would eventually make war unthinkable, the 1914-18 war did develop a new glamorous sort of warfare, with Gary Cooper[69] gallantly[70] dueling[71] Von Stroheim[72] across the bright heavens. By 1918 the American government

---

[62] *Harper Lee*: (1926-2016) American woman writer, the author of *To Kill a Mocking Bird* (1960). See Page 116, Note 55 & 56.

[63] *Nova Scotia*: a Canadian province located on the country's North Atlantic coast

[64] *Norman Mailer*: (1923-2007) American writer and journalist

[65] *Orville Wright*: The Wright brothers, Orville Wright and Wilbur Wright, are generally credited with the design and construction of the first practical airplane.

[66] *kicked*: defied

[67] *eugenics*: 优生学

[68] *Glenn H. Curtiss*: (1878-1930) American aviator and pioneer in aircraft construction

[69] *Gary Cooper*: (1901-61) American movie star; here Cooper is the representative of the American fighter flyers.

[70] *gallantly*: bravely

[71] *dueling*: fighting a duel

[72] *Von Stroheim*: Erich (1885-1957), Austrian-born star who played a German air force captain von Rauffenstein.

had an airmail service. In 1927 the twenty-five-year-old Lindbergh flew the Atlantic and became, overnight, the most famous man on earth, the air age beautifully incarnate.[73] In 1928 Amelia Earhart flew the Atlantic and took her place in the heavens as *yin*[74] to Lindbergh's *yang*.[75]

It is hard to describe to later generations what it was like to live in a world dominated by two such shining youthful deities.[76] Neither could appear in public without worshipers—no other word—storming[77] them. Yet each was obliged to spend a lot of time not only publicizing and selling aircraft but encouraging air transport. Of the two, Lindbergh was the better paid. But, as a deity, the commercial aspect was nothing to him, he claimed, and the religion all.[78] On the other hand, Earhart's husband, the publisher and publicist George Palmer Putnam (known as G.P.), worked[79] her very hard indeed. The icons of the air age were big business.

TAT's headquarters were at St. Louis, and my only memory of the summer of 1929 (other than bleeding eardrums) was of city lights, as seen from a downtown hotel window. For anyone interested in period detail,[80] there were almost no colored lights then. So, on a hot airless night in St. Louis, the city had a weird white arctic glow.[81] Also, little did I suspect as I stared out over the tropical city with its icy blinking signs, that a stone's throw away,[82] a youth of eighteen, as yet unknown to me and to the world, Thomas Lanier Williams,[83] was typing, typing, typing into the night, while

---

73 *incarnate*: appearing in a human form

74 *yin*: 阴

75 *yang*: 阳

76 *deities*: great persons

77 *storming*: running after and besieging

78 *the religion all*: The religion, by contrast, was all to him.

79 *worked*: gained profit from

80 *period detail*: detail about this historical period

81 *arctic glow*: 北极光

82 *a stone's throw away*: nearby

83 *Thomas Lanier Williams*: (1911-83) American playwright, later known as Tennessee Williams

across the dark fields of the Republic.[84]

Simultaneously, the Great Depression[85] began. Small airlines either merged or died.[86] Since a contract to fly[87] the mail was the key to survival, the postmaster general,[88] one Walter F. Brown was, in effect, the most powerful single figure in aviation. He was also a political spoilsman of considerable energy. In principle, he wanted fewer airlines; and those beholden to[89] him. As of 1930, United Air Lines carried all transcontinental mail. But Brown decided that, in this case, there should be two transcontinental carriers: one would have the central New York-Los Angeles route; the second the southern Atlanta-Dallas-Los Angeles route. As befitted[90] a Herbert Hoover[91] socialist, Brown did not believe in competitive bidding.[92] The southern route would go to Brown-favored American Airlines and the central route to an airline yet to be created but already titled Transcontinental and Western Air, today's Trans World Airlines.

Brown then forced a merger between TAT (willing) and Western Air Express (unwilling). But as neither flew the mail, Brown's promise of a federal contract for the combined operation did the trick.[93] Since Brown was not above[94] corporate troilism,[95] a third airline, a shy mouse

---

[84] *across the...the Republic*: suggesting that Williams was to be nationally famous

[85] *the Great Depression*: the severe economic problems that followed the Wall Street Crash of 1929; in the early 1930s, many banks and businesses failed, and millions of people lost their jobs in the US and in Europe.

[86] *died*: went bankrupt

[87] *fly*: deliver by air

[88] *postmaster general*: person in charge of the postal system of a country

[89] *beholden to*: indebted to

[90] *befitted*: be appropriate for

[91] *Herbert Hoover*: (1874-1964) US politician in the Republican Party who was the President of the US from 1929 to 1933, during the first years of the Great Depression

[92] *bidding*: offering a price for doing work, providing a service, etc.

[93] *did the trick*: solved the problem

[94] *not above*: not feel ashamed to have or practice

[95] *corporate troilism*: a combination involving three companies

of a company[96] called Pittsburgh Aviation Industries Corporation (PAIC), became a member of the wedding. How on earth did such a mouse get involved with two working airlines? Well, there were three Mellons on PAIC's board of directors, of whom the most active was Richard, nephew of Andrew, former secretary of the Treasury.[97] The nobles missed few tricks[98] in the early days of aviation. As it turned out, the first real boss of TWA was a PAIC man, Richard W. Robbins. And so, on August 25, 1930, TWA was awarded the central airmail route even though its competitor, United, had made a lower bid. There was outcry,[99] but nothing more. After all, the chief radio engineer for TWA was the president's twenty-eight-year-old son, Herbert Hoover, Jr. In those days, Hoover socialism was total;[100] and it was not until his successor, Franklin D. Roosevelt, that old-fashioned capitalism was restored.[101]

In September 1930, the Ludington Line began regular service. Tickets were sold in railway terminals. Gene Vidal personally built the first counter in Washington, using two crates[102] with a board across. Everything was ad hoc.[103] On one occasion, in Philadelphia, passengers from New York to Washington were stretching their legs while passengers from Washington to New York were doing the same. Then each group was shepherded[104] into the wrong plane and the passengers to Washington went back to New York and those to New York back to Washington.

---

[96] *a shy...a company*: a small company with *mouse* suggesting not only the size but also its timidity

[97] *the Treasury*: the government department that controls the money that the country collects and spends

[98] *missed few tricks*: employed almost all the tricks

[99] *outcry*: strong public protest

[100] *total*: dominant

[101] *restored*: brought back into existence

[102] *crates*: large wooden containers for transporting goods

[103] *ad hoc*: not planned but arranged only when necessary

[104] *shepherded*: guided

At the end of the first year, the Ludington Line showed the profit duly noted by *Time*. As organizer and general manager, my father persuaded Amelia Earhart to become a vice-president; he also hired Felix du Pont[105] to be the agent in Washington. He persuaded Herbert Hoover to light up[106] the Washington monument at dusk because, sooner or later, a plane was bound to hit it. On the other hand, he ignored the mandatory fire drills at the Washington terminal on the sensible ground that "We have a real fire," as one of his mechanics put it, "most[107] every day." Between New York and Washington, he put up twenty-four billboards. Slowpoke passengers on the Pennsylvania railroad could read, at regular intervals, "If you'd flown Ludington, you'd have been there." Were it not for Hoover socialism, so successful and busy a passenger airline would have got a mail contract. But Postmaster General Brown chose to give the franchise[108] to Eastern Air Transport, who were eager to carry the mail at eighty-nine cents a mile versus Ludington's twenty-five cents. But that has always been the American way; who dares question it? The Ludingtons lost heart; and in February 1933 they sold out[109] to Eastern—even though Hoover socialism had been rejected at the polls[110] and there was now a new president, eager to restore prosperity with classic capitalistic measures.

Franklin Roosevelt was something of an aviation freak[111] and, thanks in part to some backstage maneuvering on the part of Amelia Earhart and her friend Eleanor Roosevelt, Eugene L. Vidal became the director of the Bureau of Air Commerce at the age of thirty-eight. He was a popular figure not only in aviation circles but with the press. Henry Ladd Smith

---

[105] *Felix du Pont*: Alexis Felix du Pont, Jr. (1905-96), American aviation pioneer, soldier, philanthropist, and a member of the prominent Du Pont family

[106] *light up*: provide illuminations for

[107] *most*: almost

[108] *franchise*: formal permission to run business

[109] *sold out*: sold their business

[110] *polls*: election votings

[111] *freak*: an ardent enthusiast

wrote: "Gene Vidal had fared so badly[112] at the hands of Postmaster General Brown and the Republican administration that there was a certain poetic justice[113] in his appointment..."* But Smith felt that there was more honor than power in the job. The bureau was divided into three parts and Vidal "had all the responsibilities that go with the title, but few of the powers. Unhappy Mr. Vidal took all the blame for mistakes, but he had to share credit with his two colleagues..." I don't think Gene felt all that powerless, although he certainly took a good deal of blame.

Although a lot of out-of-work engineers and craftsmen would be employed, Ickes saw nothing public in private planes, and Gene was obliged to use his power to buy planes for the bureau's inspectors. He ordered five experimental prototypes.[114] The results were certainly unusual. There was one plane whose wings could be folded up; you could then drive it like an automobile. Although nothing came of this hybrid, its overhead rotor[115] was the precursor[116] of the helicopter, still worshiped as a god by the Vietnamese. Finally, there was the Hammond Y-I, which I was to fly.

Along with the glamor of flight, there was the grim[117] fact that planes often crashed and that the bodies of the passengers tended to be unpretty,[118] whether charred[119] or simply in pieces strewn[120] across the landscape. Knute

* Smith, *Airways*, p.283

---

[112] *fared so badly*: was so unsuccessful

[113] *poetic justice*: a situation in which someone suffers, and you think they deserve it because they did something bad. Here, by extension, retribution.

[114] *prototypes*: model versions

[115] *rotor*: a part of a machine that turns around on a central point

[116] *precursor*: a machine that is later developed further

[117] *grim*: serious

[118] *unpretty*: This is a vast understatement.

[119] *charred*: burned until it is black

[120] *strewn*: spread by scattering

Rockne,[121] Grace Moore,[122] Carole Lombard[123] died; and at least half of the people I used to see in my childhood would, suddenly, one day, not be there. "Crashed" was the word; nothing more was said. As director, Gene was obliged to visit the scenes of every major accident, and he had gruesome tales to report.

In 1934 the Democratic senator Hugo Black[124] chaired[125] a Senate committee to investigate the former Republican postmaster general Brown's dealings with the airlines. Black's highly partisan committee painted Brown even darker than he was.[126] Yes, he had played favorites in awarding mail contracts but no one could prove that he—or the Grand Old Party[127]—had in any specific way profited. Nevertheless, Jim Farley,[128] the new postmaster general, charged Brown with "conspiracy and collusion,"[129] while the president, himself a man of truly superhuman vindictiveness,[130] decided to punish Brown, the Republican party, and the colluded-with airlines.

What could be more punitive—and dramatic—than the cancellation of all US airmail contracts with private companies? Since the army had flown the mail back in 1918, let them fly the mail now. The president consulted the director of Air Commerce, who told him that army flyers did not have the sort of skills needed to fly the mail. After all, he[131] should know; he

---

121 *Knute Rockne*: (1888-1931) Norwegian-born American football player

122 *Grace Moore*: (1898-1947) American operatic soprano and actress in musical theater and film

123 *Carole Lombard*: (1908-42) American actress

124 *Hugo Black*: (1886-1971) American politician

125 *chaired*: served as the chairman of

126 *painted Brown...he was*: criticized Brown unfairly, given the fact he was bad

127 *the Grand Old Party*: the nickname for the Republican Party

128 *Jim Farley*: (1888-1976) American politician

129 *collusion*: an secret agreement or cooperation especially for an illegal or deceitful purpose

130 *vindictiveness*: disposition of seeking revenge

131 *he*: the director of Air Commerce

was one.[132] Undeterred,[133] the president turned to General Benjamin D. Foulois,[134] the chief of the air corps, who lusted for appropriations[135] as all air corps chiefs do; and the general said, of course, the air corps could fly the mail.

On February 9, 1934, by executive order, the president cancelled all airmail contracts; and the Army flew the mail. At the end of the first week, five army pilots were dead, six critically injured, eight planes wrecked. One evening in mid-March, my father was called to the White House. As Gene pushed the president's wheelchair along the upstairs corridor, the president, his usual airy[136] self, said, "Well, Brother Vidal, we seem to have a bit of a mess on our hands." Gene always said, "I found that 'we' pretty funny." But good soldiers covered up for their superior. What, FDR wondered, should they do? Although my father had a deep and lifelong contempt for politicians in general ("They tell lies," he used to say with wonder, "even when they don't have to") and for Roosevelt's cheerful mendacities in particular, he did admire the president's resilience:[137] "He was always ready to try something new. He was like a good athlete. Never worry about the last play.[138] Only the next one." Unfortunately, before they could extricate the administration from the mess, Charles Lindbergh attacked the president; publicly, the Lone Eagle[139] held FDR responsible for the dead and injured army pilots.

Roosevelt never forgave Lindbergh. "After that," said Gene, "he would

---

[132] *one*: one of the army flyers

[133] *[u]ndeterred*: not discouraged

[134] *General Benjamin D. Foulois*: (1879-1967) US general who learned to fly the first military planes purchased from the Wright brothers

[135] *appropriations*: a sum of money to be used for a particular purpose, especially by a government or company

[136] *airy*: carefree and light-hearted

[137] *resilience*: toughness

[138] *play*: an action in a sports game

[139] *the Lone Eagle*: a nickname for Lindbergh

always refer to Slim[140] as 'this man Lindbergh,' in that condescending[141] voice of his. Or he'd say '*your* friend Lindbergh,' which was worse." Although Roosevelt was convinced that Lindbergh's statement was entirely inspired by the airlines who wanted to get back their airmail contracts, he was too shrewd[142] a politician to get in a shooting match[143] with the world's most popular hero. Abruptly, on April 20, 1934, Postmaster General Farley let the airlines know that the Post Office was open to bids for mail contracts because, come[144] May, the army would no longer fly the mail. It was, as one thoughtful observer put it, the same old crap game,[145] with Farley not Brown as spoilsman.

Today it is marvelous indeed to watch on television the rings of Saturn close[146] and to speculate on what we may yet find at galaxy's edge. But in the process, we have lost the human element; not to mention the high hope of those quaint days when flight would create "one world." Instead of one world, we have "star wars," and a future in which dumb, dented human toys[147] will drift mindlessly[148] about the cosmos long after our small planet's dead.

Author

Eugene Luther Gore Vidal (1925-2012), US novelist, playwright, and essayist, was one of America's most prominent literary figures on the basis of an enormous quantity of work. Vidal began publishing his writings soon

---

140 *Slim*: another nickname for Lindbergh

141 *condescending*: behaving as though you think you are better, more intelligent, or more important than other people

142 *shrewd*: having or showing good judgment and common sense

143 *shooting match*: a fight

144 *come*: next

145 *crap game*: a gambling game with two dices

146 *close*: in a close manner

147 *human toys*: spacecraft

148 *mindlessly*: in an utterly stupid manner

after his wartime army service. He is best known for his irreverent and intellectually adroit novels. *The City and the Pillar* (1948) became notorious for its homoerotic subject matter. *Myra Breckinridge* (1968) was acclaimed for its wild satire. His other novels, many of them historical and most of them best-sellers, include *Julian* (1964), *Washington, D. C.* (1967), *Burr* (1973), *1876* (1976), and *Lincoln* (1984). He also published several essay collections and the memoir *Palimpsest* (1995). Known for his iconoclastically leftist political analyses, he twice ran unsuccessfully for Congressional office. He was also well known to the public through frequent appearances on television opinion programs.

What We Think of America

by Harold Pinter

On September 10, 2001 I received an honorary degree at the University of Florence. I made a speech in which I referred to the term "humanitarian[1] intervention"—the term used by NATO[2] to justify its bombing of Serbia in 1999.

I said the following: On May 7, 1999 NATO aircraft bombed the marketplace[3] of the southern city of Nis,[4] killing thirty-three civilians and injuring many more. It was, according to NATO, a "mistake."[5]

The bombing of Nis was no "mistake." General Wesley K. Clark declared, as the NATO bombing began: "We are going to systematically and progressively attack, disrupt, degrade, devastate and ultimately—unless President Milosevic[6] complies with the demands of the international community—destroy these forces and their facilities and support."

---

1 *humanitarian*: concerned with improving bad living conditions and preventing unfair treatment of people; the whole phrase sounds like political gobbledygook: intervention with others' internal affairs in the form of destructive bombing in the name of humanitarianism.

2 *NATO*: North Atlantic Treaty Organization, an alliance of several European countries and the US, giving each other military help

3 *marketplace*: a public place frequented by civilians instead of a military target

4 *Nis*: a city in Nisava District, Serbia

5 *mistake*: a bald-faced understatement

6 *President Milosevic*: Slobodan (1941-2006), president of the Federal Republic of Yugoslavia (1997-2000) who initiated a campaign to drive the ethnic Muslim majority out of the province of Kosovo. He was later charged with crimes against humanity and died in his prison cell in The Hague.

Milosevic's "forces,"[7] as we know, included television stations, schools, hospitals, theatres, old people's homes—and the marketplace in Nis. It was in fact a fundamental feature of NATO policy to terrorise the civilian population.

The bombing of Nis, far from being a "mistake," was in fact an act of murder. It stemmed from a "war"[8] which was in itself illegal, a bandit act, waged outside all recognised parameters of International Law, in defiance of the United Nations, even contravening NATO's own charter. But the actions taken, we are told, were taken in pursuance of a policy of "humanitarian intervention" and the civilian deaths were described as "collateral damage."[9]

"Humanitarian intervention" is a comparatively new concept. But President George W. Bush is also following in the great American presidential tradition by referring to "freedom-loving people" (I must say I would be fascinated to meet a "freedom-hating people").[10] President Bush possesses quite a few "freedom-loving" people himself[11]—not only in his own Texas prisons but throughout the whole of the United States, in what can accurately be described as a vast gulag[12]—two million prisoners in fact—a remarkable proportion of them black. Rape of young prisoners, both male and female, is commonplace. So is the use of weapons of torture as defined

---

[7] *forces*: ironic in that peaceful civilian institutions follow

[8] *war*: an invasion and an act of aggression in the name of war—although undeclared

[9] *collateral damage*: now a widely used euphemism for "civilian casualties" in military action

[10] *I must..."freedom-hating people"*: Obviously, no people will hate freedom.

[11] *President Bush...people himself*: bitterly ironic in presenting prisoners deprived of freedom as "freedom-loving"

[12] *gulag*: Russian acronym for "Chief Administration of Corrective Labor Camps"—a group of prison camps in the USSR, where conditions were appallingly bad; the term was largely unknown in the West until the 1973 publication of Aleksandr Solzhenitsyn's *Gulag Archipelago*. It has since become a generic term.

by Amnesty International[13]—stun guns,[14] stun belts,[15] restraint chairs.[16] Prison is a great industry in the United States—just behind pornography when it comes to profits.[17]

There have been and remain considerable sections of mankind for whom the mere articulation of the word "freedom" has resulted in thousands of people throughout Guatemala, El Salvador, Turkey, Israel, Haiti, Brazil, Greece, Uruguay, East Timor, Nicaragua, South Korea, Argentina, Chile, the Philippines and Indonesia, for example, killed in all cases by forces inspired and subsidised by the United States. Why did they die? They died because to one degree or another they dared to question the status quo, the endless plateau[18] of poverty, disease, degradation and oppression which is their birthright. On behalf of the dead, we must regard the breathtaking discrepancy between US government language and US government action with the absolute contempt it merits.[19]

The United States has in fact—since the end of the Second World War—pursued a brilliant, even witty, strategy. It has exercised a sustained, systematic, remorseless and quite clinical[20] manipulation of power worldwide, while masquerading[21] as a force for universal good. But at least now—it can be said—the US has come out of its closet.[22] The smile is still

---

[13] *Amnesty International*: an organization professedly supporting human rights and watching over abuses of them

[14] *stun guns*: a weapon producing a very strong electric current which can make people unconscious

[15] *stun belts*: a restraining device used in the treatment of "unruly" prisoners

[16] *restraint chairs*: designed for violent prisoners to restrain their movements

[17] *Prison is...to profits*: operating prisons as a profit-maker next to pornography

[18] *plateau*: raised terrain used figuratively

[19] *merits*: deserves

[20] *clinical*: coldly objective, unfeeling

[21] *masquerading*: pretending to be something or somebody else as if wearing a mask

[22] *the US...its closet*: Now that it is engaged in undisguised acts of war in public, we can see what the US intention actually is; a term that is made widespread by homosexuals making their sexual orientation open.

there of course (all US presidents have always had wonderful smiles) but the posture[23] is infinitely more naked and more blatant[24] than it has ever been. The Bush administration, as we all know, has rejected the Kyoto agreement,[25] has refused to sign an agreement which would regulate the trade of small arms, has distanced itself from the Anti-Ballistic Missile Treaty, the Comprehensive Nuclear-Test-Ban Treaty and the Biological Weapons Convention. In relation to the latter the US made it quite clear that it would agree to the banning of biological weapons as long as there was no inspection of any biological weapons factory on American soil. The US has also refused to ratify[26] the proposed International Criminal Court of Justice. It is bringing into operation the American Service Members Protection Act which will permit the authorisation of military force to free any American soldier taken into International Criminal Court custody.[27] In other words, they really will "Send in the Marines."

Arrogant, indifferent, contemptuous of International Law, both dismissive and manipulative[28] of the United Nations: this is now the most dangerous power the world has ever known—the authentic "rogue state",[29] but a "rogue state" of colossal military and economic might. And Europe—

---

23 *posture*: a way of carrying onself, an attitude

24 *blatant*: unashamed

25 *the Kyoto agreement*: an protocol (initially adopted in Kyoto, Japan on Dec. 11, 1997) under which industrialized countries will reduce their collective emissions of greenhouse gases

26 *refused to ratify*: The reason for refusal is given below, showing that the US would not hesitate to use wanton force to rescue its captured soldiers.

27 *It is...Court custody*: So the US has legally enabled itself to rescue its soldiers detained by the International Criminal Court.

28 *dismissive and manipulative*: an accurate description of US attitude toward the UN, a mere tool in its hands: now disregarding UN decisions, now coercing other nations to follow the US example as the case may be

29 *rogue state*: This is a label used by the Clinton administration (1993-2001) to characterize states that are hostile to the US, notably Iraq, Iran, and North Korea. Later it was replaced by "state of concern." Here Pinter means that the US hoists with its own petard, thus paying the US back in its own coin.

especially the United Kingdom—is both compliant and complicit,[30] or as Cassius in *Julius Caesar* put it: we "peep about to find ourselves dishonourable graves."[31]

There is, however, as we have seen, a profound revulsion and disgust with the manifestations of US power and global capitalism which is growing throughout the world and becoming a formidable force in its own right. I believe a central inspiration for this force has been the actions and indeed the philosophical stance of the Zapatistas[32] in Mexico. The Zapatistas say (as I understand it): "Do not try to define us. We define ourselves. We will not be what you want us to be. We will not accept the destiny you have chosen for us. We will not accept your terms. We will not abide by your rules. The only way you can eliminate us is to destroy us and you cannot destroy us. We are free."

These remarks seem to me even more valid now than when I made them on September 10. The "rogue state" has—without thought, without pause for reflection, without a moment of doubt, let alone shame—confirmed that it is a fully-fledged, award-winning, gold-plated monster. It has effectively declared war on the world. It knows only one language—bombs and death. "And still they smiled and still the horror grew."[33]

Author

Harold Pinter (1930-2008) was an English playwright, screenwriter, actor, director, poet, author, and political activist considered by many to be "the most influential and imitated dramatist of his generation" (*New York Times*). His best-known works include *The Birthday Party* (1957),

---

[30] *complicit*: involved in or knowing about something; here *complicit* alliterates with *compliant*. Such examples are numerous throughout the essay, such as *mistake* and *murder*.

[31] *peep about...dishonourable graves*: See Shakespeare's *Julius Caesar* I , ii, 136.

[32] *the Zapatistas*: Mexican armed insurgent groups engaged in guerrilla wars named after the country's agrarian revolutionary leader Zapata; the following statement is a paraphrase of one of its repeated declarations.

[33] *And still...horror grew*: lines 215-16 from Oliver Goldsmith's *Deserted Village*

The Caretaker (1960), *The Homecoming* (1964), and *Betrayal* (1978), each of which he adapted to film. Pinter was awarded the Nobel Prize in literature in 2005. He was also active in human rights issues and public political activities, forcefully accusing the US abuse of power around the world. He was a bitter critic of the US-led intervention against Milosevic's Serbia and an even harsher critic of the US-led war in Iraq.

The World as India

The St. Jerome Lecture on Literary Translation In Memoriam W. G. Sebald

by Susan Sontag

To translate means many things, among them: to circulate, to transport, to disseminate, to explain, to make (more) accessible. I'll start with the proposition[1]—the exaggeration, if you will—that by literary translation we mean, we could mean, the translation of the small percentage of published books actually worth reading: that is to say, worth rereading. I shall argue that a proper consideration of the art of literary translation is essentially a claim for the value of literature itself. Beyond the obvious need for the translator's facilitations in creating stock for literature as a small, prestigious import-export business, beyond the indispensable role that translation has in the construction of literature as a competitive sport, played both nationally and internationally (with rivalries, teams, and lucrative prizes)—beyond the mercantile and the agonistic[2] and the ludic incentives for doing translation lies an older, frankly evangelical[3] incentive, more difficult to avow[4] in these self-consciously impious[5] times.

In what I call the evangelical incentive, the purpose of translation is to enlarge the readership of a book deemed to be important. It assumes that some books are discernibly better than other books, that literary merit

---

[1] *proposition*: a statement that expresses a judgment or an opinion

[2] *agonistic*: of, or relating to agnosticism, a belief that nothing is known or can be known of the existence or nature of God

[3] *evangelical*: of the teachings of the gospel or Christianity

[4] *avow*: make a public statement about something you believe in

[5] *impious*: lacking respect for religion or God

exists in a pyramidal[6] shape, and it is imperative for the works near the top to become available to as many as possible, which means to be widely translated and as frequently retranslated as is feasible. Clearly, such a view of literature assumes that a rough consensus can be reached on which works are essential. It does *not* entail[7] thinking the consensus—or canon[8]—is fixed for all time and cannot be modified.

At the top of the pyramid are the books regarded as scripture: indispensable or essential exoteric[9] knowledge that, by definition, invites translation. (Probably the most linguistically influential translations have been translations of the Bible: Saint Jerome,[10] Luther,[11] Tyndale,[12] the Authorized Version.[13]) Translation is then first of all making better known what deserves to be better known—because it is improving, deepening, exalting; because it is an indispensable legacy from the past; because it is a contribution to knowledge, sacred or other. In a more secular register,[14] translation was also thought to bring a benefit to the translator: translating was a valuable cognitive—and ethical—workout.[15]

In an era when it is proposed that computers—"translating machines"—will soon be able to perform most translating tasks, what we call literary

---

[6] *pyramidal*: organized in different levels, so that there is much less at the top than at the bottom

[7] *entail*: involve something as a necessary part or result

[8] *canon*: a sanctioned or accepted group or body of related works

[9] *exoteric*: suitable to be imparted to the public

[10] *Saint Jerome*: (c347-420) the best known translator of the Bible from Greek and Hebrew into Latin; his translation is known as the Vulgate.

[11] *Luther*: Martin (1483-1546), German religious leader whose ideas have had great influence on religion in Europe; he translated the Bible from Latin into German.

[12] *Tyndale*: William (c1494-1536), English religious reformer and translator of the Bible, on whose translation the Authorized Version is partly based

[13] *the Authorized Version*: one of the most important English translations of the Bible, published in 1611 as the work of 54 independent scholars revising the existing English versions

[14] *register*: any of the varieties of a language that a speaker uses in a particular social context

[15] *workout*: a test of one's ability, capacity, stamina, or suitability

translation perpetuates the traditional sense of what translation entails. The new view is that translation is the finding of equivalents; or to vary the metaphor,[16] that a translation is a problem, for which solutions can be devised. In contrast, the old understanding is that translation is the making of choices, conscious choices, choices not simply between the stark[17] dichotomies of good and bad, correct and incorrect, but among a more complex dispersion[18] of alternatives, such as "good" versus "better" and "better" versus "best," not to mention such impure alternatives as "old-fashioned" versus "trendy," "vulgar" versus "pretentious," and "abbreviated" versus "wordy."

For such choices to be good—or better—was assumed to imply knowledge, both wide and deep, on the part of the translator. Translating, which is here seen as an activity of choosing in the larger sense, was a profession of individuals who were the bearers of a certain inward culture. To translate thoughtfully, painstakingly, ingeniously, respectfully was a precise measure of the translator's fealty[19] to the enterprise of literature itself.

Choices that might be thought of as merely linguistic always imply ethical standards as well, which has made the activity of translating itself the vehicle of such values as integrity, responsibility, fidelity, boldness, humility. The ethical understanding of the task of the translator originated in the awareness that translation is basically an impossible task, if what is meant is that the translator is able to take up the text of an author written in one language and delivers it, intact, without loss, into another language. Obviously, this is *not* what is being stressed by those who await impatiently the supersession of the dilemmas of the translator by the equivalencings[20] of better, more ingenious translating machines.

Literary translation is a branch of literature—anything but a

---

[16] *to vary the metaphor*: in other words

[17] *stark*: clearly obvious to the eye or the mind

[18] *dispersion*: the result of being spread or distributed from a fixed or constant source

[19] *fealty*: loyalty

[20] *equivalencings*: things made equal in value

mechanical task. But what makes translation so complex an undertaking is that it responds to a variety of aims. There are demands that arise from the nature of literature as a form of communication. There is the mandate,[21] with a work regarded as essential, to make it known to the widest possible audience. There is the general difficulty of passing from one language to another, and the special intransigence of certain texts, which points to something inherent in the work quite outside the intentions or awareness of its author that emerges as the cycle of translations begins—a quality that, for want of a better word, we call translatability.

This nest[22] of complex questions is often reduced to the perennial debate among translators—the debate about literalness[23]—that dates back at least to ancient Rome, when Greek literature was translated into Latin, and continues to exercise translators in every country (and with respect to which there is a variety of national traditions and biases). The oldest theme of the discussion of translations is the role of accuracy and fidelity. Surely there must have been translators in the ancient world whose standard was strict literal fidelity (and damn euphony!), a position defended with dazzling obstinacy by Vladimir Nabokov[24] in his Englishing[25] of *Eugene Onegin*. How else to explain the bold insistence of Saint Jerome himself (ca. 331-420)—the intellectual in the ancient world who (adapting arguments first broached[26] by Cicero[27]) reflected most extensively, in prefaces and in letters, on the task of translation—that the inevitable result of aiming at a faithful reproduction of the author's words and images is the sacrifice of meaning and of grace?

This passage is from the preface Jerome wrote to his translation into Latin

---

21 *mandate*: mission

22 *nest*: a group (of similar things)

23 *literalness*: exactness

24 *Vladimir Nabokov*: (1899-1977) Russian-born American novelist and poet

25 *Englishing*: the act of translating a text into English

26 *broached*: mentioned a subject that might cause an argument

27 *Cicero*: (106-43 BC) Roman statesman, orator, and writer

of the *Chronicle* of Eusebius.[28] (He translated it in the years AD 381-82, while he was living in Constantinople[29] in order to take part in the Council[30]—six years before he settled in Bethlehem,[31] to improve his knowledge of Hebrew, and almost a decade before he began the epochal[32] task of translating the Hebrew Bible into Latin.) Of this early translation from Greek, Jerome wrote:

> *It has long been the practice of learned men to exercise their minds by rendering into Latin the works of Greek writers, and, what is more difficult, to translate the poems of illustrious[33] authors though trammeled by the farther requirements of verse. It was thus that our Tully[34] literally translated whole books of Plato... [and later] amused himself with the economics of Xenophon.[35] In this latter work the golden river of eloquence again and again meets with obstacles, around which its waters break and foam to such an extent that persons unacquainted with the original would not believe they were reading Cicero's words. And no wonder! It is hard to follow another man's lines... It is an arduous task to preserve felicity[36] and grace unimpaired in a translation. Some word has forcibly expressed a given thought; I have no word of my own to convey the meaning; and while I am seeking to satisfy the sense I may go a long way round and accomplish but a small distance of my journey. Then we must take into account the ins and outs of transposition, the variations in cases,[37]*

---

[28] *Eusebius*: (c264-c340 AD) bishop of Caesarea in Palestine and is often referred to as the father of church history

[29] *Constantinople*: the capital of the Byzantine Empire

[30] *Council*: a group of people elected to manage church affairs

[31] *Bethlehem*: a town on the West Bank of the River Jordan, near Jerusalem

[32] *epochal*: uniquely or highly significant as if marking off an epoch

[33] *illustrious*: famous

[34] *Tully*: Marcus Tullius Cicero

[35] *Xenophon*: (431-c355 BC) Greek historian

[36] *felicity*: well-chosen wording

[37] *cases*: any of the inflected forms of a word that denotes grammatical relationships

the diversity of figures,[38] *and, lastly, the peculiar, and, so to speak, the native idiom of the language. A literal translation sounds absurd; if, on the other hand, I am obliged to change either the order or the words themselves, I shall appear to have forsaken*[39] *the duty of a translator. (tr. W. H. Fremantle, 1892)*

What is striking about this self-justifying passage is Jerome's concern that his readers understand just how daunting a task literary translation is. What we read in translation, he declares later in the same preface, is necessarily an impoverishment of the original.

If any one thinks that the grace of language does not suffer through translation, let him render[40] *Homer word for word into Latin. I will go farther and say that, if he will translate this author into the prose of his own language, the order of the words will seem ridiculous, and the most eloquent of poets almost dumb.*

What is the best way to deal with this inherent impossibility of translation? For Jerome there can be no doubt how to proceed, as he explains over and over in the prefaces he wrote to his various translations. In a letter to Pammachius, written in AD 396, he quotes Cicero to affirm that the only proper way to translate is

... keeping the sense but altering the form by adapting both the metaphors and the words to suit our own language. I have not deemed it necessary to render word for word but I have reproduced the general style and emphasis.

Later in the same letter, quoting Evagrius[41] this time—one must assume that there were many critics and cavilers—he declares defiantly: "A literal translation from one language into another obscures the sense." If this makes

---

[38] *figures*: figures of speech

[39] *forsaken*: abandoned

[40] *render*: express in another language, translate

[41] *Evagrius*: Evagrius Ponticus (345-99), Christian monk and ascetic

the translator a coauthor of the book, so be it. "The truth is," Jerome writes in his preface to Eusebius, "that I have partly discharged[42] the office of a translator and partly that of a writer."

The matter could hardly be put with greater boldness or relevance to contemporary reflections. How far is the translator empowered[43] to adapt—that is, *re-create*—the text in the language into which the work is being translated? If word-by-word fidelity and literary excellence in the new language are incompatible, how "free" can a responsible translation be? Is it the first task of the translator to efface the foreignness of a text, and to recast it according to the norms of the new language? There is no serious translator who does not fret about such problems: like classical ballet, literary translation is an activity with unrealistic standards, that is, standards so exacting[44] that they are bound to generate dissatisfaction, a sense of being rarely up to the mark,[45] among ambitious practitioners. And like classical ballet, literary translation is an art of repertory.[46] Works deemed major are regularly redone—because the adaptation now seems too free, not accurate enough; or the translation is thought to contain too many errors; or the idiom, which seemed transparent to the contemporaries of a translation, now seems dated.

Dancers are trained to strive for the not entirely chimerical[47] goal of perfection: exemplary,[48] error-free expressiveness. In a literary translation, given[49] the multiple imperatives to which a literary translation has to respond, there can only be a superior, never a perfect, performance.

---

[42] *discharged*: performed

[43] *empowered*: given lawful power or authority to act

[44] *exacting*: making great demands on one's skill or endurance

[45] *up to the mark*: correct or appropriate

[46] *repertory*: a type of theater work in which actors perform different plays on different days, instead of doing the same play for a sustained period of time

[47] *chimerical*: impossible

[48] *exemplary*: serving as a desirable model

[49] *given*: taking into account

Translation, by definition, always entails some loss of the original substance. All translations are sooner or later revealed as imperfect and eventually, even in the case of the most exemplary performances, come to be regarded as provisional.[50]

[...]

Our ideas about literature (and therefore about translation) are necessarily reactive.[51] In the early nineteenth century it seemed progressive to champion[52] national literatures, and the distinctiveness (the special "genius") of the national languages. The prestige of the nation-state in the nineteenth century was fueled[53] by the consciousness of having produced great "national" writers—in countries such as Poland and Hungary, these were usually poets. Indeed, the national idea had a particularly libertarian inflection[54] in the smaller European countries, still existing within the confines of an imperial system, which were moving toward the identity of nation-states.

Concern for the authenticity of the linguistic embodiment of literature was one response to these new ideas and gave rise to intense support for writing in dialects or in so-called regional languages. Another altogether[55] different response to the idea of national identity was that of Goethe, who was perhaps the first to broach—and at a time, the early nineteenth century, when the idea of national identity was most progressive—the project of world literature (*Weltliteratur*).

It may seem surprising that Goethe could have fielded[56] a notion so far ahead of its time. It seems less odd if one thinks of Goethe as not only Napoleon's contemporary but as Napoleonic himself in more than a few projects and ideas that could be the intellectual equivalent of the Napoleonic

---

50 *provisional*: likely or able to be changed in the future

51 *reactive*: reacting to events or situations rather than starting or doing new things

52 *champion*: support the cause of

53 *fueled*: sustained

54 *inflection*: mental turning

55 *altogether*: entirely

56 *fielded*: sent forward

imperium.[57] His idea of world literature recalls Napoleon's idea of a United States of Europe, since by "the world" Goethe meant Europe and the neo-European countries, where there was already much literary traffic over borders. In Goethe's perspective, the dignity and specificity[58] of national languages (intimately tied to the affirmations of nationalism) are entirely compatible with the idea of a world literature, which is a notion of a world readership: reading books in translation.

Later in the nineteenth century, internationalism[59] or cosmopolitanism[60] in literature became, in powerful countries, the more progressive notion, the one with the libertarian inflection. Progress would be the natural development of literature from "provincial" to "national" to "international." A notion of *Weltliteratur* flourished through most of the twentieth century, with its recurrent dream of an international parliament in which all nation-states would sit as equals. Literature would be such an international system, which creates an even greater role for translations, so we could all be reading each other's books. The global spread of English could even be regarded as an essential move toward transforming literature into a truly worldwide system of production and exchange.

But, as many have observed, globalization is a process that brings quite uneven benefits to the various peoples that make up the human population, and the globalization of English has not altered the history of prejudices about national identities, one result of which is that some languages—and the literature produced in them—have always been considered more important than others. An example. Surely Machado de Assis's[61] *The Posthumous Memories of Brás Cubas* and *Dom Casmurro* and Aluísio

---

[57] *imperium*: an empire

[58] *specificity*: individuality

[59] *internationalism*: the belief in the need for friendly cooperation between nations

[60] *cosmopolitanism*: the belief in having worldwide rather than limited or provincial scope or bearing

[61] *Machado de Assis*: (1839-1908) the most important Brazilian realist novelist, poet and, short-story writer

Azevedo's[62] *The Slum*, three of the best novels written anywhere in the last part of the nineteenth century, would be as famous as a late-nineteenth-century literary masterpiece *can* be now had they been written not in Portuguese by Brazilians but in German or French or Russian. Or English. (It is not a question of big versus small languages. Brazil hardly lacks for inhabitants, and Portuguese is the sixth most widely spoken language in the world.) I hasten to add that these wonderful books *are* translated, excellently, into English. The problem is that they don't get mentioned. It has not—at least not yet—been deemed necessary for someone cultivated, someone looking for the ecstasy that only fiction can bring, to read them.

The ancient biblical image suggests that we live in our differences, emblematically linguistic, on top of one another—like Frank Lloyd Wright's[63] dream of a mile-high apartment building. But common sense tells us our linguistic dispersion cannot be a tower. The geography of our dispersal into many languages is much more horizontal than vertical (or so it seems), with rivers and mountains and valleys, and oceans that lap around the land mass. To translate is to ferry,[64] to bring across.

But maybe there is some truth in the image. A tower has many levels, and the many tenants[65] of this tower are stacked one on top of the other. If Babel is anything like other towers, the higher floors are the more coveted.[66] Maybe certain languages occupy whole sections of the upper floors, the great rooms and commanding[67] terraces. And other languages and their literary products are confined to lower floors, low ceilings, blocked views.

Some sixteen centuries after Saint Jerome, but barely more than a

---

[62] *Aluísio Azevedo*: (1857-1913) Brazilian writer

[63] *Frank Lloyd Wright*: (1867-1959) one of the most prominent architects of the first half of the 20th century

[64] *ferry*: carry things a short distance from one place to another

[65] *tenants*: people who live in a house, room, etc. and pay rent to the owner

[66] *coveted*: longed for

[67] *commanding*: having a wide view

century after Schleiermacher's[68] landmark essay on translation, came the third of what are for me the exemplary reflections on the project and duties of the translator. It is the essay entitled "The Task of the Translator" that Walter Benjamin[69] wrote in 1923 as a preface to his translation of Baudelaire's[70] *Tableaux parisiens.*

In bringing Baudelaire's French into German, he tells us, he is not obliged to make Baudelaire sound as if he had written in German. On the contrary, his obligation is to maintain the sense that the German reader might have of something different. He writes:

> *All translation is only a somewhat provisional way of coming to terms with*[71] *the foreignness of languages... It is not the highest praise of a translation, particularly in the age of its origin, to say that it reads as if it had originally been written in that language. (tr. Harry Zohn)*

The opportunity offered by translation is not a defensive one: to preserve, to embalm,[72] the current state of the translator's own language. Rather, he argues, it is an opportunity to allow a foreign tongue to influence and modify the language into which a work is being translated. Benjamin's reason for preferring a translation that reveals its foreignness is quite different from Schleiermacher's. It is not because he wishes to promote the autonomy and integrity of individual languages. Benjamin's thinking is at the opposite pole to any nationalist agenda.[73] It is a metaphysical consideration, arising from his idea of the very nature of language, according to which language itself demands the translator's exertions.[74]

Every language is part of language, which is larger than any single language. Every individual literary work is a part of literature, which is

---

[68] *Schleiermacher*: Friedrich Daniel Ernst (1768-1834), German theologian and philosopher

[69] *Walter Benjamin*: (1892-1940) German Jewish Marxist literary critic and philosopher

[70] *Baudelaire*: Charles Pierre (1821-67), French symbolist poet

[71] *coming to terms with*: reconciling oneself with

[72] *embalm*: preserve (e.g., a dead body) from decay

[73] *Benjamin's thinking...nationalist agenda*: Benjamin believes in cultural open-mindedness.

[74] *exertions*: the use of power, influence, etc. to make something happen

larger than the literature of any single language.

It is something like this view—which would place translation at the center of the literary enterprise—that I have tried to support with these remarks.

It is the nature of literature as we now understand it—understand it rightly, I believe—to circulate, for diverse and necessarily impure motives. Translation is the circulatory system of the world's literatures. Literary translation, I think, is preeminently[75] an ethical task, and one that mirrors and duplicates the role of literature itself, which is to extend our sympathies; to educate the heart and mind; to create inwardness;[76] to secure and deepen the awareness (with all its consequences) that other people, people different from us, really do exist.

[...]

Author

Susan Sontag (1933-2004), American literary theorist, philosopher, novelist, filmmaker, and political activist, produced numerous works evaluating and commenting on contemporary life and literature. Regarded as a brilliant and original thinker and highly visible as one of the most prominent public intellectuals of the second half of the 20th century, Sontag became known for her vividly written critical essays on avant-garde culture in the 1960s, and her assessment of topics such as "camp," referring to exaggerated reproductions of the style and emotions of pop culture, pornography, and the Vietnam war earned her a wide readership and also controversies, well into the 1990s.

75 *preeminently*: above all

76 *inwardness*: absorption in one's own mental or spiritual life

A More Perfect Union

by Barack Obama

"We the people, in order to form a more perfect union."

Two hundred and twenty one years ago,[1] in a hall[2] that still stands across the street, a group of men gathered and, with these simple words, launched America's improbable experiment in democracy. Farmers and scholars; statesmen and patriots who had traveled across an ocean to escape tyranny and persecution finally made real their declaration of independence at a Philadelphia convention that lasted through the spring of 1787.

The document[3] they produced was eventually signed but ultimately unfinished. It was stained by this nation's original sin of slavery, a question that divided the colonies and brought the convention to a stalemate until the founders chose to allow the slave trade to continue for at least twenty more years, and to leave any final resolution to future generations.[4]

Of course, the answer to the slavery question was already embedded within our Constitution—a Constitution that had at its very core the ideal of equal citizenship under the law; a Constitution that promised its people liberty, and justice, and a union that could be and should be perfected over time.

And yet words on a parchment[5] would not be enough to deliver slaves

---

[1] *Two hundred...years ago*: the year 1787

[2] *hall*: the Pennsylvania State House

[3] *The document*: the Constitution of the United States. It has been amended twenty-seven times; the first ten amendments are known as the Bill of Rights.

[4] *until the...future generations*: During the Constitution Convention, a compromise on slavery was made to prohibit Congress from banning the importation of slaves until 1808.

[5] *parchment*: The handwritten original four-page Constitution of the United States was penned by Jacob Shallus on parchment.

from bondage, or provide men and women of every color and creed their full rights and obligations as citizens of the United States. What would be needed were Americans in successive generations who were willing to do their part—through protests and struggle, on the streets and in the courts, through a civil war and civil disobedience and always at great risk—to narrow that gap between the promise of our ideals and the reality of their time.

This was one of the tasks we set forth at the beginning of this campaign—to continue the long march of those who came before us, a march for a more just, more equal, more free, more caring and more prosperous America. I chose to run for the presidency at this moment in history because I believe deeply that we cannot solve the challenges of our time unless we solve them together—unless we perfect our union by understanding that we may have different stories, but we hold common hopes; that we may not look the same and we may not have come from the same place, but we all want to move in the same direction—towards a better future for children and our grandchildren.

This belief comes from my unyielding faith in the decency and generosity of the American people. But it also comes from my own American story.

I am the son of a black man from Kenya and a white woman from Kansas. I was raised with the help of a white grandfather who survived a Depression[6] to serve in Patton's[7] Army during World War II and a white grandmother who worked on a bomber assembly line at Fort Leavenworth[8] while he was overseas. I've gone to some of the best schools in America and lived in one of the world's poorest nations. I am married to a black American who carries within her the blood of slaves and slave owners—an inheritance we pass on to our two precious daughters. I have brothers, sisters, nieces, nephews, uncles and cousins, of every race and

---

[6] *Depression*: the Great Depression; See Page 237, Note 85

[7] *Patton*: George Smith Patton, Jr. (1885-1945), US Army officer, an outstanding practitioner of mobile tank warfare in the European and Mediterranean theaters during World War II

[8] *Fort Leavenworth*: a United States Army facility located in Leavenworth County, Kansas

every hue, scattered across three continents, and for as long as I live, I will never forget that in no other country on Earth is my story even possible.

It's a story that hasn't made me the most conventional candidate. But it is a story that has seared into my genetic makeup the idea that this nation is more than the sum of its parts—that out of many, we are truly one.

Throughout the first year of this campaign, against all predictions to the contrary, we saw how hungry the American people were for this message of unity. Despite the temptation to view my candidacy through a purely racial lens, we won commanding victories in states with some of the whitest populations[9] in the country. In South Carolina, where the Confederate Flag[10] still flies, we built a powerful coalition of African Americans and white Americans.

This is not to say that race has not been an issue in the campaign. At various stages in the campaign, some commentators have deemed me either "too black" or "not black enough." We saw racial tensions bubble to the surface during the week before the South Carolina primary.[11] The press has scoured every exit poll for the latest evidence of racial polarization, not just in terms of white and black, but black and brown as well.

And yet, it has only been in the last couple of weeks that the discussion of race in this campaign has taken a particularly divisive turn.

On one end of the spectrum, we've heard the implication that my candidacy is somehow an exercise in affirmative action;[12] that it's based solely on the desire of wide-eyed liberals to purchase racial reconciliation on the cheap.[13] On the other end, we've heard my former pastor, Reverend Jeremiah Wright,[14] use incendiary language to express views that have the

---

9 *states with...whitest populations*: The white population is a majority in these states.

10 *the Confederate Flag*: a widely recognized symbol of the South

11 *primary*: a primary election

12 *affirmative action*: the practice of choosing people for a job, college, etc. who are usually treated unfairly because of their race, sex, etc.

13 *to purchase...the cheap*: Racial reconciliation is to be bought dearly at any rate.

14 *Reverend Jeremiah Wright*: Reverend Jeremiah Wright, Jr. (1941-), American Pastor Emeritus and the former Pastor of the Trinity United Church of Christ

potential not only to widen the racial divide, but views that denigrate both the greatness and the goodness of our nation; that rightly offend white and black alike.

I have already condemned, in unequivocal terms, the statements of Reverend Wright that have caused such controversy. For some, nagging questions remain. Did I know him to be an occasionally fierce critic of American domestic and foreign policy? Of course. Did I ever hear him make remarks that could be considered controversial while I sat in church? Yes. Did I strongly disagree with many of his political views? Absolutely—just as I'm sure many of you have heard remarks from your pastors, priests, or rabbis with which you strongly disagreed.

But the remarks that have caused this recent firestorm weren't simply controversial. They weren't simply a religious leader's effort to speak out against perceived injustice. Instead, they expressed a profoundly distorted view of this country—a view that sees white racism as endemic, and that elevates what is wrong with America above all that we know is right with America; a view that sees the conflicts in the Middle East as rooted primarily in the actions of stalwart allies like Israel, instead of emanating from the perverse and hateful ideologies of radical Islam.

As such, Reverend Wright's comments were not only wrong but divisive, divisive at a time when we need unity; racially charged at a time when we need to come together to solve a set of monumental problems—two wars,[15] a terrorist threat, a falling economy, a chronic health care crisis and potentially devastating climate change; problems that are neither black or white or Latino or Asian, but rather problems that confront us all.

[...]

In my first book, *Dreams From My Father*, I described the experience of my first service at Trinity:

"People began to shout, to rise from their seats and clap and cry out, a forceful wind carrying the reverend's voice up into the rafters... And

[15] *two wars*: the Afghanistan War and the Iraq War, which broke out in 2001 and 2003 respectively

in that single note—hope! —I heard something else; at the foot of that cross, inside the thousands of churches across the city, I imagined the stories of ordinary black people merging with the stories of David and Goliath, Moses and Pharaoh, the Christians in the lion's den, Ezekiel's field of dry bones.[16] *Those stories—of survival, and freedom, and hope—became our story, my story; the blood that had spilled was our blood, the tears our tears; until this black church, on this bright day, seemed once more a vessel carrying the story of a people into future generations and into a larger world. Our trials and triumphs became at once unique and universal, black and more than black; in chronicling our journey, the stories and songs gave us a means to reclaim memories that we didn't need to feel shame about... memories that all people might study and cherish—and with which we could start to rebuild."*

That has been my experience at Trinity. Like other predominantly black churches across the country, Trinity embodies the black community in its entirety—the doctor and the welfare mom, the model student and the former gang-banger. Like other black churches, Trinity's services are full of raucous laughter and sometimes bawdy humor. They are full of dancing, clapping, screaming and shouting that may seem jarring to the untrained ear.[17] The church contains in full the kindness and cruelty, the fierce intelligence and the shocking ignorance, the struggles and successes, the love and yes, the bitterness and bias that make up the black experience in America.

And this helps explain, perhaps, my relationship with Reverend Wright. As imperfect as he may be, he has been like family to me. He strengthened my faith, officiated my wedding, and baptized my children. Not once in my conversations with him have I heard him talk about any ethnic group in derogatory terms, or treat whites with whom he interacted with anything but courtesy and respect. He contains within him the contradictions—the

---

[16] *David and...dry bones*: All the four stories are from the Old Testament.

[17] *that may...untrained ear*: They seem so different in style that people who are not accustomed to them may find them rather uncomfortably strange.

good and the bad—of the community that he has served diligently for so many years.

I can no more disown him than I can disown the black community. I can no more disown him than I can my white grandmother—a woman who helped raise me, a woman who sacrificed again and again for me, a woman who loves me as much as she loves anything in this world, but a woman who once confessed her fear of black men who passed by her on the street, and who on more than one occasion has uttered racial or ethnic stereotypes that made me cringe.

These people are a part of me. And they are a part of America, this country that I love.

Some will see this as an attempt to justify or excuse comments that are simply inexcusable. I can assure you it is not. I suppose the politically safe thing would be to move on from this episode and just hope that it fades into the woodwork.[18] We can dismiss Reverend Wright as a crank or a demagogue, just as some have dismissed Geraldine Ferraro,[19] in the aftermath of her recent statements, as harboring some deep-seated racial bias.

But race is an issue that I believe this nation cannot afford to ignore right now. We would be making the same mistake that Reverend Wright made in his offending sermons about America—to simplify and stereotype and amplify the negative to the point that it distorts reality.

The fact is that the comments that have been made and the issues that have surfaced over the last few weeks reflect the complexities of race in this country that we've never really worked through—a part of our union that we have yet to perfect. And if we walk away now, if we simply retreat into our respective corners, we will never be able to come together and solve

---

[18] *the politically...the woodwork*: The politically safe way, or the ideal one, would be to put this problem aside and to pay no attention to it, with the hope that it is forgotten by people naturally after a certain period of time.

[19] *Geraldine Ferraro*: Geraldine Anne Ferraro (1935-2011), American politician who became the first woman to be nominated for vice president by a major political party in the United States

challenges like health care, or education, or the need to find good jobs for every American.

Understanding this reality requires a reminder of how we arrived at this point. As William Faulkner[20] once wrote, "The past isn't dead and buried. In fact, it isn't even past." We do not need to recite here the history of racial injustice in this country. But we do need to remind ourselves that so many of the disparities that exist in the African-American community today can be directly traced to inequalities passed on from an earlier generation that suffered under the brutal legacy of slavery and Jim Crow.[21]

Segregated schools[22] were, and are, inferior schools; we still haven't fixed them, fifty years after Brown v. Board of Education,[23] and the inferior education they provided, then and now, helps explain the pervasive achievement gap between today's black and white students.

Legalized discrimination—where blacks were prevented, often through violence, from owning property, or loans were not granted to African-American business owners, or black homeowners could not access FHA[24] mortgages, or blacks were excluded from unions, or the police force, or fire departments—meant that black families could not amass any meaningful wealth to bequeath to future generations. That history helps explain the wealth and income gap between black and white, and the concentrated

---

[20] *William Faulkner*: (1897-1962) American novelist and short-story writer who was awarded the 1949 Nobel Prize in literature

[21] *Jim Crow*: Jim Crow Law, any of the laws that enforced racial segregation in the South between the end of the formal Reconstruction period in 1877 and the beginning of a strong civil rights movement in the 1950s in US history

[22] *Segregated schools*: schools that can only be attended by children of the same race

[23] *Brown v. Board of Education*: Brown v. Board of Education of Topeka, a case in which, on May 17, 1954, the US Supreme Court ruled unanimously that racial segregation in public schools violated the Fourteenth Amendment to the Constitution, which declares that no state may deny equal protection of the laws to any person within its jurisdiction

[24] *FHA*: the Federal Housing Administration, a US governmental agency created as part of the National Housing Act of 1934

pockets of poverty that persists in so many of today's urban and rural communities.

A lack of economic opportunity among black men, and the shame and frustration that came from not being able to provide for one's family, contributed to the erosion of black families—a problem that welfare policies for many years may have worsened. And the lack of basic services in so many urban black neighborhoods—parks for kids to play in, police walking the beat, regular garbage pick-up and building code enforcement—all helped create a cycle of violence, blight and neglect that continue to haunt us.

This is the reality in which Reverend Wright and other African-Americans of his generation grew up. They came of age in the late fifties and early sixties, a time when segregation was still the law of the land and opportunity was systematically constricted. What's remarkable is not how many failed in the face of discrimination, but rather how many men and women overcame the odds; how many were able to make a way out of no way for those like me who would come after them.

But for all those who scratched and clawed their way to get a piece of the American Dream,[25] there were many who didn't make it—those who were ultimately defeated, in one way or another, by discrimination. [...]

In fact, a similar anger exists within segments of the white community. Most working- and middle-class white Americans don't feel that they have been particularly privileged by their race. Their experience is the immigrant experience—as far as they're concerned, no one's handed them anything, they've built it from scratch. They've worked hard all their lives, many times only to see their jobs shipped overseas or their pension dumped after a lifetime of labor. They are anxious about their futures, and feel their dreams slipping away; in an era of stagnant wages and global competition,

---

25 *the American Dream*: a national ethos of the United States of America in which democratic ideals are perceived as a promise of prosperity for its people. The term was first expressed in 1931.

opportunity comes to be seen as a zero sum game,[26] in which your dreams come at my expense. So when they are told to bus their children to a school across town; when they hear that an African American is getting an advantage in landing a good job or a spot in a good college because of an injustice that they themselves never committed; when they're told that their fears about crime in urban neighborhoods are somehow prejudiced, resentment builds over time.

Like the anger within the black community, these resentments aren't always expressed in polite company. But they have helped shape the political landscape for at least a generation. Anger over welfare and affirmative action helped forge the Reagan Coalition.[27] Politicians routinely exploited fears of crime for their own electoral ends. Talk show hosts and conservative commentators built entire careers unmasking bogus claims of racism while dismissing legitimate discussions of racial injustice and inequality as mere political correctness or reverse racism.[28]

Just as black anger often proved counterproductive, so have these white resentments distracted attention from the real culprits of the middle class squeeze—a corporate culture rife with inside dealing, questionable accounting practices, and short-term greed; a Washington dominated by lobbyists and special interests; economic policies that favor the few over the many. And yet, to wish away the resentments of white Americans, to label them as misguided or even racist, without recognizing they are grounded in legitimate concerns—this too widens the racial divide, and blocks the path to understanding.

This is where we are right now. It's a racial stalemate we've been stuck in for years. Contrary to the claims of some of my critics, black and white,

---

[26] *a zero sum game*: a situation in which you receive as much money or as many advantages as the other players give away

[27] *the Reagan Coalition*: The Reagan coalition was the combination of voters that Republican Ronald Reagan assembled to produce a major political realignment with his landslide in the 1980 US Presidential Election.

[28] *reverse racism*: the black people's discrimination against the white people

I have never been so naïve as to believe that we can get beyond our racial divisions in a single election cycle, or with a single candidacy—particularly a candidacy as imperfect as my own.

But I have asserted a firm conviction—a conviction rooted in my faith in God and my faith in the American people—that working together we can move beyond some of our old racial wounds, and that in fact we have no choice if we are to continue on the path of a more perfect union.

For the African-American community, that path means embracing the burdens of our past without becoming victims of our past. It means continuing to insist on a full measure of justice in every aspect of American life. But it also means binding our particular grievances—for better health care, and better schools, and better jobs—to the larger aspirations of all Americans—the white woman struggling to break the glass ceiling,[29] the white man who has been laid off, the immigrant trying to feed his family. And it means taking full responsibility for our own lives—by demanding more from our fathers, and spending more time with our children, and reading to them, and teaching them that while they may face challenges and discrimination in their own lives, they must never succumb to despair or cynicism; they must always believe that they can write their own destiny.

Ironically, this quintessentially American—and yes, conservative—notion of self-help found frequent expression in Reverend Wright's sermons. But what my former pastor too often failed to understand is that embarking on a program of self-help also requires a belief that society can change.

The profound mistake of Reverend Wright's sermons is not that he spoke about racism in our society. It's that he spoke as if our society was static; as if no progress has been made; as if this country—a country that has made it possible for one of his own members to run for the highest office in the land and build a coalition of white and black; Latino and Asian, rich and poor, young and old—is still irrevocably bound to a tragic

---

[29] *the glass ceiling*: the attitudes and practices that prevent women or particular groups from getting high level jobs, even though there are no actual laws or rules to stop them

past. But what we know—what we have seen—is that America can change. That is true genius[30] of this nation. What we have already achieved gives us hope—the audacity to hope—for what we can and must achieve tomorrow.

In the white community, the path to a more perfect union means acknowledging that what ails the African-American community does not just exist in the minds of black people; that the legacy of discrimination—and current incidents of discrimination, while less overt than in the past—are real and must be addressed. Not just with words, but with deeds—by investing in our schools and our communities; by enforcing our civil rights laws and ensuring fairness in our criminal justice system; by providing this generation with ladders of opportunity that were unavailable for previous generations. It requires all Americans to realize that your dreams do not have to come at the expense of my dreams; that investing in the health, welfare, and education of black and brown and white children will ultimately help all of America prosper.

In the end, then, what is called for is nothing more, and nothing less, than what all the world's great religions demand—that we do unto others as we would have them do unto us. Let us be our brother's keeper, Scripture tells us. Let us be our sister's keeper. Let us find that common stake we all have in one another, and let our politics reflect that spirit as well.

For we have a choice in this country. We can accept a politics that breeds division, and conflict, and cynicism. We can tackle race only as spectacle—as we did in the OJ trial[31]—or in the wake of tragedy, as we did in the aftermath of Katrina[32]—or as fodder for the nightly news. We can play Reverend Wright's sermons on every channel, every day and talk

---

30 *genius*: a special good, creative character or spirit

31 *the OJ trial*: the O. J. Simpson murder case : a criminal trial held in the Los Angeles County, California Superior Court in which former American football star and actor O. J. Simpson was charged with the 1994 murder of his ex-wife and her friend. It is considered a trial more about racial strife than double murder.

32 *Katrina*: Hurricane Katrina, the catastrophic 2005 hurricane that devastated New Orleans and the Mississippi Gulf Coast

about them from now until the election, and make the only question in this campaign whether or not the American people think that I somehow believe or sympathize with his most offensive words. We can pounce on some gaffe by a Hillary[33] supporter as evidence that she's playing the race card, or we can speculate on whether white men will all flock to John McCain[34] in the general election regardless of his policies.

We can do that.

But if we do, I can tell you that in the next election, we'll be talking about some other distraction. And then another one. And then another one. And nothing will change.

That is one option. Or, at this moment, in this election, we can come together and say, "Not this time." [...]

There is one story in particularly that I'd like to leave you with today—a story I told when I had the great honor of speaking on Dr. King's[35] birthday at his home church, Ebenezer Baptist, in Atlanta.

There is a young, twenty-three-year-old white woman named Ashley Baia who organized for our campaign in Florence, South Carolina. She had been working to organize a mostly African-American community since the beginning of this campaign, and one day she was at a roundtable discussion where everyone went around telling their story and why they were there.

And Ashley said that when she was nine years old, her mother got cancer. And because she had to miss days of work, she was let go and lost her health care. They had to file for bankruptcy, and that's when Ashley decided that she had to do something to help her mom.

She knew that food was one of their most expensive costs, and so

---

[33] *Hillary*: Clinton (1947-), the 67th United States Secretary of State, serving within the administration of President Barack Obama. In the 2008 US presidential election, when this speech was made, Hillary was a leading candidate for the Democratic presidential nomination.

[34] *John McCain*: (1936-2018) the senior United States Senator from Arizona. McCain was the Republican nominee for president in the 2008 United States presidential election.

[35] *Dr. King*: Martin Luther King, Jr. (1929-68), Baptist minister and social activist who led the civil rights movement in the United States from the mid-1950s until his death by assassination in 1968

Ashley convinced her mother that what she really liked and really wanted to eat more than anything else was mustard and relish sandwiches. Because that was the cheapest way to eat.

She did this for a year until her mom got better, and she told everyone at the roundtable that the reason she joined our campaign was so that she could help the millions of other children in the country who want and need to help their parents too.

Now Ashley might have made a different choice. Perhaps somebody told her along the way that the source of her mother's problems were blacks who were on welfare and too lazy to work, or Hispanics who were coming into the country illegally. But she didn't. She sought out allies in her fight against injustice.

Anyway, Ashley finishes her story and then goes around the room and asks everyone else why they're supporting the campaign. They all have different stories and reasons. Many bring up a specific issue. And finally they come to this elderly black man who's been sitting there quietly the entire time. And Ashley asks him why he's there. And he does not bring up a specific issue. He does not say health care or the economy. He does not say education or the war. He does not say that he was there because of Barack Obama. He simply says to everyone in the room, "I am here because of Ashley."

"I'm here because of Ashley." By itself, that single moment of recognition between that young white girl and that old black man is not enough. It is not enough to give health care to the sick, or jobs to the jobless, or education to our children.

But it is where we start. It is where our union grows stronger. And as so many generations have come to realize over the course of the two-hundred and twenty one years since a band of patriots signed that document in Philadelphia, that is where the perfection begins.

Author

Barack Obama, born Aug. 4, 1961 in Honolulu, Hawaii, became the 44th, and the first African-American, President of the United States in 2009. He graduated from Columbia University and received his law degree from Harvard Law School. He became the first African-American president of the *Harvard Law Review* and later worked as a civil rights lawyer and as a community organizer in New York and Chicago. He was the third African-American to deliver a keynote address at a Democratic National Convention, when he took the stage at the 2004 convention in Boston. On Feb. 10, 2007, Obama entered the race for presidency of the United States. The competition for the Democratic nominee turned out to be a race between him, the first serious African-American candidate, and Hillary Rodham Clinton, the first serious woman candidate. In the end, he beat Clinton and then the Republican nominee, Senator John McCain.